Reliance
Sinclair
Book 2

IMPACT
ON
IN

HEATHER TEXLE

HEATHER TEXLE

Until It Looks Right
Minnesota

Sign up for bonus content including
On Instinct, a free *Reliance Sinclair* story at
heathertexle.com

To Shawn, Tawnie, and Rosa.
This ship doesn't run without her crew.

Previously In...

(Includes spoilers from *On Impulse*, Reliance Sinclair, #1)
FORMER DEPARTMENT OF ENFORCEMENT of Criminal Affairs agent Reliance Sinclair discovered the body of her friend, Jarrett Viorel, brutally tortured in his apartment. He had been investigating her dirty ex-partner. Fearing she would be blamed for his murder and unable to trust the Department, she went on the run to find his killer and clear her name.

The trail led her to Tazza Industries, the largest tech company in the galaxy. When Doctors Lourde and Adler caught Reliance breaking into their research lab, they kidnapped her to use her as a test subject for one of their black-market inventions. The doctors implanted an Intell neural impulse chip into her brain that allowed her to connect, hack, and infiltrate nearly every computer system that came within range. They never intended for her to survive the experiment, but she did.

While being held against her will, she discovered the Intell wasn't the only illegal product Tazza Industries was developing. They were also designing bionic weapons, which had been outlawed for the past eighty years.

Meanwhile, Agent Grayson Wright and his team tracked Reliance across the galaxy to arrest her for the murder of Viorel. Wright learned she was being held at Tazza Industries, arrested her, and brought her back to Andaress-4. Reliance convinced him of her innocence, and together, they arrested Tazza Industries' CEO Aurelian Tazza, Doctors Lourde and Adler, and the two underlings involved in Viorel's murder.

When allegations of the bionic weapons development were raised, DECA tasked Wright's team with investigating the charges and proving Tazza Industries' illegal activities. Wright invited Reliance to join his team. She accepted, knowing they would need every advantage to bring down the tech giant.

The thing Tazza Industries thought would make them invincible might be the only thing that can stop them.

Chapter 1

A GRAY-HAIRED MAN WALKED across the stage carrying a bass guitar and a case. He set up at the far end, resting the guitar on a stand and attaching an amp bot to the front panel. It lit up neon green when he linked his cuff to it and tinkered with the settings on the holoscreen. An earsplitting feedback screech drowned out the hum of conversation from the bar.

I leaned over to my boss, who sat on the cushy barstool to my left. "Are you sure we're in the right place?"

"Positive. There's only one Brackish Bar on Andaress-4," he said while scanning the room.

Lead Agent Grayson Wright had traded his usual department uniform of black tactical pants, dark Henley, and forest-green jacket for a much more casual pair of charcoal tactical pants, navy-blue shirt, and gray zip-up. He'd even gone a little crazy and let a shadow of dark-blond stubble grace his formidable jaw.

We'd both arrived early and snagged a high-top to the right of the stage. A server dropped off the plate of bacon-and-cheese crispers I'd ordered and the pitcher of craft beer Wright bought for the table. I was more of a whisky girl, but the beer was light and refreshing and just the thing to combat the dry heat of a Salin summer.

A couple in their early eighties passed by, and their cuff signals pinged my implant with notifications. She wore a fuchsia sweater set with skin-tight black leggings, a wide belt, and a chunky neck-lace that glowed in the dark. His white hair was gelled into tiny blue-tipped spikes, and he wore a leather jacket that didn't quite cover his potbelly, as well as sensible orthopedic shoes. They joined a similarly dressed group of octogenarians at the table beside ours who greeted them with a round of back-slaps and hugs.

The people-watching was fascinating, to say the least.

As the bar continued to fill, it was clear we were the youngest people there by a couple of decades. "When DeAjamae invited us to check out her band, I expected something a little..."

"More rocker and less rocking chair?" Wright supplied.

"Exactly. This crowd looks like they're out to spend their monthly pensioner credits."

A flurry of notifications splattered across my vision. My Intell neural implant chip was a greedy little bastard and sought sources of information. As each new person entered my three-meter personal bubble, the Intell tried to access any of their connected devices—cuffs and medical implants being the most common tonight. It also registered the band's equipment and the bar's payment systems, ordering stations, and cleaning bots.

Designed as a black-market device for corporate espionage and covert operations, the chip had no issues hacking its way into any of the civilian equipment it found here—whether I wanted it to or not. Information overload was a problem.

That many signals often gave me a raging headache, but I'd dosed myself with four pain tabs before heading over. At the moment, it was only a dull throb in my temples. It was worth it to support DeAjamae and spend time with the team. We'd gotten off to a shaky start—what with me being a fugitive and them tracking me down and all—but things had been good lately. The last couple of months, especially.

Being on this team was the best thing to happen to me in a very long time. I didn't want anything to jeopardize it. Besides, I wouldn't drag them into another one of my messes, not after what had happened to Jarrett. It was my problem to figure out.

Agent Ravi Singh, our team's fourth member, sidled through the crowd and slid onto the stool we'd saved for him. Unlike Wright, he'd dressed up in a tailored burgundy suit coat and a black button-down shirt.

"Wright, Reliance," he greeted us with a smile. "Wow! It isn't even dark outside yet, and this place is packed!"

"Yeah, I had to park my hoverbike three blocks away," I said. "I didn't realize DeAjamae's band was so popular."

"Have you been to one of her shows before?"

I shook my head. "The timing's never worked. Her last gig was when I was traveling."

Wright rested his hand on my forearm. It hadn't been a pleasure trip. I'd been delivering the ashes of two friends to their families—Fax's to his estranged brother on Sol-4 and Jarrett's to his parents on Ritru-6.

Ravi flashed me one of his signature smiles, attempting to derail my negative thoughts. "Well, you're in for a treat. She's amazing."

Three more band members joined the bass guitarist on stage. All were middle-aged men who looked like they'd be more at home watching holocasts of the latest sports game.

"What kind of music do they play again?" I asked, because DeAjamae was the epitome of cool, and my brain had a hard time reconciling that with the scene before me.

"Songs you'll recognize."

"Helpful."

"I don't want to ruin the surprise."

An older gentleman with a thick walrus mustache, caterpillar eyebrows, and soup-chicken skin shimmied his way over to the group next to us. He led with his bony pelvis, making little thrusting motions and shooting finger-blasters as he winked at the ladies. While the women were far too seasoned to blush at his antics, more than one gave him a perusing look, including the woman in the fuchsia sweater set. I didn't miss the possessive arm her partner wrapped around her waist.

Wright poured Ravi a glass of beer and slid it across the high-top as the lights dimmed a fraction. It was still bright by normal club standards. Scented fog rolled out onto the dance floor from a pipe built into the edge of the stage. Light and citrusy, it tickled the inside of my nose when it reached our side of the room. The guitarist strummed a lone chord, hushing the crowd as everyone spun around on their stools toward the front. Someone whooped and it was answered with a smattering of claps and whistles.

A spotlight drone flipped on, cutting a beam of bright white light through the fog to the edge of the stage where DeAjamae stood. She wore a pair of low-slung, faux-leather pants with a matching bralette that showed off her toned abs and generous curves.

"Hello, Brackish Bar!" she yelled into her microphone drone. It was decked out with shimmery silk scarves that fluttered in the draft of its propellers. "I'm DeAjamae, but you can call me Miss Dee. We are the Come-Back Comets, because everything good comes back 'round again, and that includes music. How are we feeling tonight?" She gave a high kick and then pumped her fist to a round of applause. "Let's get this party started!"

I let out a whoop that would be heard over her screaming fans, and Wright did the two-finger whistle thing that threatened to pop my left eardrum. Ravi jumped to his feet, clapping.

DeAjamae picked up a guitar and strummed a single note. "Get your asses out on that floor. I want to see you shake it!"

A barrage of old folks rushed—well, shuffled—to the dance floor. They cheered her on as she jogged to the center stage, arm raised above her head and waving. The band launched right into its first number, a thirty-year-old hard rock song that was popular several years before DeAjamae was born. I remembered my parents listening to it as a kid.

My Intell picked up a flurry of notifications from pacemakers, cochlear implants, dialysis scrubbers, and bionic hips, knees, and shoulders as people danced to the music. They appeared as rapid pop-ups in the lower half of my field of vision. Even though I denied the connections as soon as the Intell registered them, splotches of color danced across my eyes and a wave of dizziness hit me hard. I reached for the lip of the table to keep from toppling over.

Wright grabbed my elbow, steadying me and keeping me from making a fool of myself. "You okay, Reliance?" he asked. He'd leaned in to be heard over the music, and I could smell the bergamot and lime scent of his soap—clean, crisp, and bright.

"The stool's a little wobbly," I lied.

I couldn't look him in the eyes, so I focused on his fingers pressing into my bare forearm instead. His grip was firm but warm, much like the man himself. If his hand lingered a little longer than necessary, I tried not to read too much into it. Like I tried not to read too much into him using my first name. He'd been doing that more lately.

The table next to us moved to the dance floor. Ravi scooted in to let the woman wearing fuchsia squeeze by. The blue-haired guy followed her, and Walrus Mustache was close behind. They found an open section near the middle and whipped out a couple of moves that I wasn't sure I could replicate, and I was only thirty-two.

On stage, DeAjamae strutted from one side of the stage to the other, working the crowd. She looked the part of a rocker with her dark-brown curls streaked with pink highlights, nails painted electric blue, and a thick, blue bar of stage makeup across her eyes. No one would believe she was a digital forensic analyst in the Department of Enforcement of Criminal Affairs.

After the first song ended, DeAjamae stopped in the middle of the stage. "Did we like that?"

The crowd cheered.

"Say, 'yes, Miss Dee.'"

"Yes, Miss Dee!" the crowd yelled back.

Ravi choked on his beer.

DeAjamae introduced her band members. Besides the bass player, there was a man on electric drums, one on lead guitar, and a third on some kind of complicated four-tier keyboard with a hose he blew into. They launched into the second song, and I recognized it, too. It was the anthem of rebellious teenagers when I was growing up. DeAjamae's voice had a raspy, gravelly quality that suited the song well.

I snagged a bacon-and-cheese-ladened crisper from the plate and patted myself on my back for running an extra three kilometers that morning. Being planetside for the last six months had reminded me how much good food I'd missed out on while living in space for a year. Bacon was worth the extra exercise.

Half a dozen songs later, I was thoroughly enjoying the people-watching. Fuchsia Lady fanned her face with her hand. The guy with spiky blue hair who'd been dancing with her all night leaned in and said something in her ear. She smiled and nodded, and he headed to the bar.

That was all the opening Walrus Mustache needed. He swooped in, grabbed the octogenarian and twirled her around several times. She smiled and put a little extra sway in her hips as they danced, pleased with the attention. A few more turns and he plastered himself all over her like hellaberry jam on toast. He had some fast moves, and I didn't mean with his feet.

Ravi spotted the pair, too. "I hope I have half that much energy when I'm their age," he said.

Walrus Mustache grabbed her behind and gyrated their pelvises together in a way that I could never unsee. "Yeah, and only half that much."

From somewhere deep within the crowd, a bra flew through toward the stage. It arced gracefully through the air in all its beige glory to lasso the neck of the bass player's guitar. He kept right on playing like women threw their undergarments at him every day. Who was I to judge? Maybe they did.

The blue-haired man threaded his way back through the mash of dancers carrying two glasses of beer. He dropped in and out of view until he reached the pocket of cleared space around where his date and Walrus Mustache were getting down and dirty.

"Uh-oh," I said and nudged Wright's arm with my elbow.

It only took a second for him to follow my gaze and see what I saw.

Blue Hair lunged for Walrus Mustache. The beer glasses went flying, spraying the three closest people with alcohol. One hit a woman on her shoulder and crashed to the floor in a shower of broken glass.

After that, I lost sight of the group as the dancers scattered. What they lacked in speed, they made up for in disorganization. Several were jostled in the chaos, and one almost fell down before his partner caught his hand. Both men made it safely to a table, but if we didn't calm the situation, someone was going to fall and break a hip.

All three of us stood as the band stopped playing. DeAjamae had her cuff's holoscreen up and was aerial scribing commands at a rapid pace. The room lights flickered on, and she sent the spotlight drone to hover above the two brawling old men.

"Where do we start?" Ravi asked.

"Sinclair and I will separate the men," Wright said, flipping into work mode. "You work on crowd control."

A loud crack split the air and everyone hit the floor. Blue Hair stood in the center, arm raised, and pointing a gun toward the ceiling.

Fuchsia Lady screamed.

Walrus Mustache lay on the ground, clutching his chest.

Chapter 2

"Is that a combustion gun?" I asked, drawing my blaster from its concealed holster inside my cross-body bag. Wright and Ravi drew theirs, as well. We crouched beside the high-top table, sneaking glances around the corners.

Ravi crawled around to our side. The cheap wood materials wouldn't provide much cover, but it was something.

Wright tapped the black cuff strapped to his forearm. "Sophie, connect me with Dispatch."

"One moment. Connecting," his cuff responded.

"Dispatch."

"This is Lead Agent Grayson Wright out of Salin. I need a unit and a medical transpo at The Brackish Bar. One civilian down. Male, eighties, projectile gunshot wound to the chest. Suspect is on the premises but has not been detained. Male, eighties, blue hair, medium complexion, medium build, wearing a metal-studded leather jacket. Armed and dangerous."

"Confirmed, Agent Wright. I'm directing backup and a medical transpo to you now. Be advised, estimated arrival time is five minutes."

He ended the comm. "Change of plans. Singh, check the victim. Sinclair, see if you can flank the suspect." Wright twisted the power dial on the top of his blaster. "Set your blasters on low. We can't risk hitting a civilian with anything stronger."

I adjusted my setting and heard the soft, high-pitched whine, signaling a full charge for my blaster.

"Ready?" Wright asked.

Ravi and I nodded.

"Go."

Wright gave me a few seconds to get clear of our table so I wouldn't be noticed, then stood up. "This is the D-E-C-A. Drop your weapon and put your hands in the air."

The shooter spun toward Wright, slack-jawed and shaking. Confusion and panic widened his eyes until the whites showed all around. Not the face of a hardened criminal, but that only made him unpredictable. People did crazy shit when they were scared.

I eased around the edge of the dance floor as quickly as I dared. Most of the dancers had dropped to the floor after the gunshot, and I had to move slowly to avoid drawing the shooter's attention.

Wright continued talking, keeping the shooter focused on him. "We can talk this out, but the first thing you need to do is put down the weapon."

"I... I..." The old man looked down at the other man lying on the floor. "What happened?"

"We'll sort it all out," Wright said, taking one step forward. His voice was calm and measured. "But first you have to *put down the gun*."

The shooter lowered his arm and looked at the weapon, as if he didn't understand how it got there. Then he must have spotted me, because he took off at a fast shuffle toward the rear exit on the far side of the stage.

Of all of us, DeAjamae was the closest. She took a running leap off the stage but missed tackling him by centimeters. Her foot got tangled in a pile of the band's equipment bags, and she fell. The shooter made it to the door, waved his cuff across the door reader to open it, and hurried out to the back parking lot.

"I got him!" I yelled to Wright and Ravi as I sprinted across the floor.

People stayed crouched with their hands over their heads, forcing me to hurdle over the ones I couldn't avoid. I reached out with my

Intell, letting it latch onto the network signal of the door reader and triggering it to open before I got there.

Cool spring air greeted me as soon as I ran outside. The temperature had dropped several degrees while I'd been listening to the band, and the coolness cleared my head of the dull pain forming behind my eyes.

Even this early in the evening, the low altitude vehicle lot was well lit. The old man was nowhere in sight, but he couldn't have gone far. I listened for the sound of running footsteps or a LAV's engine firing up. Nothing.

Cautiously, I walked down the aisle and expanded my Intell's notification viewscreen, looking for any electronic signal that could indicate his location. The first dozen LAVs were stone cold and silent. The next one was still running through its cool-down cycle.

My Intell chewed through its privacy protocols in seconds and presented me with a list of basic information: owner's name, address, and pilot's license, registration, and insurance policy. When it pulled up the latest system diagnostic report, I made the barest of swiping motions with my middle finger to clear the screen from my vision. Once the Intell got its hacking teeth into something, it didn't know when to stop.

A whirling noise from behind startled me. I spun in time to see a personal hoverchair zip by the front of the row. It was a deep maroon color, had a cushy padded seat, and twin neon-orange slow-moving vehicle flags flapping above the shooter's head. The man's blue-tipped hair whipped in the wind as he pushed the hoverchair's thrusters to the max.

Shit. My bike was three blocks in the other direction. I sprinted after him, wishing I'd worn more comfortable shoes.

I opened a shared comm to the team. "Sinclair here. I have the suspect in sight and am in pursuit. He's in a maroon hoverchair."

Someone snickered on the other end of the comm. It sounded suspiciously like DeAjamae. Then Ravi's voice came on. "I'm sorry, can you repeat? It sounded like you said he was in a hoverchair."

I clenched my teeth. "That's because I did. Suspect is heading west on Hyssop Ave."

"Do you want backup?"

He didn't laugh, but I imagined it was only through great effort. And I got it. I was running down an old man in a flying mobility chair, but void-be-damned, that thing was faster than it looked.

My feet splashed through a puddle, soaking my shoes and the bottom edges of my pants. My next few steps felt squishy. "No, I got him. You stay with the victim."

I disconnected, and the headache I'd had earlier came back with a vengeance as I continued to use the Intell. A sharp pain shot from the middle of my brain to the back of my eyeballs.

Two blocks ahead, the shooter turned right at the intersection onto 34th Street and almost crashed into a couple walking their dog. It barked and strained at the end of its leash, trying to chase after him.

I looked down and to the left to activate the voice commands. "Show me a map of Salin with my geo location marked."

A new window popped up, obscuring half my field of vision. My toe snagged on something. I tripped and stumbled but recovered my stride. I didn't know if I'd ever get used to having the Intell's information displayed inside my head.

It only took me a moment to orient myself on the map. 34th Street was a hilly, winding pedestrian thoroughfare lined with shops. There weren't any crossroads for several blocks. Unless he ducked into a building, he would have to come out near Jasmine Avenue.

"Access program Minotaur. Set to transparency mode and overlay my coordinates. Plot the fastest course to intersection of 34th and Jasmine by foot."

At first, I didn't see anything. Then I slowed to a stop and did a complete one-eighty. The white line showing the recommended route ran behind me, back the way I had come.

Something wet tickled my upper lip. I swiped at it and my hand came back smeared with blood. "Fantastic. Just what I need."

Bloody noses were one of the side effects of using the Intell, and they'd become more common. Nothing I could do about that now, though.

The Minotaur program was designed for corporate espionage by plotting courses around guards and security measures, but it worked just as well for chasing criminals as for being one. I doubled back, following the line by cutting diagonally through the LAV parking lot. My thighs burned—still sore from that morning's run—and my stomach regretted eating so many bacon-and-cheese crispers. At least the rain had cooled the air, so it didn't burn my lungs.

I ducked under the wing of the last six-person LAV. The white line blinked, signaling I should go off the path. A small embankment ran along the rear of the lot. I scrambled to the top, my feet slipping on the wet grass.

On the other side of the hill was a two-meter vertical retaining wall that dropped straight down to 34th Street. Apparently, the Minotaur program didn't take into account elevation changes.

I leaned over the edge searching for stairs but didn't find anything helpful. I did, however, see the suspect rocketing down the path. Blue-gray smoke trailed behind the hoverchair. One flag had torn free and the other bent backward at a near ninety-degree angle from the force of the wind. His spiky, blue-tipped hair had blown out to a pale-blue fuzz.

He beelined straight down the path. Pedestrians scrambled to get out of his way.

I raised my blaster and leveled the sights at the hoverchair. It wobbled in and out of focus. The headache from using my Intell had grown to the point of distraction. My right eye felt as if a hot needle were pressing into it from inside my skull. I pulled my head back, blinked my eyes clear, and tried again. With one eye closed, I forced myself to concentrate and took aim.

My hand shook, wobbling the sights. I couldn't get a good fix on the shooter.

Stars! Not now!

There were too many people down there to risk a stray energy bolt, even if it was set on low. The hoverchair was almost to me. I shoved the blaster into the back of my waistband and sprinted along the embankment, running in the same direction.

Right before he drew level with me, I leaped from the retaining wall.

My momentum carried me forward, and then I fell. Fast.

The hoverchair flew about five decimeters above the ground. I slammed into it with a bone-jarring thud. My torso hit the handlebar. Something pointy and ungiving jammed into my diaphragm. The altitude regulator, maybe. All the air whooshed from my lungs, but I wrapped one arm around the steering column while my feet dangled over the edge.

The old guy yelped, startled by my dropping from the sky. He threw himself back, and—combined with my jump—sent the hoverchair spinning. I gripped on tight as my legs flung out from the centrifugal force. We made it three full rotations before the hoverchair finally teetered off its axis and deposited us both onto the ground. It bucked and thrashed like a wild beast until it slammed into the retaining wall.

Luckily for the shooter, my body cushioned his fall. I took a bony knee to the gut before rolling him off to the side. He didn't look injured, but he took his time climbing to his feet.

The combustion gun landed a meter away. I picked it up and shoved it into my waistband next to my blaster. It wasn't secure, but it would do until I got it into an evidence bag.

"Are you hurt?"

He shook his head. "No, I don't think so."

"You are under arrest for the unlawful discharge of a combustion gun, public disturbance, and resisting arrest. Additional charges may be added, including but not limited to, murder. You may remain silent if you so choose. If you choose to speak, your words may be entered as evidence in trial. You have the right to an appointed attorney or one of your own employment."

"I don't know what happened. One minute I was getting drinks for Moxie and me. Joe, he's always had an eye for Moxie, and when I saw them dancing, I guess I thought he'd gone too far. I remember taking out my gun, but only to scare him a little. Let him know to back off. Then Joe was lying on the ground. I ... I don't remember shooting him."

"You're going to have to come with me," I told him.

I didn't have a pair of restraints, so I walked him back to The Brackish Bar in a come-along hold with his arm twisted behind his back. It was either that or wait for Dispatch to send a Department LAV for a pickup. Between the headache, bloody nose, and shaking hands, I wasn't in the mood to wait.

It took about ten minutes to walk back. Neither of us were moving too fast. If the shooter had been any younger or even a little bit spryer, this night would have gone so much worse. As it was, I barely kept a tight hold on his arm.

I handed the suspect off to a waiting officer. She'd take him to the precinct, record his statement, and book him.

My leather cross-body bag was where I left it by the high-top table. I grabbed two migraine tabs and placed them on my tongue to dissolve. They provided little relief from Intell-induced headaches, but they took the edge off. Then I used a cleansing wipe I kept in a side pocket to clean any traces of my bloody nose.

DeAjamae stood with Ravi in the center of the dance floor, talking and pointing straight up. She had her spotlight drone aimed at the ceiling. It shone a light on a small hole.

"Hey," I said, walking over to them.

She stopped talking long enough to give me a quick once-over. "Are those grass stains?"

We all looked at my light-blue jeans.

"Ugh," I said, brushing at the loose bits of grass. "This is why DECA issues black pants and shirts."

Ravi picked a piece of something I didn't want to name out of my purple hair. "DECA has hats, too."

"Hilarious." I looked up to the place the spotlight shone on. "What's going on here?"

"Bullet hole," Ravi said.

"In the ceiling? Not it for going up there to retrieve it. I don't care if I'm the newbie."

"Turns out Mister Hot-to-Trot wasn't shot." DeAjamae snorted. "That rhymed. Anyway, the medics think he had a heart attack, likely triggered by a combination of his aerobic workout and his scare at hearing the gunshot. They took him to the hospital, but he should be fine."

"So it wasn't murder?"

"Not even attempted murder." DeAjamae aerial scribed a command into her holoscreen. The spotlight drone shut off its light and flew back to her pile of stuff beside the stage.

"That's so much less paperwork," Ravi said.

"Are we still on for tomorrow?" DeAjamae asked me.

I looked around at the orderly chaos. Things were wrapping up and with any luck I'd be out of here within the next hour. "I don't see why not."

"Great! I have a new idea I want to test."

Ravi picked up one of the microphone scarves that had been trampled on the floor and handed it to DeAjamae. "Too bad about your show, though."

She tied the sparkly fabric around her waist like a belt. "Eh, this will probably get the band some good press."

"A weapon discharge and bar evacuation is good press?"

She grinned. "In the entertainment business, all press is good press."

Chapter 3

I SWIPED MY HAND across the wall console in the common area of my ship to shut off the holocast. "I can't believe the city attorney let Aurelian Tazza off with a fine!"

DeAjamae pulled a cable from her ever-present backpack, then plugged one end into her cuff and the other into a data port on the side of the console. Code scrolled on the screen. She'd stopped over to the spaceship park where I lived on the *Soteria* to deliver the news and help me with a project.

"Her assistant contacted me right before I came over to give us a heads-up. Sounds like Tazza Industries transferred the credits for the fine this afternoon. The slimeball's already on his way back to Brione-2. That's got to be some kind of record."

My friends were dead, and the man responsible just bought his way out of punishment. A handful of credits to a man worth billions. He might even consider it a tax write-off. Just the cost of doing business.

Visions of my friends' lifeless bodies still haunted me when I closed my eyes. Neither had had an easy death. Jarrett had been brutally tortured for information. Fax—who'd received the same experimental neural implant as me—had died when Doctor Kandall Lourde ripped it out of his brain to prevent the authorities from discovering its existence.

"Hey," DeAjamae said, squeezing my shoulder. "At least Lourde got forty years. It might as well be life at his age."

"Tazza orchestrated and funded the experiments. He should be rotting in prison alongside Lourde. What was the city attorney thinking?"

Her hand dropped to her side. "Don't blame her. Six months of combing through his business records, and we didn't find anything to counter his argument that Lourde had gone rogue and acted on his own. Plus, Fax's homicide was outside our jurisdiction, and we knew going in that the evidence tying Tazza to Jarrett's murder was weak. He made sure none of the paperwork traced back to him. Everything was in Lourde's name. She weighed the odds of winning at trial and figured this was the best deal to ensure he received some kind of punishment. The plea bargain was her best option."

I blew out a breath and sat down on one of the fixed stools beside the small kitchen island. "Yeah, Tazza's good at covering his tracks."

His tech company was one of the largest in the galaxy. For a man that wealthy, it was a slap on the wrist. Void-damned attorneys.

"We'll find another way to get him. It'll just take more time," DeAjamae said.

I sighed. "I know, but it still sucks. It puts that much more pressure on the bionic weapons investigation."

"The lieutenant is getting antsy for us to show some progress, but you didn't hear that from me. I overheard her tear Wright a new one yesterday."

Our boss wouldn't be happy about that. "Anything new from the material we recovered from the lab?"

"Not much. Lourde's lackeys did a pretty thorough job shredding the hard drives, and the server we confiscated from Lourde was damaged in the LAV crash."

"Did you find anything on the medication he gave Fax and me?" I tried to make the question sound nonchalant, but judging by the look she shot me, I hadn't succeeded.

"No, I haven't been looking for that. Should I be?"

I shrugged, hating myself for lying to her. DeAjamae had a knack for anything related to computers. We'd spent the last six months testing my new capabilities. I'd learned a lot about coping with the Intell, but it hadn't come without complications.

Last night's headache and nosebleed were just the latest in a string of increasingly bad side effects I experienced when pushing the use of my Intell. The hand tremors were new, though, and they concerned me. How could I do my job if I couldn't hold a blaster?

"Just curious. It'd be nice to know what was in it."

"Probably the crushed souls of little children," DeAjamae grumbled. "That man is pure evil."

"No argument here. Isn't that right, Walnut?"

Walnut, the guinea pig I'd rescued from Lourde's research laboratory, gave a sharp *wheek* in solidarity before investigating the starting area of the new maze we'd built for him. It sat on the floor and took up most of the free space in the living room section. The base covered the access hatch to the engine room below, but since we were parked planetside, it didn't matter.

The little potato butt was a short-haired guinea pig with light-brown fur and a white stripe running from his forehead to his belly. He had shiny black eyes, and the cutest pink nose and little feet that made me want to squeeze him until he squeaked. I didn't, but cute aggression was a real problem around him.

The first time I'd seen him was in Lourde's bionic weapons lab, and my implant chip had connected with his implant chip. It told me when he was happy or hungry based on the biochemical information his chip collected. I could even elicit responses from him, like *hide from danger* or *it's safe to come out* by triggering his brain to release certain chemicals.

DeAjamae and I had studied his chip and our connection to learn how the neural impulse chips worked and how they might be combined with bionic weapons. We assumed that had been the end goal of Lourde's research. He wanted to create weapons that were concealed inside human bodies and operated without the need for an external device, like a cuff. It would be a closed system that was difficult to detect and nearly impossible to stop.

Last week, DeAjamae had run a three-dimensional imaging scan on Walnut. Both his brain and the chip were minuscule, but she was certain his chip connected to his optical and vestibulo-cochlear nerves. That meant it should be able to send and receive visual and auditory signals, similar to how mine did. The maze tested her hypothesis.

She found the section of code she'd been looking for, paused the scroll, and aerial scribed in a new line of text. Then she backed out of the program and disconnected the wire. Walnut shook his entire body as the new commands synced wirelessly to the implant in his tiny, rodent brain.

As far as we could tell, he had a simpler version of the neural impulse chip than mine. We'd been running tests for the last three weeks to see what he was capable of. I could send an image to his chip, but we had no way of knowing if that image appeared to him as a visual thing the same way it did to me. Dee had come up with the idea of using a maze to figure it out.

"I'm all set for the next run, if you are."

"Sure, let me prep Walnut," I said.

My Intell was still connected to Walnut's chip from the first run. I braced myself and opened the program that let me interface with his chip. A little viewscreen popped up in my mind's eye, and the headache that permanently resided at the base of my skull mule-kicked my brain. I ground my teeth and did my best to ignore the pain as I navigated to his health program. We'd been at it for over an hour, and I didn't know how much longer my head would hold out.

His vitals looked good. Heart rate, blood pressure, and oxygen levels were normal. Slight increase in brain activity, but I expected that since he ran the maze a few minutes ago. He seemed to enjoy it and had an excess of dopamine, serotonin, endorphins, and oxytocin floating around his system.

"Good boy, Walnut." I gave him another scratch behind his velvety ear. "Try to find the pictures I send you, okay?"

He wheeked happily, but he didn't comprehend what I said. Words weren't his thing, but we hoped he might understand the images I sent to him to lead him to the exit door we wanted.

Felix, the ship computer's avatar, chose that moment to join us in the common room. The thigh-high metal cat leaped onto the island and situated himself so he could look into the maze which was on the floor in between the couch and the walkway to the bunk rooms. His tail—made of thousands of iridescent-black, overlapping scales—swished back and forth, making a scraping sound against the stainless steel and knocking some of DeAjamae's equipment off the island.

"Did the rodent do anything useful yet?" he asked.

I picked up the cables and adapters and placed them on top of DeAjamae's overflowing backpack of parts. "*Walnut* ran the maze five times already to familiarize himself with all the paths."

"This morning, I recalibrated our hazardous gas detection sensors, *and* I extended the stellar sails to recharge my batteries without having to pay for electricity."

"It's not a competition, Felix."

"Obviously, because I'd be winning." He settled into a loaf position with his paws tucked in and stared at the wall like he was bored, but his optic lenses were wide enough to still see into the maze.

"I think we're all set," I said to DeAjamae. "Unless Felix has anything else to add?"

He didn't reply, but I heard a cleaning bot fire up in the cargo hold on the other side of the wall. Felix didn't experience emotions per se, but he often cleaned the ship when things weren't to his liking.

The first image I sent Walnut was of the enormous pile of diced carrots DeAjamae had placed as a prize behind the door with a purple circle on it. Walnut chirped and waddled his potato butt over to the starting gate.

"That's promising." DeAjamae aerial scribed a note into the holoscreen projecting from her cuff.

In prior runs, we'd let Walnut explore the maze on his own. There were four checkpoints, each with a purple shape on it—a circle, square, star, and heart. We wanted him to find each of the shapes using the images I sent him.

I used my Intell to record an image of the purple circle and sent it to him. That was the first checkpoint.

DeAjamae lifted the door slide. Walnut walked through and investigated the space, his little pink sniffer-twitcher working in overdrive. He paused and scratched his ear with a back foot. My Intell displayed his biometric readings, and I saw a spike in his brain activity. He shook his head, then scurried through the correct opening.

When he reached the circle, I sent him an image of the square. Walnut zipped through the twists and turns of the maze. Watching from above, it was clear he'd picked the shortest path. He hit each of the checkpoints with ease. At the end, he found his jackpot of carrots and made several shrill whistles before diving face-first into the pile.

"Yes!" DeAjamae's eyes sparkled with success. Her fingers flew as she aerial scribed notes into her holoscreen.

Felix simulated a yawn. "It's not like he flew through space or something. Yesterday, I ran the cleaning bots through the ventilation system, again. Salt dust from the desert gets everywhere. Do you know how bad salt dust is for a spaceship?"

"I'm going to go out on a limb and guess very bad?"

He made a sound halfway between a humph and hacking up a static hairball.

I'd moved the *Soteria* from the spacedock to a long-term parking lot after Wright offered me a position on his team. I could have sold the ship and used the money to put toward a condo or a house, but I loved it. It had everything I needed, including a sarcastic, crotchety roommate.

Felix had been fine with the move at first. He used the time to run internal diagnostic scans and presented me with a list of demands for replacement parts and system overhauls. We'd been chipping away at the list every payday, but I sensed he was getting bored.

Could a ship's computer even get bored?

DeAjamae eyed him warily, then cleared her throat. "Yeah, so, this tells us Walnut can see images that you send him. Can you reverse the feed to see what he's seeing?"

"How would I do that?" I asked.

"Hmm, maybe try visual display or the diagnostics section? There may be some way to test how the connection to his optic nerve is performing."

I dug around the settings while my headache grew. Sometimes, it gave me throbbing pains or stabbing pains. Other times, it felt like an intense pressure squeezing in or pushing out. Like there was too little or too much space inside my head. Today, it prickled with sharp little pains, like someone plucking out my hair one strand at a time. I smiled, trying my best not to let it show on my face.

My Intell didn't translate my thoughts into commands, so I couldn't just think "see what Walnut sees" and have it happen. The implant first established a wireless link to a device. Then it read the neural impulses traveling from my brain to my fingers when I thought about aerial scribing a command and transmitted that command to the device. The difference was subtle, but it was much faster than traditional cuffs. Those did something similar by mechanically detecting neural impulse signals as they passed through a person's forearm. The Intell also used my own eyes and ears for its visual and auditory interface, allowing me to interact with devices without the use of a holoscreen, camera, microphone, or speaker.

My fingers fluttered with the tiniest movements—it didn't take more than a twitch to trigger the Intell. I brought up the visual display window but didn't find anything useful. The diagnostics menu, however, was a different story. There was a whole subfolder devoted to Walnut's optical nerve integration system.

I clicked open several files, and then one viewscreen began playing a live holovid. I enlarged it to fill my entire field of view. It felt like being dropped inside a virtual reality game. There were white walls all around me, three times my height. In front of me sat a messy pile of pale-yellow cubes. The diced carrots.

"I'm in," I told DeAjamae.

Walnut chirped, and I hoped it wasn't in discomfort.

"What's it like?"

"Trippy. Everything's so ... big. And the colors are all weird."

The view shifted upward, and out of habit, I tilted my head with it. The ceiling was open. A light-brown smudge hovered in the distance. As it drew nearer, DeAjamae's face came into focus. She smiled, reached into the maze, and petted Walnut on the head.

Prickles of pain spread from the base of my neck to the top. It intensified until I imagined whole fistfuls of hair were being yanked out by the root. I placed a hand on the island to steady myself as a wave of dizziness washed over me. It only lasted a few seconds, but the spells had been increasing in frequency.

"Do you have what you need?" I asked. "I don't want to push Walnut too hard. He's already had an exhausting day."

"Yeah, we're all set. We got quite a bit of data for me to work through."

I backed out of Walnut's program as quickly as possible and severed all the connections on my way out. Blood roared in my ears. I was woozy and sick to my stomach.

DeAjamae had turned her back to me to enter in some notes. She leaned closer to the holoscreen and swiped a lock of curly brown hair that fell into her eyes. Most of it was pulled into a high ponytail, with hot-pink highlights making neon stripes across her head.

"This is fascinating. I'm going to make a copy to study on my mega-console at the precinct. Can you hand me that data dot?"

"Sure." I grabbed a data dot from the counter where she'd left it. My hand trembled, and I almost dropped it. Quickly, I placed it on the table beside her and clasped my hands behind my back so that she wouldn't see them. "Right behind you."

"Thanks." She groped at the table until her fingers brushed the data dot. She placed it on the reader and began transferring data to it. "I hate giving any kind of credit to Lourde, but this tech really is cutting edge. It has taken me months to sort out how he planned to connect the implants to bionic weapons and what that might mean for their capabilities."

I shifted my weight from one foot to the other. "Don't beat yourself up. You're not a brain surgeon."

DeAjamae turned and stretched her neck muscles by rolling her head, first in one direction and then the other. "We've been chasing bad leads and running into dead ends for months. Something has to break soon."

"It will. You said yourself you're only halfway through all that data we collected at the lab."

"Don't get me started. Lourde ran triple encryption on his files. I've got two dedicated servers chewing through them."

The reader dinged. DeAjamae removed the data dot, placed it in a carrying case, and dropped it into an internal pocket of her backpack. She slung the bag over her shoulder. "Hey, Ravi and I are getting together at his place tonight to play some VR games. He got a new one he's pretty stoked about—*Fox Hunter 15*. Want to come play with us?"

Air whooshed from my lungs like I'd been sucker punched in the gut. Jarrett had been my best friend for over a decade. We'd played every version of *Fox Hunter*. Debated strategies. Stalked the boards. Threw launch parties. It was our thing. I couldn't even imagine playing without his goofy smile lighting up whenever we completed a new level or him giving me shit when I pulled a stupid move and killed my character.

My knees wobbled, and I staggered back to the nearest chair. Felix jumped down from the counter and sat in front of me.

"Reliance? Are you sick?" The scanner behind his right eye passed a blue light over me from head to toe. "I knew that rodent was diseased. Don't move. I'm running a preliminary health scan."

I waved him off. For a mechanical cat, he could be a mother hen sometimes. "I'm okay. Jarrett and I used to play that game together."

Comprehension filled DeAjamae's eyes, and she threw her arms around me in a hug. "Oh, void-be-damned! I'm so sorry. Forget I said anything."

I sniffed, pulling myself together. "Sometimes it still hits me hard. It'll pass though. It's getting a little more tolerable every day."

DeAjamae released me. "Send me a comm if you need anything. I'm here for you. We all are."

I knew that. Like I knew they'd shift their focus from building a case against Aurelian Tazza to finding a cure if they found out how bad my symptoms had become. What mattered was shutting down Tazza's attempts to develop and manufacture bionic weapons—shutting down his whole damned tech company, if we could. The galaxy couldn't afford for our team to be distracted.

We walked to the hold, and I lowered the cargo bay door. She wrapped her arms around me, again, and squeezed. I hesitated, then returned the hug.

"See you at the office tomorrow." DeAjamae waved goodbye as she exited.

Felix sat beside me while the ramp rose back into place. My hand drifted down to pet the top of his head. His scales felt more like snakeskin than fur, but it was still soothing to run my fingers over it.

"Why did you lie to her?" Felix asked once the door sealed. "My scan returned multiple health issues. Elevated heart rate, high blood pressure—"

"Stop. There's nothing she can do to help, and she'd be required to report my symptoms to the Department. They'd put me on desk duty or give me a medical discharge. I wouldn't be able to help with the case anymore. I'd be a liability to them."

And Aurelian Tazza might never get the punishment he deserved.

"If DeAjamae can't help, who can?"

There was only one person who had answers about the Intell, and I'd rather stick a fork in my eye than talk to him.

I rubbed my hand against my breastbone, trying to ease the growing tightness in my chest. If my symptoms kept progressing, I wouldn't be able to keep them hidden from the team much longer. That would be it. I would be off the case.

I replayed the holocast in my head, picturing Aurelian Tazza's smug face as he walked out of the courthouse a free man. Free to keep on running his corporation, developing illegal weapons tech, and ruining people's lives. It wasn't right.

"Where are you going?" Felix asked, following me to my hover-bike.

"To go talk to someone. It seems I'm all out of forks."

Chapter 4

THIS WAS A PHENOMENALLY bad idea.

I removed the special helmet I'd had custom-built. All the standard electronic components had been stripped out so I could pilot the hoverbike without the weird—and dangerous—double-vision problems that occurred between a helmet's navigation panel and my Intell. My chip connected seamlessly to the bike and displayed the controls in my mind's eye. It had taken some getting used to, but over the last six months I'd practiced often and now flew my bike better than before. This was one area I had to give a point to the Intell.

Static electricity zipped through my indigo hair, lifting the fine, chin-length strands into the air and across my face. It had finally grown out enough to cover the surgical scar on the nape of my neck. I picked a piece out from my eyelashes and finger-combed my hair back into place, making sure the back lay flat. As if hiding the scar would let me forget.

What was I even doing? I asked myself for the sixtieth time since leaving the *Soteria*. That arrogant asshole hadn't cracked under weeks of intense interrogation—there was no reason to suspect he'd help me now.

Except that he loved his work more than anything else, and like it or not, he considered me his greatest work.

That thought alone almost had me flying back to my ship.

Fuck that. Lourde owed me. He put that blasted chip in my head. The least he could do was tell me the name of the medication that mitigated the side effects.

Last night proved ignoring the symptoms wasn't an option. If they continued increasing in severity at the same rate, it wouldn't matter if the team found out about them or not. By the end of the month, I wouldn't be able to do my job.

The maximum-security penitentiary cast a long shadow in the evening sun. Any moisture we'd received from last night's rain had baked off in the day's heat. Dry, crushed regolith crunched beneath my boots as I crossed the LAV parking lot. My strides were quick and purposeful to give myself less time to chicken out.

At the gate, a crusty old guard with bushy white eyebrows and mustache leaned forward and gave me a once-over through the re-inforced plastiglass window.

He pushed the intercom button. "Can I help you?"

"I'm here to see inmate Kandall Lourde."

"Visiting hours are daily between 0800 and 1800 hours. Come back tomorrow."

"I'm an officer with DECA and need to speak with this inmate about an ongoing investigation."

The guard blew out a breath forceful enough to ruffle his mustache hairs.

He pointed to a door reader secured to the wall outside his booth. "Identification and facial scan."

I found the reader on the list of nearby electronics my Intell had registered, selected it, and uploaded my DECA-issue identification credentials. Then I stepped to the side and aligned my face. A blue light passed over me from my hair to my neck, measuring my facial contours and scanning my retinas. After a beep sounded, the guard waved me through the gate.

A tall, black-haired corrections officer met me on the other side and directed me to a full-body scanner. They didn't wear a cuff inside the prison for security reasons. Instead, they had an RFID identification chip embedded in the back of their hand. My Intell grabbed onto its signal and supplied me with their name: Corrections Officer René Valdez.

CO Valdez wore a standard DECA uniform, except theirs was forest green from top to bottom. Also, their utility belt didn't contain any lethal weapons that could be turned against them if stolen by a prisoner. The way they carried themselves told me they probably handled themselves well in a fight, armed or not.

"Blaster, knives, weapons of any kind?" CO Valdez asked.

"No."

"Anything sharp or pointy?"

"No."

"Electronics or communication devices?"

"No."

"That includes your cuff. We have a lockbox you can store it in until you exit."

"I'm not wearing a cuff," I said and swiped my hand down the sleeve of my black leather jacket, turning a patch of material over my forearm transparent. The special material normally allowed the holoscreen projector of a cuff to shine through, but it also allowed the corrections officer to see my arm was bare.

They nodded and started the scan. A three-dimensional image of my body appeared on a large wall console with a green check mark signaling I wasn't carrying any weapons or contraband beneath my clothes. They gave me the thumbs-up, and I stepped out.

"You're here to see Kandall Lourde?" CO Valdez asked.

"Yes, I need to ask him a few questions. Can you bring him to a private room?"

"Follow me."

We passed through another door into a small chamber. When the door closed and locked behind us, a second door unlocked. They walked through and motioned for me to follow. At the end of the long corridor, CO Valdez unlocked the door to a visitor room with a table and two chairs and directed me to wait while they brought Lourde to me.

Sitting held no appeal. I paced the length of the room and used the time to clear out the dozens of signals pinging inside my head. Everything in the prison was controlled electronically: the doors, lights, climate control, cameras, motion sensors, loudspeakers, and fire suppression system. Even the dingy floors emitted some kind of signal, although without digging further, I couldn't tell if it was wired passively for movement detection or offensively with some type of deterrent mechanism. Although I'd been with the Andaress-4 DECA office for six months, I hadn't spent much time inside the Salin prison, and each planet ran its own a little differently.

That prickly feeling started behind my right eye. I wished I'd taken a migraine tab before coming in. They were in my messenger bag, which was locked in the storage compartment on my hoverbike. Today the pain felt like the tip of a hot needle pressing into—but not quite piercing—the thin membrane of my eyeball.

Using a visualization technique I used for managing migraines, I took a deep breath and imagined all the pain manifesting itself as that needle and dragging it from my eye. The pain subsided, or at least became more tolerable.

Sometimes compartmentalizing worked, sometimes not.

CO Valdez rapped once on the door before escorting Lourde inside and seating him at the table. They pushed Lourde's wrist restraints over a magnetic lock embedded in the table. Lourde's hands jerked three centimeters to the left until they were centered over the mechanism.

They rattled the metal chain connecting the bracelets. "The prisoner is secure. Do not approach the prisoner. Do not touch the prisoner. Do not pass anything to the prisoner or take anything from the prisoner. Under no circumstances will you release the magnetic lock. Do you understand?"

"Yes."

"You've got ten minutes," CO Valdez said. "Then I'm required to take him to the yard for his mandatory evening exercise and free time. I'll be outside if you require assistance."

After I nodded agreement, they stepped into the hall and closed the door.

This was the first time I'd been alone in a room with Lourde since before his trial. Wright had always insisted someone from the team accompany me. He'd made it sound like it was for my protection, but secretly I wondered if he thought I might go berserk on Lourde if given the chance.

His concern wasn't entirely without merit. Lourde had done some pretty horrendous things to me, and I was known to be on the impulsive side.

The doctor didn't look like much of a threat now. His wrinkled beige jumpsuit matched his slippers, and his hair lay mashed flat on one side and frizzed out on the other. In place of the custom, high-tech bionic right hand and forearm he had developed for himself was a government-issued one. It was budget grade and quality, with rubbery-looking skin and twitchy movements.

In addition, he wore a white collar around his neck that blocked signals going to and from his Insight chip—the more commercial-grade and user-friendly version of the Intell. The Insight still killed a high percentage of users, but it couldn't hack into government software and decrypt secret files, like mine. A glowing green light on the side assured me the blocker was active.

Oh, how the mighty had fallen.

I pulled out the chair opposite him and sat down.

His frizzy, black hair was threaded with more gray than I remembered, and while he'd never been a large man, he'd lost weight. It showed in the way his pale, liver-spotted skin sagged at his neck and jowls. His eyes, though. They were as sharp and cruel as ever.

"Making new friends?" I asked, pointing to a fresh bruise under his eye.

"Ach." He waved his hand dismissively, the movement stunted by the restraints. "Simpletons. Guards, inmates, all of them. I might as well converse with the pigeons in the yard for all the intellectual stimulation they provide."

"Did you say that to one of them?" I asked, eyeing his bruised cheek. "You did, didn't you?"

He huffed. "I was merely expounding on the differences between—well, that is irrelevant now. I am far more interested in what brought you here today."

A spark of excitement flashed in his eyes that hadn't been there a minute earlier. I hated that I was the one who put it there.

"Tell me, Subject E," Lourde said, using the designation he'd given me when he held me captive in his lab. "Where are your friends? The formidable Agent Wright and the delightful Agent Leahy. I believe she has potential, if she ever opens her eyes to the benefits of working in the private sector."

Beneath the table, my nails scratched into the tops of my legs. "It's Officer Sinclair, and I came alone today."

Lourde tapped a fingertip against the table. The staccato rhythm reminded me of the clicking stress cube he used to carry in the lab. "Ah, you wish to discuss something you don't want your friends to know."

My lips pressed into a thin line.

He waved his hand as far as the restraints would allow. "Come now, it's quite obvious, really. It is outside normal visitor hours, and this is the first time you've come on your own. Ergo, you wish to discuss something private."

Stars, he was infuriating. "What was in the tabs you gave Fax and me?"

His eyes scanned the visible portion of my body, but not in a sexual way. Observational. Clinical. "The side effects have increased in severity." It wasn't a question. "Headaches, dizziness, nosebleeds. Have the tremors begun, yet?"

My nails dug deeper into my thighs, and I forced the admission through gritted teeth. "Mild shaking. My hands, primarily."

He nodded. "That is consistent with the prior subjects' experience. Have you self-medicated?"

"Migraine tabs and painkillers."

Lourde scoffed and shook his head. "Mitigation, at best. They will dull the pain but do nothing to slow the progression of symptoms. It has been twenty-seven weeks since you received the Intell. This version is far outperforming its predecessors. That you survived this long is remarkable."

"Would the tabs eliminate the symptoms?"

"Eliminate?" Lourde's thin brows drew together as he gave my question serious thought. "Perhaps for a time. The neural implant chip in your brain is unique—an upgraded model from my previous round of tests. Based on data from prior experiments, I believe this version to be near perfect. With the right medication, you might survive another ten, fifteen years."

"Ten years! How is that even remotely 'near perfect'?"

Lourde leaned forward, resting his elbows on the table. "Think of all you might accomplish! Surely a decade of greatness is worth sacrificing a few feeble, doting years at the end."

Heat rushed to my face. Suddenly, the room felt too small and Lourde too close. I shoved back from the table. The metal chair legs screeched against the floor as I stood.

"I wouldn't even make it to fifty! That's hardly a *few doting years*. Stars-all, you asshole. That's half my void-damned life!"

"You had no life when I found you. A fugitive. No job, no home, no friends."

Rage I didn't know I'd been holding onto welled up from deep within my core. I lunged into the table, slamming my hands down so hard the force of it jolted through my shoulders. "Don't you dare speak to me about my friends!"

We stared each other down. My arms trembled with the effort of keeping them planted on the table's surface while images of wringing his flabby little neck flashed in my head. Prison was too good for him. It was more merciful than he deserved.

Lourde was an egotistical, narcissistic sociopath, but he blinked first. His eyes dropped, if only for a second. "That temper of yours made you a less-than-ideal subject," he said, attempting to recover.

"I can only imagine it has the same effect on your career in law enforcement."

I ground my teeth but didn't take his bait. Instead, I pulled my chair back to the table and sat down.

"How long do I have without the medication?"

Lourde leaned back as far as the secured restraints allowed. "Impossible to say without seeing more recent data. Give me access to your chip's diagnostic records. It would be child's play for the Intell to bypass this blocker." He stretched his neck to indicate the collar around his neck.

"Not going to happen. Take your best guess with the info I gave you."

"Based on Subject C's progression—three months, maybe four. Weeks once the full-body tremors begin. Days from the onset of the first seizure."

The heat and anger drained from my body, leaving me cold and numb. Three months? That wasn't right. I was finding my place on the team. We had too much to do. Aurelian Tazza was still flying around the galaxy in his private spaceship, free as an asteroid.

"What medication was in the tabs?"

Lourde frowned and shook his head. "The medication was in development and highly tailored to each subject. Doctor Adler monitored your vital signs, and I made daily adjustments to the ingredients and dosages based on your performance. How is my protégé? My lawyer tells she's receiving treatment at a psychiatric facility in Tylo."

"You'll have to ask your lawyer, but I doubt she'll be writing prescriptions anytime soon."

"Pity. She had a brilliant mind but lacked vision."

She also lacked empathy, morals, and ethical guideposts, but Lourde would probably see those as positive traits.

"There must be a medication I can take now."

Lourde tapped the pad of his middle finger against the table. *Tap, tap, tap.* The sound rang hollow in my ears, like a clock counting down the seconds of my life.

"I could formulate a new drug, one that accounts for your evolving situation."

Immediately, a klaxon sounded in my head. "What would you want in return? Because I'm telling you right now, there's no way you're getting a reduced sentence. I would rather die, and I mean that. Literally. You will never see the outside of these walls again."

"Do you know what the worst part of this confinement is? Boredom. I have nothing in common with these ... these malefactors, these common criminals. Even the reading materials are rudimentary, at best."

"You want me to visit you?"

He made a derisive sound. "Don't be ridiculous. Talking with you is no more stimulating than talking to a lab rat. No offense."

I scoffed. "Yeah, why would that be offensive?"

"What I mean to say is, I miss my research."

It took me a moment to catch on. "You want me to let you poke around in my head, again? You've got to be out of your fucking mind. Maybe you should be the one in the psychiatric facility instead of Adler."

"There's that temper impeding rational thought. This is an opportunity for us both to get what we want."

"Why should I trust anything you say?"

"Lies serve no purpose in the pursuit of knowledge. You may have a low opinion of my actions, but I never lied to you."

"Of course you didn't. I was nothing but a lowly test subject to you. You held all the cards."

"*Lowly?* You are my greatest achievement! If only you would embrace your role, we could accomplish great things together. Magnificent things!"

My nostrils flared as I drew in deep, audible breaths. I forced myself to relax my facial muscles so he wouldn't see how much his words affected me.

Embrace my role as a lab rat, my ass.

"That's never going to happen. The only reason I'm here is because this thing you shoved inside my head is malfunctioning."

Tap, tap, tap. "Stubbornness is your least attractive quality."

"What makes you think I'm trying to attract you?"

Lourde sniffed. If stubbornness was my downfall, then pride was his. I dug my nails into the palms of my hands until I was sure I'd have four little half-crescent cuts across them both. Slowly, I forced them open to lie flat against my thighs.

"Even if I considered this—and that's a very big if—my boss will never go for it."

"Ah, the stalwart Agent Wright. Does he need to know?"

"My team keeps track of you. We review your visitor logs."

Lourde paused, like a teacher waiting for a dull student to stumble upon the correct answer. When I didn't elaborate, he let out an exasperated breath. "If only you had the galaxy's most advanced hacking, decryption, and espionage technology at your disposal."

"I am not going to—" I glanced around, noting the monitoring equipment, and lowered my voice to a harsh whisper. "I will not hack into DECA's system and alter its data logs on you."

Not to mention the team would never speak to me again if they found out.

"Shortsighted fool!" Lourde lashed out against his restraints and spittle flew from his mouth in his first genuine display of emotion. "Use the gift I gave you. Don't waste it."

I slammed my hands down on the table, using the force of the movement to push me to my feet. I leaned forward until I heard the rattle of his nervous breath.

"Tell me what the void-damned medication is, or I will die, and no one will ever know the Intell existed, much less who invented it."

The corrections officer looked in through the window. Their brows furrowed together. I raised my hands and backed up a step. They nodded and turned back around.

Lourde pursed his lips, but I saw that I'd finally hit on something he cared about—his legacy.

"The primary component is hexacetaphone," Lourde said. "It will be difficult to find, as it is used to treat a rare neurological disorder affecting less than one in sixty million people. However, a near-identical compound is produced when making the street drug Blue Lace."

I rubbed at my temple, trying to stave off the growing headache. "Narcotics?"

"Several patients reported taking Blue Lace recreationally prior to coming to our research facility. That's how we first discovered hexacetaphone reduced the severity of the symptoms. It took months of isolating components, trying different combinations, and testing the formula to reach the efficacy of the medication you received in the lab. Blue Lace may lessen the negative effects of the neural impulse implant, but it won't eliminate them altogether and it won't prevent them from worsening."

"I've heard enough. Coming here was a mistake." I stood up. "Guard!"

"Think it over, but don't take too long. I may have years left, but you do not have the same luxury. The longer you go without the correct medication, the more irreversible the symptoms will become."

CO Valdez opened the door.

"I'm ready to leave," I said. "You may escort the prisoner back to his cell."

"Yes, ma'am." They flipped the polarity switch on the wall to release the magnetic cuff lock. "Wait here until I get back, and I'll take you to the gate."

The door closed behind them, and I was left alone with my thoughts. Lourde's parting shot sent me into a tailspin. I knew it was too good to be true that he would help me out of some sense of moral obligation or—I didn't know—supreme guilt over what he had done to me. No, the rat bastard saw a way to get his hooks into me again and took it.

Well, the joke was on him. No way would I subject myself to his experiments again.

What was I thinking coming here? I knew—*I knew* no good would come of it. I wasn't a person to Lourde. To him, I was nothing more than an experiment, a test subject, a set of data points to be manipulated and studied until I broke under the strain.

I kicked my chair, sending it skittering toward the wall.

May the void take him and swallow him whole.

A wave of dizziness washed over me, and I braced both hands against the table to keep from tipping over. Head lowered, eyes squeezed shut, I allowed myself one frustrated tear before pulling myself together.

Now was neither the time nor the place to throw myself a pity party. I was no worse off than I had been before coming. It was what it was. If I had two months or two years or two decades, I would live my life on my own terms. Not Lourde's.

Besides, the team would ask questions I wasn't prepared to answer if they ever found out I saw Lourde alone. And if the Blue Lace controlled my symptoms enough that I could continue to work on the case, there was really no need to make them worry. Especially Wright. He'd put me on desk duty faster than a blaster bolt.

All I needed to do was figure out how to get my hands on Blue Lace. I didn't have the same contacts here on Andaress-4 as I'd had on my home world, Brione-5, but if a bunch of idiot, twenty-year-old partyers could find it, I could, too.

I lifted the chair and pushed it under the table as CO Valdez knocked on the door again. "Are you ready, ma'am?"

"All set."

But as they escorted me back the way we had come, I was careful to access each camera, recording device, and log that proved I had visited Doctor Kandall Lourde today and erased them.

Just in case.

Chapter 5

Mondays were always rough for me, but today I found it almost impossible to stay focused. Most of the other officers and agents had cleared out for lunch, leaving the office blissfully free of personal electronic devices and snooping eyes.

This was the easiest time of day to work without the added distractions of notifications popping up every thirty seconds. I had constant anxiety that my Intell was going to hack into someone's private comms and show me a lot more about my coworker's questionable courting techniques than I needed to know. Nobody wanted to see that holo of Officer Johnson wearing nothing but his holster belt, least of all me.

I replayed my conversation with Lourde over and over in my head. What if he was right, and this thing in my brain was a ticking time bomb? Getting reinstated as a DECA officer and joining Wright's team felt like I'd been given a new lease on life. A fresh start. A purpose. I needed to figure out where to get my hands on some Blue Lace. That would buy me the time to plan what to do next.

If there was one advantage I would give the Intell, it was being able to work without prying eyes glimpsing my console or holoscreen. It required the barest amount of aerial scribing to navigate to the bookings files. I'd woken up at 0300 hours with the idea of looking through recent arrest records to find someone pinched for selling Blue Lace, and...

And what? Hit them up for a buy? Hope they didn't drop my name the next time they got busted to get out of charges?

Stupid. I closed out the file.

I reopened my earlier project of chasing down an address for Ravi. He wanted to talk to the administrative assistant of Doctor Benedict Rennali. Doctor Rennali was the employee at the Interplanetary Board of Medical Devices whom Lourde—or more likely Aurelian Tazza—had bribed to get the Insight device fast-tracked to approval. The IBMD had terminated Doctor Rennali, but they hadn't been eager to let us dig deeper into their organization.

"It's being dealt with internally" was a phrase we heard often.

Doctor Rennali's assistant, Kristyn Strann, had also been let go. Ravi thought she might feel more comfortable if he approached her outside of the auspicious offices of the IBMD.

I pulled up the file on Strann. My Intell displayed the image in my mind using my optic nerves. Female, twenty-five, never married, no kids, attractive but a little wallflowerish, judging by the few public holos of her I'd tracked down. The annoying thing was, Ravi probably could get her to talk. Charming was his middle name.

"Hey, Rel! Think fast!"

I closed the file, but not quick enough. Something small and malleable smacked into my chest and fell into my lap.

Ravi laughed. "Nice catch."

"I was looking at something," I said, swirling my finger in the area where most people would have a holoscreen projecting from their cuff. I must have looked like a space cadet staring off into nothing. No wonder people stared at me.

"A likely excuse," he teased.

"What's this?" I asked, peeking into the palm-sized bag. "Hellaberries?"

"A new food cart set up out front. Fruits, veggies, nuts. All healthy stuff."

"No pastries?"

"Not a single one."

I popped an indigo berry into my mouth and puckered my lips at the tart juice. "He's missing the mark parking so close to the precinct. DECA officers run on simple carbs, sugar, and caffeine."

"Do I smell roasted cashews?" DeAjamae's head bobbed up from her cubicle in the next row. Thankfully, her desk sat just outside my Intell's range, or I'd go crazy fending off all the electronic signals coming from it. She had gadgets and gizmos aplenty.

She'd worn her hair loose today, and the mass of curls bobbed as she zeroed in on Ravi's armful of treats. He grinned, and it was breathtaking. That man could have been a politician. Or a grifter. Same difference.

"Roasted and spiced. I bought a bag of Saper almonds, too. The merchant said this heavy rain we've been getting made for a bumper crop this year."

DeAjamae twisted her lips to the side. "Hmm..."

Ravi held out his hand. "Do you want both?"

Her answering smile lit up her entire face. "You're the best." She snatched them before he changed his mind and ducked back below the partition.

"You're welcome!" he called after her.

She waved a hand over her head. Only a few seconds passed before we heard her muttering to herself as she worked. "Son of a bee sting. Why? Why is that necessary? Yes, it does. It fucking does. I created it myself. Now I have to put whatever the fuck those are wherever the fuck they go."

Ravi grinned at the string of curses flowing from DeAjamae's cubicle. He eased his way over to Wright's desk, which was kitty-corner from mine, and cocked his hip onto the desk. He pulled a second bag of cashews from his pocket, tossing a handful into his mouth.

"You're smarter than you look, Agent Singh," I said, nodding at the nuts.

"Then I must be a certified genius."

I wheeled my chair back a few centimeters. "Do you need me to scooch over to make room for that ego of yours?"

He laughed. "Jealousy's not a good look on you, Reliance."

I let out an exaggerated sigh. "Somebody has to be the beauty and brains of this operation. It might as well be you."

"Nah." His gaze shifted to DeAjamae's cubicle. "That job's already taken. I'll have to be the muscle." Ravi flexed his right arm to show off a toned but lean biceps beneath his black, Department-issued Henley.

"Eh-hem," Wright said, coming up behind Ravi.

The poor guy jumped up so fast, you'd have thought the desk was electrified. "Hey, boss. Didn't hear you come in. Cashews?"

I stifled a laugh by chewing on another tart hellaberry.

Wright waved off the proffered treat. "DeAjamae, group meeting."

"What are you talking about? It's right there. What are you doing? What the fuck are you doing? It's right void-damn there. Don't make this hard. See? It's perfect. PERFECT. Ugh! This is giving me such a stars-all headache. Oh, there's a fucking underscore in front of it? Asshole. Now, can you please accept it?"

"DeAjamae!"

The digital forensic analyst poked her head up over the partition. "Yeah?"

"Group meeting," Wright said. "I have a briefing with the lieutenant in five minutes. She wants an update on the bionic weapons case."

"Be right there. I have to—" Something hard banged against her desk. Then, in a lower voice, she muttered, "So, you're going to ... yep, you're going to be a fucking asshole. Awesome. Just do the thing. Do the one fucking thing I told you to do."

A second later she walked over to join us, tossing the empty bag of almonds into a reclamator on the way.

"Problems?" I asked.

She shrugged. "The usual. Have I mentioned that technology is getting worse?"

"Once or twice."

DeAjamae hoisted her butt onto my desk. "Good. Because it is."

Ravi pulled his chair from across the aisle, so we all sat together. Wright leaned against his desk and faced us.

"Where are we at?"

As the senior agent, Ravi went first. "I've been following up with the IBMD. Doctor Benedict Rennali has been terminated for taking bribes to greenlight Tazza Industries' Insight neural implant chips without testing. The Board is cooperating with its local DECA office on charges of fraud, embezzlement, and endangerment of public safety. All production of the Insights is temporarily suspended while a second phase of trials gets underway. Patients who already received an Insight were notified and instructed to see their primary caregiver at Tazza Industries' expense. The company has set aside funds for the victims to cover treatment and damages as claims are made."

Wright nodded. "What are your next steps?"

"I'm hoping to speak with Doctor Rennali's former assistant, Kristyn Strann to find out if she can tie the bribe to Tazza Industries or Aurelian Tazza himself. So far, the evidence only shows the money coming from Lourde's private company, KaLo Research. Rel is tracking her down for me."

My fingers made some minute gestures, aerial scribing to my communication program. "I found her new address right before you came in. You're not going to like it."

"No?"

"She's living on Remus-3 with her parents. Sending it to you now."

Ravi groaned. Remus-3 was a newly terraformed planet on the edge of civilization. "What is that, a five-day trip?"

"Try seven, each way."

Wright frowned. "I can't spare you for two weeks. See if she'll agree to meet in a holosuite. Remus-3 is a resort planet. There should be several available for rent. Tell her to charge it to the Department." He turned to DeAjamae. "Where are we on the document review of the files from Lourde's lab?"

DeAjamae winced. "Not as far as I'd like. We retrieved a massive amount of data, both from the lab and from the backup server Lourde took with him when he fled. Tazza Industries claims it's proprietary information, and we didn't have a warrant for it, so they should get it back. The attorneys are hashing it out, but meanwhile it's here and I'm working to get whatever I can off of them. There's a lot of stuff in there not related to the implants or bionic weapons. It looks like Lourde and Adler stored side projects there. Plus, the indexing system is garbage and everything's encrypted."

"Do we have anything on the bionic weapons?" Wright asked.

"Maybe. That's what I was working on right before the meeting. Thingamajig, launch holoscreen and bring up the inventory list. Maximum display."

"Displaying now," the robotic voice of her cuff said. The holoscreen was large enough for all of us to see it.

"Our best lead so far is an inventory list for—what I believe are—five completed, prototype bionic weapons with Insights. It's dated seven months ago. I haven't been able to trace what happened to them."

Wright looked at me. "Any ideas?"

"None," I said. "There were several in the lab the night I broke in, but Lourde removed them after one of the guards found me poking around in his workroom. I assumed they were put in another part of the building."

He frowned. "I don't like the idea of five prototypes being unaccounted for."

"They're probably sitting in some janitor closet," DeAjamae said. "We tore that lab apart. On the plus side, with Lourde in prison, we know that will be the last of them."

"I could talk to Sagi Barros. Ask if he knows anything about them," Ravi said, referring to the security guard at Tazza Industries. Barros had testified against his boss and Doctor Lourde in exchange for a lighter sentence for his role in my friend's homicide.

"Barros had access to the entire building when I was there," I said. I knew that because I'd cloned his access code to break into the facility. In retrospect, not my smartest idea. "It's possible he would know where they moved the weapons."

Wright thought about it for a moment. "Do it, but get in touch with the warden first. See if he'll offer a few perks to encourage

Barros to talk. Extra rehabilitation classes, easier chore shifts, stuff like that."

"More comm time with his mother," I suggested. "They're close, and she's sick. He'll go for that."

Ravi aerial scribed a note into his holoscreen and closed it. "I have a few comms to return relating to the IBMD side of things, but I'll go to the prison tomorrow morning and talk to Barros."

"Sounds good," Wright said. "DeAjamae, keep going through the documents. Prioritize finding out what happened to those five prototype weapons. Reliance, keep on the IBMD about those financial records."

We broke apart. Ravi and DeAjamae chatted. Wright strode off to his meeting with the lieutenant. He still walked with the straight back and purposeful stride ingrained from his early career in the Ritru-6 military, but I noted the increased tension he held in his neck, jaw, and shoulders. This wasn't the kind of progress he'd been hoping for. It wouldn't be a pleasant briefing for him.

"We're going to go grab lunch. You in?" Ravi asked.

I shook my head. "No, thanks. I have to catch up on some work."

"Let me grab my bag," DeAjamae said, ducking into her cubicle. "Want us to bring you something back?"

"No, I'll grab something from the cafeteria."

Ravi followed DeAjamae to her cubicle. I wondered if Dee had picked up on his interest yet, and if she had, what she intended to do about it. It was none of my business, but romantic relationships could mess with team dynamics. We spent a lot of time together, both at work and on our off days. I didn't want that to change.

If they paired up, they'd start spending time alone together. That would leave Wright and me on our own, which would be terrible. Awful really. I definitely didn't want that. Nope, nope, nope.

I felt heat color my cheeks, so I spun my chair around and scooted in closer to my desk. Best to focus on work.

Bionic weapons. Who had them, and where were they?

The ones I saw in the lab appeared to be paired with the less-powerful Insight neural implants, but it was possible Lourde had planned to use Fax and me as test subjects for these, as well. A chill slid down my spine at the thought of being hacked apart and reassembled like some kind of Captain Stardust doll. I'd seen the lab rats and guinea pigs. They'd had healthy limbs removed and replaced with mechanical parts. There was no doubt in my mind that Lourde thought little more of me than a larger specimen for him to play with.

Bionic limbs and organs had been available for several hundred years, with significant advances made in the last twenty years by Lourde himself as the foremost expert in the field. However, bionic weapons were constructed of a synthetic material that shielded the metal parts beneath it. With a quality grade synthetic skin covering the devices, they would be undetectable on scanners. They could be smuggled between planets, on public transports, or into secure facilities and law enforcement would be none the wiser until it was too late.

Wright stormed back into the bullpen. He stopped at my desk. "Leahy, Singh. Get over here."

I spun around to find an inscrutable look on his face. Something big must have happened in the meeting. DeAjamae and Ravi hurried back from where they'd been waiting for a lift.

"Change of plans. Pack your bags, we're going to Ritru-6. I think we may have found one of the missing prototypes."

DeAjamae's eyebrows shot up. "Yeah?"

"Ritruvian Representative Damaris Delligatti was assassinated five hours ago inside the heavily secured Ritru-6 House of Representatives. The local DECA office apprehended the suspect and have him in custody. They removed what they believe to be a bionic weapon from his person. While he will be charged on Ritru-6, they agreed to let us question him and take the bionic weapon into our custody. Be ready to take off in two hours."

"Yes, sir."

The other two went to their desks to grab anything work-related they might need. I caught up to Wright and jogged alongside him as he headed toward the lifts.

"Do you mind if we take the *Soteria*? It's roomier than a cruiser, and Felix has been giving me an obscene number of alerts about being parked planetside for six months. Something about salt dust and needing to run the engine."

"I don't have a problem with that. We'll rendezvous at your ship at 1400."

Chapter 6

"What took you so long?" Felix demanded. "He's been here for fifteen minutes. On my bridge."

"Calm down," I said and finished securing my hoverbike to its rack in the cargo hold of the *Soteria*. My helmet snapped onto its magnetized hook where it wouldn't bounce around during the flight. "I'm not that late."

Felix swished his tail back and forth, the miniature scales making a rasping sound against the metal floor. *"He's in my chair."*

I chuckled and patted the oversized cat on the head before pressing the button to raise the cargo hold ramp. "He has to sit someplace," I said, "and there are only two chairs on the bridge."

The hydraulics groaned, then the end of the ramp lifted toward the ceiling. Beneath me, the floor swayed as the ship's center of gravity shifted to accommodate the new distribution of weight.

"Why can't he stand?"

"For two days?"

The cat's tail vibrated at the tip like a rattlesnake. "Yes. The preflight medical scan I ran showed Agent Wright to be in perfect health. Let him stand."

"Felix," I admonished and squatted down so that we were eye level. "You need to make room for the team. Like it or not, they're a part of the crew for the next few days."

"I choose not. It's bad enough you brought a rodent onboard. Should I even bother with security protocols anymore?"

The urge to roll my eyes was strong. I reached down to stroke the side of his shoulder plate, which he usually responded to positively. Felix dipped his back low as he stood up, staying just beyond my fingertips.

"Start the preflight check. Make sure you have enough sinnafuel and power reserves to make the trip and send a cleaning bot through the copilot bunkroom. I don't remember the last time we used it."

Felix made a huffing sound. "The last occupant was Agent Wright, and I assure you, I ran the bots in there after he vacated the ship. What do you think I do all day while you're at work?"

"Hmm, go into sleep mode?"

"It's like you don't even know me."

My headache intensified, but I didn't think it was due to using my Intell. I hoped this conversation didn't end with him barfing oil in my boots. "Just double-check, please."

"Fine. I'll be in the bunkrooms *making room* for them. We haven't pulled down the upper bunks since you did the walk-through inspection before buying me." Felix's tail twitched. "I suppose they'll need the spare jump seats released, too."

"That would make takeoffs and landings safer."

"Call me when you're ready to launch. That is, if I'm still allowed on the bridge."

Not for the first time, I wondered at his designer's decision to pick a cat to model his personality after. The man I'd bought him from had said Felix used a learning-based program, so maybe I was to blame for his shitty attitude.

He padded through the door to the common area, and I heard the distinctive whirling sound of cleaning bots turning on. Freakin' cat. If nothing else, the *Soteria* was going to be sparkling from stem to stern by the time this trip was done.

Still, odds were fifty-fifty that Wright would find a splotch of oil on his pillow tonight.

I straightened, hearing my knees pop as I did so. My strength and stamina had improved these last six months planetside, but my body still felt the toll that living for a year in space had taken on it. I debated following Felix into the common area to double-check the food and medical supplies and give Walnut a scratch under the chin, but Felix would probably accuse me of checking up on him. I'd had enough drama for one day.

That left joining Wright on the bridge while we waited for DeAjamae and Ravi to arrive.

My entire flight from the precinct to the ship, I'd thought about how to delay takeoff until I could get some Blue Lace. None of the excuses I came up with sounded even remotely plausible. We'd hoped for a lead like this for months. It would seem suspicious if I stalled. My only option was to hope we got to Ritru-6, interrogated the assassin, and got back to Andaress-4 as quickly as possible. Luckily, it was one of the closer planetary systems to Andaress-4. One day there, one day for the interview, one day back. I'd gone six months so far. What difference would another three days make?

Twenty-two hours later, we landed in Lapidea, the capital of Ritru-6. The local DECA chief and a government official met us at the security gate. I hadn't expected such a high-ranking welcome committee, but in hindsight, it shouldn't have surprised me. Bionic weapons were a touchy subject for the planet. We were lucky they were cooperating with our team and letting us question the assassin.

Ritru-6 was a mining planet. Sinna Energy had terraformed it and Ritru-3 for the planets' rich sinnalite reserves. About eighty years ago, Ritru-6 separated from the company after a vicious rebellion. Their grievances also included poor living conditions, the mistreatment of workers, and genetic engineering done to make the colonists better adapted to the stronger-than-average gravity.

The company had tried to quash the rebellion using bionic weapons during the Ritruvian Uprising Massacre. That event led to the galaxy-wide ban on the research, development, production, sale, ownership, and storage of bionic weapons. It was understandable that the Ritruvians would be sensitive to one being used to assassinate a government leader.

Ritru-6 also happened to be Wright's home planet.

I picked up my blaster from the scanner tray and holstered it. It felt heavier because of the gravity, and I readjusted how it sat at my waist.

"Chief Samuel Abara. Glad you could make it on such short notice." He wore his full uniform with all the ribbons and brass tacks, but he'd loosened his tie and removed his cap to reveal a head of close-cropped, curly, black hair. His wide, brown eyes looked tired but resolved, and I suspected he'd been doing holocast interviews with the press before we arrived.

Wright shook the middle-aged man's large hand. "Lead Agent Grayson Wright. This is my team, Agent Ravi Singh, Agent DeAjamae Leahy, and Officer Reliance Sinclair. We appreciate you calling us in."

"Let me introduce Ambassador Charlotte Rayl. She'll be working with us on any foreign relations matters."

"Please call me Lottie." The woman shook all our hands, ending with Wright.

He gave her a tight smile. "Mom."

"It's good to see you, Grayson."

DeAjamae's bony elbow nudged me in the arm, and she snuck a wide-eyed look in my direction. Wright hadn't mentioned we'd be meeting his mother on this trip.

Now that I was looking for it, I saw the family resemblance. Both Wright and Lottie were tall with athletic builds, lighter complexions, and straight, dark-blond hair, although Lottie's hair was liberally streaked with fine silver threads. Pulled into a twist, it lent her a dignified air that I bet credits to crispers served her well in her official capacity.

"Foreign relations?" Wright asked as we walked toward two sets of sleek, black, government-issued LAVs. "Have you confirmed the assassin is not Ritruvian?"

Lottie projected the holoscreen from her cuff and pulled up a file. Seconds later, my team's comms beeped with notifications for incoming transmissions. My Intell picked it up and displayed the booking holo of a man. Early thirties, medium build, light-to-tan complexion, brown hair pulled back in a low bun, dark eyes with heavy brows, and a trimmed beard. His right arm was amputated at the elbow and fitted with some kind of mechanical socket.

"The assassin. He walked through high-level security into the House of Representatives voting chamber and opened fire. Seven members and aides were severely wounded, a dozen suffered minor injuries, and Representative Damaris Delligatti from the Southern Glade region was killed when a blaster bolt hit her directly in the heart."

"He took down six security guards on his way out," Chief Abara added. "We only apprehended him because automatic lockdown procedures went into effect, sealing each individual room in the building and trapping him inside an interior room. Even so, he broke through four barriers before we pumped an airborne sedative through the climate control system."

"The bionic weapon?" Wright asked.

Chief Abara hesitated. "Removed from his person and secured."

"We'll need to take that into our custody after you've finished processing it for any evidence you need."

"Understood."

We reached the LAVs. Wright closed out his holoscreen. "This still doesn't explain why the ambassador is here."

Lottie clasped her hands together. "There was a vote on the floor concerning opening additional areas of the reserve for sinnalite mining. It was a close vote, and Representative Delligatti was the leading opponent of the measure. Rumors are that support groups are being heavily funded by Sinna Energy from Ritru-3."

"Sinna Energy has to know that Ritru-6 would never award a mining contract to them," Wright said.

"Times change. Two of our largest mines have run dry, along with the jobs they provided. Sinna Energy promises to use local labor and pay fair wages if awarded any contracts. They've been very vocal about their interest."

Ravi heaved our bags in the back of the closest LAV. "But enough to assassinate a representative with an illegal bionic weapon? Given your two planets' history, that seems intentionally inflammatory."

"I agree," Lottie said. "But we are familiar with Sinna Energy acting in illogical ways. Representative Delligatti was much loved. If Ritru-3 is behind her assassination, I fear our response will be swift and decisive."

"War?" Wright asked.

"It's not out of the question."

Chief Abara opened the gullwing door of the second LAV and held it for Ambassador Lottie Rayl.

"I'd like to speak with the assassin right away," Wright said. "We may have leverage that will make him talk."

"That's going to be complicated," Chief Abara said. "The assassin escaped custody thirty minutes ago. We tracked him heading toward the Thousand Pillars mountain range. We're hoping your team can help recapture him before he gets off-planet."

Chapter 7

"It's no good," DeAjamae said, her sculpted brows furrowing as her fingers danced over the controls. "I can't get a sensor lock on him through all that brush."

My eyes strained to spot any kind of movement on the steep slope of the mountain. "Over there." I pointed to a small clearing five hundred meters from the last place we had spotted the suspect.

Our LAV banked hard to the left. DeAjamae circled the bare patch of earth and attempted to lower the landing gear. Red warning lights lit up the main holoscreen and an angry alarm blared out a proximity warning.

"What are you doing?" DeAjamae smacked the side of the console. "What in the actual void are you doing? I did not tell you to do that." She made a grand swiping gesture, clearing the screen. "Fine. We'll start over. There's got to be an override switch in here somewhere."

The LAV listed to the starboard side when one set of legs extended but not the other.

"Talk to me, Dee."

"There's not enough room to land. This is as low as she'll go without the auto-safety features kicking in. I can try to bypass them."

"How long?"

She stared at the holoscreen, eyes flicking back and forth as she lost herself in the text.

"Leahy! How long?" I repeated.

She shook her head and grimaced. "Ten minutes. At least."

It might as well be ten days. We'd only caught one drone image of the assassin when he'd crossed an open firebreak between Lapidea and the Thousand Pillars mountain range. The bare strip of land was used to prevent the summer wildfires from spreading to the city below.

Reports were coming in, but it appeared he had two bionic arms—not one. Officers had removed the one he'd exposed during the assassination while he was still unconscious. However, because of the nature of the bionic weapon, they'd had no way of knowing about the other one. He'd waited until they'd locked him in a holding cell, then used the second one to blast his way free.

I banged my fist against the console and set off another constellation of red lights. If he got away, we would lose our best lead to proving Tazza Industries was developing bionic weapons technology.

"How far down is that?" I asked, eyeing the distance to the ground.

"Maybe two-and-a-half meters. Why?"

I unfastened my harness. "Take it as low as it will go and keep it steady."

Another alarm sounded when I forced the emergency exit bar up on the door. Cold air surged in, whipping purple strands of hair into my eyes and mouth.

"Are you nuts?" DeAjamae shouted over the roar of the wind. "You'll break your legs!"

I looked down at the rock-hard surface. It was going to hurt. No way around that.

My right hand patted the blaster holstered on my hip, reassuring myself it was still there. "You have a lock on my comm signal, right?"

"Yes. Shit. Hold on, let me at least call it in." She aerial scribed the command to open her comm.

"Wright." Our team leader's voice sounded agitated.

I maneuvered myself out of the LAV so that my feet balanced on the foot bar and my hands gripped the top of the frame.

"Sir, we lost visual of the suspect and can't pick him up on sensors. There's no place to land. Sinclair is planning to jump out of the LAV and pursue him on foot."

"Negative. Send me your coordinates. Singh and I will rendezvous with you, and we'll go together."

I double tapped my pinkie on my thumb to open my comm to the group channel. "There isn't enough time for that. The terrain is too rough. If he gets a good head start, we'll never catch him."

"Sinclair! Hold position. That's an order. We don't know what armaments the suspect is carrying. Do not go in alone."

I pretended I hadn't heard that last comm. If Wright were in my boots, he'd do exactly the same thing. Bending at the knees, I squatted until my fingers found a grip by digging deep into the seat cushion. There were no convenient handholds. LAVs weren't designed for midflight evacuation.

"Son of a sow," DeAjamae cursed as she tried to adjust for the sudden change in the craft's center of gravity.

I sucked in a deep breath, adjusted my balance, and reached down until my hands felt the cold metal of the foot bar. In one smooth motion, I slid my feet out from under me. The jolt about tore my arms from their sockets, but I maintained my hold while I dangled from the foot bar. Below me, the ground swam in and out of focus as the LAV rocked.

Not my smartest idea.

I pumped my legs to generate a small swing and let go. My landing was less than graceful. Pain shot from my toes to my hips, but I turned the momentum into an awkward shoulder roll. Loose rocks and sticks scattered around me as I slid several meters down the mountain slope. On about the fourth rotation, my feet hit a clump of tall grass that was coarse enough for purchase. I took a quick assessment and noted that the only thing I injured was my pride. That fall had to have been captured on the DECA LAV's outer cameras.

"Sinclair?" DeAjamae's voice sounded in my head.

I stood up and brushed the dirt from my thighs. "All good. Forgot to compensate for the stronger gravity. I'm heading toward the suspect's last known location."

"Confirmed. I'll keep sweeping the area and see if I can get a visual."

The LAV rose and flew off to my right.

My Intell alerted me to a new incoming visual comm—this one on a private channel. It was Wright. He wouldn't be able to see my face. Unlike the arm cuffs most people in the known galaxy wore, my neural impulse implant didn't have a camera lens that could be directed back at my face. It used my own eyes to record visual data. As I wiped my sleeve across my face to clean off some of dirt and sweat from my fall, I was glad for that fact.

I aerial scribed to the comm settings, flipping it so that Wright could see what I was seeing, and accepted the comm.

Wright's scowling face appeared in my mind's eye. His jaw muscles clenched tight. His dark-blond hair looked like he'd run his hand through it a couple of dozen times, and he had a slight twitch in his right eye. It was the look he reserved for criminals, lowlifes, and on special occasions, a certain fugitive-turned-officer who didn't always do things by the book.

"That was rash and impulsive—"

"And worked out fine."

"You could have broken your neck."

"But I didn't, and now we won't lose thirty minutes while you find a place to land. Have Leahy send up a drone. I'll signal it so you can track me."

He closed his eyes and pinched the bridge of his nose between two fingers. "All right. You may track the suspect, but do not—I repeat—*do not* engage without backup. We don't know what he's capable of."

"Aye, aye, sir!" I gave a jaunty salute, and it was for the best that my boss couldn't see me over the comm. Which reminded me of why I'd enabled visuals. I turned my head in the direction we'd last spotted the suspect.

Tall, spire-like mountain peaks stretched as far as I could see. Within them lay rich deposits of sinnalite, the energy-rich substance that made faster-than-light travel possible. From a distance, one might be fooled into thinking they were skyscrapers from a giant metropolis. Up close, however, it was obvious they would dwarf even the largest human-made structures many times over.

Clumps of coarse vegetation grew all the way to the top of the reddish-brown towers, watered by a thick blanket of mist that shrouded the mountains every morning. The mist had burned off in the heat of the afternoon sun, and I had a clear view of the entire mountain before me.

The assassin had broken out of custody, fled the city, and run straight for this pillar. Why? It didn't look any different from the others. Did he have an accomplice waiting to help? Weapons stashed? Supplies? Or did he plan to disappear into the wilderness?

Whatever it was, it was obvious he had some kind of plan, and that couldn't be good.

I raised my hand so Wright could see it and pointed to the area we'd last seen movement. "That's where I'm heading."

"We'll join you as soon as we can." Wright leaned closer to his camera and lowered his voice. "Reliance, I know you want this guy, but be safe. That's an order, and you damn well better follow this one."

He ended the comm, and I blinked to readjust my eyes. A dull pain formed behind them that often accompanied using the visual features of my Intell. It felt like somebody was pressing their thumbs on my eyeballs from the inside.

I jogged up the steep incline, watching my footing as loose pebbles skittered around my boots. Coniferous trees covered this part of the base, and it became difficult to tell which direction I was going as their dense branches blotted out sections of my view. I looked down and to the right, activating my Intell, again. A display menu popped up in the center of my vision. With a few slight movements of my fingers, I connected to Ritru-6's planetary network, pulled up a topographical map of the local area, and overlaid my geomarker with it. Once I got my bearings, it only took me five minutes to reach the firebreak.

There was a soft buzzing overhead. I cast my eyes to the clear blue sky and saw a drone hovering. It dipped up and down. DeAjamae acknowledging she had my back, even as she searched for a safe place to land.

The suspect had been headed toward the top of the pillar. I scrambled along the edge of the steep firebreak, looking for signs of where he entered the foliage on the other side. About forty paces away, I found a patch of crushed grass and fresh gouge marks on the bark of a thin tree he must have used to pull himself up.

Using the same tree to hoist myself up the bank, I noticed that my grip didn't leave scrapes on the tree. My finger traced the gashes in the splintered wood. How much force had he exerted to make them?

His trail wasn't difficult to follow—footprints, disturbed vegetation, and overturned rocks exposing the damp undersides dotted his path. He valued speed over stealth, which meant I had to, too.

I picked up the pace.

A sheen of sweat formed on my forehead, neck, back, and chest, and my thighs and shoulders burned. It was more climbing than hiking, and I was grateful for the stair work I'd incorporated into my exercise routine since settling down on Andaress-4.

Five hundred meters farther, I spotted the suspect nearing the section of the mountain where the pitch changed from steep to vertical. His build was more muscular than his booking holo had led me to believe. He still wore the beige jumpsuit they'd assigned him in jail. It was unzipped and the shirt sleeves were tied around his waist to keep them from flapping in the stiff breeze. The white undershirt popped against the green-and-brown landscape. Otherwise, I might not have seen him.

I paused in a semi-clear section and waved to the drone, pointing toward the suspect. Then I opened an audio comm. "Leahy, I have eyes on the target. One hundred and fifty meters ahead of me, heading northeast."

"Confirmed," she replied. "Landing now. We're at the base of the mountain. Try not to have all the fun before we reach you."

"Then you better hurry your asses up."

"Unpacking the switches as we speak, but you know how stubborn these two mules can be."

"Tell the guys drinks are on me if you catch up before I apprehend the suspect on my own."

"Wait for us. I can buy my own void-damned drink."

"Where's the fun in that?" I said, ending the comm before she gave me an official order to wait. I'd already ignored at least one command today and didn't know if I could get away with two.

Another ten minutes of hard scrambling, and I'd made a little ground on the suspect. He was now only one hundred meters ahead of me near the section of mountain where the steep incline at the base transitioned into the near-vertical pillar.

Ahead, his white shirt disappeared into a cut in the rock face. Despite my earlier cheekiness with DeAjamae, I had no intention of walking into the situation blind. I opened my Intell's interface, located the drone's signal, and took control. Normally, I would need an access code, but my Intell was designed for hacking and espionage. Doctor Lourde likely never envisioned it being used by legitimate law enforcement.

My stomach clenched when a viewscreen opened in my mind's eye, showing me the mountain from the drone's point of view. I grabbed onto a rocky outcropping for support and waited for the nausea to pass.

It took a few seconds to find myself from the drone's viewpoint. Like the suspect's beige jumpsuit, my forest-green DECA jacket blended in with the surroundings. Scrolling to the navigation controls, I sent the drone around the blind corner while I continued climbing.

The image that came back was of a black scar cut straight into the pillar. I flew the drone closer until the screen turned dark. Switching to a higher aperture setting brought the inside of the fissure into view. The suspect clung to the side of a near-vertical cliff wall like a spider. He reached up with his left bionic arm, dug his fingers into a groove, and *flung* his body upward by at least a meter. With the same hand, he caught a small outcropping where he dangled loose while he searched for his next handhold. Then he pumped his legs once and flung himself upward again.

Where was he going? The top of the pillar was just … the top. There was nowhere to go after he reached it.

I moved the drone higher, scanning for a hidden stash of supplies or something of value. About a quarter of the way up, a glint of light caught my eye.

Shit. I closed out the window and opened my comm to the entire team. "He's got a ship stashed on the mountain."

"Are you sure?" Wright asked.

I linked them in to the drone feed. "Positive."

"That looks like a pacer," Ravi said. "Single occupancy, fast, and capable of interstellar travel. If he reaches it, we'll have a rough time catching up in LAVs."

"Leahy," Wright said. "Get a comm through to Ritru-6's Central Command. Have them launch ships and be ready to intercept."

There was a pause, then a colorful string of curses that lasted until her breath ran out. "No can do, sir. The mountains must be interfering with my cuff's signal. I have to return to the city and send it from there."

"Go. Singh, go down with her. I'll keep heading up to give Sinclair support. If the suspect takes flight, try to coordinate with Central Command to get an interstellar ship after him."

"Yes, sir," Ravi said, and I could hear the jolts in his voice from running hard. They must not be too far up the mountain if the terrain was still clear enough for him to run.

I redoubled my efforts, using roots and the small branches to help pull myself up. My thighs and biceps burned from the unaccustomed movement and increased gravity, but within another five minutes I reached the crack the suspect had gone into. Cautiously, I rounded the corner and stared up at the cliff face while catching my breath. It wasn't as sheer as it looked from a distance, but it was still pretty damned steep.

The cut was deep and narrow, running at least one hundred meters into the heart of the mountain. It looked like a giant had removed a slice of the pillar like a piece of cake.

I guesstimated the width to be nine meters wide. A single-occupancy LAV might fit inside, but the ones we'd borrowed from the local precinct seated four. Even if DeAjamae squeezed it in without scraping the wings to pieces, she'd have no room to maneuver.

It looked like I'd be going up.

I removed my DECA jacket and tossed it on the ground, trading its protection against the sharp rocks for freedom of motion. Then I removed everything from my duty belt except my blaster to lighten my weight. I'd rock climbed a few times before, but only for fun and never for speed.

A bead of sweat trickled down the side of my neck. I took my last opportunity to dry my hands and face with the hem of my shirt and noticed a dark smear. My fingers swiped across the bottom of my nose, and they came back speckled red with blood. I'd pushed my Intell too far.

Nothing to be done about it now.

I spared a few seconds to map out a route, then grabbed onto my first handhold and hoisted myself up. A niche for my right foot. The lip of a ledge for my hand. Big stretch to the sturdy root of a bush. Next, my left foot.

"Slow is smooth. Smooth is fast," I murmured to myself as I pushed off a chunk of rock with the toe of my boot. "And don't look down."

Of course, I looked down. Dizziness washed over me. I clung on and shut my eyes until it passed.

Keep moving.

My belly scraped against the stone.

Don't forget to breathe.

Push, stretch, pull. Push, stretch, pull. I fell into a steady rhythm.

Something rustled above me. Loose pebbles tumbled and bounced off the surrounding rock—the only warning I had to duck before they pelted the top of my head. When they stopped, I looked up.

Above, the suspect paused and stared down at me, as if noticing me for the first time. I was close enough to make out a tattoo of a brown-and-gold snake coiled around his biceps.

He was almost to the ledge, and I was still too far away to stop him.

I drew my blaster and leveled it at him. "Halt! You're under arrest for the murder of Representative Damaris Delligatti."

The assassin laughed.

My hand shook, making the muzzle of my blaster wobble. Panic gripped my chest. *Not now.* I focused on steadying my blaster, but the more I concentrated, the more difficult it became. A spasm shot through my hand. My fingers jerked open of their own accord.

As if in slow motion, my blaster slipped from my grasp and fell. I didn't need to look down to know there was no hope of retrieving it.

With a giant swing, the suspect threw himself up onto the ledge. One impossibly fast pull-up, and he'd made it to his ship.

I clenched my traitorous hand, gritted my teeth, and continued climbing. There was still a chance. All I needed to do was stall him until Wright caught up to us. If my Intell was good for anything, it was hacking into and interfering with electronics, but I needed to get closer to his ship to get within range.

Push, stretch, pull. My entire left arm spasmed, the movement threatening to fling me off the mountain. I plastered my body into the cliff until the cramping eased. Precious seconds ticked by.

Again. Push, stretch, pull.

The suspect walked to the edge, knocking several pebbles free to fall around me. He held a large stone above his head and hurled it at me. It slammed into the rock face above me, sending strong vibrations through the cliff before bouncing off to my side.

I blew out a breath. He missed.

Then another chunk of rock broke free from where it had hit and tumbled down. Then another and another. Rocks rained down on me. He'd thrown the boulder with such force that he'd started a rockslide.

Pain zinged through my arm and back. One hit me hard in the shoulder, pushing me from the wall. My hands, already shaky, couldn't hold on. The next one tore me free.

I scrambled for something to grab onto, but there was nothing.

Everything happened fast after that. Air rushed by, all but drowning out the roar of the ship's engine firing up. The cliff face was a blur of browns and mossy greens until my back slammed into something pokey and springy, slowing my fall but sending me spinning. Pain lanced through the back of my left shoulder blade.

I flung my arms out and hooked one around a scraggly branch of a bush. My shoulders screamed in protest, but I held tight.

Overhead, the suspect's ship blasted off. Hot exhaust laden with the sharp chemical scent of sinnafuel flowed down the mountain to assault my lungs. I coughed and tried not to breathe it in. The ship shot up in a near-vertical takeoff toward the safety of outer space.

Feet dangling, I looked down. Because I was an idiot.

I'd fallen about half the distance I'd climbed, and the ground looked very, very far away. A lone figure stood near the base of the fissure.

My Intell alerted me to an incoming comm. This was one of the rare instances I was happy to have the neural impulse implant. Instead of needing to double-tap my pinkie to my thumb, I only had to approximate the movement.

I shifted most of my weight to my left hand, twitched my fingers, and opened my comm in audio only. Wright didn't need to see how close I'd come to becoming mycoprotein paste.

"Sinclair, report. Are you okay?" His voice was calm, but I heard the tight strain of worry leaking through.

"Oh, you know, just hanging out." Grunting, I worked my hands toward the thicker end of the branch and found a spot to wedge my foot. Relief flowed through my shoulders as some of the pressure eased.

"Hold on. I'll have Leahy break off pursuit and circle back."

"Don't." My other foot scraped along the rock until it bumped against a firm, exposed root—one that was probably attached to this same bush that had saved my life. "The passage is too narrow for the LAV, anyway. I can make it down on my own. Have her stay with the assassin."

If we lost him now, it would be my fault. I'd had him in my sights. If my hands hadn't been too shaky to shoot, we'd be slapping the augmented restraints on him right now. A heaviness formed in my chest—a black hole that threatened to suck everything into it.

Chapter 8

Thirty minutes later, I eased my butt into the rear seat of the LAV. I winced when the movement jarred my shoulder. DeAjamae handed the med kit back to Wright. He dug around in it and pulled out tweezers, a bottle of antiseptic, a sterile pad of gauze, a tube of regenerative salve, and a medium-sized GraftPatch.

As it turned out, DeAjamae and Ravi had gotten back to the ship and into the air too late, anyway. She'd followed the assassin as high as the LAV could fly, but he'd reached the lower atmosphere before she could catch up. LAVs were called low altitude vehicles for a reason. They weren't built to fly that high. She was lucky the engine hadn't snubbed out on her at eight kilometers.

The Lapidea DECA office hadn't scrambled cruisers fast enough to follow the ship into space, either. So that was that. Our best lead in months was gone, a confirmed bionic weapon was loose in the galaxy, and Ritru-6 was in turmoil over the assassination of one of its representatives—all because I couldn't take a straight shot.

Wright had me turn so my back was to him. My shirt was ruined. I didn't have to look over my shoulder to know that.

"Just cut it away."

He used a pocketknife to slice at a section of the material and teased the frayed fabric from my skin. Then he picked out any pebbles and bits of thread with the tweezers and rinsed the abraded skin with the antiseptic.

I jerked and hissed when the stinging liquid hit the raw wound.

"Almost done." He patted the area dry with the sterile pad.

DeAjamae glanced back. Her face turned a little green. *Eww*, she mouthed to me.

"How bad is it?" I asked, twisting around to assess the damage for myself.

Wright pushed my head back with a finger to my temple. "Hold still." He squirted regenerative salve over the whole thing, then pressed on the GraftPatch to hold the skin together and keep the salve from rubbing off. "It doesn't look too deep, but you're going to need stitches. You're lucky this is all you got. You could have broken your neck in that fall. I want you to report to the precinct's infirmary and have a doctor check it out."

"I'm sure it's not that bad," I said.

DeAjamae's nose scrunched up, and she nodded emphatically. "It's that bad."

Wright repacked the med kit. The two tiny clasps snapped shut with a sharp *snick*.

"What are our next steps?" I asked.

"We're dropping you off at the infirmary. While you're there, we'll meet with Chief Abara for a debriefing."

"I should go—"

Wright held up a hand. "Nonnegotiable. We'll fill you in after you get the all clear."

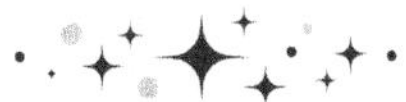

A hearty knock sounded on the door to my minuscule patient's room.

"Come in," I said and adjusted the hospital gown to make sure none of my bits and pieces showed.

A tall woman entered. She wore a blue doctor's coat and had a high-end, gold cuff strapped around her forearm. Her dark brown hair was threaded with light-blue highlights, micro-braided, and pulled into a thick braid. A golden-furred service dog padded in beside her. It sat near the wall console, and I had to restrain myself from petting it. It was on duty.

"Officer Reliance Sinclair?"

"That's me."

She smiled and extended her hand. "Hello, I'm Doctor Whalen." Her handshake was firm. "Sorry to keep you waiting. I was going over your medical file. You've had a lot of tests in the last six months. I find the neural impulse chip quite fascinating from a medical standpoint."

Her and every other doctor I'd seen. I gave her a weak smile. "I don't know much about it—from a medical standpoint."

"They haven't figured out how to remove it?"

"Not without killing me. Something about it grafting to my brain stem or central nervous system or something."

"Fascinating."

"Sure is." I retucked my hospital gown under my thighs. My feet were freezing. Would it kill them to set the climate controls a little warmer?

Doctor Whalen sat on the short stool in front of the console and waved her hand to wake up the device. After a quick scan of her cuff's credentials, the DECA logo on the lock screen disappeared. She pulled up my file. "Your diagnostic results are good. No broken bones or early signs of infection. How are you feeling?"

Her accent had a softness to it and a lyrical tone that made me think she was from one of the Fleur-de-lis systems. Avignon perhaps, although I'd only visited there a few times.

"Great. Ready to get back to work. If you could sign off on that form."

Her lips grew into a thin, pink line. "The note from your supervisor describes a pretty nasty fall. Even without your injury, you're entitled to two weeks' medical leave for mental health after a traumatic event like that."

Medical leave was the last thing I wanted. "Not necessary."

"Hmm." She sounded unconvinced. "How is that shoulder feeling now?"

I rolled my left arm. The dissolving stitches the nurse had put in tugged at my skin. "A little stiff, but nothing that'll stop me from performing my duties."

"Let's take a peek, shall we?" She moved behind me, unfastened the snap at the neck of the gown, and pulled it to the side. "Can you raise your arm?"

I did so, keeping my facial expression neutral even when pain zinged through my upper back.

"And what about this?" she asked, brushing the tip of her finger against the pink scar at the nape of my neck. "Did you hit your head at all? Any complications with the chip?"

I turned to face Doctor Whalen, using it as an excuse to duck away from her probing touch. "I didn't, and the chip is performing the same."

"Is there anything that would make you unfit for duty? Physical, mental, or emotional?"

My throat tightened. "Nope."

She sat back down on the stool and aerial scribed some notes into my file. "All right, I don't see any reason you can't return to work as long as you take it easy with that arm. Please follow up with your primary care doctor on Andaress-4 in two weeks to make sure everything is healing well. You can get dressed now. The nurse will come back with your medical clearance codes."

"Thank you." I fiddled with the hem of the hospital gown to avoid looking her in the eye. Wright needed the codes to approve my time. Once I had them, I could get back out in the field.

Doctor Whalen walked to the door. Her service dog stood with a shake and padded beside her.

Once they were out of the room, I changed back into my uniform pants, long-sleeved shirt, and green DECA jacket. The nurse knocked as I finished tying my boots and gave me the codes.

After thanking her, I left to find the team over in the main building. They'd taken over a conference room and sat around a table discussing our next steps.

Ravi slid a bag of cheesy chips over to me. I mouthed *thank you* and dug in. I hadn't eaten since early that morning.

"Chief Abara sent over security recordings from the House of Representatives, traffic camera drones, and every camera the precinct has of its holding cells," Ravi said. "It'll take some time to go through it."

DeAjamae polished off her second bag of chips. "I might be able to help with that. There's an AI program that can sift through the data faster."

"He also sent a preliminary scan of the bionic weapon, but his techs are still going over it. They won't release it to us until they're sure there's no other evidence they might get from it."

"Central Command intercepted one text transmission from the assassin before he made it out of orbit, but it doesn't give us much to go on," DeAjamae said. "It read, 'red touches yellow.' He sent it to a ghost account created under the name Ophidian, but there's no real name linked to it."

My face must have blanched, because Wright's head swiveled in my direction. "Does that mean something to you?"

I swallowed a dry lump of chips. "Red touches yellow, kills a fellow. Red touches black, friend to Jack. It's a rhyme to help you tell if a snake is venomous."

"So the assassin sent confirmation to someone that he'd killed the representative," Wright said.

My mind swirled, dredging up memories I'd thought I'd laid to rest years ago. "It must be a coincidence."

DeAjamae arched one perfectly shaped eyebrow. "You know how I feel about coincidences."

I shifted in my chair. "This has to be ten—no, eleven—years ago. I was a rookie in the Clava DECA office. We were investigating a gang called the Seven Serpents."

Wright frowned. "The gang that helped smuggle you off of Brione-5 when you were on the run?"

"Yes. There had been a coup, and the leader and his next four in command all disappeared under mysterious circumstances. We presumed Lady Ilymechina killed them to secure her place as the new leader."

"I'm not following," Ravi said. "What's the connection?"

"The former leader—the one who was presumably killed—went by the street name Ophidian. It means snakelike."

Ravi whistled.

"But like I said, we ruled him off as dead. My entire ten years at the Clava office, I never heard a whisper about Ophidian still being alive."

Wright rocked back in his chair. "The Seven Serpents helped you once. Do you think they'd help you again?"

"Doubtful. The last time I had leverage, and it was no skin off their back to smuggle me to Brione-2. We'd be asking Lady Ilymechina whether she murdered her former boss. She has no incentive to tell us if she did and every reason to say she didn't."

"Then we'll have to come up with some leverage on the way," Wright said. "Leahy, keep going over the files. Review anything DECA here put together about the assassin and the days leading up to the assassination. Do an analysis on Representative Delligatti. I want a list of her known enemies, including the ones not related to the mining contracts. Every politician has them. Singh, interview Delligatti's aides and any witnesses to the attack. Stay on the lab and take possession of the bionic weapon as soon as they're done with it."

"On it." DeAjamae had already commandeered the wall console, and all four screens played security recordings from around the House of Representatives.

Ravi gathered the trash from the table and threw it into the reclamator.

Wright stood and gathered his things. "Sinclair, you and I are going to Brione-5 to see what we can find out from the Seven Serpents."

"Are you sure that's a good idea?" I asked, but I was already on my feet, too.

"No, but right now, it's my only idea."

Chapter 9

TAKEOFF WENT SMOOTHLY, DESPITE Felix's grumbling. He perched on his charging shelf, which gave him a full view of the bridge's console. It had the added benefit of allowing him to glare down at Wright the entire time.

"Felix, take us out of orbit," I said as soon as the artificial gravity kicked in. "Then plot a course for Brione-5 and prepare the warp drive."

"Yes, Captain," my ship's avatar replied.

He only called me captain when he was annoyed, but I felt the floor vibrate and knew he'd fired the starboard thruster to reorient us toward open space.

I checked the holoscreen. Ritru-6 glowed a mix of azure, hunter green, and sienna below us. The Thousand Pillars mountain range, which rose high and imposing out of the forests to the west of Lapidea, looked like the bristles of a brush tossed in the grass. Splotches of blue from the many lakes were nothing but water droplets sprayed across the northern hemisphere.

Wright took in the view of his home planet. "It never gets old, does it?"

A smile tugged at the corner of my lips. "Never."

The planet slid off to the right of the holoscreen and was replaced with the inky blackness of space.

"Firing rear thrusters," Felix said. "Exiting restricted orbital space in five minutes."

"Systems check."

"All systems clear. Sinnafuel tank at eighty-five percent. Batteries at ninety-three percent. The warp drive will be online by the time we reach open space."

"Excellent. Thank you, Felix," I said.

He flicked his tail against the wall, making a clanking sound.

Wright leaned over and whispered, "Is he okay?"

Static crackled from Felix's side of the bridge. "*He* has a dashboard microphone right in front of you."

"Felix isn't used to sharing the bridge with anyone besides me."

Wright's eye swept the small room before looking down at the scratches on his chair's armrests. "Ah, I'm in his seat, aren't I?"

"They didn't make you lead agent for nothing," Felix said.

I clamped down my lips, trying not to laugh. From the look Wright shot me, he was, too.

"Tell you what," Wright said. "As soon as we get up to warp speed, I'll go down to the common area and start on dinner. We still have ingredients to make pizza. That way, you can have your chair back."

The cat stared at him unblinking for several beats longer than was comfortable. He turned his head back toward the holoscreen, which was now pitch black save for a few bright pixels of distant stars. "If that's the best you can do."

"Take the win, Felix," I said, shaking my head. Programmers hadn't yet achieved true artificial intelligence—not in the sense that computers were sentient beings—but sometimes Felix made me wonder.

A star chart replaced the live view on the main holoscreen. Felix plotted a direct route from Ritru-6 to Brione-5 with only a minor deviation to avoid a gas cloud that had been damaging passing ships' outer layers of shielding. It only added a few hours to our trip, so it was well worth the detour. With the added time, we'd still reach my hometown of Clava on Brione-5 in thirty-seven hours.

I eyed the secret compartment under my dash that concealed a fifteen-year-old bottle of Lonnie Powell whisky. When this trip was done, I planned on pouring myself a double.

"We have left Ritru-6's restricted space," Felix said. "Safety checks completed and passed."

The warp drive's indicator light flipped to blue, signaling it was ready to create the warp bubble that allowed us to travel at faster-than-light speeds. I used a slight hand gesture to flip the holoscreen back to live view.

"Take us out of here, Felix."

His metal tail curled around the fixed post supporting his charging station, anchoring him. "Building the warp bubble. Takeoff in ten seconds. Nine. Eight. Seven."

An iridescent shimmer passed over the front camera. It distorted the surrounding space, making the far-off stars appear to twinkle like they did when viewing them through a planet's atmosphere.

"Six. Five. Four."

I tugged on my harness straps. Secure. Wright did the same.

"Three. Two. One."

The ship no longer hummed beneath my feet. It growled and shook, like a dog with a bone. I clenched my teeth to keep them from clacking together and pressed my skull into the padded headrest of my captain's chair. Outside, the subspace field continued to form. My ears popped from the change in pressure.

With the planet and its two moons behind us, there was nothing on the holoscreen to let us visually gauge our speed. A second later, our backs slammed into our seats. Inertia dampeners only did so much.

The warp bubble snapped into place. Space contracted in front of us and expanded behind us, and we hurtled forward. The discomfort only lasted a few minutes until we reached full speed. Then we leveled out, and the ship's automated systems kicked in to counter the effects of traveling at such high speeds.

Wright unfastened his harness first. He stood and made a grand gesture of offering his chair to Felix. "All yours, buddy."

Felix yawned. His jaw hinged to an unnatural degree, showing off several rows of sharp titanium teeth.

"I'll meet you downstairs in a few minutes," I said. "There are a few things I want to look over first."

"Do you want help?" Wright asked.

"No. Get started on dinner. I'm starving."

He nodded and disappeared down the short hall to the ladder.

My neck ached from the g-forces exerted on it during the launch. I stretched it from side to side and ear to shoulder, trying to work out the kinks. Then I undid my harness and swiveled to face Felix.

"It won't be that easy to intimidate him, you know."

"I don't know what you're talking about."

"Yawning?"

Felix stood on his charging platform, then stretched with his front paws way out in front of him and his hindquarters high in the air. He jumped into the copilot chair and lay back down.

"It's a new program I'm trying out."

"Mm-hmm," I said and reached over to stroke him behind his ear. "Wright's only going to be on the *Soteria* for a few days. Try not to give him such a hard time, okay?"

His head pressed into my hand. "Fine, I'll be nice, but he better not make a mess. My cleaning bots are already working overtime from the entire team traipsing about in here."

"That's all I ask." I kissed the top of his head and left to give Wright a hand with dinner.

The scent of caramelized onions and sautéing garlic hit me as I walked into the common area. I inhaled and, for a second, forgot the throbbing pain at the base of my skull. My ship had never smelled so good.

Wright stood at the fixed island dicing four ripe tomatoes on a wood cutting board. Light from the overhead array picked up the blond highlights from his bent head. He'd removed his DECA jacket and pushed the sleeves of his charcoal-gray Henley up to his elbows. Soft music played from his cuff. The easy rise and fall of his knife matched the smooth melody.

It almost felt as if I were intruding. He looked so comfortable—so at home. I marveled at the ease with which he'd settled in. If I owned an apron, he'd be wearing it. It took me three months to visit DeAjamae at her apartment and another month to invite her onboard the *Soteria*. It seemed silly now, but trust hadn't come easy.

Walnut hunkered down across from Wright on the island, gorging himself on a chunk of tomato. I checked his vitals to make sure the launch hadn't upset him, but his chip only reported signs of happiness.

"Give me a sec," I said and ducked into my bunkroom on the left to get a painkiller tab from one of my drawers. There had been a flurry of electronic activity during takeoff. Between launching and activating the warp drive, almost every system on the *Soteria* had been used, and my Intell wanted to play with all of them. The med was a generic, low-grade kind available at any convenience store, but I hoped it would take the edge off. Keeping the severity of my symptoms a secret while spending multiple days on a small ship with Wright might prove difficult.

I changed into a more comfortable shirt that I didn't mind staining with tomato sauce, because there was a one hundred percent chance I was going to spill some on myself. While I was at it, I swapped my tactical pants for leggings and my boots for a pair of fuzzy slippers. It had been a long freaking day.

Wright's eyes traveled from my head to my slippers and back up again. "Everything okay?"

"Sure, why wouldn't it be?"

"You were quiet during launch. I thought you'd be excited to be going home, even if it's only for a quick trip."

"Like you were excited to come back to Ritru-6? I noticed you didn't take your mother up on her invite to dinner after the debriefing."

"Fair point."

"How can I help?"

He pointed his knife toward the mycoprotein proofing machine. "You can get a dough going for the crust. The sauce is almost ready to go on the stove."

Pleased to have changed the subject, I grabbed the jar of starter from the refrigerator along with yeast flavoring and a nutrient pack from the cupboard. I scooped a pea-sized amount of each into the proofer and started the machine. Might as well make a large batch since we'd be eating it for the next several days. Warm water poured in. The starter activated, quadrupling in size. Satisfied it was a good batch, I set a timer for ten minutes.

Wright's knife made quick work of the remaining tomatoes. He used the side of his knife to transfer them into the saucepan with the onions and garlic. They popped and sizzled until he gave them a stir and turned down the heat on the induction burner. After sprinkling salt, pepper, and oregano into the sauce, he wiped his hands on a towel and relaxed against the cupboard.

"Why don't we go over what you know about this Ophidian and the Seven Serpents gang while we wait for those to cook down?"

I snagged an errant chunk of tomato and popped it into my mouth before wiping down the counter. It was sweet and juicy. Tomatoes were in season in Salin now, and Wright must have picked these up fresh from a market stall.

"There's not much to tell. Ophidian was the head of the Seven Serpents when I was in the academy. They smuggled in drugs and weapons from off-planet. Tension was pretty high between the Serpents and their main rival gang, which was also heavy in the drug trade. One Serpent took two blaster shots to the chest when he walked out of a restaurant with his girlfriend. Both he and the girlfriend were high in the gang hierarchy. That sparked a string of retaliatory killings on both sides that lasted for four months. Things got pretty bloody. There was a coup. Ophidian and the four remaining lieutenants all disappeared, and Lady Ilymechina took over. We presumed the new faction had killed the old guard, but we never found the bodies."

Wright crossed his arms. The movement pulled at the fabric of his shirt, showing off his toned chest and arms. I averted my gaze when I realized I'd been staring. It wasn't the first time my thoughts had strayed in that direction. I had eyes, after all. Luckily, Wright hadn't seemed to notice.

"This Lady Ilymechina is the woman who smuggled you from Brione-5 to Brione-2?"

"Yes, but we didn't know who she was when we started investigating her. Everyone called her the Lady." I used petting Walnut as an excuse to keep my eyes down. "I worked undercover in the gang unit. Our team's main objective was to find out who the new players were. I got overzealous and arrested her before we had enough evidence to make a case. The whole thing went public. Lady Ilymechina was released, but everyone knew who she was after that. She still ran the gang, but she had to be much more sophisticated about it. Everything is run through her underlings, so she keeps her hands clean."

"How did you convince her to smuggle you to Brione-2?"

"Blackmail."

Wright rubbed a hand across his jaw. "Is that going to give us a problem now?"

I shrugged. "It won't help. I turned over everything I had on her and promised she'd never see me again."

"And here we are, six months later, asking for more help. I guess I'll have to be extra charming."

Wright's grin was a perfect mix of innocent charm and devilish promises. I snorted. No doubt that smile worked wonders for him at the bar, but Lady Ilymechina would chew him up and spit him out like last night's dinner. You didn't get to be the leader of the largest gang in Clava by falling for a pretty face, especially when that face belonged to a DECA agent.

"This may wind up being a dead end. Our team searched for Ophidian and his lieutenants for months. We never found any trace of what happened to them. It was like they just vanished. We concluded their bodies must have been dumped at a decomp facility or buried so deep no one would ever find them. If that's the case, the Lady will never cop to it. Clava doesn't have a statute of limitations on murder."

"If he's dead, we're back to square one, anyway. Let's assume he's not. Do we have any leverage to encourage her to talk?"

I shook my head. "It's been almost two years since I quit the Clava Department. Since Jarrett—" My words caught in my throat. "Since Jarrett died, I'm out of the loop."

"That's unfortunate."

A feeling grew in the pit of my stomach. It was equal parts sureness and apprehension. I had an idea, but I didn't like it. It would require us to make a quick stop once we landed—one I'd been hoping to avoid.

Wright stepped closer and leaned both hands against the island. He was close enough for me to catch a hint of his bergamot soap and squirm under the intensity of his gaze.

"What's going on in that head of yours?" he asked. "I can see the wheels turning."

"There's a couple of people who may have more current information on the Seven Serpents. We used to work in the gang unit together. Last I heard, they're still in it."

"So, what's the problem?"

My stomach soured, leaving me with a cramping sensation and an unpleasant taste in the back of my throat. While my exit from the Clava DECA office had been voluntary on the record, in reality I was persona non grata.

I'd worked in the homicide unit. Hal Cavender, my former partner, had been a dirty agent, paid by Tazza Industries to cover up several deaths caused by early models of their Insight neural implants. I'd stumbled onto a piece of evidence linking a victim to the implant, and Cavender tried to shoot me with his blaster. I'd returned fire and killed him.

"Kinnikinnic is the lead agent of the gang unit. He and my old partner were tight. Like, Sunday-barbecues and dragging-your-drunk-ass-home-after-a-bad-call kind of tight. He refused to believe I shot Cavender in self-defense. There's a high probability he'll tell me to go fuck myself in not-so-nice words."

I didn't want to see the agreement in Wright's eyes, so I picked at imaginary dirt on the stainless-steel surface of the island. Even after the Department cleared me of wrongdoing, no one wanted to work with me, especially Kinnikinnic. Not that I blamed them. How could you trust someone who'd killed one of your own? Jarrett had been the only one to stick by me, and I'd gotten him killed, too.

Maybe Kinnikinnic was right.

Wright's hand slid forward to cover mine. It was warm and strong when he gave me a reassuring squeeze. "Reliance—"

The timer dinged on the mycoprotein proof machine, saving me from tearing open any more old wounds. I pulled my hand out from under his and hopped off the stool.

Warm, yeasty steam billowed out of the top of the machine when I raised the lid. A smooth, pillowy ball of dough rested below. I divided it into two, put half in the refrigerator to keep until tomorrow, and slapped the other one on the counter to press out into a round crust.

It wouldn't taste anywhere near as good as what we could get planetside, but mycoprotein was the wonder food of space travel. A small jar of starter spores weighed almost nothing, rarely spoiled, and could feed a person for several months just by adding water, flavoring, and a nutrient packet. Bake it right away for breads or freeze it for a meat-like texture.

I tried not to think about how many mycoprotein on mycoprotein sandwiches I'd eaten over the years. Thank the stars for hot sauce and garlic powder.

"Thin or thick crust?" I asked, kneading the lump of dough into a flattened disk.

Wright straightened. My stomach clenched as I thought he was going to press me about Kinnikinnic, but he just smiled. "Chef's choice."

I snorted. No one had ever accused me of being a chef. "Thin it is. There's a great pizza joint in Clava that I used to go to a lot—Andy's. They make New York style. New York City style? I can never remember."

My fingers made little stabby motions, pushing the edges of the dough outward. Kinnikinnic loved Andy's pizza. So did his partner, Nomikou.

"It's New York style." Wright's hands rested on my shoulders as he sidled behind me to stir the sauce.

My hands jerked at his touch, and I almost tore a hole through the center of the crust. I cursed under my breath. "What?"

He grinned, clearing the last residual of heaviness from the air. "The pizza. It's called New York style. Are you sure you're okay?"

I twisted around in the cramped aisle, mouth open and finger raised to defend my sanity.

The *Soteria* lurched starboard. We both stumbled. Wright caught his balance before I did, planted his feet, and grabbed me by my waist, preventing me from falling ass over tin cups to the floor. My hands—completely of their own accord—reached out to steady myself against his chest.

"I got you," he said, tightening his grip. "I won't let you fall."

My breath hitched, and I raised my gaze. Grayson Wright stared down at me with those earnest hazel eyes of his, and for a moment, it seemed as if he meant more than keeping me on my feet. All the noise dropped away: my old team, Lady Ilymechina, Lourde, the headaches. All of it. My head was blissfully quiet.

It would be so easy to believe him. I wanted to. Desperately. Maybe if I told him about my worsening symptoms, he would figure out a way for me to stay on the team.

"Grayson, I—"

"Ahem, Captain," Felix said, walking into the kitchen.

I dropped my hands from Wright's chest and tried to step away. He held on a moment longer than necessary, then relaxed to let me slip through his fingers. I scooted back as far as the narrow aisle allowed. Heat rose to my face, and I was sure my cheeks had turned red.

Wright, for his part, looked more amused than anything.

I cleared my throat. "Felix, what was that?"

The tip of the large cat's tail flicked back and forth. When he responded, he kept his eyes locked on Wright. "Are you all right, Captain? I'm reading elevated heart and respiratory rates for both of you. Were you injured in the turbulence?"

Wright coughed, but it sounded suspiciously like he was covering up a laugh.

Captain, my ass. Felix knew we were fine. He was just in a snit.

"Status report," I said.

"Debris from a mining field drifted into our original course. I adjusted and flagged the coordinates to update the universal star charts once we reach the Brione system."

"Thank you, Felix. I should go look into that." I stepped even farther from Wright. "Can you finish up the pizza? This will take a few minutes."

I was already edging toward the door when he answered.

"Take your time. I'm not going anywhere."

Chapter 10

Thirty-six long hours later, we landed at the R. Burns Interplanetary Spacedock in Clava, the capital city of Brione-5. Wright had spent a good chunk of our free time familiarizing himself with different parts of the ship. He had his deep-space pilot's license, but he'd never owned his own ship or stayed more than a few weeks at a time on one. I appreciated that it meant fewer opportunities for awkward conversations, but it drove Felix absolutely bonkers. The cleaning bots ran nonstop during our waking hours.

I unlocked my hoverbike from its rack and glided it down the cargo bay ramp. We'd parked in the Department's designated area. Central Command had given us a bit of lip over being a civilian ship, but they'd eventually found us a spot near the edge of the perimeter fencing. Armed drones patrolled the area, so I didn't worry about leaving the *Soteria* there unattended, especially with Felix monitoring the external sensors.

Crisp, spring air whipped around the side of the ship, blowing my hair into my face and slipping down the back of my leather jacket. It still had the sharp bite of winter's chill to it.

I tugged my zipper higher and adjusted the collar around my neck.

Measured footsteps clanked behind me on the metal ramp. I held out the spare helmet, and Wright took it when he drew near. He'd dressed in casual clothes—dark jeans, a green long-sleeved shirt that matched his eyes, and a jacket long enough to conceal the blaster holstered on his right hip. We'd agreed that going in civilian clothes was our best play. There was no way we'd get into the club decked out in full DECA gear.

I swung a leg over my hoverbike. As soon as my weight settled onto the padded seat, my Intell connected to the bike's operating system.

Wright climbed on behind me as Felix closed the rear hatch. "One of these days, you're going to let me fly her again."

"Not a chance. That was a onetime deal."

"You haven't even heard my offer."

"I'm listening."

"How about a bottle of seven-year Lonnie Powell?"

"Make it a ten-year and you got yourself a deal."

"Deal." He swung his leg back over.

"Hold up, flyboy. Payment first."

"I'm good for it. We can pick up a bottle before we leave the city."

"Ha! My mamma didn't raise a fool. Whisky first. Then we'll talk." I shoved my helmet on my head and revved the engine.

"All right, all right." Wright donned his helmet, as well. My Intell connected our comms. "You drive a hard bargain, but I'll hold you to it."

His hands rested at my waist while we lifted off before he moved them to the passenger handlebars below the seat. Although he didn't crowd me, only millimeters of air separated his body from mine.

I kicked the hoverbike into gear and pulled back on the throttle. It was a cherry-red, twin-thruster Cymbeline SR9 with aftermarket sinnafuel boosters and custom trim. She was sleek, fast, and a thing of beauty as we glided toward the gate.

We paused long enough for Wright to flash his DECA credentials to the guard. She confirmed it against her log and waved us through.

I brought us up to the nearest skylane, about six stories above ground level. My bike slipped in between two mid-sized cargo LAVs. Traffic was light, but we'd get caught in the afternoon rush hour if we dawdled too long.

Part of me wanted to camp out in the slow lane, arrive late, and self-sabotage any chance of catching Kinnikinnic at the precinct before he left for the night. The other part—the bigger part—knew that if groveling at Kinnikinnic's feet got us even one step closer to putting Aurelian Tazza behind bars, then I'd do it. Happily.

I rolled my wrist back and zipped around the LAV in front of me. Squat, industrial structures soon gave way to city architecture. Clava had ample room to spread out, so the buildings never reached the soaring towers of those in Tylo, Ceti, or even Salin, but what she lacked in height, she made up for in style. The hospital sat on the outer edge of the city proper. It had curved walls of plastiglass so patients could enjoy the tranquil view of the lakes and farmland beyond the city. After the hospital, we passed the university campus, with its tilted, oval rings of bridges between buildings, and then the art and history museums that two of Brione-5's most celebrated architects had designed.

A soft smile tugged at the corners of my lips. Despite having left on less-than-ideal terms, Clava was where I'd grown up, experienced my first crush and heartbreak, attended the DECA academy, and struggled to build my dreams. It would always be home, even if I never lived there again.

Traffic slowed through the more touristy section. It picked up again when we hit the clump of municipal buildings: City Hall, the Courthouse, Public Works, the Department of LAV Licensing, and the DECA precinct. These buildings leaned more utilitarian in design, but were still elegant in their simple, flowing lines.

I parked in the public LAV lot nearest the precinct. We walked through the front entrance, and Wright requested the desk sergeant ask Lead Agent Kinnikinnic to meet with us. He and I had agreed ahead of time that Kinnikinnic would be more likely to see us if we didn't mention my name. The sergeant directed us to a private side office to wait.

Five minutes later, Lead Agent "Nicky" Kinnikinnic and his partner, Agent Georgia Nomikou, opened the door. He had his head twisted behind him, trading a jab with Nomikou. She wore an amiable smile, the remnants of a laugh still on her lips.

They hadn't changed much since I'd last seen them. He was tall, barrel-chested, and looked like he could put a serious dent in someone's refrigerator, both inside and out. She was petite, quiet, and kept her thick, curly hair pulled back into a bun. They'd both been fun to work with—even if Kinnikinnic's humor ran toward groan-inducing puns. I tried to remember that, and not how they'd frozen me out at the end.

"Sorry about that," Kinnikinnic said, turning his attention toward Wright. "How can we be of service?" His eyes narrowed when he spotted me. "You got a lot of nerve showing your face around here, Sinclair."

Nomikou's face remained passive. I'd seen that look often. It was the one she wore when questioning suspects she found disagreeable.

"Nice to see you, too, Nicky," I said, using the nickname he'd had since his days in the academy. I nodded to the other agent. "Georgia. This is Lead Agent Grayson Wright from the Andaress-4 Salin precinct."

Wright held out his hand, which both agents reluctantly shook. "We're working an illegal arms case, and we believe the leader of the Seven Serpents may have information vital to tracking the weapons down. We hoped as the head of the gang unit here, you might have intelligence that would help convince her to be more forthcoming with sharing that information."

Kinnikinnic looked from Wright to me and barked out a laugh. "You got to be kidding me. If I had dirt on the Lady, what makes you think I'd share it with you? Even when you worked her case, we didn't let you anywhere near her. You were a public relations nightmare."

My cheeks burned. "Come on, that was eleven years ago. You said yourself you would have arrested her if you'd been in my shoes."

Kinnikinnic leaned forward and jabbed a sausage-sized finger at my chest. "That was when Jarrett was here to back up your side of the story. He isn't around to do that anymore, now is he?"

And there it was. I knew it had been coming, but it still hurt like hell.

My face must have betrayed my feelings, because Nomikou put her hand on Kinnikinnic's forearm, easing him back.

"No, let him," I said. "He can't tell me anything I haven't told myself a thousand times. I'm the one who found him, Nicky. *Me*. He was my best friend, and I'm doing my best to get him justice."

"Your best is a pretty piss-poor excuse of an officer. You aren't fit to wear the uniform."

Nomikou shook her head. "Maybe it's best if you go."

"Believe me, coming back here wasn't my first choice. This concerns Ophidian."

"Ophidian?" Kinnikinnic scoffed and looked at Nomikou as if to say, *can you believe this nut job?*

"Reliance, Ophidian's been dead for over a decade," she said. "The worms who ate him are dead. Their slimy, little worm babies and grandbabies are dead."

My eyes slid over to Wright, who gave me the nod of approval. "We believe he's still alive, and that he may be involved in the manufacturing or distribution of bionic weapons."

Kinnikinnic waved his hand. "No one's made bionic weapons in over eighty years."

"We're well aware," Wright said, his Ritruvian accent coming out thicker than normal. "Not since the Ritruvian Uprising Massacre, and I plan to keep it that way."

"Please, Nicky. If you have any information we can use as leverage against the Lady, it would help us get ahead of the problem while we can still do something about it."

Nomikou shifted her weight, causing her thick-soled boots to squeak against the floor. "She keeps her hands pretty clean. We made a big bust about six months ago of a shipment of illegal tech coming in from Brione-2. One of her guys took the fall for it. We were hoping to track it to her warehouses, but he walked in with the bug we'd placed inside one of the pieces and confessed before it went anywhere. That's how she operates. Nothing gets close to her. You could try—"

"No." Kinnikinnic interrupted. "No, we're not getting dragged into one of your hare-brained conspiracy theories. It wasn't enough you killed Cavender. You had to drag his good name through the mud." He grabbed my wrist and jerked me forward until I smelled the pastrami on rye sandwich he'd had for lunch on his breath. "Did you know his wife never received his pension because of your accusations? She had to take a second job at the canning factory just to make ends meet. Even that wasn't good enough for you. You pulled Jarrett into your nonsense, too. It's a damn shame. He was a hell of an agent."

Wright angled between us. All traces of amicability vanished from his features, leaving his face cold and dangerous. It was a look I hadn't seen on him since we first met, when I'd been his prime suspect in Jarrett's murder. He grabbed Kinnikinnic around the base of the hand and squeezed against the fragile bones of Kinnikinnic's thumb and pinky finger.

"Unhand my officer."

Kinnikinnic's lips pressed into a thin line until his hand turned from bright pink to purple.

Wright's free hand drifted toward his blaster. "I won't ask twice."

My former teammate released his hold on me, but his glare could have left blaster burns on my face.

Wright let Kinnikinnic go but kept himself positioned between the big guy and me.

"Georgia, we're leaving." Kinnikinnic turned toward the doorway, but Nomikou hesitated. He turned back around. "That's an order, Agent Nomikou."

She snapped her jaw shut, nodded curtly, and left.

"Watch your back," Kinnikinnic warned Wright before following Nomikou out the door. "You're safer taking your chances out in the void than having this one as your partner. They all wind up dead."

Chapter 11

"WELL, THAT WENT WELL."

Wright ran his hand through his hair. The short ends stuck up every which way before he finger-combed them back to within regulation guidelines. "You warned me Agent Kinnikinnic might not be receptive to helping. I'd expected more professionalism from a lead agent, though."

I wished I could say the same. "Cavender was his friend."

"But you were his teammate." He said it like that's all there was to it.

"Do you still want to talk to Lady Ilymechina?"

He stared out toward the end of the parking garage where an exiting silver LAV caught his eye. "I would rather have gone in with leverage, but I'm not willing to give up yet. You know her. What do you suggest?"

I zipped up my jacket. "We talk to the Lady. Assuming Ophidian is still alive, we appeal to her sense of pride. I doubt there is any love lost between them, and it doesn't help her reputation if he rises from the ashes involved in a galaxy-news-worthy crime."

"And if she says he's dead?"

"Then we hope to the void she doesn't send us to meet him."

Wright gave me a sideways look. "So, where do we find her? The gang must have an established territory. Do we check abandoned houses, street corners, parks?"

I climbed back on the hoverbike, chuckling at the idea of Lady Ilymechina slinging credit bags of Stardust to junkies on a street corner. "Hop on. I have a good guess as to where she's holding court."

Once Wright settled behind me, I started the engine and plotted a course for The Snake Den, a bar owned and operated by the Seven Serpents. My stomach rolled as the Intell fed me information on traffic patterns, skylane closures, weather, and a high-speed chase by DECA officers in pursuit of a stolen LAV.

My vision blurred before I forced the Intell out of DECA's secure dispatch system. I raised my visor to wipe my eyes. Reducing the amount of data streaming into my head helped calm my stomach, but it still left a sour taste in my mouth.

It took thirty-five minutes to get across town and another ten to find parking. The club must be hopping tonight.

As we walked the three blocks to the club, I noticed it was already dark. The sun had set, taking what little warmth it had provided with it. We'd have a chilly ride back to the ship when this was over.

Wright's eyebrow rose as I led him through the front entrance of a grocery store. Stark, blueish-white lighting had me squinting until my eyes adjusted. Soft music played overhead, and a bored teenage clerk helped shoppers work the cuff scanners to pay for their groceries. My Intell picked up the nearest customer's cuff signal, and I closed out of the notification before it could pull her banking details.

Wright looked around, confused. "Do we need to resupply the *Soteria* before talking to this Lady Ilymechina?"

I headed down the aisle of baking supplies. "The Snake Den is in the basement. It started out as an exclusive hangout for the gang members and friends, but it turns out booze and dancing are pretty profitable. Now it's the worst-kept secret in Clava."

"Ah. So getting in won't be a problem."

"I didn't say that."

We reached the butcher counter at the back of the store. I rang the little bell for service. No one came out, so I whacked it a few more times.

"Yeah, yeah, I hear ya." A short, balding man with a wispy, black comb-over pushed through a swinging door behind the counter. He wiped his hands on a towel tucked into the strings of his bloody apron. The butcher leaned both hands on the refrigerated display case. His short-sleeved shirt showed off ashy, liver-spotted skin with sinewy muscles. He gave each of us a casual once-over. "Keep right on walkin', honey."

I frowned. "You're not even going to ask me what I'd like to buy?"

"Don't matter." He jerked his head toward a hand-scribbled sign on the wall that read, *We Reserve the Right to Refuse Service to Anyone—That Means You*. "I remember you."

"Gee, I'm flattered."

"Don't be."

"We have business with the Lady."

"Never heard of her."

"She's the one authorizing your paycheck every week."

"It isn't hard to spot a couple of *ribbits*," he said, using the derogatory nickname given to DECA officers owing to their dark-green uniform jackets. He curled back his lips and gave an earsplitting whistle. Two stock boys appeared from the aisles behind us. And by boys, I meant guys who looked like they played on the Asteroids' defensive line. "Keep pressing your luck, and we'll be running a special on frog legs."

One of them grabbed Wright by the biceps, and the other placed his hands on either side of my shoulders. They tried to steer us toward the front of the store. Wright's muscles tensed, but he let me take the lead. This was my show.

I dug in my heels. "All I'm asking is that you deliver a message and let her decide if she wants to meet with us. Tell her we're looking for Ophidian."

The butcher stilled. He held up one liver-spotted hand, and the bouncers held us in place. His dark eyes shot from me to Wright. "Not many people remember that name."

"I do, and I suspect we'll be hearing it a lot more if you don't let me talk to Lady Ilymechina."

His jaw worked back and forth, as if he were chewing over the idea. "Wait here. Don't move."

As if we had a choice.

He walked into the back room, and we overhead him talking to someone on a comm. A moment later, he returned with deep scowl lines creasing his forehead. "Follow me."

Wright and I stepped around the counter. The back room was a prep area for all the meat being sold out front. It looked like he'd been in the process of cutting up chicken parts when I'd rung the bell. I tried my best to keep my eyes front and center.

The butcher escorted us to The Snake Den's hidden entrance via a lift hidden in the walk-in freezer. I tried not to shiver when he shut the door, sealing us inside the pitch-black subzero room. As soon as the latch clicked, a strip of neon-blue lights ringing the ceiling flickered on. It was barely enough to see by and cast everything in an otherworldly glow. That was new.

With a rumble, the floor sank. The racks of frozen food must have been secured to the walls, because they didn't descend with us. It grew darker as we moved away from the light. The steady pulse of music from the club grew louder. With a lurch, the lift halted and the rear door opened.

I was bombarded with signals from the experience jockey's equipment—speakers, amps, mixing boards, headphones, light sequencers, thermostat controls, and more.

Pain formed at the base of my skull, and my fingers tingled. Numbness crept up my palms and into my wrist. I shook out my hand, trying to dispel the prickling sensation while simultaneously cutting off the excess feeds. It would have been easier if both actions didn't require the use of my hands.

We walked into a circular area dimly lit by deep red and purple lights. The hostess section had been cordoned off so that I couldn't see the rest of the room. Rough-hewn stone pavers lined the floor and cutouts of ornate buildings crowded the walls. Old-timey streetlamps and paper lanterns were strung across the ceiling. It looked like something you'd find in one of the Fleur-de-lis party cities, not Clava.

Lady Ilymechina had made a lot of changes since my last visit.

A tall, lithe woman in a reinforced bodysuit stepped out from a hidden alcove. Her jet-black hair was pulled into a high ponytail except for a fringe of bangs, which ended in a sharp line that just grazed her kohl-rimmed eyes.

"Hey, Rizpah." I recognized Lady Ilymechina's bodyguard.

Instead of returning my smile, she held up her arm and pointed her cuff at us. "Hydra, initiate weapons scan."

We wouldn't get close to the Lady carrying blasters, so we'd stored them on the hoverbike before coming in. Wright had grumbled about it but agreed with my reasoning. We didn't want to give them an excuse to turn us away.

A blue sensor beam from her cuff cut across my neck, then trailed down to the floor as she scanned me. She twirled her left hand, motioning for me to spin around. Then she repeated the process with Wright. Satisfied that we were unarmed, Rizpah led us through an arched opening.

I guessed we were supposed to follow.

Partitions had been erected into some kind of maze or labyrinth where the dance floor used to be. A soft haze of smoke blanketed the room, swirling around our ankles into little eddies as we moved through the channels. Partyers wearing glowing neon mood-enhancement bracelets and carrying glasses of liquor cut around us, laughing.

We came to a small room where an aerial silk artist hung suspended from the ceiling. A long swath of sheer white material wrapped around her body. A crowd of twenty people gathered in a circle to watch the performance. She let herself drop, rolling down the cloth at a terrifying speed, and stopping herself just seconds before hitting the ground. The crowd roared with drunken approval.

Rizpah hustled us through the corridor on our right. It opened into another room, this one bathed in green light and decorated with plants. Long vines dangled from the ceiling, crept up the walls, and were arranged in pots around a fountain with wrought-iron benches. On the far side of the room, a bartender in a white-collared shirt and black vest attended a long line of thirsty customers.

The next room showcased a belly dancer with a belt of gold coins jingling about her waist and a brown-and-black striped snake coiled around her arms. She wove through the audience, shaking her hips in time to the string-and-flute-based music. The gem-encrusted bralette top and sheer pantaloons left little to the imagination. One man reached forward to touch the dancer but snatched his hand back when the reptile snapped its head around and hissed a warning.

Rizpah's holoscreen flashed on for a moment, and my Intell intercepted a comm to security. A bouncer showed up as we exited the room to escort the man outside. Message received: don't touch the performers.

As we wound our way through another channel into a new room, the song changed to something with a faster tempo. Blue lights shifted to pink and purple speckles, reflecting on a fresh wave of scented fog. It smelled sweet, like mangoes and bananas. A group of performers were barefoot and wore animal masks. They did a complex dance that involved a lot of stomping, exaggerated arm movements, and lifts.

All around us, mood bracelets flared bright. Some of the audience members giggled, and I bet the EJ had hit them with a dose of happy drugs. That was the main draw of a club like this—an immersive experience that touched all of your senses and then amped them up with low doses of narcotics distributed through the special bracelets.

We reached what must have been the back wall of the club—although I'd gotten so turned around in the maze that it was difficult to tell for certain.

Rizpah pulled aside a heavy curtain, waved her cuff in front of a secured door reader, and led us down a dark hallway to a private room with a round, wooden table and leather-padded chairs. As soon as I stepped inside, the music dropped to a conversational level. I glanced up and saw a sound dampener on the ceiling. The walls were painted a moody burgundy shade and held expensive artwork.

Most of the paintings featured serpents of some kind, including a striking depiction of the ancient myth of Medusa. This room was meant to impress people and show off the power and success of the criminal enterprise.

"Sit," Rizpah commanded.

Wright walked around the table and selected the chair that gave him the best view of the door. I sat next to him in the seat closest to the exit. We left our chairs pulled out in case we had to get up in a hurry. If things went sideways, I wanted to secure a way out as quickly as possible.

We waited for twenty minutes. I'd just started recounting the snakes on Medusa's head when I heard the rhythmic click-clack of high heels on tile registering over the muffled music. Lady Ilymechina and her underlings, Dominique and Iko, entered the room.

Rizpah tilted her head to the Lady and moved closer to the door. Her hand rested on the blaster strapped to her thigh. I had no doubt she'd shoot us if she thought we posed a threat to her boss.

Iko sauntered to the far corner, where he had a clear line of sight to us. In his hurry to get to his place, he didn't bother assessing the room. He probably assumed Rizpah would have taken care of any threats, but it was lazy on his part. I saw the moment his eyes sparked with recognition.

The first time I'd met Iko, he'd been a scrawny kid working as a lookout for a junkie dealer in the gang. I'd been undercover trying to get an introduction to his boss. The last time I'd seen him was six months ago. He'd gone behind Lady Ilymechina's back and tipped off DECA that I'd be at the spacedock trying to get off Brione-5. Wright had almost caught me, but I'd managed to get away. Barely.

Iko's face paled, and sweat beaded along his brow. His fingers clenched into fists at his side.

Rizpah's brows drew together, and she shot him a look that told him to get his shit together.

Lady Ilymechina either didn't notice Iko's unease or didn't show it. She wasn't a real lady. No planets employed a monarchy system of governance, although a few maintained an honorific title system to reward their most esteemed citizens. However, it was easy to see how she came upon the moniker. Even in the back room of an underground club, she exuded class and sophistication.

Today she wore designer pants with a tailored suit jacket and no shirt beneath it. The deep V of the jacket plunged almost to her belly button, exposing a section of bronzed skin I could never pull off. A golden snake pendant dangled from a delicate chain.

She took the chair opposite Wright, giving her back to the door. Dominique sat across from me.

Once they settled, Wright cleared his throat. "Thank you for meeting with us. Please let me introduce myself. I'm—"

Lady Ilymechina held up her hand. "I know who you are, Lead Agent Grayson Wright of the Andaress-4 DECA office, former commander in the Ritru-6 military, survivor of the Ritru Asteroid Belt Conflict, and son of Tanver Wright and Charlotte Rayl, ambassadors of Ritru-6." She turned her piercing eyes to me. "Captain Sinclair, it was my understanding from our last meeting that our business was concluded, and you were never to darken my doorstep again. And yet, here you are. With law enforcement."

I swallowed the lump in my throat and wondered if anything fazed her. "First, love what you've done with the place. It's very carnival meets Avignon meets Ceti Red-Light district—but in a classy way."

She inclined her head. "We must give the people what they want."

"Second, you are correct. My intention had been that you and I would never meet again. So sorry. However, since our last meeting, I've uncovered information that a tech company is developing bionic weapons. The inventor is in prison, but we believe several prototypes made it out of the lab."

"Do you think I have them?"

Dominique chuckled. Rizpah remained stone-faced. Iko looked like he was about to blow a gasket. Red crept up his neck.

"No, but I think you may know someone who is involved."

Ilymechina leaned back and crossed her legs. "This sound like DECA's problem, not mine."

The muscles in Wright's jaw tightened. "Bionic weapons are everyone's problem."

"Yes, as a Ritruvian, you would believe that, wouldn't you? Let me be clear. The only reason you are sitting here and not tossed out in the back alley is because you said this had to do with Ophidian." At his name, Rizpah made a derisive sound. A sharp look from Ilymechina quieted her. "You piqued my curiosity, but my interest is waning."

"Three days ago, a man assassinated a politician on Ritru-6 using a bionic weapon. The suspect was apprehended but escaped custody. As he was fleeing, our tech specialist intercepted a comm from his ship."

She waved her hand in a hurry-up motion. "Get to your point."

I leaned forward and rested my forearms on the table. "The comm was sent to an untraceable account under the name Ophidian. It said, 'red touches yellow.'"

Iko inhaled sharply.

"Kills a fellow," Dominique finished the rhyme to herself.

Ilymechina and Rizpah exchanged a loaded look.

"That's ridiculous!" Iko spat out. "Ophidian is dead. He died over a decade ago."

"Did he?" I asked. "Because we never found a body. Not his or his top four lieutenants."

Iko stepped forward. "You lying little—"

"Iko!" Rizpah hissed out a reprimand.

He paid her no heed. "My lady, you can't believe anything they say. They're fucking *ribbits!*"

His nostrils flared, and he gave me a three-fingered hand gesture.

"Maybe so," I spat back. "But do you know what's worse than a ribbit? A *rat.*"

I instantly regretted losing my temper.

Iko bellowed and lunged across the table.

Chapter 12

Iko leaped across the table, pure rage burning in his eyes. His hands fisted the lapels of my leather jacket.

I tried to shove my seat back, but the legs stuck to the floor. The chair wobbled back onto two legs.

Wright shot up, kicking his chair out of the way. He grabbed Iko by the shirt and yanked him off me. With a twist of his hips, he redirected Iko's momentum to send him flying off the table.

Iko grunted as he hit the floor hard on his hands and knees. He recovered, leveraging his position to ram into Wright. His shoulder caught Wright in the stomach, and he drove my boss into the wall. One of the expensive paintings fell from its hook. Iko's foot ripped through the delicate canvas right before the carved wood frame splintered.

Wright kneed Iko in the gut, then delivered a double hammer-fist strike to Iko's spine. He followed Iko to the floor and cocked his arm back for a punch when I heard the high-pitch whine of a blaster beside me.

I spun to find Rizpah pointing her blaster at both men. "First man to move gets a blast to his dick."

Wright wisely unclenched his fist and held his hands at chest height. Rizpah jerked her head to the side, and Wright stepped back. Iko glared up at us from the ground, but he, too, raised his hands at Rizpah's command. A trickle of blood leaked from a split lip.

My boss tugged his jacket into place. At Rizpah's direction, he took his chair but sat farther forward with his feet balanced under him, ready to jump up if necessary.

Rizpah holstered her blaster, but she kept a vigilant eye on Iko.

Lady Ilymechina arched one delicate eyebrow. "Well, you have my attention now."

Iko got to his feet and looked around the room, searching for a friendly face. Finding none, he stepped toward Lady Ilymechina, pleading. "They're ribbits! Don't listen to them, Lady. I can explain—"

Rizpah kicked him in the balls. The sound was so loud that even I flinched.

Iko double over, clutching his privates.

She grabbed him by his hair and forced his head up. "I told you not to fucking move."

"Please, Rizpah, I—"

"Silence!" Lady Ilymechina held up her hand. Her look quelled any thought Iko had of continuing his plea. "I wish to learn more about this rat."

The way she said rat made me feel a little sorry for Iko, even if he was the scum of the galaxy. Everyone looked at me.

Moving slowly under Rizpah's icy stare, I straightened my chair and sat down. "After I helped your people load the smuggled electronics into your LAVs, I made my way back onto the tarmac. But before I reached the ship you'd hired to smuggle me to Brione-2, I ran into Agent Wright. Someone in your organization tipped him off that I was in Clava and would be at the spacedock."

"Iko?"

It was Wright who answered. "Yes. He contacted my office with a holo of Officer Sinclair taken from a security camera and a date and location of where she would be. I wouldn't have found her without that information."

"I spotted Agent Wright before reaching the ship and tried to evade him," I continued. "Iko followed me and shoved me off the viewing platform right in front of him."

Rizpah's blaster was back in her hands and aimed at Iko's head. "Traitor," she hissed.

"Wait! I can explain." Iko's wide eyes darted from me to Rizpah to Lady Ilymechina. His voice held a note of uncertainty. "I was the one who convinced Shug to give her a chance ten years ago. I didn't know she was an undercover officer. It's my fault you got arrested and put on trial back then. She does nothing but lie. Don't you see? She can't be trusted. I was *protecting* you."

Rizpah clocked him across the side of the head with her blaster. "Your job is not to question the Lady's orders. It is to follow them. By turning Reliance in, you broke the Lady's word."

Iko staggered, dazed. She raised her hand to deliver another blow, but Lady Ilymechina stopped her. Rizpah lowered the blaster.

"We will discuss Iko's transgressions later. In private."

"Yes, Lady," Rizpah made a slight bowing motion, then used her cuff to summon two bouncers.

At that, Iko shrunk against the wall. Gone was any semblance of his cocky attitude. Fear shone in his eyes. There was a reason Seven Serpents would go to prison for Lady Ilymechina. She'd earned that respect through hard work—and dirty work.

When the bouncers appeared, Iko made one last attempt to plead for her mercy, but the Lady was having none of it. "Take him away while I think of an appropriate punishment for the rat."

I was about to protest. Iko wasn't a friend by any means, but as DECA officers, we couldn't just stand by and let them murder him. The Lady cut me off with a sharp look.

"I won't kill him," she said, and I let out a sigh of relief. "But he may prefer that I did."

The bouncers dragged Iko from the room. He still hobbled awkwardly from his encounter with Rizpah's boot.

"Back to the business at hand," Lady Ilymechina said. "It is apparent that I did not uphold my end of our bargain for safe passage. To clear the slate, I will tell you what I know of Ophidian. My predecessor is not dead, or at least, not by my hand. We had already lost too many young lives under his failed leadership. Rather than endure more bloodshed, we exiled Ophidian and his four closest allies. They left understanding they could never return to Brione-5."

Wright launched a holoscreen, showing the booking photo of the assassin. "Do you know this man?"

She glanced at the holo. "He's older than the last time I saw him, but that's Sidewinder. He was banished with Ophidian."

"Does Sidewinder have a legal name?"

Lady Ilymechina shrugged. "Thomas, I believe. I never knew his last name. Everyone used street names back then, and we weren't that close."

"Do you know where they are now?" Wright asked.

Lady Ilymechina leaned over and whispered something into Dominique's ear. The younger woman nodded and left the room.

The second-in-command returned carrying a handful of mood bracelets. Unlike the normal blue bracelets handed out at the club, these glowed bright orange in the dimly lit room. She dropped them in the middle of the table. There must have been half a dozen.

"First, I have a few questions of my own. Put on these mood bracelets." Lady Ilymechina pointed at the glowing stack. "Dominique will program them to release a dose of Rhap. We'll continue this conversation once the drug takes effect, and I am assured that your answers are honest."

My jaw clenched as I looked down at the bracelets. Rhap—short for Rhapsody—was an illegal party drug imported from the Avignon system. It had the effect of putting the user at ease, lowering inhibitions, and making them say and do things they normally wouldn't.

"If we're taking you at your word, then you can take us at ours," I bit out.

"I have no desire for Ophidian to slither out from whatever rock he's been hiding under for the past twelve years. If you're lying, and your real motivation is to bring him back to Clava to stand trial for his past crimes, then his resurrection could prove problematic for me. However, if you are telling the truth, and he's involved in some ludicrous scheme involving bionic weapons, I will tell you what you want to know. Iko wasn't wrong. You swore I would never see you again, and yet, here you are." Her voice dropped to just above a whisper. "Your word means nothing to me."

"Fine," I said and reached for a bracelet.

Wright put his hand on my arm. "I'll do it. You've had enough people mucking around your head without your permission."

He let go and snapped one of the orange bracelets onto his wrist.

"Now the rest of them," said Lady Ilymechina.

"He'll be high out of his fucking mind!"

Dominique made a splayed motion with her fingers, activating her holoscreen. I saw the controls for each bracelet flash on. She slid all six control toggles to the maximum settings. "That's the point."

"You don't have to do this," I told Wright. "We'll find another way."

"Not soon enough. This is our best lead. Now stand down. That's an order."

I had no choice but to watch while Wright fastened the other five mood bracelets around his wrist. He nodded to Dominique. She pointed her finger to a button on her cuff's holoscreen, and all six bracelets pulsed bright orange.

The muscles across Wright's chest and back flexed and bunched, pulling the stiff fabric of his jacket taut. Rhap wasn't cheap, and a dose this substantial was something most junkies only dreamed about. But Wright wasn't a junkie. No, he was the exact opposite. A my-body-is-a-temple kind of guy. A control freak.

It only took seconds for the Rhap to hit his system. His pupils dilated, blown out until his hazel eyes looked nearly black. The tension in his muscles relaxed. He listed to one side, then jerked back, shaking his head.

"Ask your void-damned questions," he ground out, but his eyes drifted off to the side, unable to remain focused.

Dominique studied the readings on her holoscreen projection. "He's ready."

Lady Ilymechina stood. The supple black fabric of her suit shimmered in the subdued lighting. It was made of ov-ex material—an expensive, high-tech, and illegal cloth that reflected light to such a degree that it overexposed any images taken of it with a camera, hiding the wearer from law enforcement. Her heels clicked on the floor as she circled around the table behind us.

"Who do you work for, Grayson Wright?" she asked.

He swayed side to side, his eyes half-lidded as he tried to keep her in his sight. "I'm the lead agent of the bionic weapons task force for the Andaress-4 DECA office."

"No one else?"

"No."

"The Clava DECA office?"

"No."

"Have you ever accepted a bribe?"

"Never."

"Has a competitor of mine hired you to put me out of business?"

I twisted in my chair to follow her movements. "He's not dirty."

She flicked her wrist, and a stiletto dagger slipped out from under her sleeve and into her hand. She trailed the tip across the surface of her palm as she continued circling the table. "Forgive me if I don't rely on your judgment. You don't have the best track record for identifying dirty agents, now do you?"

My mouth snapped shut because she was right. Being fooled by my former partner was how all of this started.

"Sinclair, I'm good," Wright said, but I could see him fighting the effects of the drugs.

"Why are you interested in Ophidian?"

"We are tracking an assassin known to have used a bionic weapon. Ophidian's name was found attached to an intercepted communication."

Lady Ilymechina paused beside Wright's chair. She bent until her face was level with his and cupped his chin in her hand, studying his eyes. The golden stiletto flashed as she brought it up between them.

Wright jerked back, his movements slow but sure.

I tried to stand, but Rizpah closed the distance between us and shoved me back down onto the chair.

"Don't move," she said, and I felt the muzzle of her blaster poke me between my shoulder blades.

Wright's gaze sharpened. His right hand went to his hip, where his blaster normally sat. Only it wasn't there, because we'd left our weapons on the hoverbike.

"Nuh-uh-uh." Lady Ilymechina twisted the dagger until the tip pricked the hollow point between his clavicles.

"I'm good," I said, holding up my hands, both to signal Wright not to struggle and to show Rizpah I intended to behave.

"I think Agent Wright requires a second dose."

"Yes, my lady." Dominique pointed her finger at the button on the holoscreen again. The six mood bracelets pulsed once, and Wright's entire body heaved.

Rizpah called for an employee out in the hall. "Get a bucket." When the employee didn't move fast enough, she shouted. "Get a bucket now, or you'll be the one cleaning up vomit."

That did the trick, because the employee double-timed it out the door and returned with a grimy, yellow cleaning bucket. He tossed it down just as Wright doubled over and emptied the contents of his stomach into it. When Wright straightened, his face was clammy, with beads of sweat on his forehead.

"You didn't have to do that," I said. "We're being honest with you."

Lady Ilymechina ignored my comment. She ran her fingers through Wright's hair, fisted the blond strands, and yanked his head to face her. "What do you plan to do with Ophidian?"

Wright's eyes blinked as he struggled to focus through the haze of narcotics. "Don't know. Have to ... find him ... first."

"You will bring him back here to testify against me, won't you?"

"Lady ... I don't give a ... shit ... about you."

"Hit him again."

Wright couldn't handle a third dose—not at those levels. I closed my eyes to minimize distractions and used the smallest movements possible to aerial scribe commands to my Intell. It only took a second to open the screen connected to Dominique's cuff. As always, my

Intell's hacking program set to work breaking down her firewalls. A spike of pain at the base of my neck told me my implant was working hard, but I was in before Dominique turned back to her holoscreen.

"Give him any more Rhap, and I will lock you out of every system connected to this cuff."

To prove my sincerity, I got into her cuff's system controls and changed her passcode. Immediately, her holoscreen blanked.

Dominique's eyes flared. She tried reopening it, but it wouldn't accept her code. "What did you do?"

It was a temporary measure. She'd be able to get around it with some effort, but I only needed to show them I was serious about my threat.

"Finish your questions, and I'll return control."

Dominique looked at her boss, her shoulders lifted in a subtle shrug.

"I can make her cooperate," Rizpah offered.

Lady Ilymechina's ruby-stained lips drew into a tight line. "That won't be necessary. I only have one question left for Agent Wright." She circled back to her chair and sat down, crossing her legs with deliberate slowness. "If Ophidian is involved in the unspeakable development of bionic weapons, will you do what the legal system of this planet never did? Will you hold him accountable for his actions?"

"If Ophi ... Ophi-ie ..." Wright sucked in a deep breath and blew it out. "If he's involved ... I will see jus ... justi ... justice served. I swear."

He punctuated his statement with a wobbly head bob that threatened to tip him out of his chair.

Satisfied, Lady Ilymechina directed the rest of the conversation at me. "The last I heard, Ophidian was on Valla in the city, Newtown. An old acquaintance of ours passes through there now and again. Apparently, Ophidian fancies himself a bit of a pirate these days."

"How long ago was that?" I asked.

"Four months. Maybe Five."

"That's pretty dated information."

"You're searching for a man who has been dead for twelve years. Four months is the least of your problems."

A lot could change in four months on Valla. It was a known criminal sanctuary. The population was largely transitory and there was no governing system to speak of. Those who lived there permanently were self-sufficient or bartered for what they needed. It didn't even have a proper spacedock anymore, as criminals didn't want to be tracked coming and going and thieves kept stealing the sinnafuel, anyway.

I ripped off the mood bracelets from Wright's arm and tossed them into the cleaning bucket before resetting the passcode on Dominique's cuff. She let out an audible sigh of relief as her holoscreen projection flickered back to her starting screen.

Wright's eyes were half-lidded. He was struggling to stay alert, but we needed to get out of here before the amount of Rhap in his system pulled him fully under.

"Thank you," I said, and tapped Wright on the shoulder. "Sir, we need to go."

Wright's eyes opened enough to meet mine, and he leaned heavily onto the table as he pushed himself to his feet. His arm rested across my shoulders for balance.

Rizpah opened the door and stepped clear. "The effects of the Rhapsody will wear off within the hour. It's pure, not cut like most of the shit sold on the streets. He'll have a hell of a headache tomorrow, though."

I propped him against the wall, waited to make sure he wouldn't fall, then returned to the room. Rizpah's hand rested on the blaster at her thigh.

"Was there something else?" Lady Ilymechina asked. From her tone, I could tell that was a rhetorical question.

"Yes." I spared a glance over my shoulder to check that Wright hadn't wandered in behind me. "This is personal in nature."

She raised her eyebrows but inclined her head for me to continue.

"I need Blue Lace."

Anger flashed over her face. "The Serpents don't deal that shit. Legitimate prescription drugs, maybe a little Stardust, but that never hurt anyone. Blue Lace can kill you if you get a bad batch."

Never say the universe doesn't have a sense of humor. "I have my reasons. You may not sell it yourself, but you can find it. Can you get your hands on some? Quickly?"

"Cyril," Dominique said, naming the leader of one of the other local gangs. Minor compared to the Serpents. "He's been pushing harder stuff this year. If anyone has it, it would be him."

Cyril's territory was closer to the business district, if I remembered correctly. People with high-paying jobs and credits to wipe. I reached into my messenger bag and pulled out two hundred in legal tender, hoping it would be enough to cover at least a week's worth of Blue Lace.

"We'll make some inquiries," Lady Ilymechina said.

"I need it before we leave tonight." I handed my LTs over to Rizpah.

Lady Ilymechina looked me over with an appraising eye. "You have balls, I'll give you that. Dominique will see to it." She leaned back in her chair. "If you find Ophidian, give him my regards."

The smile she gave me was anything but friendly.

Chapter 13

WE STAGGERED THROUGH THE grocery store parking lot. I hoped the cool night air would help Wright sober up. He had one arm thrown over my shoulder for balance, and my arm around his waist kept us moving in a nominally direct path toward my hoverbike. A hovercart zipped past us on its way to an auto-return station, forcing me to pull Wright up short to avoid getting clipped.

"Whoa! Did you see that?" He tipped to the side as his head followed the cart.

I grabbed his hand and tugged. "Wrong way, big guy. The bike's over here."

Wright let me pull him back around. I looked down and realized we still held hands in a way that felt too familiar for him being my boss. When I tried to drop it, he wouldn't let go. I told myself he needed it for balance.

It took ten minutes to reach my bike. By the time we got there, Wright was walking more or less in a straight line, and he'd stopped slurring his words.

"This is such a cool bike," he said, letting go of my hand to trail his fingers along the sleek, cherry-red frame. "When I was a teenager, I used to dream about owning a Cymbeline. Did I ever tell you that?"

"I don't think so."

"Oh, yeah. I'd watch holovids of races at night when I was supposed to be sleeping. I even saved up credits from my allowance and odd jobs for a year hoping to buy one. Then my mom found out and said absolutely not."

A light shone from his eyes that wasn't just a reflection from the overhead streetlamps. For a second, I caught sight of a younger Wright, one who dreamed of fast bikes and adventures—who hadn't yet joined the military or shouldered the burden that came with being a homicide detective.

"Let me guess—no child of hers would ride one of those death traps? My mother told me something similar."

The smile wavered from his face. "Mom has a tendency to be overprotective. It hadn't been long since my brother—well, she had her reasons. It didn't stop me from dreaming, though. I always thought I'd get one. Just haven't gotten around to it yet."

Wright rarely talked about his life prior to joining DECA. In fact, that was the most he'd ever shared about his childhood. I didn't know what to make of a chatty Grayson Wright.

Even though he moved with more assuredness, a closer look confirmed his pupils were still dilated from the Rhap. It hadn't occurred to me that Wright might be unable to ride in his inebriated state.

"Maybe we should call an auto-LAV," I suggested.

Wright straightened and scrubbed his palms up and down his face. "No, we need to get to Valla as soon as possible. My head is already clearing."

"It's more your body I'm worried about. It'll slow us down if you fall off thirty stories up and kill yourself. The paperwork alone will take me a week."

He released his helmet from the magnetic lock above the rear thruster and gave me one of his half-smiles. "I appreciate your concern for my body, but I can hold it together long enough to get back to the *Soteria*."

My lips tightened into a thin line, but I unlocked my helmet, slipped it on, and threw my leg over the bike seat. A notification for the bike's operating controls popped up in my mind's eye. A familiar burning sensation at the base of my skull accompanied the increased activity of my neural chip. I aerial scribed to open the panel and started the preflight check. All systems were a go. The engine purred to life, causing the bike to bob in the air as it readied for takeoff.

Once Wright fastened his helmet, I connected to his comm. "If you feel off, tell me right away, okay? I'll leave the comms open the entire way."

It took him two tries to get his leg over the hoverbike, and he had to grip onto my shoulder to do it. When his thighs settled around mine, I activated the cargo tie-down program. A long strap released from beneath the right side of the seat.

"Cross that over your legs and fasten it to the clip on the other side," I instructed. It was designed for securing packages during transport, but it would give Wright extra support in case he wobbled again.

Soft grumbling transmitted over the comm as he belted himself in. Despite that, his arms wrapped around my waist tight enough that I knew he took his impaired state seriously.

My fingers trembled as I tried to form the minute signals that engaged the main thruster. I shook out my hand, hoping Wright hadn't noticed. What a defective pair we made tonight.

I got it going on the second attempt. We rose straight up in a hot burst of sinnafuel exhaust. Thankfully, I didn't need to access a map of the city to know the fastest route to the spacedock. This was my hometown. I'd grown up navigating these skylanes and then patrolled them for a decade.

For the first twenty minutes, Wright sat with his helmet resting against the back of my shoulders. If it weren't for his ironlike grip around my waist, I might have worried he'd passed out.

It wasn't until I slowed and dropped back down to ground level that I felt his muscles relax. The bright-white lights of the spacedock enveloped us as we hovered in the entrance line. It was late, and traffic was light.

We made it through without any fuss, although I felt like my head might explode when I called up our credentials for the guard at the gate. Between that, flying the hoverbike, and hacking Dominique's cuff, my brain had taken about all the Intell chip's processing power that it could handle.

Felix lowered the cargo bay door as we approached the *Soteria*. I coasted straight in, cutting the engine so the interior didn't fill with exhaust.

"We're here," I said, nudging Wright with my elbow before removing my helmet.

His hands loosened from their locked position, sliding back to settle low onto my waist just above my hip bones. Their warmth sank through the wind-chilled material of my shirt. I tried not to think about how comfortable they felt there.

"Grayson? Are you all right?" I asked, as the moment threatened to drag into awkwardness.

"I'm waiting for you to untruss me."

"Untru—? Oh, right." I scrambled to release the strap across his thighs.

He wobbled a bit, regained his balance, and then unmounted the bike in one smooth motion.

Instinctively, I offered my hand to steady him. "Hold on to me. I don't want to peel you off the floor."

Wright removed his helmet and secured it on the rack. His pupils were almost back to normal. Their hazel coloring looked more green than brown in the ship's light, and they held my gaze steady as he reached over to smooth a lock of my hair that had been mussed by my helmet.

"I promise not to make a mess on your ship, Captain."

"Humph," Felix said and jumped down from the second floor with a loud clang. "See that you don't. My cleaning bots have enough to do around here without following you around all night. Aren't you a little old to be drinking past your limit, Agent Wright?"

I used the excuse to break eye contact, never more grateful to see that rusty bucket of metal. "Cut him some slack, Felix. He's not drunk. He's high."

"Oh, well, in that case…"

"Give me a hand, huh? Close the door while I help him to the common room." I got off the bike and locked it into its rack.

Wright leaned forward until his chest pressed against my back. His voice came from just above my ear. "*He* is standing right here and not nearly as high as you think he is."

The feel of his warm breath on my neck sent a shiver down my spine. I stepped forward, and he stumbled without my support. "Uh-huh. You were saying?"

He laughed. "My head is clear—mostly. I just can't feel my feet."

I circled back and took some of his weight onto my shoulders. He didn't argue and let me guide him back to the common area.

While he went to his bunk to clean up and splash water on his face, I poured him a glass of cold water from the potable water tank. He managed the walk back without bumping into anything.

"Drink." When he didn't move, I nudged his foot with the toe of my boot. "Drink. It'll help flush out the Rhap."

He grumbled but raised the glass to his lips and drained it in one go. A tremor raked through my hand as I took it from him. My hand shook so badly that I almost dropped the glass.

Stars! I needed to get that under control.

"Whoa, easy there. Are you okay?"

Wright took the glass back from me and set it on the counter. The concern in his voice was genuine and just about undid me.

"Yeah, I'm fine." I shoved my hand through my hair to disguise the shaking. "I should get to the bridge to help Felix prepare for takeoff. Why don't you lay down in your bunk for a bit?"

"Reliance—"

"Rizpah said the effects would wear off within the hour, but resting couldn't hurt." I started for the exit, remembering I might have a few pain tabs up on the bridge. And if not, there was always the bottle of whisky I kept stashed for emergencies. This certainly qualified.

As I squeezed between Wright and the wall, he snagged my hand and tugged me back toward him. His hold was firm but not hard. I could have pulled away if I wanted.

But I didn't.

"Tonight couldn't have been easy on you," he said, "seeing your old teammates and then Lady Ilymechina. I know she and you have a complicated history. Do you want to talk about it?"

Granted, seeing Kinnikinnic and Nomikou, or even Ilymechina and Iko, weren't the highlights of my day, but they weren't what was sending me fleeing for solitude. I wished I could tell Wright about the problems the Intell was giving me, but there was nothing he could do to help. All he could do was force me into extended medical leave where the Department doctors would poke and prod me like some kind of lab animal.

Been there, done that, got the souvenir brain chip. Hard pass.

I looked down at our hands. His thumb rubbed in a soft, reassuring circle across the top of my hand, which did nothing to settle the storm of emotions swirling in my stomach. It killed me to lie to him, but I couldn't lose the team. Not when I'd just become a part of it.

"There's nothing to talk about," I said.

"I can see something is bothering you."

"Then you should get your eyes checked."

He ignored my halfhearted attempt at lightening the mood. His finger brushed along my jawline, then curled beneath my chin to tip my face toward his so that our eyes met. "I don't think I've ever seen things more clearly."

"Grayson, I..." To my horror, my voice came out low and breathy. I wasn't even sure what we were talking about anymore.

The pad of his thumb skimmed over my bottom lip, and then he lowered his head to mine.

"Ahem," Felix said from the doorway.

We broke apart, both of us looking guilty.

Stars, what was I doing? There was no way this didn't end in a colossal shitshow.

"Someone is at the door requesting permission to enter," Felix continued.

Wright's eyes never left mine. "I'll go speak with them."

"No. No, I'll go." My lip still tingled from where he'd touched it. I needed out of this room.

"Rel," Wright said, reaching for me.

Blood pounded in my ears, and I was sure my face was flushed. "I said I'll go. It's my ship."

Felix's tail whipped from side to side. His heterochromia eyes flashed in the dark hallway. "Orders, Captain?"

For all his snark and sarcasm, Felix's programming was exceptionally good at reading human emotions. He was, after all, created to serve as the crew's companion. Obviously, he picked up that something had changed between Wright and me. As if Felix needed another reason to antagonize Wright.

I breathed in to calm the feelings threatening to overwhelm me before he threw a hissy fit. "Go to the bridge and prepare a flight plan for Valla. Transmit copies to Brione-5 Central Command, our office on Andaress-4, and to Ravi and DeAjamae. They should still be on Ritru-6. Then initiate the preflight check. I want to leave as soon as we're space-worthy."

Felix's ears flattened. "What about him?"

Excellent question. "It's been a long night. Neither of us are feeling quite ourselves, so Wright's to rest. Isn't that right?"

"You can't pretend that just didn't happen," Wright said.

Watch me. "It shouldn't have."

I fled for the cargo hold before he could respond.

Shit. Fuck. Void. Damn. Stars.

I looked for something to kick, but Felix had everything buttoned down tight. How could I be so stupid? Wright would come to his senses in a few hours and reach the same conclusion.

Echoes bounced around me as I clomped through the cargo hold. I circled a finger to bring up the *Soteria*'s outer cameras, although I was pretty sure I knew who it was. Two viewscreens opened in my mind's eye. For a second, my vision swam in and out of focus as my brain struggled to process another series of inputs from the Intell. When it cleared, it left me with a sick feeling.

As suspected, Rizpah stood outside. The harsh cut of her black bangs and the jut of her sharp chin emphasized her angular features. She looked pissed to be playing errand girl, and I didn't blame her.

I lowered the ramp and met her at the point where the light from the ship faded into shadow.

"I only got three doses of the Blue Lace. It was short notice," Rizpah said without preamble.

"Only three? I gave you enough LTs for at least ten tabs."

"You're lucky I procured this much." She handed me a slim packet with the drugs. It weighed next to nothing.

Rizpah put her hand on my wrist. "Are you certain you want that? It is highly addictive. The Lady doesn't allow it to be sold within our territory."

I spun my hand in a counterclockwise motion, breaking her hold. "It's a good product, though, right?"

The lithe bodyguard's face showed no emotion. "It comes from a competitor. Cyril has a reputation for selling quality products, but there's no guarantee."

My fingers clenched around the packet of tabs. "Thank you."

"The Lady wanted me to tell you that this was a onetime thing. Having DECA officers hanging around is bad for business."

"I understand."

"Do you? Because you didn't understand the last time or you wouldn't be here now."

"Fine. Message received."

Rizpah glared down at me, her dark eyes gleaming with intensity.

"Is there something else?" I asked.

The muscles along her jaw and neck clenched. "If Ophidian is involved in this, you shoot that rat bastard the second you get a chance. He is a poison that kills everything he touches. The Lady was magnanimous in letting him slither away to hide and scheme beneath some distant rock. She should have cut off his head when she had the chance, but she feared more bloodshed would have torn the Serpents apart. It is a risk I would have taken."

"We will bring him to justice," I said.

"The only justice fitting for Ophidian comes from the end of a blaster."

I watched Rizpah slip away, her gray bodysuit soon blending in with the ships' hulls and concrete pavement until I could no longer distinguish her with any accuracy. When I was sure she was gone, I opened the packet she had given me and peeled off a lacy, light-blue tab. It reminded me a bit of a snowflake, and when I placed it on the tip of my tongue, it dissolved like one, too.

An artificial calmness settled over me, and almost immediately, my headache disappeared.

Chapter 14

Valla was the only moon of the only planet in the Searcy system. It was near Ritru-6 and took three days to travel there from Brione-5. The moon had been one of the earliest to be terraformed, and the scientists and engineers hadn't yet perfected the process.

Everything started off well. The tropical and temperate zones were warmer and wetter than on Earth, but well within range of habitability. Multiple cities spanned its eight continents with citrus products and insect proteins being their chief exports. Marketing firms for its tourist board coined it *The Emerald Jewel of the Galaxy*.

Unfortunately, miscalculations in the atmosphere-building stage led to a buildup of greenhouse gases. Temperatures rose and weather patterns destabilized. The equatorial zone grew too hot to support life. Plants died. Desertification took over the central band of the moon and spread toward the poles. Within decades, once-thriving cities were buried beneath drifting sand dunes.

Most people immigrated away. By that time, terraforming technology had advanced to a point where once a planet or moon was declared colonizable, there was a ninety-five percent certainty it would stay that way. Other people were too stubborn to leave Valla or lacked the funds to do so. Generations of families chased the ever-narrowing bands of livable land as they pushed toward the north and south poles. It was a hard life. Companies refused to invest in new development, and local governments collapsed under the constant need to pick up and move.

Then the criminals moved in. A lack of resources and functioning government created a safe haven for those looking to hide until the heat cooled down or to disappear altogether. I'd tracked nine offenders to Valla myself during my decade as an officer in Clava. It didn't surprise me that Ophidian had been hiding there, but it did make our job more difficult. Looking for a criminal on Valla wasn't like looking for the proverbial needle in a haystack. It was like looking for a needle in a stack of needles, and each one wanted to stab your hand.

I spent the entire first day avoiding Wright, which was no easy feat on a ship as small as mine. He'd attempted to join me on the bridge for the first shift. After a couple of awkward conversation nonstarters, I'd escaped to the first level, claiming I had routine maintenance work to do on the engine. He'd tried again at lunch. That time, I excused myself to the restroom and waited until Felix told me Wright had given up and gone back to the bridge. Wright probably thought I had a gastrointestinal problem with how long I'd been in there, but that was infinitely preferable to the horror show that would be our next real conversation.

Oh, I knew we had to have it soon. I was just putting it off as long as possible.

I set down my book tablet, yawned, and stretched. Since I was headache free for the first time in months, I'd given reading another shot. It was a good story about a deep-space explorer making first contact with alien life in the void. DeAjamae had recommended it.

Unfortunately, I'd reread the same paragraph three times because my brain kept wandering. As Lourde had suggested, the Blue Lace suppressed the negative effects from my Intell. However, two days later it still messed with my concentration and left me feeling sluggish and irritable as the depressant flushed out of my system.

The tabs I'd taken in Lourde's lab hadn't done that, but then again, I'd taken them every day. Since I only had two of the Blue Lace tabs left, I didn't have the luxury of seeing if another dose would take the edge off.

Felix perked up from his place on the copilot seat. His iridescent-black scales reflected a soft pinkish-blue glow from the main holoscreen. The star chart on the autopilot display tracked our progress to Valla. We'd arrive in twelve hours, assuming we didn't run into any interference.

"Time for bed?" Felix asked.

Stars, I hoped so. "Where is he?"

Felix blinked his eyes—he did that sometimes when processing data. "Agent Wright is in his bunkroom. Motion sensors have detected no movement for the last fifty-nine minutes."

"Finally," I grumbled and stood up. A kink in my lower back protested the motion, so I twisted from side to side and arched my back to stretch it out. I'd been waiting on the bridge for three hours for him to fall asleep.

I gathered my empty glass, plate, and book tablet, and we headed downstairs. The common area was dark, with only soft-amber safety lights illuminating the area. Felix went straight into my bunkroom while I put my dishes into the sanitizer unit. I winced when the plate clanked against the rack, but I didn't hear any movement from Wright's room.

Walnut rustled out of his hut to investigate the commotion, or more likely, to see if I would drop any food into his habitat. His whiskers twitched as he sniffed the air for clues.

I plucked a ripe cherry tomato and a fresh lettuce leaf from the hydroponics station and lifted Walnut from the plastiglass enclosure. "How about you sleep with me tonight?"

Before joining Wright's team, I'd spent weeks alone in space. I should be used to the silence, but this felt different. Heavier. Lonelier. A little company might be nice.

Walnut wheeked his agreement.

"Shh," I said and scratched behind one of his ears. "We have to be quiet."

"Not on my account." Wright spoke at a normal volume, but the words thundered in my ears.

I spun around, clutching Walnut to my chest. "I thought you were asleep."

"Yeah, it took a while, but I figured out you were using the ship's sensors to track me. After that, it was only a matter of staying in my bunk until you came down."

"So you were literally lying in wait for me? For an hour?"

He gave me one of those devastating half-smiles. "I'm a patient man."

"Some people might find that creepy." I tried to scoot around him.

He blocked my path. "Reliance, you can't avoid me forever."

"I'm not avoiding you."

He cocked one eyebrow. We both knew that was a lie.

"Fine. I was avoiding you." I set Walnut down and sent an image of my bed to his little guinea pig brain. He'd gotten better at understanding the images I sent him and had even figured out how to send a variety of them back to me.

"Wheek!" he chirped and scurried off to my bunkroom, his chubby potato butt wiggling all the way.

"Why?"

I'd been hoping to put this off until after we'd caught the assassin, secured the prototype, and returned to Andaress-4. Or forever. That would have worked, too. But Wright seemed determined to do this now.

"Things got carried away last night. You were high. I shouldn't have let it go that far."

"The Rhap was out of my system."

I gave him a skeptical look that said I didn't buy it.

"All right, mostly out," he amended. "Enough that I don't regret what happened. Do you?"

"It's complicated."

He stared at me with an intensity that made my heart pound faster. It was all too easy to remember how he'd looked at me last night with that singular focus, to remember the feel of his fingers brushing my face. All I had to do was take one small step to close the distance between us.

I looked away.

It was bad enough keeping my symptoms secret from my teammates. Wright deserved someone who could be honest with him. Someone who had a future to give him.

"It's late. I'm going to turn in."

Wright stepped back to let me pass, but the aisle was narrow, and I couldn't help smelling the citrusy scent of his soap as I slid past him. The clean, crisp notes were at odds with the murky tones of my feelings. I hurried the few steps to my bunkroom before I lost my resolve and did something stupid.

Felix waited for me, his blue eye glowing, no doubt scanning my vitals for abnormal readings. I held my index finger to my lips in a *shh* sign. When I turned to shut the door, I saw Wright still standing in the kitchen, arms braced against the island and head bowed.

Once again, my problems were causing a friend pain.

I closed the door with a soft click. It was better this way. He would feel much worse if he found out I'd been lying to him.

A weight leaned into my lower thigh, and Felix's head pressed up into my hand. My fingers ran over the smooth scales, letting their coolness sap the heat from my mood.

"Come on, Felix, you're bunking with me tonight."

I sat on my bed and unlaced my boots. Felix jumped up, making the mattress dip on his end. Walnut waddled over to check out the fresh vegetables. I changed into a set of pajama leggings and a tank top that read, *Just Five More Minutes.*

Walnut munched on the lettuce while I crawled into bed. He'd started in the middle, and ruffly green leaves comically stuck out from either side of his mouth as he munched on it. It was hard to muster up a smile.

Once I settled, Felix lay down by my feet. "Your facial expression and vital readings suggest you're experiencing sadness. Should I initiate a counseling program? I added five new ones since we last tried. They are specialized for people dealing with medical issues."

Bless his processor. In the absence of my willingness to see a therapist, he'd tried to help me cope with being held captive, forcibly receiving the neural implant, and adjusting to life back as a DECA officer. So far, none of the programs clicked with me.

"Thanks, Felix. I'm sure they're great programs, but I don't want to talk tonight."

I scratched my nail against the sheet, and Walnut snuggled up with me. Sometimes, he made quiet purr sounds that lulled me to sleep. I hoped he did that tonight, but I suspected sleep wouldn't find me for some time.

"I could throw him out the airlock," Felix said.

"What?"

"Agent Wright. He made you sad. I could wait until he walks by the airlock and then just ... *whoosh*. We could alter the logs to make it look like an accident."

"No! Who programmed you? We're not killing anyone. Especially Agent Wright. Now go into sleep mode."

Homicidal cat.

He lowered his head onto his giant paws. "It was just an idea."

Chapter 15

"Entering the Valla system," I said over the ship's comms.

I waited sixty seconds for Wright to secure himself down on the lower level and collapsed the warp bubble around the *Soteria*. Inertia pushed my body forward as the ship stuttered out of faster-than-light speed. My harness did its job, digging into my shoulders and waist. It pinned me to my chair while my head snapped and my stomach felt like it launched several thousand kilometers in front of us.

The reverse thrusters kicked in. Their familiar rumble sent vibrations through the floor.

"Felix, bring up the view from the front cameras." A pale-yellow dot materialized on the main holoscreen. "Magnify."

The image enhanced until a planet and moon filled the screen. It was summer in the southern hemisphere of Valla. A chartreuse band wrapped around the moon near the negative-sixty degree longitude mark, but it was difficult to make out any topographical details through the yellowish haze of the atmosphere. Hard to believe it was once called The Emerald Jewel of the Galaxy. Citrine, maybe.

I checked the clock. Newtown would face the Valla star now. It should be early afternoon when we touched down. Normally, I would hail the moon's Central Command to request permission to land and refuel, however Valla didn't have a Central Command. It lost its last official spacedock a decade ago when it was swallowed by the desert. Sandstorms made keeping the launch area clear difficult, and the citizens packed up their belongings and migrated south or immigrated to a less hostile planet. No one bothered to re-build.

Felix entered the bridge and took his usual spot in the copilot's chair. He had something silver in his mouth.

"What do you have?" I asked.

"Nothing."

I gave him a side-eye glance. "Is that Wright's cuff?"

The big cat dropped the object on the dash and stared at it. His green eye pulsed brighter, a sign that his processors were working extra hard.

"Maybe."

"Why do you have it?"

"Agent Wright was in the water shower."

"Hmm, so you thought you'd take his cuff?"

Felix batted the cuff with one paw. "He wasn't using it."

My gut said something else felt off. "What else did you do?"

Silence.

"Felix?"

He batted Wright's cuff again until it balanced precariously close to the edge of the dash. "I took away his access rights to the hot water."

"Felix!"

"Agent Wright has been in there for seven minutes and twenty-five seconds. He's using up all my resources! Let him take sonic showers."

"Give it back. Now." Damn cat.

"Fine." Felix's green eye pulsed. "He made you sad. I thought you didn't like him anymore."

"No, it's not like that."

"Then why haven't you talked to him in two days?"

"We've talked."

"Barely."

I let out a long breath. "It's hard to explain."

Felix returned my side-eye but said nothing.

"What are our sinnafuel levels looking like?" I asked. We'd had a full tank when we left Clava, but I had zero desire to get stuck on Valla because of a miscalculation in fuel consumption.

"Sixty-two percent," Felix said. "Batteries at seventy-three percent."

"Adjust our course to swing around to the star side of the moon. We'll drop in fast. I want to spend as little time in atmo as possible. The less time you're sucking that filth through your vents, the better."

"Do you have a landing site in mind?"

"Yeah, Lady Ilymechina said she'd last heard Ophidian was in Newtown." I pronounced it Newton like the locals, not New Town. They'd stopped bothering with clever names a long time ago. "Let's see if we find someplace inconspicuous to put down around there."

Something pinged against the hull of the ship. "What was that?"

Felix changed the image on the main console to show a closer view. "I'm picking up bits of debris."

"Where's it coming from?"

His green eye glowed as he processed the incoming data from the ship's sensors. "Refined metals. Inorganic shapes. They appear to be parts from a ship."

I sifted through the data myself on the holoscreen. "More like ships, plural. That's a lot of debris out there." Two more pings echoed through the bridge. "Hull integrity?"

"No breaches, but there are larger fragments floating in our current trajectory."

"Get us clear of the debris field," I said as a hunk of twisted metal the length of my arm passed by the camera. The *Soteria* banked sharply to its portside, and I was grateful I still had my harness buckled. "Scan for potential causes."

Something scraped across the belly of the ship. A sick, grinding sound reverberated up from the engine room before being drowned out by an alarm. My console lit up like the night sky on Exploration Day.

"Captain, I have a hypothesis on what caused the damage to the other ships."

Felix calling me captain put me on alert. The main console switched views to a side camera. Three skiphoppers approached from the moon on our starboard side.

Two were painted slate gray and had silver battle scars slashed across their surfaces. The third was different. A much-higher class, painted a void black that all but disappeared against the vacuum of space. Each of the spaceships was only large enough to carry two people, but they were fast and agile. They split to approach us from three separate angles.

A fist grabbed hold of my stomach and twisted it into a snarled knot. "Wright!" I yelled into the comms. "You better get your ass up here!"

I connected to Walnut and sent him the run-and-hide signal with an image of his hut.

"The three ships are approaching fast, Captain. Scanners detect weapon armaments on all three."

"Are they broadcasting any identifiers?" I asked.

"Negative," Felix replied. "Should I send out ours?"

Tough call. There wasn't a DECA office on Valla. The Department and citizens shared a mutual philosophy of *don't bother us, and we won't bother you*. I doubted sending over our official credentials would win us any points, no matter who piloted those ships. Giving them nothing could also be risky.

"Send them the *Soteria*'s civilian identification pack. Strip out anything related to DECA, our official titles, or our warrant for Sidewinder. And mute the alarms."

The sound cut off, and I heard Wright's footsteps pounding down the short hallway to the bridge.

"Report," he said, taking in the flashing lights on the console and the ships moving into flanking positions on the holoscreen. His shirt was untucked, and his hair was damp from the shower.

"We've got company, and something tells me they're going to wear out their welcome sooner than the traditional three days."

It was the most we'd said to each other in almost two days.

"They're responding to our comm," Felix said. His speaker squelched a high note. "It says, 'prepare to be boarded.'"

"Void-be-damned. They're space pirates."

"Move it, cat," Wright said. He slid into the copilot's chair after Felix begrudgingly jumped down.

I pointed to his cuff on the dashboard. "You might need that."

His eyebrows rose, but he said nothing as he fastened it around his forearm. No time for questions I didn't want to answer.

I stopped giving audible commands to Felix and took direct control using my Intell. My eyes blurred for a moment as they adjusted the multiple viewscreens that popped up in my mind's eye.

"Tracking heat signatures using thermal sensors. I have eyes on all three ships. They'll have us surrounded in two minutes."

"Dive back into the debris field," Wright said.

"They're smaller and more maneuverable than us," I argued. "It'll slow us down more than them."

Wright pulled the harness straps over his shoulders and buckled them at the chest. "True, but we have the lead. If we can get through the field first, we'll have a clear path to the moon."

I nodded, already entering the course corrections. "Then it's a race to Valla and hope we can lose them in the atmosphere. The gases will play havoc with their sensors. It's a good plan."

The ship vibrated when the thrusters fired in reverse to push us back into the minefield. We were traveling at thirty thousand kilometers per hour. Any of those fragments could tear into our hull and blow us out into space.

As a precaution, I triggered all the interior airlock doors to seal shut. That way, if one area of the ship was compromised, the entire ship wouldn't be lost.

"Felix, initiate emergency protocol J Thirty-Seven. Authorization Sinclair-Foxtrot-Mike-Lima-Ten-Four." If we were killed, incapacitated, or taken hostage, Felix would send a distress call back to the team and lock down the ship's computer tighter than a Ceti casino vault.

Proximity alerts flared all over my internal viewscreens, and the main holoscreen as well, judging by the string of curse words coming out of Wright. This was one time when having a neural implant chip was to my advantage. I responded to each warning with more speed than possible using a standard cuff and holoscreen.

Wright swiped through several screens of programs. "Does this ship have weapons?"

"It's a personal transport vehicle, not a DECA cruiser. Weapons don't come standard."

"So that's a...?"

"Yes, obviously. I was a woman traveling the galaxy by myself. It was the first upgrade I added."

"What am I looking for?"

"Ah..." I rolled my neck at the sudden tension headache gripping the base of my skull like a vise clamp. The Intell was reaching its processing limit.

"Reliance?"

"Two rail guns—one on either side. You've only got ten rounds of ammunition in each, though, so make your shots count."

A warning message popped up, telling me the weapons system had been engaged. Good, Wright was on top of it. I swiped the notification away with a shake of my left hand.

The lead skiphopper pressed closer. It was following us into the debris field.

Another alarm sounded, sending a hot needle of pain through my right eye. "Shots fired. Initiating evasive maneuvers."

My stomach flip-flopped as I steered us into a turn. The enemy slug sailed through our previous location and embedded itself into a deformed fragment of a ship's hull five hundred kilometers ahead of us. I pivoted us again, avoiding chunks of flying metal as the old ship's pieces careened off each other like trilliards balls.

"Returning fire," Wright said and shot an ammunition plug from our rail gun.

We watched the blinking light that represented our shot on the holoscreen. It found its mark in the lead skiphopper, clipping the port thruster. There was a brief burst of flames as the sinnafuel ignited and burned out. Then the ship sat dead in space.

One down, two to go.

A small droplet of blood leaked from my nose. I swiped at it, annoyed at the distraction. The tabs of Blue Lace were in my room. I should have kept one on the bridge.

Shoulda, woulda, coulda did me no good. I shoved it out of my mind and tried my best to compartmentalize the pain.

One of the flanking skiphoppers drew closer, more cautious after watching its buddy take one to the thruster.

"Not as easy prey as you thought, huh?" I murmured to myself while plotting out the clearest path.

Wright sent off another slug. It missed but kept the ships off our tail.

We were close enough to Valla to feel the pull of its gravity. I compensated, using a program designed for navigating planetary ice rings to help us avoid the larger chunks of debris.

The two remaining skiphoppers divided. The black one hung back in an empty section of space while the gray one followed us in. They must have agreed on a plan, because the one tailing us wasn't being cautious anymore. It burned sinnafuel to catch up, using its smaller size to thread its way nimbly through the drifting chunks of debris.

The *Soteria* dipped and swayed as we wove between hurtling engine parts, fuel containers, hull fragments, and furniture.

"Wright, we're never going to make it with him on our ass."

One of the skiphoppers fired two shots in quick succession.

I took us into a higher orbit, abruptly slowing our speed. The slugs flew past us, missing the space trash and burning up in Valla's toxic atmosphere in twin flares of bright-white light. Moments later, the second skiphopper zipped by.

"Excellent," Wright said. "Now take us—"

"On it."

I changed course, bringing us closer to the moon again and on the same plane as the skiphopper. It was looping back around but fighting against the natural pull of Valla's orbit. That bought us the precious few seconds we needed to get into position.

"Get ready," I told Wright.

His fingers were a blur as he aerial scribed in the new targeting parameters. He fired three rounds in a triangle pattern. We wouldn't get a better shot than this.

The skiphopper was too slow—saw the shots coming too late. It dodged to the side, but most of its power was already going toward battling Valla's orbital rotation. The little ship didn't have enough juice left to get out of the way.

It turned toward the moon—the path of least resistance. Wright's first slug missed. Too far to the outside by the time it reached the ship. The second slug went too low, skimming the bottom of the hull, but not doing much more than adding another battle scar to the paint.

Pain stabbed at my eyes. Internal pressure filled my skull such that I feared my Intell chip had finally fried it. My vision blurred. I white-knuckled both armrests, and my harness was the only thing keeping me from toppling out of my chair.

"Target neutralized." Wright's voice was distant, hollow. Like he was speaking through a tunnel.

I clawed my way toward his voice. Focused on it until I wrestled the pain back into its box. It was still there—void, was it still there—but I could think through it.

An ammunition slug slammed into the cargo bay hull, rocking the *Soteria* with the force of its hit. My head jerked forward so fast I thought my neck might break. Angry red lights flashed all over the console and in my internal vision.

Fuck me.

"Breach in the cargo bay," Felix reported from behind me. "Venting oxygen. Air pressure is dropping."

"Are the ... seals holding?" I asked. My words came out in between halting gasps. If the hole was any bigger than my fist, the rear compartment would be out of breathable air within minutes.

"Airlocks are functioning within safety protocols. Life support is stable on the bridge, bunkrooms, and common area."

"Where in the void did that come from?" Wright asked, making a circling motion with his hand and changed the outside camera view to the ones on the top of the *Soteria*. He pointed to the middle of the main console. "There."

At first, all I saw was the blackness of space speckled with stars. Then there it was, two small, faint stars twinkled. Stars don't twinkle when there isn't any atmosphere to interfere with their light rays. It happened again. This time, a different star winked in and out.

Another slug hit us somewhere near the engine room. There was a terrible screeching sound—metal rending. My ears popped as the air pressure rapidly decreased.

"Engine room hull breached," Felix reported. "Minor breaches in the bridge and additional minor damage in the cargo hold."

The *Soteria* tipped hard to the starboard side.

"Hang on!"

The sudden movement sent Felix sliding across the floor. His metal feet scrambled for purchase on the metal floor, scratching long gouges into the slick surface but not finding grip. Excited static crackled from his speakers.

"Felix!"

My hand shot out, but he was too heavy and going too fast for me to grab hold. He picked up speed as he hurtled toward the wall and certain destruction.

Wright reached back and hooked his arm around Felix's body. His muscles strained as he hauled the metal cat into his lap.

I pointed our nose toward Valla and burned as much sinnafuel as I dared to sink us into a decaying orbit before I lost complete control of the ship. It was our only shot. If we stayed up here, we'd be boarded, looted, killed, and then blown to pieces to add to the debris field. Preferably in that order, but not guaranteed.

Wright saw what I was doing and nodded. He knew the odds the same as me and shot off our remaining slugs as cover.

We entered the atmo. Our heat shields burned hot as we hit air molecules. The sickly yellow clouds that made up Valla's atmosphere grew bigger and brighter. Then they enveloped us, blocking out land and space alike. Thick and glowing with the star's refracted light. I had no sense of where I was or where we were going. It wouldn't be a graceful landing, if we landed at all. Parts of the ship were damaged. Probably important parts.

Fear threatened to take hold of me.

Felix raised his speaker volume to be heard over the deafening noise. "Impact in one minute forty-five seconds."

Chapter 16

The force of the Gs plastered my body into my chair. I thanked the stars my harness kept me from flinging into the wall like a spoonful of mashed potatoes in a food fight.

My head might as well have been clamped to the headrest. I couldn't rotate it, but I saw Felix and Wright out of the corner of my eye. Wright had his arms wrapped around the avatar's body, but I didn't know how he kept his grip.

Sending commands through my Intell, I diverted all available power to the reverse thrusters. Our descent slowed, but not enough for a safe landing. We broke through the upper layer of clouds. Off to one side, a vast plain of desert sand stretched into the dark. Far below, dried, brown vegetation skimmed along beneath us.

Our point of entry had put us on the northern border of the habitable zone but at a shallow angle. I hoped my calculations were correct.

Eighty seconds. No sign of pursuit from the skiphopper.

We were heading west, toward daylight. The first glimpses of true green appeared.

"Felix," I called out through clenched teeth. "Deploy ... emergency ... parachute."

"Deploying now, Captain."

There was a *bang* and a *whoosh*, then a sound I'd never heard my ship make. I would have grimaced if I'd had any control over my facial muscles.

My entire body jerked against my harness as the aramid-reinforced material expanded behind us, creating drag and rapidly slowing our descent. An alert popped on the main console that the parachute had been successfully deployed and the tethering cables were holding.

We weren't out of the woods yet. Or rather, we weren't *into* the woods yet. I'd aimed to put us within a dozen kilometers of Newtown, but crash-landing wasn't an exact science.

Forty seconds. The ground wasn't just a blur of browns and greens anymore. I made out distinct outlines of rock formations and forested areas. A deep gorge cut through the landscape. Sunlight sparkled off the river at the bottom.

Twenty seconds. The vegetation was thick and lush. Individual trees took shape as they raced beneath us.

This was going to hurt.

At ten seconds, the tips of the treetops scraped against the hull. More alarms. I shut them all off. There was nothing I could do about them.

"Brace for impact," Wright said.

Tree limbs slapped at the camera lenses, turning the main console screen into a disorienting kaleidoscope of flashing whites, greens, yellows, and blacks.

The ship thrashed and bucked. Anything not bolted down became miniature missiles. Something small and hard hurtled through the air and punched into my shoulder with the power of a galactic boxing champ. Pain radiated out from my shoulder blade and down my right arm. I didn't have time to dwell on it, though, as the *Soteria* dropped the last fifteen meters to the ground, crushing a dozen trees in its wake.

We came to a standstill. Nausea threatened to upend my stomach. My shoulder would need to be addressed, but it wasn't urgent. The pressure around my head was the worst it had ever been, like a watermelon with a hundred rubber bands squeezing around the middle. I needed the Blue Lace in my bunkroom. If the crew quarters were even still attached to the ship.

"Wright? Felix?" I gasped out. My breaths came in short, quick bursts.

"Still kicking," Wright said.

Felix jumped down from Wright's lap. "He saved me, Rel. I was going to hit the wall and smash into a thousand pieces, but Agent Wright saved me."

I tried to reach down to pet him on the head, but my shoulder screamed in protest. "Glad you're okay, buddy."

It wasn't the smartest decision, but I searched for my link with Walnut. My Intell instantly connected to his Insight chip. His little heart was racing, and his adrenaline levels were the highest I'd ever seen, but he was alive. His hut and habitat—which were both secured to the ship—had protected him from the worst of the crash.

I sent him a comforting image of me stroking the fur between his ears, wishing I could check on him in person. However, first I had to make sure that the skiphopper hadn't followed us to the surface.

Wright unbuckled his harness and twisted to face me. He looked at me with concern. "Did you hit your head? Your nose is bleeding."

His hand reached for my face to look for an injury, but I ducked my head under the guise of getting out of my harness. He couldn't find out how much using the Intell had damaged me.

"I'll live. Is the main computer online? How about our sensors?"

Felix wedged himself between our seats. "All computer systems are functional, but I'm getting heavy interference from the atmosphere gases. Sensors, comms, and planetary net are unavailable. Superficial damage to the underside of the ship. Full hull breaches in the cargo hold and engine room. I'm running diagnostics to ascertain the extent of internal damage."

"We need to get outside and see if we can get a visual on that skiphopper," Wright said.

"Go. I'm right behind you."

He made his way down the tilted hallway, avoiding bits and pieces that had come loose during the crash. I heard the airlock seal disengage, then the sound of his boots on the metal rungs of the ladder going down to the cargo hold floor.

I winced as I got up, rolling my shoulder to test its range of motion. Luckily, it was the opposite shoulder from the one I'd hurt falling off the cliff on Ritru-6. Scanning the floor to discover what had hit me, I spotted a sheared-off bolt that must have broken free from a wall panel during the crash.

"How bad is it?" I asked, lifting my shirt and kneeling with my back to Felix.

"My scan shows a contusion with a nine-centimeter radius and an abrasion six centimeters by ten centimeters. No injury to the underlying bone. Recommended treatment is the application of regenerative salve and intermittent use of cold compresses. Limit movement for the next five to ten days."

I stood and tugged my shirt back down. "Thanks. Let me know when you have a full damage report. I want to know how soon we can get the *Soteria* space-worthy."

I flushed the toilet after emptying the contents of my stomach. If I ever ate a hellaberry meal bar again, it would be too soon. I flipped the sonic sink to water-mode and rinsed out my mouth. The water from the gray water tank wasn't safe to drink, but I hurt too much to drag myself to the kitchen.

While the water still ran, I wet a clean cloth and wiped the sweat and blood from my face. My nose had stopped bleeding once I ceased overtaxing my Intell, but I didn't want Wright to see any trace of it.

My fingers trembled as I peeled a tab of Blue Lace from its film of packaging—so much so that I almost dropped it into the sink. Quickly, I stuck my finger in my mouth.

The tab dissolved on my tongue, and I hoped my head would stop feeling like a watermelon about to explode. It was impossible to think straight. As much as I hated giving Lourde any credit, he'd been right about the drugs. They reduced the headaches considerably. Too bad they'd get me kicked off the team if anyone found out about them.

I leaned against the sink and hung my head between my arms while the drug kicked in. Like the first time I'd taken Blue Lace, an artificial calmness passed through me. My senses dulled to a tolerable level. Lights didn't make me squint, and sounds didn't grate my ears so much. Best of all, the pressure around my skull eased. No more watermelon mush for brains.

"Sinclair!" Wright called from outside.

My jaw clenched, and my fingers flexed around the rim of the stainless-steel sink.

"Coming," I yelled back.

I activated the holoscreen above the sink and set it to mirror mode to make sure I'd cleaned away all the blood. My pupils were dilated—either from the drugs or the Intell overstimulating my optical nerves—and my hair was a mess. I ran my fingers through it to sort out the worst of the tangles and headed out to see what Wright needed.

"Wheek-wheek-wheek!" Walnut scurried over to press his pink little feet against the wall of his enclosure as I passed by it.

A few of his tunnel tubes and bridges had been knocked around during the crash, but nothing that couldn't be fixed. I reached my hand in to pet him and make sure his food bowl had nuggets and his water bottle hadn't spilled. His nose twitched at warp speed, and his neural implant chip fired off readings to my Intell.

The little potato butt was fine. I shut down the signals and set up a block between us. Thankfully, the Blue Lace started reducing the pressure, but I could do without the extra signals.

"You were a brave boy, Walnut," I told him. In response, he shoved his cold nose into my hand, making me smile. I scratched his chin. "You little goofball."

Thirty seconds later, I shuffled down the ramp, grateful to be on the ground and that all the alarms had shut off and stayed off.

Hot, humid air greeted me outside. It smelled a bit like ozone. If I inhaled deeply, the air scratched at my lungs. We'd landed in thick jungle vegetation. The canopy stretched high overhead except for a narrow band of about two hundred meters where the *Soteria* had trampled everything in its wake. That band revealed a soupy yellow sky of toxic clouds.

Wright stood atop the ship, shading his eyes against the hazy sun.

"Any sign of the skiphopper?" I asked. An insect buzzed my face, and I swatted at it.

"None," he called back, then half-climbed, half-slid down the side of the ship. He dusted his hands off on his pant legs. "It looks like we might have lost it. It was a good plan, although I wish the landing had been a little smoother." When he turned to face me, his brows drew together in concern. "Your eyes ... they're dilated. Are you sure you didn't hit your head in the crash? You may have a concussion."

He tilted my chin with the side of his finger to turn my face toward the light.

"No. I mean, yeah, I got shook around a bit, but my head is fine." Lies, lies, lies.

"Hold still while I check." Wright used his commanding-officer voice—the one which left no room for debate and sent a shiver down my spine.

He pressed his fingers along my hairline, searching for signs of injury. His fingertips moved to my hair, lightly sifting through my strands. It felt ... nice. I closed my eyes and leaned into the sensation. His hand cupped the back of my head.

Wright cleared his throat, and my eyes snapped open.

I stepped back, putting some space between us. A lump the size and texture of a mycoprotein dough ball formed in my throat. "I'm fine, really. Just a little rattled."

Damn Blue Lace. I needed to only take it when I would be alone. It eased the side effects of the Intell, but it was still a narcotic.

"Do you have any other injuries?" Wright asked.

"A loose bolt hit my shoulder. Superficial only. I was on my way to get a GraftPatch when you called out." Not a lie, but a half-truth.

Felix joined us, walking five meters out from the ramp, which was as far from the ship as he could wander. In his mouth, he carried the ship's med kit.

Wright moved behind me. "May I?"

I nodded and held the hem of my shirt up with my hand when he lifted it over my shoulder. The movement was strangely intimate even though he sterilized the area, coated it with salve, and applied a GraftPatch with professional detachment. He took the fabric from my hand, and his fingers gently skimmed down my back as he settled my shirt back into place.

Another shiver tickled my spine, but for an entirely different reason.

"I have completed the damage report," Felix said.

"Let's have it," I said, grateful for something else to focus on.

"Hull damage in the cargo bay and engine room. Both slugs penetrated all the way inside but were not armed with explosives. The first slug damaged the hoverbike rack and the hoverbike fuel tank. The second slug lodged in the high-pressure pump. I can 3D print patches for the hull and parts for the rack, but we don't carry replacements or materials sufficient for me to fabricate the high-pressure pump."

"What about the bike's fuel tank?" I asked. "Can you repair that?"

Felix sat down. "We can use material from other items onboard, reclamate them down to raw materials, and then use them to print replacement parts, but it will take time."

"How long?"

"Depending on the priority list of repairs, three to four days."

"Can we contact the team?"

"Negative. There is too much atmospheric interference to reach the subspace relay, and I have been unable to connect to a planetary net."

"That's because there isn't one. They lost it a few years back." I sat on the edge of the ramp. Standing felt like too much work. "So we're stranded—on Valla, the criminal hideout of the galaxy—with no way to fly out or call for backup." I didn't have the brainpower to compute how screwed we were.

Wright remained quiet during the exchange. He paced to the edge of our small clearing and stared into the thick underbrush of the forest.

"Not necessarily. Newtown"—he pronounced it incorrectly like New Town—"isn't a large city, but there must be some legitimate businesses still running. We hike there, buy the parts we need, and get back here to repair the ship."

"I know a guy there, or at least, I used to. He might help us send a message to Ravi and DeAjamae. How far do you think it is?"

"It's hard to tell where we landed without being able to connect to a global positioning system."

"I haven't been here in a couple of years, but I don't remember the clouds being this yellow. The terraforming measures may be breaking down faster than predicted."

He scratched his chin. "That might work in our favor. If we haven't picked up any signs of that skiphopper, maybe it hasn't picked up any of us."

"Or maybe you destroyed it with that last round of slugs."

"Possibly," he said, but he didn't sound like he believed it.

"I know Newtown is to the southwest, but beyond that..." I shrugged. My attention had been on making sure we didn't die when we landed. Anything after that was gravy.

Wright sat beside me on the ramp and used his cuff to project a predownloaded map of Valla. He zoomed in on our approximate location in the southern hemisphere. "Did you see that big gorge when we flew over? I think that's here." He pointed to a dark line on the map. "And from the top of the ship, I saw this rock formation." He pointed to a smaller dot on the map with a marker showing an area of sharp, pronounced elevation.

I frowned. "Are you sure that's the same one, because that would put us—"

"At least fifty kilometers from Newtown."

"Shit."

I was a city girl, through and through. Dark alleys and abandoned warehouses? Bring them on. Urban exploring? I'm your girl. But I didn't know jack shit about camping. "It'll take us days to get there and back."

"Then we should get on our way."

"What about Ophidian?" I asked. "Do we try to find him when we get to Newtown?"

For once, Wright didn't look like he had a plan. That worried me, because Wright always had a plan. Sometimes it was a bad plan, but there was always a plan.

"We'll cross that bridge when we get to it. For now, pack a light bag. Lighter than you think you can carry. Food, water, dry socks, a small, water-resistant blanket if you have one. It's hot now, but it will cool off at night. If you have legal tender or something lightweight you think we can barter with, bring it. The Department will reimburse you."

"I have some LTs that should be enough to cover a new pump." I'd increased the amount of emergency legal tender I kept stashed onboard since taking the job at DECA. If there's one thing my temporary status as a fugitive had taught me, it was that you never knew when you might need it.

"Batteries are down to fifty percent," Felix said. "Should I extend the solar sails to charge them until you return?"

I looked up at the hazy-yellow sky and frowned. "No, we won't get much of a charge through that cloud cover. Besides, the reflective material of the sails will be too visible from the sky. We can't risk those pirate ships circling back and spotting you."

Felix bristled, the sharp little points on his scales lifting along his back. "Let them try. My weapons system is still intact."

I squatted down and stroked my hand from his head to his tail, smoothing his scales back into place. He never liked being damaged. "Wright used all our slugs getting us here, and your other weapons are primarily defensive and designed to be used in outer space. I'm afraid they won't work very well down here. It would be better to be stealthy now."

He blinked. His one green eye glowed as he processed the information. "I can move the ship's internal holo-emitters to the top of the hull to project a treetop canopy."

"It wouldn't fool anyone up close," Wright said. "But assuming the other ship experiences the same sensor difficulties that we do, it may be reduced to relying on visual scans."

My head bobbed, following his train of thought. "They might not notice the *Soteria* at all."

Felix jumped to his feet. "Until we ambush them!"

"Right, until we—wait, no. No, we aren't ambushing anyone, you suicidal cat. You stay hidden and work on repairs until we get back from Newtown with the pump. Then we all fly out of here, safe and sound and in one piece."

"They. Broke. Me. They deserve to die."

I rolled my eyes. "All right, little Butcher of Bellarouxdonda, back on the ship. Get those maintenance bots started on patching the tears in the hull. Those are the top priority."

Felix marched up the ramp, his clomping paws anything but cat-like.

"Well," I said, smiling at Wright. "The good news is, I think the pirates have taken your place at the top of Felix's shit list."

"You think?"

"Don't get too excited. That list is long and old. He won't let me park at the main spacedock on Nephali-7 because the ground crew scratched the *Soteria*'s thruster while moving around cargo five years ago. I didn't even own the ship back then."

"Then I'll have to hope that other people continue to piss him off more than I do."

I laughed, forgetting the awkwardness that had been between us for the last few days. Wright was nothing if not persistent. If anyone could wear Felix down, it would be him.

Chapter 17

I SMACKED A MOSQUITO biting my neck and cursed the Valla terraformers for the millionth time since we started hiking. Early on, scientists had insisted the bugs were a vital link in the food chain for birds and other insects. I didn't care if they'd been genetically modified not to carry disease. They were a pain in the ass, and I hated the little bloodsuckers.

Ahead, Wright paused at the top of the hill we'd been climbing.

"Let's take a break," he said when I caught up.

"No argument here."

I dropped my pack and found a rock to sit on that wasn't too wet. My heel hurt in that special way that told me I'd find a blister when I took off my boot. We'd only been walking for an hour, but it wasn't like there was a road. The entire way had been climbing over tree roots and elbowing our way through bushes. It was slow going, to say the least, and the Blue Lace hadn't helped. Half the time, I was tripping over my own dang feet.

I grabbed a water pouch from a side pocket of my bag and drained it. It hit my empty stomach like a rock. Wright took a slower approach, nursing it while he sat on a mossy stump and stretched his feet out in front of him. He tossed me an apple from his bag, and we spent the next five minutes enjoying our snack in silence.

As I finished gnawing it down to the core, my neck prickled. I scanned our trail of broken twigs and scuffed dirt. Nothing moved, save for a couple of birds ruffling their feathers and flitting between trees at our passage. Several times since leaving the ship, I'd gotten the sensation of being followed.

Wright looked like he'd stepped out to the corner shop for a cup of coffee. His shirt wasn't even sweaty, for star's sake. I told myself it was due to him having genetically manipulated DNA, and not me still being out of shape from living in space for a year.

"Did you see something?" he asked, following my gaze.

"No, just nerves."

"This looks like a good place to check our progress," Wright said, standing up and wiping his hands against his thighs.

We'd been making our way toward the rock formation, but we only caught glimpses of it in clearings or areas of high elevation. This was the highest hill we'd climbed so far, and it was covered in trees.

"How do you plan on doing that?" I asked, tossing my apple core into the woods for the local wildlife to find.

"One of us is going to climb that tree." He pointed to a large tree with two thick trunks branching out in different directions. The silvery leaves were only half the size of my hand and sparse. Theoretically, a person could see a long distance once they got above the other trees.

I eyed the smooth trunk warily. "Don't let me stop you."

He itched at the back of his neck. "How about I boost you up to where the trunk divides? You're lighter, so you can climb higher, and the branches will support you."

"So that's how it's going to be."

"Unless you want to boost me."

"Sure, why not?" I curled my arm to flex my biceps in a body-builder pose. The toned muscles popped up, but I didn't think it would impress any judges.

Wright chuckled, and it felt good to be ribbing each other again. Maybe our friendship wasn't doomed after all.

"But," I said, "since I happen to be an *excellent* tree climber, I volunteer to go up."

We inspected the tree. The bark was thin and smooth like paper, not like the trees I'd climbed back in Clava as a kid. Those had thick, rough bark that bit into my palms like sandpaper. I ran my finger down the trunk, making sure the bark wouldn't flake off once I put my weight on it. It held firm.

The trunk split over two meters up. High enough that I couldn't touch it with my arms stretched overhead. I reached up, prepared to grab onto the branches, and hiked my leg foot-to-butt so Wright could use my shin to boost me without getting his hands dirty. "Ready when you are."

Wright moved in close behind me and suddenly having him lift me didn't seem like such a good idea. I fought the urge to lean back against his chest when he pressed against me. He grasped my ankle with both hands and counted to three.

I gave a little bounce, and on three jumped, using his hands as a springboard. My arms reached the forked branches without issue, and I scrambled to leverage my torso into the crook. Wright let go of my leg and a second later, I felt his hands on my ass, pushing me the rest of the way up.

Consider me motivated.

Two curses, one wobbly armed push-up, and a solemn vow to visit the gym later, I crouched between the two main branches.

"You good?" Wright called from the ground.

My upper back muscles protested at the exertion, both where I'd injured them in the fall on Ritru-6 and when we crashed. They were dull aches, though. The regenerative salve had numbing agents that eased the worst of the pain.

I stood, using the smaller limbs to steady my balance. The thicker of the two branches stretched up to my right, so I planted my foot on the lowest limb, tested another with my hand, and hoisted myself higher.

"So far, so good."

It took a few minutes, but I made it halfway up before the branches became too thin to support my weight. I secured myself and looked out into the distance.

The rock formation was easy to spot—a craggy needle of pale-yellow limestone that towered over the surrounding forest. Wind and rain had whittled away at it until most of the rock lay in a conical mound at the base like an upside-down funnel. In another three hundred years, there might be nothing left at all. Nestled near the bottom sat a small cluster of houses, their pointy roofs peeking out from the forest.

I grinned and scrambled down the tree as quickly as I could without breaking my neck.

"Good news," I said and told Wright about the houses. "We won't be camping outside after all."

"When did you become such an optimist?"

"Right after I killed my fiftieth mosquito. Just let me mark our current location on your map, and we can get going. We can make it before dark, if we hurry."

I took down all the safeguards I'd erected around my Intell after the crash. It was blissfully quiet on Valla. Without the *Soteria* or a planetary net to connect to, the usual barrage of signals and electronics was almost nonexistent. In fact, I only detected Wright's cuff and...

"You've got to be kidding me."

Wright drew his blaster faster than I thought possible. His eyes darted around us, searching for what had caused me concern.

"No!" I slapped my hand up, forcing the barrel of the blaster straight up. Not standard procedure, but I didn't want him firing an energy bolt at the ground by accident.

I knelt down and made little clicking sounds while rustling my fingers across some dead leaves. Walnut waddled out of the underbrush, and a flurry of images popped into my brain.

"How did he find us?" Wright asked.

A quick check of his vitals confirmed he was okay—scared and exhausted, but happy to be with us again. Then I went into his diagnostics program and into the optical nerve integration system subfolder. Inside, there was a twenty-four-hour temporary cache of his visual recordings. I'd noticed the folder when DeAjamae and I ran Walnut through his maze a few days ago. I assumed it was to help troubleshoot any glitches with his chip, but it would help me trace his movements from the ship.

I selected a timestamp of about seventy minutes prior and set it to run at triple speed. Just like when I'd watched the live feed while he ran the maze, I was dropped into a three-dimensional view from Walnut's perspective. Colors shifted to primarily yellows, blues, and greens and anything more than a few feet away was a blur.

Through Walnut's eyes, I watched myself reach into his habitat to pet him, check his food, and walk away. Ten minutes passed, and then Walnut made his escape.

"He climbed up one of the broken tunnel pieces in his cage and slipped out while Felix patched the hull. I think he followed our scent trail. Poor little guy ran all the way here."

Wright stared at his boots for a solid count to ten, then holstered his blaster. "The guinea pig wasn't part of the plan."

I tore open a second pouch of water and dribbled a little into my palm. Walnut gulped it down, so I added more. When he finished, I drank the rest and scooped him up. He squirmed over my shoulder and settled onto the top of my backpack.

"Could be worse," I said.

"How?"

"It could have been the cat."

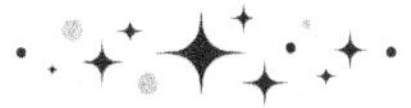

It took us three more hours to reach the cluster of houses, even though darkening storm clouds hastened our steps. I'd tried to send a comm to Felix telling him Walnut was with us, but the atmosphere had already caused too much interference for it to go through. He'd probably noticed Walnut's absence. Not much happened on the ship without his knowledge. He might be throwing a party to celebrate the *Soteria* once again being rodent-free.

Wright and I hadn't spoken much all evening, but it was a companionable silence unlike the tension-laden avoidance we'd practiced on the ship. It was better. Nice even.

We stopped at the edge of a gravel clearing. The residents had spread limestone rubble from the rock formation to help keep the forest at bay. Even so, runner vines stretched deep into the clearing and little sprouts of green poked up from the loose stone. Nature always found a way.

Ahead sat five derelict houses. Even from the distance, we saw they were abandoned. The roofs had caved in on all of them—one even had a tree poking through a window and what was left of the roof.

"Looks like the owners moved on," Wright commented.

"Not unusual. We're on the trailing edge of the habitable zone. Another fifteen or twenty years and this will all be desert."

"Wait here," he said. "I'll check it out."

"You got it, boss."

Wright headed for the buildings. Shoulders back, stride purposeful. His head stayed pointed straight ahead, but I knew his eyes took in everything.

I kept one pace behind him and half a step to the right.

"You were supposed to stay back," Wright grumbled.

"Oops."

No one came running out waving a blaster at us, so that was a good sign. I brushed my fingers against the grip of my blaster, taking comfort in its reassuring weight at my hip.

We reached the first building. It was a little two-room mycelium house with broken windows and rotting bamboo floors. Mushrooms sprouted all over the walls, telling me the construction had been shoddy from the get-go since the mycelium hadn't been fully cured before the blocks had been laid. Without maintenance, the spores grew and spread.

The next three buildings were in similar condition. One looked like a store, but the shelves were stripped bare.

We paused outside of the last building at the sound of space-ships in the distance. A couple of black specks stood out against the graying clouds.

I pulled Wright close to the door where the eaves would block us from view. We held our breaths as two ships passed overhead. Skiphoppers.

Wright's brows drew together. Credits to crispers, we were thinking the same thing.

"Do you think they're the pirates who shot us down?" I asked.

"Could be. It would be a big coincidence if they weren't." We watched the ships disappear into the distance. "It doesn't look like they spotted us, though."

A peal of thunder rolled through the sky. I didn't like the look of the clouds. They shouldn't be the color of watered-down tea. "We should set up camp for the night."

"This looks like our best option for a dry place to sleep," Wright said. "It's the sturdiest of the lot, and the roof is still partially intact."

I assessed the dilapidated structure with skepticism. A thick layer of moss coated the siding, and a scraggly tree grew out of one side where the roof had collapsed. Still, it had half a roof, which was one-half more than any of the other buildings.

As if to prove my point, a few fat water drops splattered onto my head. Walnut gave a startled *wheek* in protest and burrowed deeper into my backpack. Weather wasn't really his thing.

Wright tried the door. The reader was busted, its connecting wires and batteries long since rusted through. He pushed, and it opened a crack before sticking firm. With a grunt, he rammed his shoulder into it. The stubborn wood held for a second, then gave way in a rush. Rot and debris rained down on his head, along with an entire nest of blue nipping beetles.

"Gah!" Wright ducked farther into the house, slapping his hands against the back of his neck and shoulders.

Creepy, crawly shivers slithered down my arms and neck as I watched hundreds of beetles scurry across the floor. Most of them darted for the outside, and I hotfooted it after Wright. No way, no how did I want any of them scuttling up my pant legs.

Nipping beetles were vicious little buggers with twin sets of sharp pincers they used with abandon. They'd been introduced to Valla as a fast-breeding, high-protein source of food for the bird population they wanted to establish. Unfortunately, most birds preferred other insect species, and with no natural predators, the nipping beetles multiplied unchecked. They were almost as bad as the mosquitoes. Almost.

Balancing ecosystems was a delicate business.

Smacking and crunching sounds echoed in the small room as Wright flicked off a few remaining nipping beetles and crushed them under his boot heel.

"You good?" I asked.

He dropped his backpack and shook out his shirt, dispelling a few caught in the folds. "I may never be good again."

That earned him a snort.

We checked out the rest of the house and found it much like the others. Without a roof, the two bedrooms were complete losses, and I'd seen cleaner bathrooms in dive bars. Nature had begun reclaiming the spaces for itself.

No house is complete without a tree in the living room, and this one came with thick clumps of moss draped over the branches. In addition, a small waterfall feature appeared along the far wall once the rain picked up in earnest. That left the kitchen as the only option for sleeping quarters. It was sort of dry. Dry wasn't really the right word. Damp, maybe, or clammy. Moist. Blech!

A few trickles of water coming from the living room crisscrossed the floor, and it was not as critter-free as I would have preferred.

"Help me flip this over?" Wright asked, grabbing onto the side of an overturned table.

We righted the heavy piece and discovered one leg cracked near the bottom. Wright snapped off the loose piece and propped up the broken section with two chunks of mycelium from a crumbling wall.

He brushed the dirt off the top and gave it a test shake. "It's not a Ceti hotel bed but not too bad for being out in the middle of a jungle."

I pulled Walnut out of the bag, along with a meal bar and my extra shirt. He got a quarter of the crumbled bar and attacked it with vigor while I scrunched my only long-sleeved shirt up into a makeshift nest for him at the far end of the table. Of the three of us, he'd have the most comfortable bed tonight. I hopped up on the table and sat with my feet dangling.

"So there's two of us and only one table," I said, struggling to maintain a serious expression.

He laughed. "We can sleep in shifts—" Wright stopped mid-sentence to slap at his back. He contorted into a weird position, trying to reach the space between his shoulder blades.

"Here, let me see," I offered. He spun around, still swatting at his back. My hands ran across his shoulders, feeling the muscles twitch at my touch. I smoothed the fabric of wrinkles but didn't find any bugs. "It must be under your shirt."

The words hadn't even finished leaving my lips when Wright whipped his shirt off in one smooth motion and started shaking it out. Strong, toned muscles bunched and flexed with the movement. A tattoo of a dragon, wings flared and teeth bared, covered his right shoulder. Its tail curled down his side and under his arm, out of view. That surprised me, because I hadn't pegged Grayson Wright as a tattoo kind of guy.

My mouth went dry—probably because it was hanging open.

A shimmer of blue on the dragon's scaled foot caught my eye, and I brushed the nipping beetle away with my palm. My hand lingered, absorbing the heat of Wright's body. A hint of the bergamot and lime from his soap still clung to his skin.

"Did you find it?"

"Hmm?" I shook my head to shoo my thoughts from the dangerous path they traveled. "Yep, got it." Then I patted his shoulder twice like I was signaling an LAV pilot it was time to go.

He twisted out from between my legs while pulling on his shirt, giving me a front-row seat to the Grayson Wright abs show. It was an award-worthy show, too.

I thought I'd kept my perusal to a quick glance, but when I lifted my eyes, I found him watching me. Heat burned up my neck to the top of my head.

Laughter filled his eyes. The asshole was playing with me.

"Rel—"

"Nope."

The room felt claustrophobic despite the broken windows and lack of a ceiling. I hopped off the table and busied my hands tugging at my shirt hem, patting my pockets, and checking that my blaster hadn't magically disappeared from its holster in the last five minutes. The whole time, I backed my way toward the door.

"I'm going to do a perimeter sweep. Make sure there aren't any more nipping beetles trying to get in." My hip rammed into the door handle. I winced at the sharp pain that went straight to the bone, spun, and fled from the small house.

That—whatever that had been—was a terrible idea.

Chapter 18

COOL RAIN GREETED ME the moment I stumbled out the door. It soaked my thin top and made my hair hang in stringy, violet clumps that fell into my eyes.

I didn't mind. The water rinsed the sweat and dirt of the day's hike from my skin and cooled my body from whatever-the-void it had been feeling inside the house.

My head fell back, and I let the rain splash down my face. I shouldn't be feeling anything for Wright. I'd let the moment on the ship go too far. He'd been under the influence of Rhap. Even if he hadn't been, he wouldn't be interested in me if he knew the secret I kept from him.

He was a stickler for the rules and valued honesty and loyalty above all else. If he found out I'd been hiding a medical condition from him—a condition that might make me unfit for duty—well, he wouldn't wait for the results of a doctor's examination. He'd fire me on the spot for dereliction of duty, insubordination, and fifteen other infractions I didn't even know about.

At six months, I'd be the shortest-tenured officer in DECA history. It didn't escape my notice that this would be the second time I left DECA under less-than-honorable circumstances. Maybe Kinnikinnic was right, and I wasn't fit to wear the uniform.

But both times I'd used Blue Lace, it had gone a long way in combating the side effects of using my Intell. I just needed to find a good supply once we got back to Andaress-4. Then there'd be no reason I couldn't keep working. Wright and the team might not see it that way, but it was my life. I wanted to spend what time I had left doing the thing I loved with the people I cared about—not in hospitals with doctors.

I walked the perimeter twice, sticking close to the houses and then sloshing through puddles on a wider circuit along the jungle's edge and near the rock formation. On the second pass, I noticed a dilapidated trail heading in the general direction of Newtown. It was only a footpath, but the next day's hike would be faster if we didn't have to fight the brush every step.

Dozens of rivulets streamed down from the tower of limestone, forcing me to hopscotch my way through a four-meter section. I shouldn't have bothered, because by the time I made it back to our temporary shelter, I was soaked to the bone—feet included.

Wright looked up from preparing dinner when I walked back in. He was—thankfully—fully clothed.

"See anything?" he asked.

"All clear. Nothing's moving in this rain, not even the mosquitoes."

"At least something is going our way."

"No kidding."

I unlaced my boots, tipped out the water, and set them aside. Then I peeled off my socks, wrung them out, and laid them so they dangled over the edge of a block. There were clean socks in my pack, but I wanted to let my feet dry out before putting them on. As suspected, blisters graced the backs of each of my heels.

Walnut slept on the only other top I'd brought, so my long-sleeved shirt would have to dry on the rack. Me being the rack.

"Hungry?" Wright pushed a meal kit from the *Soteria*'s emergency rations across the table. It claimed to be beef stew.

"You said to travel light. I only packed meal bars."

He shrugged. "I knew I could handle the extra weight, but if you don't want it..."

"No takesies-backsies," I said and snatched the box before he rescinded the offer.

He withdrew his hand with a smile, but it wasn't the same playful smile he'd given me earlier.

I rotated the knob on the bottom of the box, triggering a chemical reaction that had the precooked food steaming hot within forty-five seconds. It came with a spoon, three crackers, and a chocolate chip cookie for dessert. Wright's was the same, and we both dug in while it was hot. After we finished, I placed the boxes in an exposed section of the room, turned the knobs again, and watched while a second chemical reaction lit them on fire. No trash to carry with us.

I returned and saw Wright had removed something else from his pack—a travel med kit. Antiseptic, sterile pad, regenerative salve, and a new GraftPatch lay lined up on the table. My eyes slid to his bag. How much stuff did he cram into that thing?

"It's time to change your bandage," he said.

Any excuse sounded childish. It's not like I wanted the wound to get infected. I fought to pull one arm out of my wet sleeve and lifted the hem of my shirt over my shoulder. Not my most graceful move.

Wright wiped away the moisture that still clung to my skin. In a quick motion, he ripped the old bandage off.

I grimaced at the smarting sensation. The cold squirt of antiseptic wasn't much better.

"It's healing well," he said, preparing the sterile pad with the salve. "You're lucky the bolt didn't hit the cut from your fall. The skin is turning purple, but the abrasion is already healed over. One more application and you should be as good as new."

I craned my neck to look, but the wound was too far back to see. The movement brought my face close to Wright's as he leaned in close to examine the scrape in the waning light. His breath was warm and sweet from the cookie that came with our meal kit. He pressed the pad and GraftPatch into place and smoothed the edges to form the watertight seal.

When he finished, Wright looked up, and our eyes locked. His had shifted toward a clear, honey brown, the lighter-green bits all but swallowed by the black of his pupils.

My heart pounded, and my breath hitched. Why did my stomach have to flutter when he looked at me like that?

"Reliance," he said, his voice low. "We should talk about what happened."

"No, Grayson, we shouldn't."

"Tell me you don't feel this, too." His hand slipped over my bare shoulder to run down the length of my arm. Goosebumps peppered my skin, every nerve electrified by his touch. "Tell me I'm not imagining this spark between us. Tell me I'm not the only one who feels it."

Of its own volition, my body swayed into his. We fit like two puzzle pieces coming together. His hand covered mine, fingers intertwining, and I closed my eyes.

"You're not the only one," I whispered.

Wright's forehead rested against the back of my head. The tension released from his muscles as he exhaled. His head dipped to the side, so that his lips brushed against the shell of my ear. "I thought I'd ruined everything on Brione-5."

He pressed a soft kiss against my shoulder, sending a delicious shiver of awareness down my spine. My traitorous neck bent to the side, inviting Wright to do more.

Each kiss was slow and deliberate as he worked from my shoulder to that spot behind my ear.

His free arm slid around my waist, pulling me closer. A soft moan escaped my lips, and he smiled against my neck. I reveled in being held in his arms.

Wright kissed his way down my neck until he reached the pink surgical scar. The one Doctor Lourde had put there when he implanted the chip.

That thought shocked me back to my senses like I'd been doused with a bucket of ice water. What was I doing? Nothing had changed, and starting any kind of relationship with Wright was a bad idea. Not with that big of a lie between us.

It took all my willpower to pull myself from his arms.

He didn't let go immediately and tried to draw me back to him. "Reliance—" His voice was low and rough with desire.

Mine was much the same, but I doubled down on my resolve and twisted away. "We can't do this."

His hands dropped to his sides. "Is it because I'm your supervisor? The Department frowns on relationships between team members, but it's not against regulations. There are workarounds. Forms we can file."

"That's not it," I said, struggling to shove my arm back through my wet sleeve. "I mean, yeah—fuck, I hadn't even thought about that—but this…" I waved my hand, sending the shirt material flapping between us. "This is going to get real complicated, real quick."

Wright took my arm, untangled the sleeve, and pulled it over my hand. "It doesn't have to."

"I don't see how it can't, and I love being on this team too much to jeopardize it." That, at least, was the truth. Not the whole truth, but a version of it.

His jaw tightened, and I imagined it was with the effort of biting back his next argument. It wasn't in Grayson Wright's nature to back down from a fight.

But he did.

"If that's what you want," he said and stepped back to put distance between us. It was only a meter, but it felt like the cold void of space between stars.

Wright placed his bag on the table and repacked his supplies. "I'll take the first watch."

I plucked at my wet shirt, tugging the hem back into place. "Let me go first. Walnut had an exhausting day, and I don't want to wake him getting my spare top. It'll give me time to dry off."

Wright pulled a shirt from his pack and tossed it to me. "You had a long day, too. You can borrow this until yours dries."

"Thanks," I said, catching the army-rolled shirt and clutching it awkwardly to my chest.

He was right, as usual. My thighs and calves hurt, and the scrapes on my shoulders burned from where my pack had rubbed against them all day. Even though I'd started running four days a week since moving to Salin, my stamina wasn't up to a five-hour hike through the virgin jungle. That table was looking pretty damn comfy.

I went into what used to be a bedroom and changed into Wright's dry shirt. It was one of his work Henleys—charcoal gray, long-sleeved, and three sizes too large for me. I sniffed. It smelled of his laundry detergent. If we'd been back on the *Soteria*, I'd be tempted to wear only it as a nightshirt. Since we weren't, and since I didn't want to invite more trouble, I kept my tactical pants on but conceded to taking off my belt and holster. No way could I sleep with them jabbing into my hips all night.

Back in the living room, Wright gathered some of the loose mycelium blocks and fashioned a kind of chair that faced the door. It was far enough from the table to give me a modicum of privacy. Or maybe that was for his benefit, not mine.

After a quick check on Walnut, who still slept soundly, I hung my damp shirt up to dry. Then I lay on the table and tried to get comfortable.

Despite my physical exhaustion, sleep did not come quickly.

Chapter 19

Wʀɪɢʜᴛ sʜᴏᴏᴋ ᴍᴇ ᴀᴡᴀᴋᴇ. "I let you sleep as long as I could, but I need a few hours of rest if we want to make it to Newtown by the afternoon."

My eyes opened slowly, dry and irritated from too little sleep. It was almost as black as the void, save for a light shining from his cuff. I sat up and stretched, feeling every centimeter of the rock-hard table in my joints. The numbing properties of the regenerative salve had worn off, and my bruised shoulder muscles ached from lying on them. I checked the clock on my Intell and estimated that I'd slept for about five hours.

"Thanks," I said, yawning. "I'll wake you at dawn, or whatever passes for it here."

Walnut woke as Wright took my place. No surprise, he was hungry. So after packing up the shirt he'd been sleeping on and slipping into my boots, I busted out another meal bar and broke off a chunk for the bottomless pit. He gobbled it down, sitting on my lap on the makeshift chair.

Like a true soldier, Wright wasted no time falling asleep. He didn't even remove his boots or blaster.

I stroked Walnut's slick fur, wondering what had possessed him to break out of his habitat and chase after us. To pass the time, I connected to his neural implant chip and checked his health stats. Since he had been a test animal in a lab, his chip monitored all his vital signs and then some. I'd spent a great deal of time familiarizing myself with guinea pig health information, and everything I saw looked to be within normal ranges. He snuffled my hand, tickling my palm until I scratched behind his ears.

It had stopped raining during the night. The last vestiges of the downpour dripped from the living room tree, and the sounds of night animals drifted in through the open half of the ceiling. A lone mosquito whined in the room. I didn't know what was worse, the shrill noise it made as it flew or the ominous silence when it stopped. It had been a long time since I had experienced true silence.

I scratched my arm where the little bastard and several of his friends had bitten me while I slept.

Out here, the only electronics were Walnut's chip and Wright's cuff. No city nets, advertisements, LAVs, news broadcasts, comms, notifications, or even automatic lights. Not since Lourde had used me as a test subject rather than turn me over to the authorities had I experienced so much peace inside my own head.

It felt like ... like I could *breathe*.

Maybe after this was over, I'd fly the *Soteria* to some deserted corner of the galaxy for a long vacation. Someplace with warm weather, a beach, and not much else. The team could visit. DeAjamae was always talking about how she wanted to travel away from Andaress-4. She'd barely have to bat her long, dark lashes, and Ravi would pack his bags. That boy had it bad for her, even if neither one of them wanted to admit it yet. Wright... Wright didn't seem as keen on vacation time, but maybe we could tell him it was a team-building exercise or secret training mission or something. Ravi would come up with a good excuse.

We could make a good time of it until the Intell finished frying my brain.

White static flashed across my vision for a second, then it was gone.

I held my breath, but it didn't repeat.

Stars, it was happening already. I counted to ten, forcing myself to take slow breaths. I'd about chalked it up to too little sleep and an overactive imagination when Walnut's ears perked up. He lifted his nose high in the air, sniffing. His chip sent me images of his hut back on the ship. Home. Safety.

Something was out there.

I couldn't give him his hut, but I did the next best thing by nestling him into my backpack, making sure the top was open enough for him to wiggle out if needed. He burrowed down without any of his usual wheeks or chirps.

I crept to the side of the nearest window and peered into the dark. The light from Searcy-1 that reflected down to the moon was weak through the heavy cloud cover. It cast a dim, amber light on the trees that didn't penetrate to the forest floor. I didn't see any movement. Didn't hear any sounds through the broken plastiglass panes.

In fact, no sounds at all. No insects buzzing or nocturnal animals calling to each other. Even the water dripping from the leaves seemed to have quieted.

The white static flashed again. This time, my Intell picked up a bit of data with it. Stray fragments that didn't give me any clear information about what was sending the signal. However, that my Intell was picking up anything at all meant someone or something was there, and it wasn't an animal.

A viewscreen popped up in my mind's eye. My Intell had latched onto the signal and launched one of its hacking programs. The data scrolled in front of me, and I skimmed it while easing back from the window. Whatever it was, it was running in some kind of stealth mode. The Intell normally chewed through security protocols and firewalls like Walnut through a carrot stick, but this one gave it trouble. Already, the first pangs of a headache pressed against my temples.

I slunk over to the table. Like the soldier Wright had been before joining DECA, he hadn't wasted precious sleep time rehashing our conversation. No, that had just been me. He'd fallen asleep the minute he'd closed his eyes.

I touched his shoulder. Also, unlike me, Wright woke up alert. His hand clamped down hard on my wrist until he registered it was me hovering beside him.

"Shh," I whispered, holding my index finger up to my mouth. "Company."

He rolled off the table and onto his feet without a sound. His blaster appeared as if by magic.

"How many?" he mouthed.

I closed my eyes and concentrated on the hacking program interface. That program was still the most nebulous to me, as Lourde had designed it to run autonomously from the user. It had been meant for corporate espionage or black-op situations where time was of the essence. As near as I could tell, the Intell actively searched for secure systems and then attacked them. I supposed the assumption being anything valuable enough to protect was valuable enough to steal.

DeAjamae would have read the code much faster. It took me half a minute to parse out what I saw. There were two distinct signals the Intell was trying to break into. I held up two fingers, then pointed to Wright's cuff to indicate that I was likely tracking the signals from their cuffs.

Together, we scooted to the front of the room, each taking a window. Wright edged his face around the frame. He looked out, then at me, and shook his head. Nothing.

I drew my blaster and felt my hand shake. Stars, not now. I'd barely used my Intell.

Deep breath. Focus. I transferred my blaster to my other hand, shook out my arm and fingers, and repositioned myself with a two-handed grip.

Outside, the amber moonlight lent a surreal quality to the landscape. It was like looking through glasses with heavy radiation shielding in the lenses. Movement near the store building caught my eye. It was only for a second, but someone ducked through the door.

An energy bolt lit up the night sky before slamming into the building a decimeter from where I stood.

"Shit!" I dropped to the floor and lost hold of my blaster. It clattered toward the center of the room.

Electricity burned through the organic construction material, creating a blackened and charred spiderweb of veins on the inside of the wall. A thin trail of smoke curled up from the hole and drifted to the ceiling.

"Found one," I said.

Wright fired off two rounds, then ducked away from his window. Answering shots shattered the remaining plastiglass.

"Female, brown shirt, no armor," he said. "There's a second one posted in the building across the street. Male, dark clothes. Can't get a good look from this angle."

I bobbed my head past the window ledge for a quick look. Another energy round sizzled into the mycelium blocks as I hunkered back down. "Confirmed. He's moving from the door to the window, but we have a bigger problem."

"Yeah?"

"That woman out there isn't firing a standard blaster. She's got one of the prototype bionic weapons."

"You're sure?"

"Unless a full sleeve of blasters is a new fashion statement."

Wright's jaw clenched. "Not the exact circumstances I wanted to find them under."

A bionic weapon's most dangerous aspect was its ability to go undetected and take the target by surprise. However, even removing that element, the weapon still had several advantages over nonintegrated blasters. A larger power reserve, for one, and an extreme unlikelihood that the user would ever become separated from it another. Unless we literally removed her arm, she'd just keep firing at us. That made capture and detainment much more difficult.

I snagged my blaster from the floor, checked the power level, and changed the intensity to medium. If we could stun one of them and interrogate them, we might track down the other four prototypes sooner than we'd hoped.

Of course, using a less-than-lethal setting also increased our chances of getting killed ourselves.

"We're sitting ducks in this room. I need to get higher," Wright said. He scanned the slick algae-and-moss-covered walls. The only furniture in the place was the table, and that was too heavy to move far. He nodded toward the tree growing in the living room. "That'll have to do."

He holstered his blaster, took three running steps, and launched himself into the upper branches. The young tree bowed under his sudden weight, but the springy limbs held. Wright executed a quick up-and-over pull-up, got his feet under him, and jumped onto the roof. I held my breath as his foot slipped, but he steadied himself.

"What the void was that?" I demanded.

Wright peered down at me from his perch. "What was what?"

"You said you couldn't climb trees."

"Pretty sure that's not what I said." He flashed me one of his most devastating smiles before crawling to the peak of the roof.

I hurried back to the window. Hopefully, Wright could get a clean line of sight to the shooters from his new position, but it would help if I could draw one out. Maybe I could crack open the door like I was coming out or wave a shirt on a stick in front of a window.

It would be easier to think of a brilliant plan if I didn't have a raging headache.

Outside, the two shooters stopped firing. The woman posted up behind one of the houses, but the man went inside the one across from us. He poked his head out from different openings every few minutes.

My hand trembled as I aimed my blaster across the street. I'd be lucky to hit the ass end of an arrowhead ship. There was a program on my Intell I could use that would help me target, but it required me to give control of my body movement over to the chip. Because of that, I'd practiced very little with it and didn't know what side effects it might trigger.

I mopped the sweat from my forehead with my sleeve and rested the barrel of the blaster against a part of the frame. That technique was better situated for a long barrel, but it was the only chance I had to keep the muzzle steady. The man came into view, and I fired.

Before I could tell if I'd hit my mark, a new viewscreen opened in my head, blocking my vision.

I ducked back behind cover, reading the new information. My Intell had broken through one device—a cuff. The tremors in my fingers made some of the minute aerial scrolling more difficult, but I called up another program to copy whatever information I could.

"Geomarker, geomarker," I chanted to myself as I sifted through the target's programs. Every cuff had one. It's how maps, informational searches, and advertisements worked. "Got it!"

I pulled the geomarker, imported it into Wright's map—which I snagged from his cuff—and got three blinking dots showing all our locations. It would have worked better if there was a planetary net to show me buildings and such, but it was something to work with. By moving a few meters in either direction, I saw where I was in relation to Wright and, therefore, where I was in relation to the target's cuff.

After some quick math—squinting at the map, looking outside, and squinting at the map again—I decided the cuff belonged to the mystery man behind door number two. His dot moved toward the far end of the house nearest the open doorway. I jerked my fingers in a sideways motion to clear the screen from my view.

Anticipating his appearance, I aimed for where his chest would be and rested my finger on the trigger. As if we'd choreographed it, the man edged around the doorframe, and I fired three shots in quick succession.

He cried out. His blaster fell from his hands as he dropped to his knees, hands clutching his chest. A dazed expression passed over his face.

I opened a comm to Wright, thankful the signal went through. "Wright! I stunned the—"

The man's body rocked as multiple energy blasts pummeled his head. He toppled through the doorway into the pebble-strewn dirt. Blood covered the half of his face I could see. It looked black in the amber light of the moons, but there was no mistaking what it was. His eyes stared blankly off into space.

"That wasn't me," Wright said over the comms.

A battle cry jolted me out of my momentary shock. The woman stood outside the store with her arm stretched toward the fallen man. A ring of five blaster barrels expanded outward from her forearm like a ship's Gatling gun. She'd shot her companion herself rather than let us interrogate him.

She swung the monstrosity in our direction.

"Take cover!" I screamed loud enough that I didn't bother using the comms.

A barrage of energy bolts bit into the side of the house, making the mycelium blocks look like a crater field. I sniffed, catching a whiff of acrid smoke that hadn't been in the air before. Glancing around the room, I spotted the source. Bright-orange embers glowed from the network of cobweb-like veins streaking across the wall. I placed my hand on the wall and found it hot to the touch. The blaster fire must have ignited the mycelium blocks, which were burning from the inside out.

Fire would travel up the semi-hollow walls and spread to the roof. My eyes mapped the distance from where the fire would reach first to the spot where Wright had settled into his makeshift crow's nest.

"Wright," I called up, concern ratcheting my voice higher. "Fire! You've got about thirty seconds before this place goes up in flames."

"Copy that," he yelled back. "Go out the back. Rendezvous at the northernmost building."

"What about you?"

"I'll be right behind you."

I swung his pack onto my back, and stars was it heavy. It weighed twice as much as mine, if not more. With a grunt, I yanked on the adjustable straps until the bag settled into a position where I could keep my balance. Then I strapped my bag—with Walnut inside—onto my front.

"Hang on, buddy. We're going for a run."

His nose poked out for a second before burrowing deeper into the bag.

I hurried to the back door. It hung off one hinge, its door reader and lock long since broken away. I yanked it open and ignored the handful of beetles that dropped from the crumbling wall.

After I cleared the building, I glanced over my shoulder. Wright worked his way down the back side of the steep roof. Dark smoke rose from the front half of the building behind him.

He was about a third of the way down when I spotted the woman flanking us from the far side of the house. She had that void-damn Gatling gun of an arm aimed at the roof. In a few seconds, she'd round the corner and have a clear shot at Wright.

I was halfway between houses with no cover in sight, but she was so focused on Wright that she hadn't noticed me yet. My heart raced. I fumbled for my blaster, the double packs making it an awkward draw. The muzzle jumped all over the place. My shaking hands couldn't hold it steady, even with a two-handed grip.

"Wright!" I screamed as I fired. Three bolts zinged by the woman. One came close to clipping her thigh, but they weren't enough to stop her.

She whipped around, zeroing in on the source of the blaster bolts. I was easy to spot, standing in the middle of the path with fifty kilos of bags strapped to my body. The woman charged across the short expanse of the street. An almost berserker-like rage contorted her face.

My heart pounded in my chest. I fired a few sloppy cover shots over my shoulder while running for the nearest building, but they all went wide. My fingers spasmed so badly, I could hardly hold on to my blaster.

She closed the distance to about ten meters and raised her bionic arm. There was no way she'd miss that close.

The closest building was still too far away. In a panic, I pulled up the hacking program window, hoping to jam the controls to her bionic arm. It spun, still unable to get past whatever security protocols had been installed.

Above the sound of her boots pounding against the loose limestone gravel, I heard the high-pitch whine of her blasters. I wasn't going to make it.

I slid to my knees, tucking my head into the backpack strapped to my front to make myself as small a target as possible. Wright's stuffed pack would offer me some protection. I wrapped my arms around the front pack, shielding Walnut as best I could and squeezing my eyes shut as I waited for the energy pulse to burn into me.

Chapter 20

I HEARD THE SHOT FIRE but felt no pain. Had she missed?

A strangled grunt sounded behind me, then the dull thunk of a body falling to the ground.

"You're clear," Wright said over the comms.

Air whooshed from my lungs, hot and sharp from being held too long. A glance over my shoulder confirmed the woman was down.

I unclamped my fingers from where they'd dug into the bag and peeked in at Walnut. He expressed his extreme displeasure with a series of wheeks and chitters but otherwise seemed unharmed. Satisfied, I shrugged out of both packs to make standing easier.

Wright half-slid, half-jumped down from the roof, landing on his feet. He swept the area, keeping his blaster raised. "Are you detecting any more signals?"

I opened the hacking program and wobbled as a wave of vertigo overcame me.

My boss caught me by my elbow.

"All good." I lurched away from him and made it two steps before heaving up the contents of my stomach.

"Sinclair?"

Concern colored his tone, but he didn't take his eyes off our surroundings to look at me. We were too exposed.

I spit to clear my mouth. "I'm fine. It's just the adrenaline dump." And the Intell scrambling my neural circuits.

Carefully, I looked over the scrolling data. "There's only one signal now. The cuff of the guy I shot is sending out an emergency medical beacon. Not that anyone is going to receive it."

"I got a good look from up top. He's dead. No medical team in the galaxy is bringing him back from that headshot."

"It would have been nice to question him."

Wright's lips drew into a thin line. "I suspect that's why she killed him."

"I'm not detecting a signal from the woman," I said. "You must have damaged her cuff when you shot her."

Thick, dark smoke poured from the building. The scent and taste of it polluted the air. We gave the building a wide berth when we circled back to where the woman lay.

She'd fallen on her back. Mid-forties, stocky build. She wore a dirty brown tank top and olive-green pants. No insignia or identification. Her navy-blue hair was cut short except at the top, where damp curls stuck to her forehead. Even in death, her face looked hard, and I imagined her life hadn't been easy.

Her left forearm had been replaced with a bionic limb at the elbow, similar to the one Lourde designed for himself. Whereas his only used a single, normal-sized blaster neatly tucked inside where the radius and ulna bones would be, hers sported five extremely thin-barreled blasters. Less powerful, but they fired faster between shots.

I peeled off the largest pieces of synthetic skin, then lifted the arm to look at the connection points. The team spent a lot of time studying the bionic weapon Lourde had worn when I'd arrested him, so I had a vague idea of what I was looking for. I spotted the lock, rotated it to the release position, and the entire arm popped off the artificial socket.

There were a few differences between Lourde's bionic weapon and this one. Besides being on the opposite arm, his had a certain elegance this one lacked. Tazza Industries had spared no expense in giving him the highest quality materials to work with. This one looked industrial—almost cobbled together. The metals were mismatched in color.

Wright scanned the weapon with his cuff and made notations in the evidence log.

"I don't see a cuff," Wright said. "She'd need one to interface with the arm, right? Unless..."

Unless she'd also been implanted with a neural impulse chip.

Wright rolled the woman onto her stomach. Her pixie cut revealed a jagged red incision at the nape of her neck. Bright-pink, swollen tissue surrounded the cut. The skin was stretched tight to the point of looking shiny and like it might split open at any moment. Infected.

"She has a chip, like me." Subconsciously, I reached up to run my finger along the scar at the base of my neck. It had been infected like that when Wright had rescued me from Lourde's lab and took weeks to heal with Andaress-4's best doctors overseeing my recovery. They'd jumped at the chance to study the Intell.

"Lourde must have implanted the chip and bionic weapon before we took him into custody," Wright said.

"That's a long time to deal with an infection. She must not have had access to good medical care."

"Out here? Not surprising."

"They might have a ship or LAV nearby," I offered. "It could save us some walking."

Wright stared off into the foliage, contemplating. "Possibly, but it'll be difficult to trace their path back to it with all the rain tonight. They would have landed at least a half kilometer away for us not to notice it. Or they could have been dropped off. We could spend days searching and never find it. Once we arrive in Newtown, we can get an LAV and do an aerial search. We'll need one to get back to the *Soteria* anyway."

"What's that?" I asked, bending down to look at a circular mark on the side of her neck. "A body mod?"

It was four centimeters in diameter and contained a raised image of the head of a snake tattooed in florescent green that glowed in the dim light. I rubbed my thumb across it to clear the dirt, and five miniature spikes poked out from her skin like venomous teeth. Startled, I jerked my fingers away, cautious of drugs or poisons that may be concealed in such a mod, and eyed them warily. They were placed on the snake's jaws—three on the top and two on the bottom.

"Have you ever seen a snake that looks like that?" I asked.

Wright shook his head. "Not even in a holovid. What about Lady Ilymechina's gang? The Seven Serpents. Could be she's tied to that."

That didn't sound right. "The Serpents like their tattoos. They're into snakes, but I've never seen any this stylized. Their stuff is always generic snake images. It makes it difficult for DECA to declare someone a gang member based on tattoos or mods."

"Smart."

"If the Lady wanted to, she could run the whole damn planet. Stars, I might even vote for her."

Wright searched the woman's pockets and boots, but didn't turn up anything. He pulled a pocketknife from his belt and unfolded it. "Why don't you go check the other guy?"

"You're going to cut the chip out of her?"

"We can't leave it here for someone to find. The tech is too dangerous."

And there was no DECA office on Valla to call for assistance moving the body to a secure facility.

I understood and was grateful I wouldn't have to watch. Six months ago, Lourde's protégé, Doctor Yelena Adler, had tried to cut my implant out of me after Wright had rescued me from the lab. He'd taken me to a hospital, and Adler had attacked me in my room. Tazza Industries hadn't wanted their tech falling into the government's hands. She hadn't cared that I'd been alive at the time, either.

Wright waited until I reached the other body to begin.

A search revealed nothing of interest about the man, save for a similar five-toothed snake tattoo on the back of his hand. His was of a rattlesnake. He was pushing forty, shoulder-length hair tied back, and fighting scars that crisscrossed his skin. Some were new, but most were so old they were little more than silvery threads on his arms and chest. No bionic weapon. No implant scar.

The man had a cheap, unregistered cuff. It looked like he'd only used it for comms on this job. There was no home address or identifying information on it. I scanned the comm log. Messages had been few and brief, starting with their approach to this abandoned settlement. Not surprising, since they would have walked close enough to talk and only switched to comms when they wanted to be silent.

Why attack us? Had they happened upon us, or had they tracked us from the *Soteria*? Was Felix okay?

I turned east, in the direction of my ship, even though I couldn't see more than a few meters beyond the tree line. The sun would rise soon. Already the clouds glowed with a golden light along the horizon.

We needed to get moving.

I recorded an image of the cuff, made a note on the evidence log, and slid the cuff off the man's forearm. Maybe DeAjamae could get more information off it. Once I was done, I walked back over to Wright. He wiped the blade of his knife clean on the woman's pant leg.

"I saw a trail heading that way." I pointed northwest. "It's overgrown, but it was big enough for a hovercart. I bet it goes to Newtown. That's the largest town in this region."

Wright hefted his backpack onto his broad shoulders and adjusted the straps. "Let's put some kilometers between us and this place before their friends come looking for them."

"Agreed."

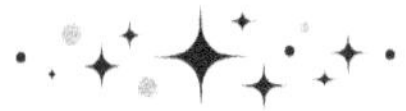

We hiked for six or seven kilometers on the winding trail. It followed a dried-up stream bed cut into a layer of limestone. The landscape grew increasingly rugged as we went. At times, the trail dipped and became slick and muddy, with loose debris washed down from the rain. Other times, we climbed over toppled trees and scrambled up rockfalls. My feet were blistered, and my hands were scraped, but it was still easier than hacking our way through the brush.

"How far are we from the gorge?" I asked. That was our next big landmark. We hoped this path would lead us to a bridge. After we crossed it, we'd turn north and follow it most of the way to Newtown.

Wright took over plotting our course on his map. He'd spent more time in the wilderness than me, and the lack of a civilized grid pattern didn't bother him. I could navigate my way around almost any city, but out here, time and distance were elusive concepts. It was impossible to maintain a steady pace, and we only got glimpses of the overall terrain when the trail crested a large hill.

"Not long. Ten minutes if we continue at this rate. This should be the last major incline."

How he knew that by looking at the little squiggles and lines on the map was beyond me. Give me a star chart any day.

"Did you hear that?" I whispered, putting my hand on Wright's arm to stop him for the fifth time. We hadn't seen any signs of pursuit, but that hadn't tamped down the feelings of unease dogging us the entire morning.

Wright turned around, studying the thick foliage. "No—"

"There it is, again."

This time, we both heard the rustling sound coming from behind us. We were at the bottom of one of the mini ravines, and the sound echoed off the rock walls that rose four or five meters on either side.

"Go." Wright pushed me in front of him and drew his blaster.

I sprinted forward, eyeing a bend in the trail up ahead. I rounded the curve with Wright at my back. He snagged the strap on my pack, pulling me up short, and pointed at the rocky incline out of the riverbed.

The bank was sloped and had decent handholds. It only took me a few seconds to scramble to the top, draw my blaster, and position myself to cover my boss.

Wright moved several paces up the trail before making a deliberate footprint in a patch of soft mud. Then he backtracked, being careful not to leave additional impressions. He scaled the small cliff in half the time it had taken me. His long arms and legs easily negotiated the nooks and crannies, even taking the time to smooth a few scuff marks I'd made.

I eased myself down without rustling too many leaves and lay as flat as possible. Wright used his knife to cut large fronds and placed them over me as camouflage before doing the same for himself and stretching out beside me. For my part, I used my Intell to shut down Wright's cuff and throw up a strong firewall around my and Walnut's implants. It would prevent our signals from giving away our location to whoever had followed us from the houses seeking revenge.

We heard the clomp of many feet and the skitter of pebbles. I aimed my blaster at the first point in the trail they would appear.

A reddish-brown doe rounded the corner, trailed by two spotted fauns, then a second doe and her fawn. They were short, standing not much higher than my waist, and had two bulbous sacks that stretched from just below their eyes to their nostrils that flared as they breathed. Mutations from generations of surviving on toxic air and water.

They stopped, the lead doe raising her head high and swiveling her velvety ears in all directions. She snorted, the nostril sacks swelling like balloons. The doe stomped her leg and made a sound that was a cross between a bark and a cough. She'd probably sensed we were there but still hadn't seen us.

Wright laid his hand on the barrel of my blaster, pushing the tip to the ground. "I think we'll be okay," he whispered, and his voice held a hint of a laugh.

I closed my eyes and let my forehead rest against my hands. Running on high alert for hours had been exhausting. I returned control of Wright's cuff to him and took down my firewall. It required too much processing power to maintain, especially when there was no need for it in the middle of nowhere.

After a moment, the little group continued on, passing right below us. I tossed off the fronds and climbed unsteadily to my feet. Once again, a wave of dizziness had me reaching for the nearest tree trunk to keep myself upright.

There was no stopping the nausea, and I dry heaved until my empty stomach felt like I'd run it through a cheese grater. It hadn't even been twenty-four hours yet, but the soothing effects of the Blue Lace I'd taken after the crash were already gone. In fact, my headache was worse now than it usually was. I wanted another tab so much, but I only had one left and needed to save it for an emergency.

When I turned back around, Wright was standing with his arms folded across his chest, staring at me. "Are you ready to tell me what's wrong?"

I slung my bag onto my shoulders and tried to laugh it off. "Maybe I should have checked the expiration date on those emergency meal kits."

"Your hands are shaking, and you can barely stand on your feet—this is the third time you've thrown up since we got to Valla. Something's wrong."

"It's been a hard day, and this is only the second time," I said, downplaying my symptoms.

"Just now, back at the houses," Wright counted each incident out on his fingers, "and after the crash."

My face warmed. "How did you—?"

"It's a small ship, and you're not as stealthy as you think."

"You were outside. On top of the *Soteria*."

Wright's expression softened. "Your cat is worried about you. I think he's right to be."

Felix. Damn meddling cat.

I clutched at the straps of my backpack, nails digging into the sturdy fabric. "I'm fine. The hiking is getting to me is all. Not all of us are genetically modified for physical labor."

It was a low blow, and I regretted saying it instantly. Wright's ancestors hadn't agreed to the genetic modifications. Sinna Energy had told them they were getting required immunizations for a new colony. They hadn't known about the gene resequencing until it was too late.

That was one of the primary contributing factors to the Ritruvian Uprising and the miners' bid for independence. They didn't like being reminded of it, even if it meant Ritruvians tended to be taller, faster, and stronger than the general population of the galaxy.

"Something's going on with you, Sinclair, and I will figure out what it is." Wright didn't wait for my apology, although it was on my lips when he stalked off into the jungle.

I didn't want to lie to Wright, but I didn't see any way around it—not if I wanted to stay on the team. Besides, it was only for a little while longer. Once we found Ophidian and tracked down the remaining four prototypes, we'd return to Andaress-4. I'd get my hands on a bunch of Blue Lace to stop the symptoms from getting worse and get back to doing my job like normal. I just needed to make it through the next few days.

Chapter 21

It took another seven hours of rough hiking—including discovering there was no bridge, scrambling to the bottom of the gorge, fording the shallow river, and climbing back out—before we saw the lights of Newtown ahead. We'd pushed ourselves hard, hoping we wouldn't have to sleep outside.

Valla only took twenty hours to complete a full rotation, making for short days and nights. By the time we reached the edge of the city, night had already fallen.

Newtown wasn't a large city now, but it had been bustling back in the days of early settlements in space. At one time, it may have had around two hundred thousand residents. Old government buildings, grocery stores, and schools defined the city borders, but most had been abandoned and reclaimed by the jungle. If there were seven thousand stragglers still hanging around, I'd be shocked. People were always coming and going, but overall there were more going than coming.

I'd changed back into my short-sleeved shirt around midday when I couldn't take the heat any longer. Wright, however, still wore his tactical pants and DECA Henley. Add in the regulation haircut, uniform holster, and overall Grayson Wright attitude, and he screamed law enforcement.

We stopped outside a two-story building with a row of cobbled-together tiny homes off to one side with a *For Rent* sign shoved in the window of the first one. A dozen LAVs were parked in the grassy lot and music poured out of the open windows.

"This is your friend's bar?" Wright asked. He didn't sound impressed.

I could see where he was coming from. The stained wood was bleached to gray, the lawn was more weeds than grass, and a drunk guy lay passed out under the wing of a rusted-out LAV.

I squinted and made out the faint rise and fall of the man's chest. Yes, just passed out.

"How did you meet him?" Wright asked as he fell into step beside me.

"It's … complicated."

"Sounds like a lot of things are complicated these days."

"Pierce is a good man—for the most part. Sometimes he's a little fast and loose with the rules, but to be fair, he grew up on Valla and rules don't mean a whole lot here. He rented me a room to stay in and helped me track down a few criminals when I worked for the Clava office, but this isn't the kind of place you go around advertising that."

Wright eyed me from the side. "Why would he do that?"

"Like I said, it's complicated."

Mercifully, Wright didn't press me for more information.

"We're going to have to do something about"—I waved my hand up and down his body—"this."

He looked down, like I was talking about the mud on his shoes. "What's 'this'?"

I made a face. "It's all very DECA-officer chic, which isn't in style here. Did you pack any non-work clothes? A different shirt, maybe?"

"Do you really think this is necessary?"

"Yes."

He pulled off his Henley, revealing a black short-sleeved shirt underneath. It fit him tightly across the chest and arms, showing off his impressive physique. Definitely not a regulation look.

"Better?" he asked.

"Remove the holster, too." I'd already moved my blaster and holster to my bag.

Wright took off his belt and holster and tucked his weapon into his waistband behind his back. "Best I can do."

"That's fine. Everyone in there will be armed. It's the Department-issued holster that'll draw attention. Now for your hair." I reached up and mussed his hair, pulling some of it forward over his face. Luckily, after two days of hiking, he was in need of a shave.

"Is there anything else that doesn't meet your approval?" he asked. He'd lowered his voice, and I realized just how close I'd moved to him. One deep breath and my chest would be plastered against his.

"No, you look good. I mean, you look less like you—less like an agent. You look less conspicuous." I turned toward the bar, hiding my face. Stars, why did I get that way around him? "Come on, let's see if my guy's still here."

We approached the front entrance of the bar with me leading and Wright trailing a half-step behind me. My Intell lit up as we neared—cuffs, lights, climate control system, personal music drones, and a whole host of other electronics.

"Take it outside!" someone yelled.

Two men crashed through the door and slammed into the porch railing. The bigger bloke landed an uppercut to the little guy's stomach, who countered with a jab to the big guy's face. They traded blows, staggering back and forth across the porch until the little guy jumped on the big guy's back, and the big guy tried scraping him off against the doorjamb.

"Yard!" the same voice yelled from inside the bar.

Both men fell down the porch steps to the gravel yard, where the fight devolved into a wrestling match.

Wright moved to break them apart. I placed a restraining hand on his arm and shook my head.

"Welcome to The New Bar," I said.

"Nice place."

"It has its charms."

We sidestepped the bar fight and went inside. Two steps in and a rush of signals bombarded me. I gritted my teeth and scanned the room. Not much about the dive bar had changed in the last couple of years.

Music blared, drowning out most of the conversations. There must have been about twenty guys and half a dozen women knocking back drinks at the bar or one of the three picnic tables. I clocked at least a dozen blasters on the customers and an antique blaster rifle hung over the mirror behind the liquor bottles. That was just for show. No doubt there were several more modern weapons within easy reach behind the bar.

The bartender was serving a beer to a customer. He didn't look up as he pocketed the legal tender and wiped a spill from the varnished top of the bar. "I said keep it outside, you bloody morons, or you're paying for the next thing you break!"

Pierce had cut his black hair short since the last time I'd seen him and let his facial hair grow into a devilishly sexy beard. He was every bit the tall, dark, and handsome rake he fancied himself to be.

"Is that how you treat all the ladies around here?"

He wiped his hand on a rag, then turned our way. His brown eyes flashed with mischief and delight. "Boots?! Is that you?"

I shucked off my bag and set it on the closest stool before grinning back at him.

"It is you!" A smile broke across his face, revealing a set of straight white teeth. He hopped over the bar, scooped me into a bear hug, and spun me in circles.

I squealed, slapping him on his back. "Hey! Put me down!"

My toes barely touched the floor when Pierce planted a giant kiss on my lips. He tasted like junipers, and I flashed back to a night sharing too many gin and tonics, among other things.

"Damn, Boots. I almost didn't recognize you with that purple hair." He ran his hands through it. "It looks good on you."

Wright cleared his throat. He stood with his feet planted shoulder-width apart, arms crossed, and a stern expression on his face. That man shouldn't be let within a thousand light-years of an undercover operation.

I patted Pierce twice on his chest and extricated myself from his arms. He held onto me a moment longer than necessary before letting go.

"Who's the muscle?" Pierce asked.

"This is my friend, Grayson. Grayson, meet Pierce, the owner of this very fine establishment."

The bartender shook Wright's hand vigorously. "Nice to meet you, mate. Can I pour you a glass?"

"I was hoping we could talk to you for a moment," I said. "In private?"

"It's like you read my mind." Pierce's accompanying grin was infectious, and I remembered how easy it was being around him. "Let me get Jerry to take over. You go on back."

Pierce jerked his head toward a swinging door behind the bar that led into a small kitchen. He called out to a skinny guy with a bushy mustache and receding hairline and walked over to talk to him. Jerry, I presumed.

"Boots?" Wright asked, cocking an eyebrow.

"It's a long story—one I'm not about to share."

"Mm-hmm. How did you say you know this guy?"

"I told you, I met him a few years ago working a case."

"Are you sure we can trust him?"

"As much as we can trust anyone on this moon."

Wright's jaw clenched, and his right eye twitched.

"Unless you have a better idea on how to contact Ravi and DeAjamae?"

"No," he admitted.

"Okay, then. We'll see if Pierce has a way to get a comm off of here. Let me do the talking and try to be a little less … you. Maybe give smiling a shot."

Wright's lip curled up into a smile that sent a shiver down my spine that was equal parts nervousness and straight-up lust.

My foot caught on absolutely nothing, and I stumbled a half-step before regaining my balance. "Forget what I said. Nix the smile."

Wright chuckled.

We walked past the picnic tables on our way around the bar. One group had ordered some baskets of greasy bar food, and my stomach rumbled at the hot, delicious smell of onion rings, fries, and crispers.

The galley-style kitchen was small. A little dirty but not unsanitary. Honestly, for a city with no ordinances, health inspectors, or law enforcement, it could have been a lot worse. Pierce had a refrigerator, a griddle, and a zapper for making simple bar food. To the left, a narrow, carpeted staircase led up to the living area and bedrooms. On the right, an alcove jutted out from the back wall, with a circular table and four chairs.

My lips quirked up in a half-smile. Something told me if I looked around, I'd find cards and poker chips nearby—and maybe a box of cigars from Avignon.

"I didn't know if I'd ever see you again," Pierce said from the door.

"Neither did I." I nodded to the table. "Are you still running your weekly game?"

He opened a drawer and pulled out a deck of cards. "Fancy a game? If I recall, you were pretty good."

I tossed the cards back into the drawer. "Some other time. Unfortunately, this isn't a social call."

Pierce sized up Wright. "So I gathered."

"We were hoping you might help us. Our ship crashed, and we need to send a message to our friends on Ritru-6."

"Good thing you were in my neck of the galaxy." Pierce grabbed a dusty bottle of whisky from the top of a cabinet and three glasses. "This sounds like a conversation best shared over drinks." He looked at the swinging door to the bar. "Why don't we go upstairs? Fewer eyes and ears."

Up in his apartment, Pierce set the glasses on a coffee table made of empty liquor crates. He poured two fingers of golden liquid into each glass. Muffled sounds from the bar carried up through the floorboards.

"I assume you still drink Lonnie Powell," he said, handing me the first glass.

"Is that the bottle I gave you?" I asked, taking it before sitting down on the couch.

"It didn't seem right drinking it without you."

Pierce handed Wright the second glass, then took the chair opposite us. Wright sat beside me, his arm casually thrown across the top of the couch. Not touching me, but not *not* touching me either.

I mentally rolled my eyes and leaned forward, resting my elbows on my knees.

Wright sipped his whisky, taking in the room. "Nice place you have here."

It was nice. While the bar was furnished with cheap stools, cobbled-together shelving, and empty bottles for decoration, the upstairs had been painted, and he'd hung some art on the walls. The line drawings were one step classier than scantily clad women in impractical settings, but it wasn't a big step.

"Pierce's family were some of the original settlers on Valla," I said. "They've been here, what? Four hundred years?"

"Closer to five hundred, but that doesn't hold much water with folks these days. Most don't stick around much more than a month or two. Those who do aren't looking to compare family trees. Too much root rot, if you know what I mean."

"How does it work on Valla?" Wright asked. "Without laws or government or a planetary network?"

Pierce sipped his whisky. "We keep to ourselves, don't ask too many questions, and of course, LTs if you please."

Wright drained his glass. "Why stay?"

Pierce relaxed into his seat. "Business is good. The scientists say it'll be another twenty years before Newtown dries up. I figure I'll ride it out until then, see how it goes. Besides, somebody has to make sure these lowlifes don't go thirsty. But you didn't come all the way to Valla to inquire about my little bar. What mess did you get yourself tangled up in this time?"

My glass dangled from my hand between my knees. I swirled the whisky while I gathered my thoughts and figured out how much I wanted to tell Pierce. "We're tracking down a shipment of weapons.

There's a guy involved who used to run a gang out of Clava until he got run out. We think he's hiding here."

Pierce scratched his chin. "That describes a lot of people that come through here. There are always a few weapons guys hanging about. What are we talking about? Civilian? Military? Planetary- or space-based?"

I looked at Wright, who only raised one eyebrow at me. Clear enough. He was leaving it up to me to decide how much we shared.

It would be easy to dismiss Pierce because of his pretty-boy good looks and laissez-faire attitude, but that would be at your own peril. His dark-brown eyes studied me, not missing a single nose twitch or shift in my posture. It was what made him an excellent poker player. For as much as he bent the rules, he had a kind heart and strong moral compass.

I gave him the highlights. He listened, taking in all the information. I ended by describing the two people who attacked us in the jungle.

"All right, let me see if I got this straight," he said. "You need to message your team, find a high-pressure pump, and track down these Ophidian and Sidewinder characters. That about sum it up?"

"And seize any of the prototype weapons we find," I added.

Pierce whistled. "You don't ask for much, do you?"

"I understand if you don't want any part of this."

"Now I didn't say that, but we might have to get creative to get what you need. We stopped being able to transmit messages about six months ago. The tech was having a hard time getting through the atmosphere anyway, but then someone stripped the equipment for parts. You'd have a better chance using my zapper to send a comm than it."

"So, how do you communicate with other people in the galaxy?" I asked.

He laughed. "Well, that's a big assumption now, isn't it? That we want to talk to other people or that other people want to talk to us."

"That seems like an elaborate excuse for why you haven't returned any of my comms."

Wright muttered something under his breath that I refused to pay attention to.

Pierce grinned. "See, I knew you missed me. But as it happens, I have a friend who makes frequent runs to other systems for … well, let's just leave it at *reasons*. For a fee, she takes comms with her and transmits them once she breaks orbit. She'd probably send yours, but I'd be cautious how you word it and who you send it to. I can't guarantee it'll be kept private. In fact, I pretty much guarantee it won't be."

"We can work with that," I said.

Pierce finished his drink and poured himself another. "The pump is going to be difficult. People have been nicking any kind of scrap technology they can get their hands on. LAVs, ship parts, hovercarts, you name it. Spare parts are pretty scarce these days. Wouldn't surprise me if they were the ones that shot your ship down. Salvaging has become a big business around here."

Wright finished his drink and set the glass on the coffee table. "If you get a message to our team, they can bring the part from Ritru-6."

"Shouldn't be a problem. Prati got back from her last run a few days ago. She should be going again in a day or two."

"I'll write something up and address it to DeAjamae's personal account to avoid any association with DECA," Wright said.

Assuming this Prati could send the message tomorrow, it would take Ravi and DeAjamae at least another day to obtain the part and fly here. I didn't like the idea of leaving the *Soteria* out in the jungle for that long, but we didn't have a choice. Felix's repairs would take that long to complete, anyway. Hopefully, he got the holo-emitters running for camouflage.

"Now, about this Ophidian character. I can't say as I've heard of him, but some of my regulars mentioned seeing a few members of the Five Fangs gang sporting new hardware. Real high-tech stuff. I didn't pay much mind to it at the time, but it might be a fit for the people you saw in the forest."

Wright and I shared a look. "Five Fangs?" he asked.

At Pierce's nod, I felt several pieces clicking into place. "Ophidian's old gang is called the Seven Serpents," I said. "Seven Serpents, Five Fangs. Not a big creative leap there."

Wright tapped on his cuff and launched the holoscreen. He pulled up a holo of the tattoos on the people from the jungle and made a twisting motion to spin the image toward Pierce. "Is this their mark?"

"Yeah, that's it. Ugly sucker, isn't it?"

I wrinkled my nose in confirmation.

Pierce nodded. "They've set up shop somewhere on the outskirts of town to the east. Been there a year, year and a half. Pretty small potatoes. Keep to themselves. Valla's got no shortage of potential recruits for an organization like that."

"What else can you tell us about them?" Wright asked.

"Not much. My clientele lean more toward the don't-play-well-with-other types. They're in Valla to lie low for a bit, not make friends."

Wright blew out a breath and shoved his hand through his hair, forcing the dark-blond strands to stand on end. "It's not a lot to go on."

"But it's more than we started with," I said, elbowing him in the side. "Thank you."

"If you want, I could make some quiet inquiries," Pierce offered. "Mind you, I might not find anything. For health reasons, people around here tend not to stick their noses in other people's business."

Wright's eyes narrowed ever so slightly. "What makes you different?"

Pierce's easy smile grew into something more mischievous as his gaze slid from Wright to me. "It's been rather dull lately, and Boots here never fails to make things interesting when she's in town."

"Why don't you prepare a comm for DeAjamae?" I asked Wright, attempting to change the subject.

"There's a guest room down the hall, if you want some privacy," Pierce offered. "It's nothing fancy, but you can use it for the night. Boots is more than welcome to bunk with me."

The wink he tacked on to the end of the statement sent a flush to my cheeks. I wasn't embarrassed about the time we'd spent together, but I also wasn't ready to pick up where we'd left off two years ago.

"It may be best if we keep the sleeping arrangements separate," I said, standing up. Pierce and Wright followed suit.

"Ah, well. You can't blame a bloke for trying, can you?"

Wright handed me my pack. "*Boots* can take the extra room. I'll sleep on the couch, if that's available."

"Knock yourself out."

"Do you mind if I use your sonic shower to clean up and run my clothes through a cleaning cycle?" I asked.

"No problem. You know where it is. I'll grab some towels for you."

"Thanks. For everything. I owe you one."

"We can discuss payment later."

Wright retreated to the guest room to record the message for DeAjamae, and I hopped in the sonic shower. I would have killed for a hot water shower, but clean water was a luxury on Valla. Because of the toxins in the atmosphere, all water needed to be filtered and sanitized before it could be used. Without a functioning government, individuals had to handle the process themselves, and most of Pierce's water resources went to supplying the bar. Still, the thin layer of soap and sonic waves vibrated off two days' worth of dirt, sweat, and grime, leaving me feeling clean if not refreshed.

I found a comb and some styling products under the sink—Pierce spent more time on his hair than I did. I finished combing through some kind of gel when there was a knock on the door.

It was probably Wright wanting to know if I needed to add anything to the message.

"One second," I said, checking the time on the clothes cycle. It still had ten minutes to go.

I wrapped a towel around myself and tucked in the end. It was on the short side, but all the important bits were covered. I cracked open the door to find Pierce, not Wright. He held a small pile of folded clothes. "I thought you might like these. They'll be a little big, but I remember how much you hated wearing dirty clothes. These will be cleaner than anything you carried around in that pack through the jungle."

"Thanks." I took the clothes, which looked to be a pair of soft pajama pants and a t-shirt from a tequila company specializing in spicy flavors. It had a cartoon pepper on the front doing a rather suggestive act with a sexy lime.

Pierce looked me up and down, taking his time on my legs. "That offer to share a bunk is still good, if you changed your mind."

"Sorry, but I do have another favor I'd like to ask you." I pulled him into the bathroom with me and shut the door. I wished I was wearing something other than a towel.

His gaze slid down to my chest. "Have I ever mentioned how much I admire your negotiating skills?"

"You're hilarious." I lowered my voice to make sure Wright couldn't overhear us. "While you're out, could you get your hands on some Blue Lace?"

Pierce dropped the flirtatious banter. "Why do you want Blue Lace?"

"That implant I told you about? Well, I'm not handling it as well as I said. It has some unpleasant side effects if I use it too often. The Blue Lace helps keep them under control. If Wright finds out, he'll say I'm unfit for duty and kick me out of the Department."

"I don't know, Boots. That's some pretty wicked stuff. Are you sure?"

"I'm sure."

He gave me a long look. "Then I'll see what I can find."

With one hand, I held my towel firmly in place. With the other, I gave him a giant hug and kissed him on the cheek. "Thank you."

Chapter 22

THE NEXT EVENING, I paced across the living room, waiting for Pierce to return. He left five hours ago to talk to his contact about delivering our message to DeAjamae. It was almost dark again. I couldn't fathom what was taking him so long. How did Vallagorians function without a reliable comm system?

My head throbbed. The bar had stayed open until the wee hours of the morning. Not only had the loud music kept me up, but there had been about fifteen customers right below my bedroom wearing cuffs, playing trilliards, and throwing e-dice at the bar hoping to win free drinks.

At one point, I'd given up shutting down all the signals. That had been a big mistake. The things on those people's cuffs weren't things I wanted to know about. At least not in this situation where we needed to keep a low profile, and there wasn't anything I could do. I'd held out as long as I could, but after the relative peace and quiet of the jungle, that many signals was overwhelming. So, banking on Pierce being able to get me more, I'd taken my last Blue Lace tab and drifted to sleep on the high it gave me.

It was less than fifteen hours later, and I already craved my next fix.

The downstairs door opened and closed, then footsteps jogged up the steps. Pierce's lithe frame popped out of the stairwell with the energy of a collegiate athlete. Sometimes I had to remind myself that he was only twenty-seven. Growing up in the harsh reality of Valla matured him faster than most guys his age.

He set a cloth bag with groceries on the kitchen counter. "Where's the buzzkill?"

"Wright's pretty fun once you get to know him."

Pierce unloaded the food. "Yeah, but you knew right away who I was talking about, didn't ya?"

"Touché. He's out for a walk. He wanted to scout the area. The latest map we have isn't very accurate."

"Right-o. If Valla prides itself on one thing, it's being off the map."

I grabbed a box of Clavan whole wheat crackers from the bag and raised it in a silent question. Pierce pointed toward a cabinet at the end of the row. I put it away, along with a container of cereal with freeze-dried hellaberries, also from Clava. "You trying to make me feel at home?"

Pierce laughed. "Nah, Prati just got back from a run to Brione-5. She loads up on supplies and flips them for a pretty profit. Greenhouses do well here, but grain's been trickier to grow in large quantities. Thought I'd put that DECA money to good use."

That morning, we'd agreed on a price for Pierce's services and lodging. We'd talked about renting one of the tiny homes, but Pierce said we'd be too visible so close to the LAV lot. He didn't want it getting out that he was housing law enforcement. So the guest room and couch it was.

Wright had come prepared to pay for local help in legal tender, although we'd planned on staying on the *Soteria*. Pierce may have been a friend, but this was business for him, and he drove a fierce bargain. After paying extra to get a message to the team, our reserves were running low.

I handed Pierce a box of locally sourced insect protein powder and wobbled when a sharp needle of pain zinged the back of my head.

He grabbed my forearm to steady me. "You okay?"

I waved off his offer to help. "Did you pick up the other stuff?"

Before Pierce had gone, I'd slipped him all the legal tender I'd brought with me to buy Blue Lace.

He put away the box of mycoprotein starter in his hand, then withdrew a square paper envelope from his back pocket.

I held out my hand, which had been shaking ever since the morning crowd had shuffled their hungover bodies into the bar for some hair of the dog. Pierce had a small greenhouse out back filled with hydroponic tomatoes for making his infamous Bloody Marys. The almost nonstop whirling of the blender had been a fun little kick to my already throbbing headache.

Pierce's full lips pressed into a thin line, but he handed over the envelope of Blue Lace tabs, along with half my legal tender. "Be careful with this, Boots. It's changed hands a lot before getting here, and I don't know how pure it is. Plus, Prati only had three tabs on her."

"Only three?" What was with these drug dealers only keeping three tabs on hand?

"Someone bought most of her supply, and she isn't going to the Nephali system for another month. She sounded suspicious, so I didn't press. I usually only score a little Stardust off her."

I heard Wright coming up the stairs and squirreled the envelope of drugs in a hidden pocket inside my pack.

"Thank you." I went up on my tiptoes and kissed Pierce on the cheek. "You're a good friend."

Wright entered as we were putting away the last of the groceries.

"I talked to my contact," Pierce said. "She's heading to the fox hunter races in Alpha Bohn-ri and can deliver your message tonight."

"That's great! Ravi and DeAjamae might get here by tomorrow night."

Pierce leaned against the counter. "I also asked around about the Five Fangs. One of my buddies is seeing a girl who waits tables over at an east-side bar called The Wandering Star. She's been complaining about a new group hanging out there—loud, obnoxious, gets a little handsy with the staff. A regular tried to teach them some manners. Get this—the guy caught his fist mid-punch, squeezed, and crushed the regular's hand. Broke a couple of bones, I guess."

"A bionic hand?" I asked.

"The server didn't say, but I thought you might be interested."

"Lots of people have bionic limbs, but it's worth checking out. You said the Five Fangs territory was on the east side, right?"

Pierce shrugged. "That's where their tags are. The old city was pretty big. There's plenty of abandoned buildings up for grabs, and most of the population is transient. Fighting over territory hasn't been a big issue."

"It'd be helpful if we had a detailed map of the city and identified areas to look into," Wright said. "The map I have is outdated and topographical only."

"I can help with that," Pierce offered.

"If it's okay with you," I asked Wright, "I'd like to go check out The Wandering Star. See if I can spot anyone who looks interesting."

He agreed. "Recon only. The assassin got a look at you on Ritru-6, and you could spook him. I want to wait for the entire team to get here before we go in."

I should have packed a sandwich.

My stomach gurgled, reminding me I'd missed dinner. The little packet of dried fruit and nuts that I'd swiped from Wright on the hike had suspicious bite marks on the bag. I didn't need a forensic team to tell me they were a close match to guinea pig teeth.

Stupid little potato butt.

I picked through the pile and found an almond that looked unassailed and popped it into my mouth. Desperate times and all.

The motion reminded my thighs and shoulders that I hadn't moved in over an hour. I eased myself from a sitting position to lying down and scooted forward to keep the street below in view. The rough roofing material scraped against my elbows, but the cramps eased from my legs.

The Wandering Star was about two kilometers southeast of The New Bar in the oldest area of town. I'd passed by empty factories, schools, and a recreation center—leftovers from a time when New-town had a population to support large gathering places. Back when it had a name other than the New Town.

Some buildings showed signs of habitation, like a sheet of unbro-ken plastiglass over a window or an aggressive number of locks on the door, but most looked cold and barren. I'd noted green smears of algae and water-soaked moss clinging to most of them.

For shits and giggles, I tried sending a comm to Felix. We weren't often this long out of touch, and I missed the sarcastic little avatar. I hoped he was okay, that those spaceships hadn't discovered the *Soteria*, and that the repairs were going well. As expected, my comm terminated with no connection.

Worry gnawed at my already raw stomach, but like my hunger, there wasn't much I could do about it. How did people live without a planetary net?

Voices drifted up from the street. Two guys joshed each other as they crossed the gravel pedestrian road overrun with weeds. New-town didn't have working streetlamps, but a few of the businesses along this stretch had installed their own outside lights—mostly flashing holovids advertising cheap food and cheaper beer. It was enough to make out people's faces as they entered and exited the bar. So far, I hadn't seen anyone who struck me as belonging to the Five Fangs gang.

The air whirled as a LAV approached, hot and fast. It was dark green or navy blue—hard to tell against the night sky. I tucked myself against the rusted-out climate control mechanical box. It didn't hide me from being viewed overhead, but it camouflaged my silhouette better than the rest of the bare rooftop. That, plus the darkness, would keep my position concealed.

The LAV made an ugly landing on my side of the street, slam-ming down hard on the front left leg, then rocking back off-kil-ter before settling to the ground. The gullwing door rose, and a woman climbed out. She had a lean figure clad in a pencil skirt and blouse—very corporate attire. That alone set her apart from everyone else I'd observed so far. The wing closed behind her, and she strode across the street with fast, purposeful steps. I couldn't see her face from my angle, but something about the way she moved felt familiar.

I twitched two fingers in quick succession, activating the recording program on my Intell. It translated the signals coming from my eyes and optical nerve into digital information and saved the image—as good as any camera system. So far, I'd recorded twenty-eight bar customers, most of them within the last hour. Hopefully, DeAjamae could trace them with her facial- or gait-recognition software. Otherwise, we'd have our work cut out for us running down all these identities, especially since a good portion of them had likely taken countermeasures to remain anonymous.

A mosquito bit my ankle, and I jerked reflexively to smack it. Maybe the Vallagorians had fled because of the desertification of their moon, or maybe it was because of these nasty, little bloodsuckers. I itched at the welt and the three others beside it.

When I looked back at the street, the woman was stepping through the front door of the bar. Music drifted out for a moment, the lyrics muted by distance and humidity. Blue-tinted light from inside silhouetted her form. She paused and looked to the side, letting me catch the profile of her face for a split second before the door swung shut behind her.

My breath caught.

Heart pounding, I scooted back from the ledge on my knees and elbows until I was out of view from the street. My back pressed against the climate control box, but the chill of the metal did nothing to temper the sweat that broke out along my forehead and chest.

It couldn't be her. She was supposed to be on Brione-2, locked away in a psychiatric treatment facility.

My mind raced, thinking through the implications. Her presence here changed everything. Five prototype bionic weapons were now the least of our concerns. There was no limit to how many weapons they could make if Doctor Yelena Adler was involved.

Chapter 23

I scrambled to my feet, careful to stay back from the edge so no one below would see me. A wave of dizziness and nausea rolled through me. I twitched all five fingers of my left hand together like I was making a fist. That shut off the recording program in my Intell, but for once, it wasn't to blame for making me feel sick. No, the cause was much more human this time.

Precious seconds passed while I stood doubled over at the waist with my hands on my knees, waiting for the world to stop spinning. It hadn't righted itself yet when I stumbled for the maintenance ladder fixed to the rear wall of the building. I climbed down the rungs, wondering why the ladder seemed four times longer than it had on the way up.

My boots sank into the rain-softened dirt. I slid on the mud before finding my footing and bolting around the corner. The gravel street between buildings was empty, save for a few parked LAVs I wove between.

I yanked open the bar door and collided with a set of pectorals roughly the size of my first apartment.

"Whoa, there now," the guy said, giving me a sloppy smile and appraising look. He'd tinted his skin in an aquamarine-giraffe pattern and dyed the tuft of hair sprouting from the top of his head silvery-white. "What's the big rush? If you wanted me to stay, all you had to do was ask."

I tried to move past while he chuckled at his own drunken joke. He moved with me, stepping back to keep himself between me and the rest of the bar. It was impossible to see around his massive chest, even when I rose to my tiptoes and leaned to the side.

His head dipped into my view. "All you're looking for is right here." He jabbed his thumb backward, pointing to his chest. "One hundred percent, grade-A, interstellar-class man." He flexed his pecs and did that thing where he made the right and left sides bounce in an alternating pattern.

"Maybe next time, big fella." I patted his chest, forcing space between us. It was like pushing a boulder.

The gap allowed me to scan the room. Standard layout with a long bar to the left and scattered tables dotting the floor. A smart-dart board with flashing lights occupied the far right. Restrooms in the back. The color scheme was somewhere between muddy brown and dirty-mop-bucket-water gray.

There were about three dozen customers, a bartender, and a haggard server darting between tables and swatting off the roving hand of a man trying to cop a cheap feel. Every single one of them looked like they were armed. That included the staff.

Doctor Adler stood with her arms crossed beside two men and a woman seated at a round table. She'd lost weight during her stint in the psychiatric facility. Now she looked gaunt with sharp cheekbones angling across her face. And then there was her eye.

Six months ago, she'd tried to kill me in a last-ditch effort to keep DECA from discovering the Intell in my head. We'd fought, and I'd stabbed her in the eye in the process of trying not to die. Instead of getting a realistic replacement for it, she had a raw-metal bionic eye inserted into the socket. A glowing red light swiveled in whichever direction she looked.

Adler scowled down at the group with her finger jabbed at one man. By the look of everyone's body language, they were in a heated conversation.

"At least let me buy you a drink, honey," the guy in front of me said.

I leaned to my right. The man with Adler shoved back from the table and shot to his feet. Middle-aged. Tall, with broad shoulders.

Head shaved and tattooed in the pattern of snakeskin. Body mods made the scales ripple and flex as a flush of blood rushed to his face.

I had no recent holo to compare his image to, but it was possible the man was Ophidian. His age, height, and complexion—what I saw of it—matched the holos from Ophidian's DECA file. However, Ophidian from twelve years ago hadn't had facial tattoos or body mods. They were numerous enough that it was difficult to make a positive ID. Maybe that was their purpose.

The woman had hot-pink hair in an asymmetrical cut and wide shoulders like a swimmer. The other man was broad all over, from his thighs to his chest to his shoulders to his big fat forehead. Both looked like they kicked puppies on the weekend for fun.

These weren't misguided youth. They were seasoned criminals.

I took a fast recording of the group with my Intell before my new companion stepped closer, blocking my view again. He attempted to herd me toward the bar.

"Thanks." I took a step back. "But I'm not thirsty."

"Then why come to a bar?"

"Look, fella. It's nothing personal, but you and me? It ain't happening tonight." A glimmer of hope still flickered in his eyes, so I amended myself. "Not any night."

"Ah, to the void with you then." He waved his arm, almost clocking me in the head.

I bobbed back, out of reach.

He stumbled, caught himself on a chair, and straightened. "Where was I going? Oh, right. To take a piss."

By the time he staggered out the door, the group was no longer at the table. My stomach tightened as my eyes darted around the room. They'd been there a second ago. It wasn't a large enough place for them to disappear into the crowd.

Movement in my peripheral vision caught my attention. A back door partially hidden by the smart-dart board swung shut.

I sprinted for the rear of the bar, banging my hip into a chair and shouldering past the server who'd stopped to see what the commotion was about. Beer sloshed out of the glass she held and onto my pants.

"Watch where you're going!" The glass slipped from her hand and smashed to the floor. Her customers clapped and whistled. "Yeah, yeah, ya bunch of assholes," she said, knocking one of the men on the back of his head.

"Sorry," I called over my shoulder but didn't slow down.

The door led to an alley. With no sign of people in either direction, I spotted a derelict LAV parking lot at one end and sprinted toward it. The group from the table piled into two LAVs. Neon-blue sinnafuel flames shot out beneath the first vehicle, blowing exhaust fumes my way. I coughed and watched as it rose thirty meters before blasting off to the south.

The engine of the second LAV sputtered twice before catching. It was too far away to reach before they lifted off, but it was pointed in the opposite direction to its companion. It would need to turn around.

I opened the gate on my Intell, pushing the hacking program to latch onto the now-rising LAV. Pings from dozens of electronic devices flashed in my head—cuffs from the patrons inside the bar, the smart-dart board, trilliards table, holoscreens, music drones, automatic lights, sonic faucets in the bathroom, and the zapper behind the bar. I made a small waving motion with my hand, discarding each one as it popped up.

Pain wrapped around my skull. Squeezing. Constricting. Tears blurred what was left of my vision. I wiped them away with my sleeve and focused on the craft rotating one hundred and eighty degrees above me.

Its thrusters swiveled from their lift-off to forward-flying positions, pushing the LAV in my direction. I'd have about two seconds as it passed overhead when it would be within my Intell's range.

Hot, dry wind swirled around me, pelting bits of sand and loose regolith stones against my skin. The LAV swung as close to me as it would get.

"Come on," I whispered, willing the LAV's signal to appear.

More useless notifications popped up as patrons walked in and out of range. I swiped them away.

There! A hit for an active low altitude vehicle filled my vision. That had to be it. I selected it and signaled my Intell's hacking program to search for weaknesses in the security settings. I'd hoped for an older model or even a stolen one that had already been tampered with. If I could access the controls, I could force it into an emergency landing.

My Intell pinged, a sound only I heard. It was through the first layer of security.

The LAV completed its turn and drifted away from me. I ran toward it, trying to buy a few more precious seconds. A bright pulse of blue light lit up the parking lot as the thrusters engaged. The accompanying roar of the engine drowned out my scream of frustration as the ship sped out of range.

I'd been too slow.

Overhead, Doctor Adler's navy-blue LAV zipped by, headed in the same southernly direction as the other two crafts.

"Shit!" I clenched my fist, wishing I had something to punch. Doctor Adler's smug face came to mind.

Blood from my nose trickled down my lip. I shut down all the nonessential programs and rubbed my temples to ease the pain. It didn't help.

I knew this time I wouldn't be able to stop it. I fell to my knees and emptied the contents of my stomach onto the gravel. When there was nothing left, I dry heaved acid until my throat burned and tears stung my eyes. I straightened and wiped my nose and mouth with the back of my sleeve. As much as I wanted to lie in a dark corner for the next hour or six, Wright needed to know that Adler was on Valla and not locked up like we'd assumed.

Her presence here changed everything. She may not have invented the bionic weapons herself, but she was Doctor Lourde's protégé. Where he'd conducted his experiments with a clinical sort of detachment, she'd reveled in the torture she'd inflicted on Fax and me. Fax—my friend and the sole-surviving recipient of the Intell when

I'd been taken hostage at Tazza Industries. He hadn't made it out alive.

My stomach clenched, but I wasn't going to be sick again. I'd rather be strapped to the cold side of an asteroid than let her pick up where she'd left off. With her working for Tazza again, there was no limit to how many bionic weapons they could make.

A hard knot of determination formed, pushing me into a fast jog. We couldn't afford to wait. We had to find where she'd set up her base, and we had to do it now. Before she "recruited" any other innocent people to serve as her subjects.

Chapter 24

"What happened?" Wright demanded when I stumbled through the upstairs door to Pierce's apartment.

He wrapped his arm around my waist and half carried me to the couch. I wasn't proud of myself, but I let him. It had taken everything I had to run the two kilometers back to The New Bar. Sweat soaked through my shirt, and my hair clung to my face in ugly purple clumps.

Wright crouched in front of me. He scanned me for visible injuries, then cupped my face and stared into my eyes as he turned my head side to side. His thumb stroked my cheek just below my eye.

"Your pupils are dilated, your skin is pale, and your pulse is racing. You could be in shock."

I supposed those symptoms could be attributed to shock instead of the malfunctioning chip in my brain. Fingers crossed.

"Water?"

Wright made sure I was settled before retrieving a glass of water from the purifier. As I drank it, my gaze drifted to my backpack on the kitchen floor. Inside were the three tabs of Blue Lace Pierce had bought for me. I desperately wanted one but not with Wright in the room. If I could get to step out of the room for just a minute—no. I willed myself to take deeper, slower breaths. My head needed to be clear for this discussion.

"Adler," I said after my breathing returned to normal. "I saw her. She's working with the Five Fangs."

"Doctor Yelena Adler? Are you sure?"

"Hers is not a face I'm likely to forget."

Wright's brows furrowed. "But she's on Tylo. How did she get out of the psychiatric facility?"

I shrugged, still feeling lightheaded.

"No wonder you're in shock." Wright brushed my hair from my face and held my gaze for a moment. Then he had me lie down and lifted my feet onto the arm of the couch so they were elevated above my heart.

Even though it caused my headache to flare stronger, I opened the connection between my Intell and his cuff to send him the recordings I'd made of Adler and the people she met.

He pulled the chair across from me closer and reviewed the data while I walked him through everything I saw at the bar. Then he asked me questions. A lot of questions.

"This was supposed to be recon only. You shouldn't have gone after them, especially without backup. There were four of them and one of you. What would you have done if you'd brought down the LAV?"

I eased up to a sitting position and pulled my feet up under me. "Honestly? I hadn't thought that far ahead. Seeing Adler kind of threw me."

At that, Wright's expression softened. "I imagine that would throw most people, but you can't go off on your own like that. Do you understand? We work as a team. I have to trust that when I send you out to do reconnaissance, you'll do that and report back so we can make a plan."

"But you know what this means, right? She's probably the one who installed the bionic weapon and neural impulse chip into that woman out in the forest. The three unaccounted-for prototypes are almost assuredly active now. We need to find them."

I uncurled my feet in preparation to stand.

Wright placed his hand on my thigh. "Reliance, you are driven, brave, and have some of the best instincts I've ever seen in an officer."

I didn't see where he was going with this but sat back onto the couch. "Thank you?"

"Those aren't always good things."

"Oh." I sank the rest of the way down.

"They make you reckless at times. The assassin almost dropped you off that cliff, and the woman in the forest would have shot you if I hadn't gotten to my blaster quick enough. And then there was the crash-landing." He scrubbed both hands over his face before looking up at me with exasperated eyes. "You run into danger without a moment's hesitation. As your lead, I need to know that you can stick to the plan. For your safety and the team's."

"The pirates were hardly my fault," I grumbled.

"You've almost died three times in the last two weeks!"

I sighed. "I see your point. It won't happen again."

"Good, because I don't know if my blood pressure can take a fourth time." He leaned back and gave me one of those half-smiles. "Now, despite how you gathered it, perhaps we can put your information to good use. That is, if you feel up to it."

My skull still felt like someone had taken an impact hammer to the back of it, but it would feel that way whether we were figuring out how to catch Adler or not. "Where do we start?"

"Pierce got his hands on several drone recordings taken around the city over the last five years, and we used an AI program to compile a partial map. We spent the afternoon going over it, trying to identify likely locations for the gang to hole up on the east side of Newtown. It's a large area."

"Can I see it?"

Wright cleared off the coffee table. He placed his cuff in the middle. "Sophie, initiate holographic map of Newtown, Valla."

"Initiating holographic map," a robotic feminine voice answered from his cuff.

An image of the town projected between us. "Nothing has been surveyed, but Pierce has been adding to the map bit by bit. It's fairly complete except for this far western area." Wright pointed to the part of town with the densest population. "He says people move in and out too quickly for the data to be reliable."

"I don't think that's where the Five Fangs are, anyway. My credits are on the southeast side," I said, manipulating my hands to spin the map around and zoom in on that corner. The movements felt big and clunky compared to the subtle commands my Intell could detect. "See this building here? That's The Wandering Star." I squiggled my finger over the gray building, turning it blue, then pointed at the parking lot behind it. "From here, all three LAVs flew south. Maybe a little southeast. There's no reason for them to all go in that direction, unless they were heading to the same place."

"Let's say you're right. That eliminates everything to the north and west of the bar." Wright bladed his hand, cut two perpendicular lines through the holo, and swiped those sections away. The map blinked and reformed to show only the southeast portion of Newtown.

While largely abandoned now, that section had been a bustling suburban district at one time. We leaned over, assessing the options.

"A hospital would be the logical choice."

Wright located the old hospital on the map and enlarged it. The complex must have sat on the edge of a lake before the terraforming failed. Increased rainfall over the last few decades had doubled the size of the lake, flooding half the floors and turning it into an island.

"Probably not our best bet," Wright said.

"Agreed. I think we can eliminate the single-family residences." I thought back to my time in the Tazza Industries lab. "If Adler is implanting chips and bionic weapons into people, she'll need a whole surgical suite. That kind of equipment takes a lot of power."

"She could be using generators," Wright countered.

I pursed my lips. "Even so, the wiring couldn't support that level of energy. It would be easier to set up someplace already designed for heavy equipment, especially when there are so many options available."

Wright rubbed a hand across his jaw, thinking. "That looks like an old LAV repair shop. It could handle that kind of power load."

"Also difficult to make sterile for surgery," I said. "Ophidian might not give a shit, but Adler is very particular. I don't think it would be her first choice."

"Agreed." Wright swiped his finger over the building, turning it yellow, as well as two other round structures near it. "That holds for the wastewater treatment facility, too."

"And the mycoprotein processing plant. Even if it hasn't been used in a decade, those spores are impossible to eradicate one hundred percent. What about the old school?"

"Pierce eliminated that earlier today. He said a group moved in there about a year ago and set up a spaceship chop shop. Apparently, there's good business to be done on Valla taking stolen or suspect ships, replacing the identification codes, and refurbishing them into new ships."

I was familiar with the process from prior trips. Criminals came here to hide from DECA until the heat cooled down. Having a "clean" ship to leave in was worth a lot of credits.

Wright spun the map for a closer look at the far eastern side. Our eyes landed on a six-story apartment building.

"It's residential," I said, "but they'd have commercial-grade power for the central climate control and utilities."

"Plus, it's on the edge of the city. Less traffic and people poking around. Worth checking out." Wright shaded it green on the map.

We worked our way around the map, designating buildings as gray, yellow, or green. Residential houses and small shops got gray. We added a grocery store, shopping center, and a factory to the list of most likely places for Adler and Ophidian to be occupying and designated them as green. We couldn't tell from the drone recording what the factory had manufactured, but the sheer size of it suggested it had supported heavy machinery. Everything else got bucketed as yellow. In the end, there was a lot more green and yellow on the map than we would have liked.

"Let's scope some of them out," I said, rising from the couch. It was almost midnight, but with a strong cup of coffee, I'd be good to go.

"It can wait," Wright said, staring down at the map.

I opened my mouth to object, but he held up a finger.

"You need to rest." He made a swiping motion to close the program, then snapped his cuff back onto his wrist. "Hopefully, DeAjamae and Ravi will arrive tomorrow, and the four of us can surveil the green-marked locations. After we have more solid intelligence, we'll make a plan on how to arrest them. Together."

It wasn't what I wanted to hear, but I understood. We said goodnight, and I snagged my backpack from the kitchen on my way to my room. I tossed it on the bed, attempted to toe off my boots without unlacing them, tripped over my own void-damned feet, and stumbled into the bed. My shin hit the frame, sending a jolt of pain up my leg.

Defeated, I flopped onto the mattress and stared at the flaking paint on the ceiling. I felt dirty and gross from running and should take a shower but that required effort. Now that I'd lain down, I didn't want to get back up again. Instead, I replayed our conversation over in my head. It wasn't the first time I'd been reprimanded, and it wouldn't be the last. Anger I could take. Superiority, sure. Void, even straight-up asshole I could handle. But Wright had looked ... disappointed.

The worst part—the absolute *worst* part—was that Wright made a good point. Following the gang to the parking lot and trying to bring down their LAV hadn't been my brightest idea. Even if I'd caught them, I'd had no way to contact Wright or haul them back to Pierce's bar, let alone to Andaress-4. What was I going to do? Sit on them until Wright came looking for me?

I'd never been one to check the depth of the pool before jumping in. I just assumed everything would sort itself out after the splash. It made me a lousy teammate and partner.

Tomorrow there would be four of us, which were much better odds. Plus, they'd have a DECA cruiser and the pump to repair my ship, so transporting everyone we arrested back to Ritru-6 or Andaress-4 wouldn't be an issue. Wright had a plan. I just needed to stick to it.

A soft *wheek* chirped from the head of the bed. Walnut's pink nose poked out from between the two pillows, twitching.

"Wheek, wheek!"

I blew out a breath, and with it, a lot of the steam I'd been building up inside. My head hurt too much to keep holding it in.

Walnut wiggled out from his hidey-hole to investigate the hand I stretched toward him. He sent me a mental picture of an empty bowl and a carrot. Receiving the image sent a zing straight to the back of my eyeballs. He was getting better at showing me what he wanted. They weren't thoughts exactly, but I got the gist of it.

"Sorry, buddy. It's way past dinnertime for you."

He snuggled into my hand and sent me an image of his hut onboard the *Soteria*.

I stroked him between his ears with the tip of my finger. "I want to go home, too."

My head rolled to the other side. At the foot of the bed, my backpack lay on its side where I'd dropped it. Some of its contents had spilled onto the blanket. The packet of Blue Lace poked out from under a strap. I licked my lips.

The smart thing to do would be to save it for an emergency. My finger traced along the edge of the packet. The paper was dirty and worn. It had changed hands many times before finding its way to Pierce's friend.

A new group entered the bar below me. Four, judging by the number of cuffs that pinged inside my brain. One of them had a personal drone that buzzed in and out of my range, lighting my head up like an aurora on a dark winter night. I tried to build my firewall to keep the signals out, but it kept collapsing. My concentration just wasn't there.

Screw it. I didn't want to feel any of it tonight—not the pain and not the guilt.

I fished out a tab and placed it on my tongue to dissolve. Within seconds, the calming effects slid into my bloodstream and flowed into my brain. The pressure eased, like waves receding from a shoreline.

Numbness crept over my senses. I lay back, feeling my connection to the world slip away with the tide. My thoughts became syrupy. This batch of Blue Lace was stronger than the one Rizpah gave me. It was all right, though, because I didn't want to think anymore.

Downstairs, someone fired up a music drone and transferred a few credits into the smart-dart board. I rolled over, not even caring when the notifications flooded my vision. Instead, I let them fall into the ocean of my thoughts and smiled as they floated away with the tide.

Chapter 25

Ravi and DeAjamae arrived late the next evening. They stashed their ship in a small clearing half a kilometer away and then followed me back to The New Bar. For obvious reasons, Pierce didn't want a DECA cruiser parked in front of his place of business. Something about scaring away his customers.

"Did you have any trouble with pirates on your approach?" Wright asked once we were all upstairs.

"Piece of cake," DeAjamae said, looking around for a place to put her backpack. Pierce's apartment was a little cramped with all five of us there. She settled on dropping it beside the couch. "Thanks for the heads-up in your message. I grabbed a better long-range scanner on our way out of Ritru-6. It was so chaotic there, I don't think anyone will even notice it's missing."

Wright's jaw clenched. He may not go home often, but it was part of who he was. It couldn't be easy knowing the situation was so precarious.

DeAjamae fiddled with her cuff. "We dropped out of warp on the edge of the system and waited until there was a clear opening and beelined it for the coordinates you sent. If there were any pirates out there, we didn't see them and they didn't see us. Is there really no planetary net here?"

"You get used to it," Pierce said. DeAjamae looked horrified.

Ravi removed his jacket—no doubt regretting his choice to wear it in the humid heat—and laid it across the arm of the couch above Dee's bag. "The landing could have been smoother. It's been a while since I've had to bring a ship in without navigational assistance from a Central Command."

"That atmo is *wild*," DeAjamae added. "How long has it been that shade of ... of ..."

"Piss?" Pierce supplied.

"Oh, no. I was going to go with, um, pine pollen?"

Pierce thought about it amount. "Yeah, that works, too. It's been a couple decades, probably. I was still a kid. It was gradual at first. You didn't right notice it until one day you looked up and realized, yeah, the sky's yellower than a mug of beer."

I motioned for them to sit at the kitchen table. Pierce had brought up one of the chairs from his poker table so we could all sit around it together. He grabbed a salad from the fridge while I carried over the pot of soup he'd thrown together from the tomatoes and basil in his little greenhouse out back. I always appreciated a man who could cook, because stars knew I couldn't.

Walnut parked his butt in front of Ravi, who sneaked him slivers of carrot from the salad bowl when I wasn't looking. However, Walnut's chip registered a dopamine hit each time he ate one, and his little buck teeth had orange bits stuck on them. I'd have to remember to grab some fresh hay for him when we went back to fix the *Soteria*.

Wright sliced up a loaf of Clava bread at the head of the table and passed it around. I itched to get a more in-depth update on how things were in the Ritru system, but Wright waited until everyone had gotten a good start on dinner before asking any questions.

"Report?"

Ravi brushed the breadcrumbs from his hands. "Someone leaked surveillance footage of the assassination to the media. People are convinced this Sidewinder guy is the next Butcher of Bellarouxdonda."

Wright grunted. "He killed one unarmed politician. I wouldn't go that far."

"The Southern Glade district is holding an emergency election in three weeks to replace Representative Delligatti," Ravi continued.

"She had been expected to carry her seat, so there's no real front-runner yet."

"What about the military?"

"A lot of fluffed feathers and posturing. Shuffling around existing assets. So far no one wants to make the first move until there's more proof of who the assassin is, who hired him, or what organization he belongs to."

DeAjamae pushed up her sleeve to expose her cuff. "The lieutenant sent this over right before we left. Thingamajig, play visual recording from file 2418.09.03—Tylo Psychiatric Facility."

"Okay!" the cheery cuff responded. "Playing now!"

A holoscreen projected from the cuff on her left hand. On it, a vid from a security cam played. Pierce moved the pot of tomato soup to the kitchen counter so it wouldn't block the projection.

I leaned closer, munching on a cracker. The sterile corridor in the holovid was unfamiliar to me, but I recognized the stone floors and walls as those typical in Tylo and the people wearing blue scrubs and knee-length coats as medical staff. An orderly guided a patient in a hoverchair down the hallway and around a corner. Two nurses chatted while filling out forms at a console.

Thirty seconds later, an explosion rocked the vid. One nurse flew back, slamming into the wall behind him. The other lay crumpled on the floor. Dark liquid trickled down her forehead.

Dust and debris clouded the air and settled to the ground. Squinting through the glowing specks of hologram light, I saw a hole had been blown through the wall. Emergency lights flashed. Two men stepped over the crumbling blocks into the corridor. Both wore ov-ex masks that protected their airways from the dust and caused the camera to overexpose their faces until they were nothing more than white blobs.

The orderly came running back, a shocked expression on his face. One man—who had snakeskin tattoos covering his shaved head—lashed out with a front kick. The orderly crumpled like a tissue, the force of the kick propelling him unnaturally far. He slid along the floor to the edge of the frame and didn't get up.

The two men walked off camera, then came back a minute later escorting Doctor Adler. She wore baggy pants, a sweatshirt, and slippers. No drawstrings, zippers, or buttons. Her chestnut hair fell in unkempt waves halfway down her back—loose save for the eye patch strap that wrapped around her head. It wasn't the fancy metal one she'd worn at the bar the night before. All three exited through the hole in the wall.

DeAjamae backed up the recording and paused it on the figures.

Ravi gave his last slice of carrot to Walnut, then hooked his thumb toward the image. "This happened last month at the hospital treating Adler. As you can see, these men facilitated her escape. The hospital only notified our office a day ago. They claimed to have waited, because they believed it was possible to retrieve her on their own. I suspect they either didn't want the bad press or somebody paid them to keep quiet."

"And by someone, you mean Aurelian Tazza," I said.

"He would be at the top of my suspect list."

DeAjamae narrowed her eyes at me. "I expected you to be more surprised by this."

I glanced at Wright. "Yeah, we have some stuff to fill you in on, too."

Wright and I took turns catching them up on the details from our meeting with Lady Ilymechina, the space pirates, crash-landing, being attacked in the jungle, and what I'd discovered at The Wandering Star the night before. Even Pierce, who'd heard most of it before, listened intently.

"Both of those men were at the bar last night. That guy," I said, pointing at the taller man, "could be Ophidian. Granted, that's based on holos over a decade old. The big guy didn't say anything, but he sat at the table with Ophidian and another woman. They all left with Adler."

"How can you tell they're the same guys with the ov-ex masks?" Wright asked.

I sent the recording I'd taken at the bar over to Ravi's cuff since I had no way of projecting it on my own and hacking into their cuffs to do it was just plain rude. "Can you put that up besides DeAjamae's holovid?"

He did so and pushed the two images together so we could compare them side by side.

"Same tattoos," I said. Then I pointed to the second guy. "And same boots."

Ravi zoomed in. The snakeskin lines were a little blurry, but they were definite matches.

"Why didn't she receive an ocular implant at the facility?" I asked.

The technology to replace her eye with a bionic one was not all that dissimilar to how the Intell used my ocular nerve to translate what my eye saw into digital information—just reversed.

DeAjamae flicked her middle finger against her thumb to close the holoscreen. "Her file says she refused, claiming that any device the government supplied her would be 'so inferior to her own creations as to be barbaric.' That's a direct quote."

Yeah, that attitude tracked with my impression of Adler. The only person with a bigger ego was her mentor, Lourde.

"This would have been helpful to know a month ago," Wright said. He speared a hydroponic cherry tomato with his fork. "The crux of it is that at least two people received the full bionic weapon and neural implant chip package—the man who assassinated Representative Delligatti and the woman who attacked Reliance and me in the abandoned village outside of Newtown. We are no longer trying to recover bionic weapon components. With Adler involved, we have to assume she has either already implanted the remaining three prototypes or has plans to do so soon. It's imperative that we stop this operation now."

Pierce gave a low whistle. "Seems like a lot of fuss over a couple of weapons. Wouldn't it be easier to wait and see what they do with them, then round them up after? I mean, how much damage could they do? There's only four of them left."

Across from him, Ravi's affable expression and relaxed body language stayed the same, but his voice lost any hint of jovialness. "When we left Ritru-6, the government was in a state of disarray.

Officials refused to leave their private estates without full teams of armed escorts, the media is in a frenzy, and accusations are running wild. No one claimed credit for the attack, but Ritru-3 has the most to gain. Tensions between the two planets have intensified with each side pointing their finger at the other. Both have beefed up military deployments along their border zones and restricted civilian travel between planets, including commercial shipping. People are hoarding food and supplies in anticipation of shortages. Ambassador Rayl believes if we don't deliver the assassin within the next few days and prove that Sinna Energy was not behind the attack, Congress may open debate about going to war."

"All that over the death of one person?" Pierce asked.

"A match is just a match," I said, "unless you strike it near a ship's oxygen generator. Then it's a bomb."

Wright got that stony look that reminded me he served in the Ritruvian military before joining DECA. He'd flown on similar missions and patrolled those borders himself.

"Relations have always been strained within the system," he said. "Ritru-3 is still under the control of Sinna Energy, which took a big financial hit when Ritru-6 gained its independence. Their mineral deposits aren't as rich, require more refining, and are primarily located near the poles, which are difficult to access because most are under oceans. There have been minor border skirmishes since before I was born."

"Was that Aurelian Tazza's goal all along? To start a war in the Ritru system?" Ravi asked.

DeAjamae's eyes widened. "The IBMD has issued an injunction on Tazza Industries' production related to the Insight chips while the investigation is ongoing. Tazza Industries bet a lot of credits on that product. They might be financially strapped and looking to make up the loss."

Wright nodded. "Tazza uses the bionic weapons to instigate a full-on war, then sits back and sells his high-tech ship parts, medical devices, security systems, and computer components to both sides."

"And with the mutual aid agreements between various planets, a war would have the potential to spread to every corner of the galaxy."

"Nah, that's insane, mate," Pierce shook his head. "Two hundred thousand people died in that Ritruvian war. All the planets signed the Treaty of Alpha Bohn-ri, even Valla, back when it still had a governing body. There hasn't been a major interplanetary war since. I've spent my time with a fair number of criminals and lowlifes, but no one wants to go back to that again. Nobody's that crazy."

He looked around at the team, and the team looked at me. I knew they were thinking about how Wright had found me in a Tazza Industries' lab and what we'd discovered when we went back to arrest Lourde and Aurelian Tazza. The high-priced attorneys may have been able to get Tazza off with a plea deal, but he had ambitious plans for the technology Lourde was developing. Maybe we hadn't guessed *how* ambitious.

An image of my friend, Fax, flashed in my mind. They'd preyed upon him when he was in his most desperate state, implanted an In-tell in his brain, and pushed him through so many tests he couldn't survive outside of the shielded lab. When he became a liability, they disposed of him like a lab rat. Human life meant nothing to them.

Wright projected his city map with the buildings that were good possibilities for the gang's hideout. There were a lot of green "good" prospects and even more yellow "maybe" prospects.

Beside me and under the table, Wright's hand drifted toward mine. For a second, I thought he would take it. Then he clenched his fist and turned back to the map. "All right then. It's up to us to make sure that doesn't happen."

Chapter 26

THE NEXT MORNING, I borrowed Pierce's LAV and picked up DeAjamae at the cruiser where she and Ravi had slept. We flew out to the *Soteria* with the replacement high-pressure pump while Wright and Ravi prepped for our stakeout later that night. Luckily, between the *Soteria*'s 3D printers and mechanical bots, Felix had made excellent progress on the repairs. He'd even patched up my hoverbike by reclamating the material from the busted hull fragments and printing patch pieces that his bots riveted into place.

"Hand me that screwdriver?" I asked DeAjamae, sticking my arm out behind me. My head was buried deep inside one of the access hatches to the warp engine compartment. We'd been here for ten hours putting things back together.

"Here you go." She slid the screwdriver into my palm.

"Thanks."

"No problem."

Felix wedged his head beneath my other arm, his miniature scales slick and cold against my bare skin. "Does it fit? Did she bring the right part?"

I yelped. "Stars, cat! You're freezing. Go sit under a heater."

He ignored me and scooted closer until the back of his head blocked my view.

"We're almost done." I elbowed his fat face out of the hatch. "It would go faster if you got out of my way."

His speaker crackled in what I took to be Felix's version of *humph*, but he backed up and sat down behind me. Somewhere in the crew cabin above me, I heard a cleaning bot fire up.

I clicked the button to activate the spinning function of the screwdriver and tightened the last four screws on the titanium plate, securing the pump into place.

"Are you ready for me to run the engine diagnostics scan again?" DeAjamae asked.

"Yeah, it's as ready as it's going to be until we're back at a space-dock with a maintenance wing. Run a whole system test when you're done with the engine. Make sure it's talking to the computer. I hope it doesn't want to connect to a network for updates."

"Not a problem. If it does, I can bypass the request."

My knees popped as I backed myself out of the compartment. They'd spent too long in a cramped position and protested audibly. I grunted and rotated so I could sit and stretch my legs while we waited for the results. "You've picked up a lot about astronautics. Thinking about a career change?"

She snorted and reached over to run her hand down Felix's back. "Nah, nothing like that. I just find it interesting." DeAjamae shoved her bulging pack of tech supplies out of the way and sat beside me. "You have a lot of cleanup to do. When you said you crashed, I expected things got tossed around a bit, but it looks like everything you own fell out of their storage bins. Even if the central computer system went down, the magnetic closures should have all still held."

I cleared my throat. "Want to take this one, Felix?"

He wrapped his tail around his legs. "This is why rodents don't belong on ships."

"Once Felix realized Walnut wasn't in the habitat, he tore the ship apart looking for him. I think he was worried about the little guinea pig. You ol' softie."

"I was only concerned about what further damage a loose rodent might cause. There's a reason ships have strict vermin eradication protocols."

DeAjamae laughed and petted his head. "You're a pretty sophisticated model to make an exception to your programming like that."

He slow blinked at her. "Yes, I am."

I bonked the back of my head against the wall. Freakin' cats.

"So," DeAjamae said. "Things were kind of strained at Pierce's last night. Anything I should know?"

"You noticed that, huh?" I glanced over, expecting to see accusations but only finding concern in her warm-brown eyes. "Wright didn't like how I got the info on Adler and gave me a well-deserved dressing-down. He's right, but my ego is still a little bruised. We'll get past it." I hoped.

DeAjamae pursed her lips and nodded. "Wright is a stickler for the rules."

"Stick being the operative word."

We laughed. It wasn't the first time Lead Agent Grayson Wright had been described as having a stick up his ass, the most recent in memory being by his own lieutenant.

"We, um, kinda almost kissed," I blurted out.

"What?! Bury the lead, why don't you?" She bumped her shoulder against mine.

"Yeah, suffice to say, it was a mistake and shouldn't have gone that far. For *so* many reasons."

"Well, I can't say as I'm surprised, what with the way you two act around each other. I can see how that could complicate things, though."

My jaw dropped. "The way we act around each other? How do we act?"

"Oh, you know, the banter, the looks when you think nobody's watching. Y'all aren't as sneaky as you think."

"Just kill me now." I drew up my knees so I could bury my head in them. "What am I going to do? It's been awkward ever since."

"There's not much you can do if you don't want to pursue it further. Give it time. Things will go back to normal."

Back to normal. Is that what I wanted? The feeling in my stomach made me think I wasn't so sure anymore.

The wall console beeped, saving me from that line of thought.

DeAjamae stood and checked it. "All systems clear. We should be good to fire her up."

Felix's green eye glowed brighter, and his speaker rumbled with his purring sound. "Yes, yes! All checks coming back clear. Recalling the bots now. Let's go up to the bridge so we can get out of this jungle."

He trotted to the ceiling hatch that led to the floor of the common area and launched himself up to the next level. We humans had to take the more mundane route of climbing the ladder.

DeAjamae exited the ship through the cargo bay. She'd follow us in Pierce's LAV back to where the cruiser was parked in case there was hidden damage we hadn't found.

We waved goodbye, then Felix and I headed to the bridge. I buckled in with the full five-point harness—just in case. Felix settled into the copilot's chair. He coiled his tail around one of the arm posts, securing himself for takeoff.

"Let's see how well your repairs hold," I said.

"My repairs are exemplary, and they were only necessary because you crashed us."

I rolled my eyes. "Begin preflight check."

"Initiating preflight check. Systems are coming online."

Lights flickered across the console, and the engine hummed as it purred to life. I patted the dashboard. "That's my girl."

My Intell automatically connected, but I'd become comfortable with the *Soteria*'s network. I couldn't ignore the buzz of pain caused by so many signals, but it felt akin to an old pair of shoes that fit too snug at the toes. The pain was there, but I'd become accustomed to it.

"Electrical systems go. Guidance systems go. Communications go. Environmental levels go. Oxygen and nitrogen tanks at seventy-two percent. Batteries at forty-four percent. Sinnafuel cells at forty-one percent."

That last one was concerning, but it would be enough to get to Ritru-6 if we didn't take any detours.

"External cameras on. Begin safety checks."

The main console screen lit up, showing me a live feed from outside. DeAjamae's LAV had already taken to the air and hovered a hundred meters off our port side. To my right, the copilot's console ran a list of all the preflight and safety checks. Each one came back green. Good to go.

"All right, Felix, take us up."

The thrusters rotated to their vertical takeoff positions and fired. A cloud of slate-gray sinnafuel exhaust obstructed the cameras, causing the console screen to go black. We rocked side to side, the landing gear buried deep into the soft jungle floor. With a lurch, we broke free. The smoke cleared as we rose to reveal a hazy setting sun off to the west.

"So far, so good," I said. "Watch that tree on the starboard side."

"My sensors detect it," Felix grumbled. "It's not the first time I've taken off from a forest."

"It's not?"

"My former pilot used a lot of public parks. He hated paying docking fees, and sometimes he preferred not to appear on any official registration logs."

"Ah, that explains how you knew to use holoprojectors to camouflage the outside of the ship from aerial detection." And the secret compartments in the cargo bay only accessible by ladder or in zero-gravity. Credits to crispers, Felix's former owner was a smuggler of some sort. Which made sense now how my pawnbroker friend, Seddy, was in possession of it in the first place.

We cleared the tree line, and I opened a comm to DeAjamae. "Everything's looking good here. What do you say we get back to the guys and get on with this investigation?"

"Stars, yes," she said. "The sooner we find and catch the assassin and his friends, the sooner we can get back to civilization. This moon gives me the creeps."

Chapter 27

In the end, we went back to The Wandering Star to see if we could get lucky twice. There were too many locations where the Five Fangs might be staying to check them all out. We planned to scope out the bar for a few hours, and if nothing turned up by then, we'd split into pairs to check out the places we'd marked green on the map.

As our team member with the least fighting experience and most technical knowledge, DeAjamae opted to act as overwatch from the same rooftop I'd been on the day before. She'd brought along a surveillance drone and had reprogrammed it as a communication relay. It extended our comm range up to half a klick and allowed her to surveil the nearby streets while we waited.

Wright sat inside the bar, posing as a customer. I'd volunteered, arguing that I'd spent the most time undercover, but Wright overruled it. If the assassin showed up, he may recognize me from Ritru-6 and that would blow our shot at following him or a Five Fangs back to where they were staying. We'd rather do that than capture and question one of them. It would make recovering the prototypes a lot easier.

That left me on my hoverbike and Ravi in Pierce's LAV. Pierce hadn't been thrilled about his vehicle being connected to a DECA operation, but Wright threw in a pile of the Department's legal tender, and he agreed on the temporary loan.

We'd parked a few blocks from the bar. Close enough to get back in a hurry if Wright needed help, but far enough away to give us a decent perimeter to work with if Wright lost visuals on them.

"Possible match for Ophidian coming from the south. He's on foot." DeAjamae's voice came over the comm line.

"Solo?" Wright asked quietly. He was belly-up to the bar nursing a beer. He'd left his comm open, and I heard the din of muffled conversations and music in the background. It sounded busier than the night before.

"Sending a drone on a perimeter sweep now." DeAjamae paused. "I'm not seeing anyone else approaching."

A moment later, Wright reported the man had entered the bar. Minutes ticked by without further updates.

A warm breeze blew through the narrow slot of the alley I'd nestled myself into. It stank of mold, mildew, and rotting vegetation. Water from a light drizzle in the afternoon still clung to the mycelium bricks of the buildings, making them slick with algae.

I rechecked the system status of my hoverbike for the seventh time. Fuel reserves good. Battery charged. Felix had done a decent job with the repairs, although the body panel would need to be replaced.

No question, I would one thousand percent rather be on the other side of an op. Waiting and not knowing what was happening sucked space dust.

With a quick aerial scribe, I opened the link to DeAjamae's surveillance drone. It was as small as a songbird and had four dragonfly-like wings. She set it to fly in a slow loop over the bar. By toggling between settings, I accessed the different lenses, including ones that showed night vision, thermal, and multiple magnification ranges.

I flipped to the long-range view and spotted a woman approaching. Zooming in, I saw she was in her early-to-mid forties dressed in a tank top and cargo pants, straight dark hair and a short, petite build. It was hard to make out much detail without redirecting the drone closer, but it wasn't Adler. She entered the bar through the front door.

I zoomed the camera back out. The parking lot was filled with LAVs and a few hoverbikes. Most registered between a cool blue and warm yellow on the thermal lens, suggesting they'd been off for a while.

The drone flew through the westernmost point of its loop, and I spotted Ravi in the LAV. He'd parked behind an old coffee shop.

"Suspect is talking with a woman who just arrived," Wright said over the comms. "She handed him a small bag. They're arguing."

The background noises were difficult to distinguish, but they increased in volume. Something crashed. Shouts. Cheering.

I wish we'd fitted Wright with a micro-cam, but DeAjamae hadn't brought one.

"Assault in progress." Tension laced his words.

"Keep your cover," I said. "You can't intervene."

Sitting back while a crime took place—especially a violent one—was one of the toughest parts of undercover work.

"The woman is on the ground. Possible broken arm. Suspect exiting the front door. I'm following."

I studied the drone feed as the suspect we assumed to be Ophidian left the building and walked south along the street.

DeAjamae took the drone off autopilot. "The woman is exiting the rear door. She's leaving on foot. Do you want me to stick with her?"

"No," Wright answered. "Stay with the suspect."

Wright waited for the man to get a short lead, then slipped out of the bar during the commotion. He'd worn the darkest clothing he'd packed. If it weren't for the thermal imaging, I'd have a difficult time picking him out against the dilapidated buildings.

I tightened the chin strap on my helmet, powered up the hoverbike, and connected to the controls via my Intell. It responded instantaneously, almost as if more to my thoughts than my commands. For as much trouble as the Intell gave me, I had to admit that the experience of flying with it—either the hoverbike or the *Soteria*—was as close to the real thing as I could imagine.

I rose a meter into the air, careful to watch my sightlines. The short building didn't give me much room to maneuver before losing my cover.

"Singh, I'm going to follow three blocks over to the west."

"Copy that," Ravi replied. "I'll loop around from the east. Same three block buffer."

I eased out of the alley, ignoring the pinprick of pain growing behind my eyes. High above and to my right, I found DeAjamae's drone, but only because I knew where to look. The live feed from it ran in the upper right-hand corner of my vision. Below it, I pulled up the fragmented map of the city we'd cobbled together and overlaid my geomarker signal to it.

My fingers trembled as I swung the hoverbike onto the pedestrian street. I eased the throttle back to bring the bike up to a jogging speed. There were almost no other vehicles around, and I didn't want to come roaring down the street and draw unnecessary attention.

Ophidian kept a brisk walk for five blocks. I watched Wright trail behind him, keeping about a block and a half between them and sticking close to the shadows. Ravi and I kept pace a block behind Wright, three streets to either side of him. Several times, Wright broke into a jog to keep up to Ophidian.

The sixth block contained a blocky building with tall, ivy-covered pillars in the front. A bank or financial institution judging by the architecture. Ophidian cut across the front steps and onto the smaller cross street toward Ravi.

"He's running," DeAjamae said.

Wright sprinted for the bank. "Did he spot me?"

"I don't think so. He's not trying to hide. He's just running fast. Really fast."

"Point taken." Wright passed the bank, taking the steps three at a time. By the time he made it onto the cross street, he'd fallen behind another block.

The drone struggled to keep them both in view. DeAjamae stuck with the suspect. Even with his long legs and genetic advantage, Wright became nothing more than a dark smudge on the image growing smaller by the second.

"He's too fast," Wright said, breathing hard. "He must have ... bionic ... legs. Singh ... you're up."

"Copy that," Ravi said.

I overshot the cross street and turned left two blocks past it to maintain a parallel path.

Seconds later, Ravi's LAV nosed out onto the street. He flew low for four blocks, then climbed altitude until he reached a normal flying height. Any farther and it would have been suspicious. LAVs were terrible options for following someone on foot. Luckily, Ophidian didn't seem to pay him attention and kept running on a straight path.

I cut over and picked up the tail. It gave Ravi time to swing back around. It would be better if there was more traffic. Or any, for that matter.

At least I didn't have to creep along at a walking pace. A glance at my hoverbike's readouts confirmed we were flying sixty kilometers an hour, and Ophidian showed no signs of slowing. His strides ate up the ground in a kind of swinging side-to-side movement as his powerful legs launched him inhumanly far with each step. No question they were bionic.

Ravi and I leap frogged behind Ophidian, trading off the lead, then rushing ahead to pick it back up.

We entered a residential district of Newtown, although most of the houses loomed empty and dark. Some bore the ugly snake symbol of the Five Fangs Gang painted on their outer walls.

The jungle encroached on that section of town. Tall, moss-laden trees sprouted inside and around the crumbling buildings. Overgrown lawns and broken fences lined both sides of the street. Yards were strewn with electrical boxes, climate control systems, and water reclamation units, their guts ripped open and stripped of usable materials. There were few reasons someone would be flying low through the city, and it became difficult to follow without being conspicuous. I slowed, dropping back another half block.

I zoomed out on the map. The road ended at a walled-in wooded area not far ahead. It had been a park, but now it was a tangle of trees and bramble. He'd have to turn north or south at the junction. Hopefully, he'd go north, and Ravi would pick up the tail again. It would look suspicious if I picked it up again too soon.

"Leahy?"

"I see it, Sinclair. Break off now and turn south. Be prepared to reengage if he turns your way. I'll follow with the drone while you lose eyes."

"Copy that."

As I leaned into the corner, a wave of dizziness washed through me. I listed to the side, then overcompensated in the other direction when I felt my body falling. My hoverbike wobbled, bucking at the sudden uneven distribution of weight.

"Not now," I said under my breath and came to a full stop while my world righted itself. Pressure built around my head, like a clamp tightening between my temples.

"Can you repeat that?" DeAjamae asked. "I see you stopped."

"Nothing. Mechanical issue." Not a complete lie. "It's fine."

I gunned it for the next three blocks to make up the time I'd lost, then turned left to reach the potential intercept position before Ophidian. Once there, I landed beneath a tree with long, drooping branches and killed all the lights on my bike. If he came my way, I would follow in dark mode.

With a twitch of a finger, I pulled the drone feed to the center of my vision and enlarged it. He neared the end of the road. I watched for any sign of which direction he would take. We were almost at the edge of the city. Wherever he was holing up must be close.

Ophidian ran straight for the two-meter wall. Without slowing a beat, he leaped over it, legs pinwheeling in the air.

"Fuck me sideways," DeAjamae cursed through the comms.

Ophidian winked from the camera's view as he ran beneath the thick foliage. He popped in and out as he dodged between trees. Within seconds, he all but disappeared.

DeAjamae dropped the drone below the canopy. My stomach flip-flopped as the feed twisted from an overhead bird's-eye view to a swooping and swerving street-level perspective. She closed the distance to decrease the chance of losing Ophidian. The little drone dipped and wove around branches. Its proximity alert alarms flashed bright red. It wasn't designed for this type of acrobatic flying.

My choices weren't great. I could fly over the park, but it would be a dead giveaway that we were following him and eliminate the possibility of him leading us back to his hideout. We'd have to capture him and hope we could break him into telling us where the other prototypes were. I didn't care for the odds of us being able to do that. The other option was to go around and pick up his trail wherever he exited. There was a risk we'd lose him, though.

I scanned the map for the fastest way to the opposite side of the park. Unfortunately, there wasn't a great one. The roads devolved into a tangled warren of cul-de-sacs, dead ends, and circular drives. Through-streets weren't all that important when you weren't strolling between stores and you could zip up to a skylane overhead.

I opened the Minotaur program Lourde had developed for my Intell. He'd intended to offer it as part of a black-market espionage suite of capabilities. While designed to work off blueprints of buildings and space stations, it would still run if I fed the map of Newtown into it. It could chart a course around the park far faster than I could on my own. The only downside was that it used a tremendous amount of processing power.

No time to worry about that now. I'd just have to deal with any side effects as they arose.

"Not seeing a clear path through those trees," Ravi said.

"Go around the north end," Wright ordered. He no longer sounded out of breath, but frustration laced his words. "Sinclair—"

"Taking the south side."

The Minotaur program opened. I loaded our map and linked the live feed from the drone to it. It was sophisticated enough to match the terrain from the feed to the graphics of the map even without access to a city net. The next part was where Minotaur proved its worth.

I latched a marker to the moving image of Ophidian and asked it to plot out the fastest route to interception, accounting for Ophidian's speed, direction, obstacles, and anticipated course changes. Seconds passed while it calculated, and the spot in my brain where the neural impulse chip sat grew warm. I cracked my neck, trying to relieve the uncomfortable sensation.

A pulsing dot appeared on the map, crossing the park at an alarming rate. A yellow line shot out from my location, around the park, to a point deep within a cluster of houses.

I rolled back on the throttle, throwing up a cloud of dust and gravel in my wake. Minotaur took me on a zigzag course through the maze of city streets. I flew too fast to follow my progress on the original map. Instead, I relied solely on the three-dimensional rendering Minotaur fed to my optic nerve. My senses, thought process, comms, connection to the drone—even my hoverbike—all worked together in a flawless symphony of technological design.

DeAjamae brought the drone back up to normal tracking height as Ophidian made another giant leap over a second fence. "Suspect exited the park. Running southeast along the perimeter. How in the void is he keeping up this pace?"

The clamping pressure around my skull from the Intell continued to grow. It felt like a ratcheting band circled my head while someone cranked the strap tighter and tighter with each passing minute.

Ravi cut a diagonal path toward Ophidian following a shallow drainage canal that ran between subdivisions until it intersected with the curving street around the park. He turned onto it, right behind Ophidian's running form.

Ophidian must have heard the LAV, because he darted between the next two houses and increased his speed to seventy kilometers per hour.

"He made me!" Ravi said.

"Move in to apprehend him," Wright said. "He won't lead us back now."

"Yes, sir." Ravi and my voices echoed over each other through the comms.

Minotaur adjusted to Ophidian's new course. The yellow line designating my route shifted to cut through the crumbling remains of a row of townhouses, its central unit long since collapsed.

"He's turned into the courtyard of an apartment complex," DeAjamae said. "There's no other outlet. This might be it. Going in closer in case he enters the building."

I reached a straight stretch and switched my focus to the drone feed. "Thirty seconds out."

The drone followed Ophidian through a small arched entrance and into the circular courtyard. A marble fountain stood in the center. It had a carved globe of Valla that would have had water cascading over it into the pool below.

Ophidian used his bionic legs to vault himself to the top of the fountain. He pushed off, flipping his body one hundred and eighty degrees. The force of his movement cracked the globe like an asteroid crashing into the planet.

"Son of a bee sting!" DeAjamae cursed into the comms and jerked the drone backward.

It was too late. Ophidian snatched the drone in midair. The feed blurred with its rapid descent, then went black.

"Oh, for fuck. Asshole." Command codes scrolled across the black viewscreen that used to show drone feed. "It's out. We've lost the void-damn drone. I can't track him from the sky."

The target dot in my Minotaur program burst apart. A deafening roar filled my ears, much like what I imagined the mythical Minotaur would have sounded like. Lourde had built negative reinforcement measures into the program for any failures. At least outside of his training simulators, I wouldn't also receive the accompanying electrical shocks.

I jerked my left hand to close the program. The three-dimensional image built by Minotaur collapsed. I blinked away the distortion as my real-world surroundings reasserted themselves into my view. It forced me to reduce my speed by almost half.

Ravi reached the target area before me. He left his comms open as he landed his LAV and jumped out with his blaster drawn. "Halt!

Department of Enforcement of Criminal Affairs. Put your hands above your head!"

I arrived at the courtyard in time to see Ophidian hurl the mangled drone at Ravi. It flew like a tiny rocket and only missed hitting Ravi because he ducked behind the LAV's door. The drone crashed into the door, leaving a dent the size of my head. Pierce wouldn't be happy about that.

Ravi got off two shots with his blaster, but Ophidian had used the distraction to get behind the cracked globe fountain.

I swung wide to come at him from a different angle. The circular courtyard held little in the way of cover for any of us.

Ophidian's right leg swelled. The fabric of his pants ripped apart at the seam. No, not just his pants. The artificial skin beneath split, as well.

He reached inside the cavity of his thigh and removed a blaster. Quicker than I could react, he pointed the barrel at me and fired.

I braked hard, spinning my hoverbike in a dizzying circle on its front end. The energy bolt missed my shoulder by centimeters, a streak of neon-blue electricity glowing bright against the dark sky. Two more bolts followed. Those were aimed at my head. I ducked, using the body of the hoverbike for cover, and pulled my blaster out from the holster at my hip.

The high-pitched whine reassured me it was charged, but I glanced at the dial to confirm it was on a medium setting. He was no use to us dead.

"Give it up, Ophidian!" I called down. I was close enough to see the surprise on his face. "Yeah, we know who you are."

He wore a black shirt with cutoff sleeves that showed off some impressive biceps, especially for a man in his fifties. There was no cuff on his arms, which confirmed our suspicions that he either had an Insight or an Intell along with his bionic legs.

"Doesn't matter if you're dead," he yelled back and fired another shot. It slammed into my left thruster, sending my hoverbike careening.

I steered into the spin, gripped the bucking seat hard with my legs, and tried not to get thrown. The increasing pain in my head made focusing difficult, but I trained my blaster on Ophidian's center mass and fired. My hand spasmed, and I missed.

"Void blast it," I cursed and fired again. My hand shook so bad that time, the only thing I wounded was my pride.

Ophidian looked at the black char mark on the fountain left by my energy bolt and laughed. "DECA's not what it used to be."

"See if you can get him to turn to the side and give me a clear shot," Ravi said over our comms.

I dropped two meters of altitude to avoid another round of blaster fire. "No problem. I love playing the bait." Moving away from Ravi, I yelled down to Ophidian. "You should have stuck to the petty crime that kept you off our radar for the past decade. We all thought the Lady had killed you."

"Ily's nothing but a bleeding-heart hack. She couldn't stomach what it meant to be in the Serpents. None of them could." He fired again.

I scooted forward a few meters, creating more distance between Ravi and me. A little farther and Ophidian wouldn't be able to keep both of us in view at the same time. "Funny! I heard she ran you out of town."

His shaved head turned a brilliant shade of red, and the body mods under his scalp made his snakeskin tattoo undulate.

Ravi stood and fired while Ophidian glared at me. It hit low, grazing the outside of the gang leader's leg. The fabric sizzled. Beneath it, a blob of artificial skin bubbled and melted. It glopped down Ophidian's leg like hot candle wax, revealing more of the metal interior.

The man bellowed, but I knew it was out of rage, not pain. A second blaster burst from his other thigh. He turned them both on Ravi and unleashed a hail of blaster fire at my teammate.

Ravi dived behind the LAV. Through the comms, I heard him grunt in pain.

"Ravi! No!"

Ophidian turned and sprinted for the building's door. No, not the door—for the building itself.

He leaped up, planting one foot on the wall above the door, leaped to reach the balcony of the second-floor apartment. Using his powerful legs, he scaled the next two floors, weaving between balconies.

"Are you okay?" I asked, torn between running to my friend's aid and keeping Ophidian from slipping away.

"Go! It only clipped my side."

Ophidian reached the fourth floor. He only had two more to go before reaching the roof.

I had a clear line of sight and raised my blaster. Stars! My arms felt weak, and my hands wouldn't stop shaking, even in a two-handed grip. The blaster felt like it weighed twenty kilos. I couldn't hold it steady.

Screw it. I opened another program exclusive to my Intell—Artemis. It aimed at, well, aiming. It used the signals from my optic nerve, calculated the trajectory, and let the neural implant control the signals to my hand for positioning. I hadn't practiced with it much. Losing control of my body gave me the creeps, but I wouldn't let the team down again because the Intell made my hands shake.

Artemis whirled to life. Reticle lines appeared over my vision and fixed Ophidian into the center of the cross hairs. My hand steadied as the muzzle of my blaster came into line.

Searing heat flared at the nape of my neck, and dark splotches appeared around the outer edges of my sight. I squeezed the trigger as Ophidian crested the roof.

Vertigo washed through me and my body convulsed. The sky spun.

My hands slipped from the handlebars. Alarms rang from my hoverbike. It threw itself into its emergency landing procedure.

Darkness closed in.

I tipped sideways, and for the briefest of moments, I was weightless. Like being in space.

Then I crashed to the ground.

I lay there for seconds. Minutes. My vision faded in and out of consciousness.

Ravi's face swam into view. His lips moved, but I couldn't understand him. It felt like I was underwater—the surface too far above to reach. He might have said my name.

"Pierce," I whispered. "Blue Lace."

And then I let the blackness swallow me.

Chapter 28

I woke up on the couch in Pierce's apartment to the indistinct murmurs of Ravi and DeAjamae talking in the kitchen. Their hushed tones made it difficult to make out what they were saying. Wright and Pierce sat silently in the chairs across from me. Pierce slouched back with an ankle crossed over his knee, and Wright leaned forward with his forearms resting on his thighs.

Between us, the packet of Blue Lace tabs lay on the coffee table. Only one of the three tabs remained.

I groaned and attempted to sit up. My thoughts had the telltale sluggishness that came from using the drugs.

"Boots?" Pierce slid out from his chair to kneel beside me. His hand pressed against my chest. "Don't sit up yet. You had a nasty fall."

That explained the aching in my shoulder and hip.

"Hmm?" I asked, when I realized Pierce had asked me a question.

"Are you thirsty?" He raised a glass to my lips.

The cold water made me sputter and cough, and I struggled into a sitting position despite his protests. I took a smaller sip. It helped chase away some of the brain fog.

Ravi and DeAjamae wandered over to stand behind Wright's chair. From the looks on their faces, they'd been talking about me. DeAjamae's hand rested at her waist. Her fingers drummed against her hipbone.

That packet of tabs loomed like an elephant in the room.

Wright finally looked up at me. His hazel eyes held a mix of anger, concern, and disappointment. "Are you okay?"

I sat up straighter, winced, and nodded. "Ophidian?"

"Gone. After you fell, Singh abandoned pursuit to get you back here. To your drug dealer, apparently. How long have you been on Blue Lace?"

Pierce bristled beside me. "Can you give her a bloody moment before you start the interrogation?"

"This doesn't concern you." Wright used his lead-agent voice, the one that had criminals tripping over themselves to get out of his way.

However, Pierce never had much use for authority figures. He turned to me. "As far as I'm concerned, it's your own damned business. I haven't spent much time in other places, but here on Valla, people get blasted for sticking their noses where they don't belong. You say the word, luv, and they'll be looking for a new set of accommodations."

That, coming from the guy who'd given me his own lecture before agreeing to get me the drugs. I placed my hand on his arm. "It's all right, Pierce. He has a right to know. They all do."

Pierce rocked back on his heels, giving me space. "If you're sure."

"I am. It's time."

"Excellent," Wright said. "We're all ears."

"I've been taking it for less than a week. Before we left, I spoke to Doctor Lourde—"

"Why in the hell would you talk to that asshole?" DeAjamae interrupted. "We all agreed it was better if you didn't have any contact with him."

"You all agreed," I corrected her. "I had questions only he could answer."

Her lips pursed. "As if you can trust anything that comes out of that sack of Vesian slime's mouth."

"When?" Ravi crossed his arms over his chest. "I monitor all of his visitor and comm logs, and I've never seen your name on them."

I forced myself to meet his stare. "You didn't see it, because I erased the information from the system."

"That's a planetary offense!"

"Yes, but..."

"But what?"

"I was afraid that if any of this wound up on an official report, DECA would force me into a medical discharge. I couldn't walk away from the Department a second time."

"Any of what?" Wright asked. "Start at the beginning."

"The Intell is giving me more problems than I've let on. For the last couple months, the symptoms or side effects—whatever they are—have gotten a lot worse. Headaches, dizziness, nausea."

"Nosebleeds," Wright added.

I nodded. "Yes. Sometimes my hands shake, like when I pursued that older guy in the hoverchair. It's hard to aim straight when that happens. That's why I had to tackle him. I've also passed out a few times, like tonight. It gets worse the more I use the Intell. Usually, I catch it in time and shut down all the programs, but that doesn't always help."

"Can't you take anything for it? Painkillers or something?" Ravi asked.

"When I was being held in the Tazza lab, Lourde and Adler gave me tabs every day to mitigate the symptoms. Once I left the lab"—I shrugged—"no more tabs."

"Why didn't you say anything?" Wright asked. "We'd have taken you to see medical experts."

My fingers curled into fists. "I've seen all the experts. Believe me, once they heard about the Intell, every doctor in Salin wanted to gawk at it. It's far more advanced than anything they've dealt with. When I asked them to remove it, no one would even attempt the surgery. The chip has fused itself to my nervous system. There's too great a risk that I'd end up blind or paralyzed, if I survived it at all. Lourde was my last option."

DeAjamae's fingers squeezed into her hips until the tendons rose against her skin. "That still doesn't explain why you didn't tell us—tell *me*. I could have been there for you."

"Dee, I—"

"No, you know what? I don't want to hear it." She waved her hand and stormed off to the kitchen.

The apartment was small. I watched as she busied herself filling a glass of water but didn't drink it.

I let her have her space. "After living alone on the *Soteria* for a year, it was nice to be on a team again. I hadn't realized how much I missed it and didn't want to risk getting discharged."

"So you visited Lourde in prison," Wright said.

"Yes."

Ravi frowned. "And you used your Intell's programs to hack into the prison's record system and delete your log entry."

"The camera recordings, too. I left no trace." If I was telling them any of it, it might as well be all of it. "Lourde's work means everything to him. Even worse than being locked up with no ability to continue his research was learning his experiment failed. He'd been so sure that he'd solved the integration problem with the version he put in me. The tabs were his big breakthrough."

"They were just Blue Lace?" Wright asked.

"No, but they were based on it. Lourde said the tabs needed to be tailored to each patient—well, he called them subjects, not patients. He's willing to formulate them for me, but..."

"There's a catch," Wright guessed.

"In exchange, he wants access to my implant—to me."

The thump of a glass being slammed on the counter came from the kitchen, followed by a derisive *humph*.

"When I told him that wasn't an option, he said taking Blue Lace might mitigate the effects, but it wouldn't make them go away. It's like putting a GraftPatch on a stab wound."

Wright leaned back. "Does it work?"

"Sort of." I waffled my hand back and forth. "It takes the edge off the headaches and the tremors, but it leaves me feeling high. That's why I've only taken it when I wouldn't be out in the field. I swear, I would never risk putting any of you in danger."

DeAjamae stomped into the room. "Putting *us* in danger? What about yourself? That stuff can kill you. What if you get a bad batch?"

I touched the back of my head, remembering the burning sensation from the Intell pushing its processing limit. "The alternative might not be too different."

She glared at me but shoved a fresh glass of water in my face. "Here."

After making sure I took a sip, she walked over to stand beside Ravi. Maybe I hadn't completely destroyed our friendship.

An idea struck me. "You know, if I need to take something to manage the side effects of the Intell, then the Five Fangs might need to, too."

"You think Adler is giving them Blue Lace?" Wright asked.

"It's a possibility. Lourde said he was the only one who could formulate the tabs." I turned to Pierce. "Your supplier was low on Blue Lace. It's possible Adler bought her out."

Pierce shifted in his chair. "Anything's possible, I suppose. I'm not in the habit of inquiring after her customer list."

"Would you be willing to set up a meeting?" Wright asked.

Pierce scratched at the back of his neck. "That's not how we do things here. I don't mind making a few LTs on the side giving you a place to stay and sharing the local gossip, but I prefer none of it be traced back to me. Besides, my friend's not a real big fan of DECA, if you get my drift."

"We'll pay. Handsomely. Her for the information, and you for a finder's fee."

"And immunity for both of us. If what you've said about these weapons is true, there could be a whole shitstorm of trouble raining down on anyone it touches. Prati's good people. If she's helping them somehow, she doesn't know what they're involved in."

Wright's jaw clenched. The idea of giving blanket immunity without conditions grated against his ideals. However, we didn't have the time to dig up a new lead now that Ophidian knew we were onto him. We had to find him and Adler fast before they moved the operation to another planet. The Ritru system could be at war by the end of the week.

"Fine, as long as she cooperates. Get me a meeting with her as soon as possible. Now would be ideal."

Pierce shook his head. "The only way this is happening is if Boots goes with me. No offense, but I don't know any of you, and I'm not vouching for you. I know her."

"Sinclair is off of field work until further notice."

"Then it isn't happening."

The two men stared at each other. For a moment, I thought neither would back down, and we'd be back to square one. That was just plain stupid.

"I can do this," I said. "It's a meet and greet. As long as I keep the use of my Intell to a minimum, I'll be fine."

DeAjamae scowled and crossed her arms over her chest.

"Look, I messed up, and I'm sorry. To all of you. You didn't deserve to be kept in the dark about my symptoms when you trusted me to have your backs. But we're so close to finding the prototypes and might not get another chance like this. Let me go with Pierce to find out what his friend knows. Don't jeopardize the case because I screwed up."

Ravi and DeAjamae shared a look, then gave a small nod to Wright.

He ran his hand through his hair and blew out a breath. "All right, set it up. But after this, you're grounded. No more field work until you get that implant under control."

Not a resounding vote of confidence, but I'd take it. "Thank you. You won't regret this."

Chapter 29

WE PAUSED AT THE EDGE of a dirt-packed yard in front of a farmhouse with faded-white paint. It was worn, but the windows were intact and scarlet-red poppies brightened the flowerpots on both sides of the covered porch.

The woman we'd come to meet stood on a ladder beside an arrowhead-class spaceship a little larger than the *Soteria*. With a compact bridge up front and large cargo hold in the back, it was aerodynamic when flying in atmo and had loads of storage space for transporting goods between planets. She'd jerry-rigged a light stand and solar battery to illuminate half of the triangular ship.

A hull panel hung loose by one bolt, and her head was stuck deep in the wing's guts. Clanking sounds echoed from inside. She wore an olive-green tank top, and her bare arm sported a thick bandage around the biceps. When she finished what she was doing, she backed out of the wing, stuffed the wires back inside, and closed the access hatch.

"Well, we're in the right place," I said.

Pierce glanced at me, his dark eyebrows raised in question. "Why's that?"

"Because that's the woman from the bar last night—the one who argued with Ophidian after giving him a package."

Her skin was tanned and leathered from years spent outside—unusual for someone who captained a spaceship. Only after she put her tools back into their box did she notice us.

"Didn't expect to see you so soon," said the middle-aged woman.

Pierce looked up with a teasing smile. "Disappointed?"

"That depends on what brings you here."

"Business, unfortunately."

She climbed down the ladder—black hair swinging from a braided ponytail—and wiped her dirty palms on the sides of her cargo pants. Standing on level ground, she only came up to my shoulder. Despite her age and small size, I got the distinct impression that she could hold her own in a fight.

"Pratibha, I'd like to introduce you to my friend, Reliance."

She looked me over, then stuck out her hand. "Any friend of Pierce's is a friend of mine. You can call me Prati."

We shook. Her grip was firm despite the injury to her arm. "Pierce tells me you got him the Blue Lace for me."

She scowled at Pierce. He dipped his head in encouragement.

Prati wiped a smudge of grease off her hand with a rag from her back pocket. "Yeah, but I'm clean out, if that's what you're after. Won't get more until next month."

"That's okay, I appreciate you sold me what you had. What I need now is information."

"Information's even harder to come by than drugs. More expensive, too." She stuffed the rag back into her pocket.

I pulled out two hundred credits worth in legal tender. "What can you tell me about the other customers who buy Blue Lace? Specifically, the guy who did that to your arm."

Prati snorted and picked up a pair of pliers, a wire cutter, and a container of loose nuts and bolts. She added them to the toolbox, then shut and locked the lid. "Lady, I don't care whose friend you are—you could play mah-jongg with my own sweet mother, and Pierce's friend or not, I wouldn't tell you shit about that guy."

"Your mother's dead, Prati, and she used to cheat at mah-jongg," Pierce said. "I should know. I lost a fortune to her."

"She always liked you."

"So help us out. For old times' sake."

I added another fifty credits to the stack. "All I want to know is where he and his friends are staying. No one will ever know the information came from you."

"Sorry, wish I could help."

Pierce shoved his hands in his pockets. "Remember that time your brother had that little dustup with those boys from Nephali?"

Prati's lips pressed into a flat line. "You damn well know I do."

"And do you remember who gave him a place to hide for a week while they tore through the city looking for him?"

"You did."

"He snores, Prati. Real loud. I didn't sleep all week."

Prati shook her head. "He's a sweet boy, but dumber than a box of rocks. Look, I appreciate what you did for him, but the only thing that money will buy is a heap of trouble. Trust me on this." She picked up her toolbox in one hand, patted Pierce on the shoulder with the other, and walked to the house. When she reached the porch, she hesitated, then turned back. "Used to be you could get anything you wanted in Newtown, all in one place. Now it seems the only thing you can get is stabbed in the back. Watch yourselves out there."

She trudged up the steps, letting the screen door bang shut behind her. I shoved the LTs back in my bag, and we headed down the path to the LAV.

"Sorry, Boots. I thought Prati would help."

"I was so sure Blue Lace was the key to finding them."

"You said using that thing"—Pierce twirled his finger at my head—"made your symptoms worse."

"That's right."

"Well, you also said you didn't use it as much on Valla because there's no net. Maybe they don't need the Blue Lace, because living on Valla is easier for them." Pierce took my hand into his, threading our fingers. "If you lived here, you wouldn't need it, either."

My heart rabbit-kicked inside my chest. "Pierce, I—"

"Hear me out, Boots. It sounds like your symptoms are the worst when you're doing some hare-brained Captain Stardust shit for

DECA. So don't work for them anymore. Come live here. Valla's not so bad once you get used to it." He flashed a smile that reminded me how charming he could be when he wanted. "I'll even let you bunk with me."

I laughed. "Oh, will you now? How chivalrous."

Pierce pulled me closer, his free hand going to my waist and reminding me of the familiarity of his touch. "It's okay if you're tempted."

It would be hard not to be with his soulful brown eyes staring down at me and his fingertips pressing into my lower back, encouraging me to take the last step between us.

I squeezed his hand before releasing it and stepping away. "While I'm flattered, I can't. My place is with the team."

"Is it? Because it sounds to me like Wright benched you. DECA's never going to let you on active duty once he tells them you're on Blue Lace."

"Maybe DECA doesn't need to know … officially."

Pierce snorted. "I've known that guy for two seconds, and I promise you, he doesn't bend the rules for anybody. When it comes down to it, he'll choose the job over you every time."

He was right. I just wasn't willing to admit it yet. Not even to myself. "I need to see this through, or at least, as far as they'll let me."

For a moment, I worried Pierce would be mad. Rejection always stung, and he'd done nothing wrong. Six months ago, I may have jumped at his offer. Then he gave me one of his mischievous smiles.

"Can't blame a guy for trying, can you?"

"I'd be disappointed if you hadn't."

As we neared his dented LAV, I put my hand on Pierce's arm, pulling him to a stop. "Hey, will you pull up the map?"

"How come?"

"Did Prati's last comment sound kind of odd to you?"

"Not particularly." He aerial scribed a few commands and the city map projected in front of us. I pointed to a building that encompassed four city blocks. He zoomed in. "The old shopping mall?"

"She said, 'you could get anything you wanted in Newtown, all in one place.' That sounds like a mall to me."

Pierce scratched at his short beard. He hadn't had one the last time I was on Valla, and it added a bit of maturity to his youthful face. "Maybe? I haven't heard of anyone setting up there for years. A bunch of squatters lived there when I was a teenager—refugees from a failed colonization project. They put up temporary walls and divided it into several hundred separate living units. They moved on, like most people around here do. Then parts of the roof caved in a few years back. Without it, the place is too big to cool. That's pretty much the only thing anybody cares about when they get to Valla. Well, that, and where to get a cold drink."

I thought my idea deserved better than a "maybe." A facility that big would have commercial-grade electrical wiring, rooms for the gang members to stay, and large open spaces for equipment and a surgical suite. Wright and I had designated it green on the map.

Pierce wrenched on the door handle of his LAV. It swung up with a groan. "I expect DECA to spring for a new LAV when this is all done. A nice one, too."

"If we catch the guy who assassinated Representative Delligatti and bring in all five prototype bionic weapons, DECA will buy you any LAV you want."

I shifted in my captain's chair on the *Soteria* and set the steaming cup of artificial coffee into the holder on my left. Felix jumped into the copilot's chair, his metal tail making scraping sounds as it lashed back and forth. He peered at the drone feed displayed on the main console.

"You never told me stakeouts were this much fun."

"Because they aren't. Not on this side of them, anyway."

"You're just sore they left without you."

Damn skippy. Wright liked my idea of checking out the old mall, but he'd refused to budge on letting me join the search. Instead, DeAjamae and I swapped places. She took my spot out in the field while I was stuck coordinating the comms via the last drone DeAjamae had brought. We'd chosen to use the *Soteria* because it was less conspicuous than the DECA cruiser. Plus, the cargo hold was large enough to transport anyone we found back to the bigger ship.

Just in case we had to leave in a hurry, I'd packed all my stuff from Pierce's apartment and put Walnut in his habitat. I checked his signal and confirmed he was sleeping.

I took a big swig of artificial coffee, begging the caffeine to kick in. "What time is it?"

"0700."

No wonder my internal clock was all messed up. While it was around bar closing time in Newtown, back in Salin, I'd be eating breakfast right about now. These short days were killer on the circadian rhythm.

Ideally, we'd have spent a day scouting and planning our approach to a place this size. However, we didn't have that luxury since Ophidian knew we were onto him. If they were at the mall, we needed to stop them before they moved. If they weren't there, we needed to cross it off the list and keep searching.

Plus, there was that whole looming war thing.

I zoomed in on Wright, DeAjamae, and Ravi picking their way through the jungle. We'd landed about a kilometer south of the old mall to avoid raising suspicion. The downside was that the underbrush was thicker on the edge of town, and coupled with the creepy yellow light from the three moons, the team had a slow walk to the mall. DeAjamae cursed and smacked at the back of her shoulder. She hated the mosquitoes almost as much as I did.

The drone functioned within parameters, except for a slight delay between the relay because of the interference. I panned out, flipping the lens to thermal. Nothing bigger than a house cat showed in their immediate vicinity. I switched back to night vision as they stepped out of the foliage and onto a regolith gravel road that led to the mall.

They passed a few boarded-up restaurants before reaching their biggest obstacle—an enormous public transport hub and LAV parking lot surrounding the shopping mall. Heaps of scrap metal pockmarked the area so that it resembled a junkyard. It was difficult to identify exact shapes, but some looked to be stripped-out LAVs, construction materials, and even parts of spaceships along the outer rim. Their hulls had been ripped open, wires and cabling spilling out onto the gravel, like prey fed upon by wild animals.

I thought about the pirates who had attacked us and shivered. It could have been the *Soteria* lying down there.

Wright called for the group to stop at the parking lot. "Sinclair?"

I circled the drone over their immediate area and then in a wider arc around the entire shopping mall. "Nothing new since our initial sweep," I reported. "Still clear to entry point A."

Ravi and Wright fanned out, hurrying between piles of scrap metal with their blasters raised. DeAjamae covered their rear. A small holoscreen projection glowed near her wrist. On my screen, I saw she'd tapped into the drone feed and checked it as they made their way across the lot.

"Reliance, I see movement on the northeast side." Felix's green eye pulsed brighter. "It's a person."

I pushed the drone in that direction and verified what Felix had seen. A man had exited the building. He had dark hair that was tied back and a prominent nose. No cuff. Except for possessing two functional arms, he looked very much like the assassin. Looks like we found the right place.

"Hold up. Someone's approaching from the east side. It might be Sidewinder. Stay sharp. He's got a replacement bionic arm."

"Copy that," Ravi said through the comms.

Wright signaled for Ravi to move to the next pile. "Leahy, stay back. Find a spot with a clear view and provide cover for us. Singh, keep low. I'm going to draw him over here. When he gets to this open area, Singh and I will move in to arrest him."

"Copy that, sir." DeAjamae's voice sounded tighter than normal, but she found an old mycelium-block maker tipped on its side and climbed to the top. She crawled through the broken windshield and into the cab.

"Switch to visual comms only," Wright said and aerial scribed the commands to launch a small holoscreen above his wrist.

Once Ravi and DeAjamae were in place, Wright took off in a crouched jog, winding his way toward the building.

Seven meters ahead, I sent to his comm as he neared the assassin.

He slowed and kept close to one of the scrap heaps.

Six. Five.

Sidewinder stopped to take a slow drag from a cafaco vaporizer. It flared red for a second on the thermal lens, then died back down to a pale yellow.

Wright darted across an open path in plain view of the assassin.

A spot of yellow streaked to the ground when the vaporizer fell from Sidewinder's hand. In the same motion, he raised his arm. There wasn't even synthetic skin on the replacement arm. Just a raw, plastic-like coating that split open along the inside of his wrist. A blaster was nestled inside. It shot forward using some kind of spring-lever action and slid in his palm. He swung in Wright's direction, but Wright had already rounded the next bend.

I watched the two men play hide-and-seek between the piles, wishing I was there to help my team. It was a solid plan. Wright and Ravi both had a lot of field experience, and DeAjamae had proved herself an excellent shot, if only in the practice range. Finding one of the Five Fangs outside and alone was a good thing. It would allow them to even the odds and maintain the element of surprise.

Wright reached the target zone first and turned hard right to take cover behind a junked LAV. His position created a kill box between the team members.

The assassin barreled around the corner and stopped short when he clocked the three blaster barrels trained on him.

I zoomed the camera in, snapped a holo of his face, and ran it through facial recognition against the booking holo we had for Delligatti's murderer. *Identification confirmed. Street name, Sidewinder,* I sent over the comms.

Wright took a cautious half-step away from the LAV. "I am Lead Agent Grayson Wright of the Salin Department of Enforcement of Criminal Affairs. I'm placing you under arrest for the murder of Representative Damaris Delligatti. Drop your weapon, put your hands in the air, and get down on your knees."

Laughter erupted from the assassin. "Woo-hoo, you got me." He raised his arms but waved his hands in a mocking gesture. "Salin, you say? You're a long way from home, aren't you now? In fact, you're a long way from anywhere."

"Drop your weapon," Wright repeated.

"Oh, this?" He waved his blaster, again. "Naw, I don't think I will."

Sidewinder jerked his blaster down and fired two quick shots at Wright and Ravi. They ducked behind their junked vehicles. Spinning, he grabbed onto a protruding bar of metal and flung himself up onto the scrap heap behind him. That pile seemed to be comprised of loose construction material. Another two energy bolts streaked toward DeAjamae. They hit the outer shell of the cab and dissipated.

DeAjamae sent a return volley, but her shots were scattered, the bolt sparking in red-hot showers on either side of his head. Sidewinder ripped chunks of equipment free from the pile and hurled them at her in quick succession. They slammed into the support post of the cage. The force caused the reinforced steel to bend at a dangerous angle.

I swung the drone around, trying to record as much as possible. Each thrown object, each blaster shot, was evidence of resisting arrest and attempted assault on an officer and could be used at his trial. Not that we didn't already have enough to put him away for the rest of his miserable life.

Sidewinder jumped toward the top of the pile, grabbed onto a pole, and dangled over a three-meter drop. He pumped his legs, gaining momentum for another leap.

Wright adjusted his aim and fired. His energy bolt hit the aluminum pole, heating the metal until it snapped in two.

With a startled grunt, the assassin fell. He didn't have bionic legs like Ophidian to absorb the shock and landed hard. The impact jarred the blaster from his hand, and he went down to his knees.

Wright dove forward and tackled the assassin to the ground. His right arm wedged under Sidewinder's chin into a rear choke hold.

They scrambled in the dirt. The assassin threw his weight to the side, trying to dislodge my boss. When he grabbed onto Wright's arm with both of his bionic hands and pulled, I knew from the look on Wright's face he couldn't hold the position for long.

Ravi sprinted forward and locked a pair of augmented leg restraints around Sidewinder's ankles. The assassin lashed out with both feet, knocking Ravi square in the chest and sending him hurtling backward.

The movement caused Wright's grip to break. He tried to get his other arm around Sidewinder's neck. Even without a weapon, the bionic limbs gave the assassin a significant advantage in strength.

Wright rolled off the man and onto his feet. He and Ravi watched and waited. The microdoses of sedatives in the augmented restraints should have been injected when the assassin kicked Ravi.

The assassin wobbled to his feet.

A woman with hot-pink hair raced out from the building. I recognized her from The Wandering Star.

Second hostile incoming from the north, I sent across the comms. The assassin must have called for backup using his neural implant.

The team was too busy to pay attention to the little light flashing above their cuffs.

She sprinted for the team, weaving between the piles.

"Behind you!" I yelled out loud while sending another comm.

The woman rounded the last pile. No one saw her as she raised both palms flat in front of her. Twin cords snaked out of her wrists to coil at her feet. She snapped her hands down, and the whips cracked.

I opened my Intell's hacking program and directed it at the comms unit. It only took a second to wrest control from their cuffs and flip them all back to audio.

"Duck!"

Wright dropped to the ground. The whip cracked right where his head had been, burying itself into the wing panel of the junked LAV behind him. She yanked hard, wrenching the panel from the LAV, and pulling it toward her. It landed on Wright's back.

She released her whip and turned her attention to Ravi.

He tried to move out of the way but wasn't fast enough. The pointed end of her whip lanced clean through his shoulder. Barbed ends expanded out, effectively creating a grappling hook.

A strangled grunt came over the comms. Ravi clawed at the thick cord threading through his shoulder, but there was no way to pull it free.

She pulled hard. Ravi stumbled forward, losing his footing and tripping over Wright as she retracted the whip back into her forearm.

Wright threw off the panel that was pinning him down.

She cracked her free whip, sending a sinewy s-curve rolling through its length. The sharp tip struck Wright's blaster. Sparks flashed from the energy pack, and he dropped it.

Wright rushed the woman.

She snapped her whip again, this time lassoing Wright's ankle. She jerked her hand back, pulling his foot out from under him. The thin cable dug deep into his leg before the grappling hooks opened to lock it in place.

A chill ran through my veins. I'd never seen a weapon like that before.

Sidewinder hobbled over to where his weapon lay on the ground and picked it up. He aimed it at Wright's head.

DeAjamae rained blaster fire down on the pair, trying to buy Wright and Ravi time to free themselves.

A long slit appeared in the assassin's left arm and a slender rod the length of an ulna bone rose out of the cavity. He shook his head, no doubt struggling to shake off the effects of the sedatives from the augmented restraints on his ankles.

Oh, shit. "Dee, get out of there!" I screamed into the comms. "He's going to blow the whole thing!"

DeAjamae swung her blaster from the woman to the man in time to see a blue-hot flame shoot out the back of the munition. She scrambled out of the cab window and leaped to the ground.

The blast slammed into the mycelium block maker, setting off a horrific explosion. Fire erupted. Shards of twisted metal and plasti-glass flew out in all directions.

A blast of hot air hit my little drone, sending it spinning and frying its circuits. The feed blinked twice, then went black.

Chapter 30

"No!" I beat my fist against the dash. The console screens stayed pitch black. "What happened? Are they okay? What are the biometric readings from their cuffs?"

"I am no longer receiving any signal from the drone. Attempting to reconnect," Felix said. "Reconnection failed."

"Damn it! Keep trying."

The artificial coffee turned sour in my stomach as I worked through possible scenarios. Best case, the team rallied, took control of the fight, and arrested Sidewinder and Whip Girl. They could have killed the Five Fangs members. Another option was that they were injured, incapacitated, or taken hostage. Worst case—there was no worst case. I refused to consider the possibility that they hadn't made it. That thought got wrapped up tight and shoved to the far recesses of my brain.

All I knew for sure was that I wouldn't get any more information sitting on the bridge.

I raced down to my room to get my weapons with Felix right behind me. I strapped on my thigh holster and secured my blaster. From a drawer under my bunk, I pulled out an electric baton I'd acquired on a previous job. Blue electricity buzzed at the tip when I pressed the activation button. It clipped onto my holster in front of the blaster.

"Agent Wright left an extra blaster in his room after the crash. It only has a thirty-eight percent charge," Felix said.

"Better than nothing. Grab it for me."

Felix disappeared into the other room while I dumped the contents of my cross-body bag onto my bunk, making space for the extra supplies. The team had taken most of our weapons, but besides my blaster and baton, I had two pairs of augmented restraints and two pairs of basic restraints. Not knowing what kind of shape they'd be in when I got to them, I tossed in a travel first-aid kit and a few water packets. Felix returned carrying Wright's blaster in his mouth and dropped it on my bed.

The mall was an immense building. The only thing going for me was the element of surprise. It would be nice to have a drone to scout out the area ahead of me, but the one Sidewinder destroyed in the blast had been our last one.

Walnut wheeked from the common room. He knew something was up.

I recorded a brief update to our lieutenant and saved it in an easy-to-access file.

"Felix, if we're not back within two hours, you need to get off of Valla and send this message to the nearest DECA station."

"Safety protocols restrict me from autonomously launching or traveling at FTL speeds without a human pilot present."

I squatted down until I was at eye level with him. "I'm preauthorizing the launch sequence, but there's nothing I can do about the FTL restrictions. You may be stuck in orbit until someone from DECA arrives."

"What should I do if the pirates return?"

I ran my hand down the side of his head and neck. The sleek, metal scales felt cool against my clammy palm. "Try to avoid other ships if you can. Hide in the debris field and run dark. Shut down any unnecessary systems. Use evasive maneuvers if confronted."

"Yes, Captain."

I stood and slung the messenger bag across my chest. A flash of silver caught my eye. The packet containing the last tab of Blue Lace poked out of a fold in the blanket. My fingers flexed and curled at my sides.

If I took the tab, it would impair my cognitive function, but it would stave off the side effects of using the Intell. I could push it harder and use it longer. Going into the field while benched and under the influence would mean Wright would have to turn me in to the Department for a full evaluation. They would discharge me. No question about it.

But if I didn't take the Blue Lace, I would be giving up my biggest advantage, and I needed every weapon at my disposal.

I peeled the delicate, pale-blue tab from its backing and placed it on my tongue. Like spun sugar, it dissolved almost immediately. The painkillers flowed into my bloodstream, easing the aches and pains from my injuries. At the same time, it suppressed the panic I felt at watching my friends fight for their lives.

The ocean waves washed over my brain and lapped at my feet, their steady rhythm drawing me out with the tide. It would be so easy to let my mind drift away on their rolling swells. My vision rippled, and my torso swayed in sync with imaginary waves.

Felix nudged my thigh with his head, bringing me back to the present. I rubbed my temple, but working through the effects of the Blue Lace was a struggle.

"Thanks, buddy."

Walnut wheeked and pressed his little pink paws against the plastiglass of his habitat when he saw me step from my bunkroom into the common area. I reached in to pet him, when I noticed his maze secured to the wall where I'd stowed it during the flight. He chirped and sent me a mental image of a carrot.

I gave him a chunk of dehydrated veggie mix from a bag on the counter but kept staring at the maze. I may not have a drone to help scout the mall, but maybe I had something better.

Wright's donated shirt lay on the counter by the treats. I shoved it into my bag and made a soft nest on top of the restraints.

"Hey, buddy. How would you like to help me find our friends?"

"Wheek-wheek-wheek!"

"I'll take that as a yes," I said, and helped him snuggle into the bag.

The junkyard leading up to the mall appeared empty. I dropped the firewalls I'd built around my Intell to check for any sign of electronic surveillance or cyborg gang members patrolling the area. No notifications pinged, so I hurried forward between the piles of scrap metal.

They looked much larger in person than they had on the drone feed. What I had taken to be one or two LAVs crumpled into each pile were, in reality, more like four or five. They also looked freshly dumped. Anything that sat on Valla too long gained a film of mold, algae, moss, or some combination of the three. All this metal was clean. Dead leaves and vegetation from the surrounding trees hadn't even blown in.

Why were they here? Valla wasn't the kind of place that cared about tidying up old machinery. Most residents would just as soon dump vehicles off in the desert. Less traceable or susceptible to discovery that way. It would take effort for the Five Fangs to haul it all over here. Knowing what I knew of Ophidian, I couldn't picture him in the metal resale market. It was a lot of work for a small payout, even here, where resources were scarce. Why were they pirating and salvaging so much material?

I found the clearing where the team had fought with Sidewinder and Whip Girl. Black smoke still streamed from the scrap heap DeAjamae had dived from. The smell of hot metal, ash, and oil stung my nose.

The Blue Lace made concentrating difficult, but I did my best to piece together the scene. There were no bodies, but a pair of augmented ankle restraints lay mangled on the ground. Blood dotted the gravel in two places. At least one would belong to Ravi. That injury to the front of his shoulder looked bad. The second one might also be his, or someone else may have been injured. That was good, though. Wounded meant not dead.

A trail of scuffed dirt led toward the mall. I picked out two distinct groups of footprints in the damp earth. The first group had three sets of prints. Smaller shoes on the left, and larger ones on the right. The center set often contained long drag marks. Two people on the outside supporting a third in the middle. Overlaid on that grouping was a second set of two prints. Based on the depth of the prints, they both carried a lot of weight.

I closed my eyes to picture the scene. DeAjamae walked on the left with Wright or Ravi on the right side. One of the guys was injured. He was in the middle, being supported by the other two. Sidewinder and Whip Girl walked behind them—their bionic weapons made them heavier than the average person. They marched my team to the mall at blasterpoint. Or whippoint?

The image sat in my stomach like a rock. Every minute Ophidian and Adler held the team was a minute too long. Ophidian had no use for DECA officers, and Adler—Adler had too many uses for them.

Again, I checked to see if my Intell detected any electronic signals. Nothing.

I followed the trail, keeping a sharp eye out for signs of a guard on the ground or the roof, but the area looked deserted. It petered out as the ground became more compacted closer to the mall.

As I approached, the sheer size of the mall hit me. It rose six stories high and spread out for four city blocks. I couldn't even see the other end of it. Pierce's map had shown it was laid out like the diagram of a molecule—multiple circular hubs connected to each other via hallways and bridges. From this spot alone, there were six visible entrances, and I had no way of knowing which one they'd used.

Stars, how was I ever going to find my friends?

I picked the closest entrance to my right. A sign above the doors read, *J WING*. I entered through a double set of cracked plastiglass doors and cringed when they groaned. Inside, the air was hot and stale. A broken guidepost in the hallway pointed the way to the pool, amusement park, food court, retail stores, holovid suites, hotel, and kid zone. There were fifteen circular wings, each with its own central atrium that had eight floors of stores, restaurants, and attractions ringing it. The J Wing was the largest and housed a small amusement park in its center, complete with a roller coaster with a six-story drop.

None of that was visible from where I stood, because walls had been erected across most of the walkway. One end had a gap just big enough for me to walk through without scraping my elbows on the sides. I followed it until it divided off into multiple narrow pathways. Little light made it in over the tops of the partitions, shrouding the skinny corridors in darkness. Not for the first time, I lamented that without a cuff, I had no portable light source on me.

After investigating a few of the branches, it seemed it must be the refugee housing Pierce had mentioned. Some paths led to old stores, which had been converted into living quarters. Ratty furniture, busted crates, broken dishes, and other detritus littered the floor, making walking difficult. Other paths led to communal gathering spots or restrooms with makeshift sonic showers. The refugees had done their best to turn the space into a temporary shelter, but they hadn't been too organized about it.

I stumbled down multiple pathways and through dozens of rooms. Holes were cut between the old stores to connect them, and some exits had been sealed off, making the original floor plan completely irrelevant. There were signs that a few of the rooms had more recent habitants—a tidier space, a stash of fresh food, and bedding that was free of dirt and animal droppings but no sign that my team was nearby.

Ten minutes later, I still hadn't even reached the central atrium of the J Wing. I pulled Walnut out of my bag and set him on the floor. He rose on his hind legs and sniffed the air.

"Okay, buddy, here's the deal. It's going to take me a long time to search this entire mall for the team. They may not have that kind of time, so I'm going to need your help."

I connected my Intell to his neural chip and sent him an image of his maze. He chirped in recognition and sent me back his picture of a carrot—his typical reward for completing the maze.

The next part would be tricky. I pulled up a visual recording of Walnut's last run and selected a frame from his starting position. I took a snapshot of our current surroundings and sent him that. Then the starting position, and then our current position again.

Walnut twitched his nose and turned in a circle.

"Here's the hard part. I need you to find Wright, and then come back to me."

I sent him images of his ending position in the maze and of Wright. Walnut turned in another circle and sniffed at some dirt on the floor. I held my breath. This was asking a lot of an animal whose brain wasn't much bigger than a—well, an Andarian walnut.

He came back to me and pawed at my bag. I sighed and opened it for him to hop back in. It had been a long shot, anyway. Instead, he stuck his head inside and sniffed at Wright's shirt. He sent me an image of Wright and a gigantic pile of carrots.

"Yes!" I sent him the images back. "If you find Wright, I will give you lots and lots of carrots. *All* the carrots."

"Wheek-wheek-wheek!"

He shot off down a pathway, a guinea pig on a mission. I hoped I hadn't made a mistake sending him off on his own.

I tapped into Walnut's visual feed and was disoriented by the shift to blue, violet, and green tones that made up his visual spectrum. His eyesight wasn't great for long distances, but he didn't let that slow him down. He ran through the cluttered room quicker than I could, and he'd already reached the opposite wall.

His head turned as something caught his attention. Seconds later, a cockroach that came up to his chin skittered across his path, forcing him to pause while it passed. Then he was on the move again, racing parallel to the wall until he found a doorway.

I kept the feed running as I climbed over a stack of pallets barricading the next exit. Walnut went through the door. It was difficult to make out much of what he saw. Guinea pigs had a good sense of smell and hearing, but they were near-sighted. It was brighter though, and he crossed over multiple leafy vines as he hurried along. The little potato butt was surprisingly fast on those short legs.

My Intell lost connection with his chip.

The room I entered was different from the one Walnut had chosen. It was almost pitch black, and my progress slowed ever further as I stumbled around, searching for the next exit point. Compounding the issue was the Blue Lace dulling my senses and making it hard to concentrate. Twice I tripped over something on the floor I hadn't noticed.

The team's fight was on autorepeat in my head. The whip lancing through Ravi's shoulder. Wright crushed under the heavy panel of an LAV. DeAjamae leaping from the junk pile as it exploded behind her. The team didn't have time for me to wander around. Who knew what Adler and Ophidian were doing to them right now?

Many long minutes later, I found a locked plastiglass door that led to the mezzanine around the amusement park. Grime-covered plastiglass shards littered the floor. I used the side of my electric baton to knock out the jagged pieces around my head and torso area before climbing through the empty frame. So far, I'd seen no signs of people, but I kept my right hand close to my blaster as I stepped onto the walkway.

I eased closer to the edge for a better look, testing for stability before transferring my weight to my front foot. It held.

At the railing, I looked out over an amusement park. It stretched the full six stories up and an additional two levels down that had been dug out below ground level. Eight total levels of stores and restaurants ringed the park.

Weak, yellow light filtered through the gaping hole that used to be the ceiling, but it was enough to see by. Broken rafters and support beams had fallen at odd angles, crisscrossing the central opening of the mall like a giant child's game of pickup-sticks.

Even from here, I saw parts of the mezzanine floors were damaged or missing altogether. There were sizable gaps between stores with little-to-no paths to safely cross over them.

In the middle, a huge free-standing waterfall splashed into a pool below, although probably with only a fraction of the volume it once sported. Some of the ceiling panels remained intact, which must funnel rainwater into the system.

Thick vines hung from the railings, winding around support beams and clinging to the twisted rails of a derelict roller coaster. The cars from the coaster lay in broken bits on the ground floor. Trees grew between the chunks of concrete, carnival-game-style booths, and food stalls. They were slender and spindly, but the tips of their branches reached almost to my level. Nature was reclaiming the mall.

My breath hitched at the size of it.

And this was just one of fifteen sections. My team could be any-where in there or in any of the stores around the edges, or not even here at all. It would take me days to search all of them, assuming I could even reach all the sections. Looking at the broken and missing chunks of floor around the rings, I doubted that was even possible.

The enormity of the task weighed down on me, and I felt myself sinking under the waves again. The Blue Lace beckoned me to slow down, give in, and let go.

I shook my head, attempting to clear the fog. Slowly, I clawed myself back to the surface, although my thoughts still felt thick and syrupy.

The first thing I did was use my Intell to scan for signals again. Nothing. I scanned the park, using one of the thick support pillars as cover. For a place built to attract thousands of people at a time, it was eerily silent.

As much as the Blue Lace encouraged me to do so, I couldn't sit there all day. I didn't want to get bogged down in the warren of living quarters. Since they seemed to stick to the old stores in the outer loop, I figured checking out the central atria would give me the best lay of the land in the shortest amount of time. Plus, the ground floors should offer the fewest obstacles. I might have to climb over a few things, but I wouldn't need to figure out how to get across the missing sections of the floor.

A switchback staircase beside the nonfunctioning lift connected all the levels. I trotted down it, feeling exposed and keeping a sharp eye out for any signs of movement.

There was a sturdy-looking ticket booth near the stairs that provided some cover while I assessed the rings above me. No lights or sounds came from any of the old stores. No signs of recent activity.

I followed the walking trail between rides and game stalls until I came to an archway that led out of the J Wing. A wide hall led to an intersection of five walkways. Above each was a sign for a different wing of the mall. None looked more promising than the rest.

Starting with the one to my right, I investigated the short hallway for signs of recent use. A thick layer of grime and plant debris coated the floor. I backed out and tried the next one.

There, the dead leaves and plant litter had been disturbed. A trail about half a meter wide had been blown clear—about the width of a small hovercart. I followed it. Halfway down the dark corridor, I noticed a foul smell emanating from the end. It overpowered the damp and mildew permeating the air in the rest of the mall.

I gagged and tried to take shallow breaths through my mouth. As I neared the end, light from the next atrium cast a sickly yellow hue over a macabre scene.

Bodies—and body parts—lay dumped in an unceremonious heap. There were a dozen, maybe more. Some had exposed bionic parts attached to them. Others were ... incomplete. Of those whose heads were turned away from me, all showed wounds from having chips removed. Victims who hadn't survived Adler's experiments.

I forced myself to look for the faces of my friends. When I didn't find them, a wave of relief washed through me. There was a chance they were still alive. I backed away, unable to look any longer. Each of these people were somebody's friend, somebody's loved one. They hadn't needed to die.

When I made it back to the central hub between wings, a rustling sound came from the corridor to my right. I spun, drawing my blaster and taking three quick steps forward to crouch behind a stone planter. Shadows cloaked the hallway in darkness.

The sound came again, followed by soft scratching.

A notification pinged in my Intell, and I let out a breath.

"Walnut!" I holstered my weapon.

He wheeked and scurried out from a pile of debris. I scooped him up and brushed little bits of dirt from his honey-brown fur. His neural implant chip spit out a health report, and besides an elevated heart rate and some extra adrenaline, he seemed okay.

I poked a hole in the water packet for him to drink, then fished out a few pieces of dried apple chips from my bag and set them on the ground. He munched away while I accessed his memory storage and replayed the last thirty minutes at high speed.

A lot of it was dark and difficult to make out. I wasn't used to viewing the world from shoe height, and Walnut didn't take a direct path. He'd gone down dead ends, doubled back on his trail, and squeezed into crevices far too small for me to fit through.

There! He'd found them!

I stopped the recording, picked up Walnut, and gave him a kiss between his ears. "You did it, buddy! Who's the best guinea pig? That's right. You are."

"Wheek!" He wiggled in my hands until I set him back down to finish his snack. I added some dried carrots to the pile.

I played the recording at regular speed. Wright, Ravi, and DeAjamae were secured to three chairs in the middle of a room. Walnut had been on the floor, hiding under a stainless steel table, so the view was largely of their pant legs. They each shifted their feet from time to time, so at least I knew they were all conscious.

I made out the boxy shapes of a commercial-grade refrigerator, several stoves, and reclamator units. They were being held in a commercial-grade kitchen. Probably in the back of one of the many restaurants.

Walnut had started to go to DeAjamae when voices sent him scurrying behind the table leg. Sidewinder, Ophidian, and Doctor Adler entered the room.

"We found them skulking around outside," the assassin said. "They say they're with DECA."

Adler walked over to Ravi, blocking my—Walnut's—view of the team. "This one is no use to me. If you're going to bring me subjects, do not damage them before they get here. I require healthy controls. Clean up the other two, and I'll see what's left to work with."

"What about him?" Sidewinder asked.

"Find out how much DECA knows about our operation, then dispose of him."

At the first sound of Adler's voice, Walnut backed up the way he had come. As soon as he reached the end of the table, he dashed across the floor, through a doorway, and into the adjoining room. He'd dodged around dozens of table and chair legs until he was back in a store.

I stroked his slick fur, regretting that he'd seen Adler. Walnut had been a test subject at Tazza Industries, the same as me. Adler hadn't been kind to any of us—human or animal.

I paused the recording and tried to figure out where he was within the mall. Bright, generic overhead lights. Not an upscale restaurant. The tile floor matched the tile that ran throughout the main hallways. I advanced the recording. He'd run through that room and the next, only slowing down when the sound of voices was too far away to hear. No separate entryway into the restaurant.

The food court. They had to be in the food court!

"You did great, little buddy. You found them." I held him up so that his shiny, black eyes were level with mine. "Now let's go get them back."

Chapter 31

I MOVED FASTER AFTER I stumbled across one of those kiosks with a map of the mall on it. Somehow, I'd turned myself around enough that I'd wandered into the H Wing without realizing it. The map showed the food court as being in the central atrium of the F Wing, so at least I was headed in the right direction.

Once I entered the F Wing, I took another set of stairs up to the second level for a better vantage point. The atrium was much smaller than the one with the amusement park. A seating area made up the interior portion with a ring of restaurant counters surrounding it. Signs above each one advertised the food they used to sell: burgers, tacos, soups, meatballs, noodles, and more. There were over a dozen.

Notifications for lights, fans, and other systems popped up, and I swiped them from view. The seating area between the restaurants had been cleared of vegetation. Tables, chairs, and cooking appliances lay in a giant heap on one side of the courtyard. Walkways had been busted through the counters, providing easier access to the kitchen spaces. The low hum of a generator sounded loud compared to the silence I'd found in the rest of the mall.

A large, industrial-grade reclamator sat near an exit to the outside. There was a pile of scrap material to one side of it, and neat stacks of reclamated bars on the other, sorted by metal type and ready to be manufactured into bionic weapons.

Through the open doorways, I saw new equipment had been brought in—equipment that looked a lot like the stuff in Lourde's lab back at Tazza Industries. Patient monitors, a 3D imaging bed, and a surgical suite filled two rooms. Mechanical items like smelters, 3D printers, weapons parts, bionic limb components, and hardware were in the others.

Wright and DeAjamae sat tied to chairs in the kitchen of a Vesian meatball restaurant. Blood dripped from the gash on Wright's forehead, and DeAjamae had the start of a shiner on her right eye. I didn't see Ravi, but I hoped he was just out of view from the doorway.

Sidewinder exited from the old burger place. He wore jeans and a black sleeveless shirt that showed off the snake tattoo around his biceps. His right bionic arm consisted of raw metal, circuitry, wires, and a slim blaster with a short handle. He pulled a cafaco vaporizer from his pocket and inhaled.

Whip Girl stepped out of the kitchen area of the noodles restaurant. I flattened myself against the floor so she wouldn't see me.

I lifted Walnut from my cross-body bag and set him on the ground. "Go hide," I whispered and sent him the hide-from-predator command.

He hurried off into one of the storefronts and dropped out of signal range.

Below, the assassin took another puff and exhaled smoke rings.

"Doctor Adler is going to throw a fit if she catches you smoking that shit near her fancy equipment," Whip Girl said.

"Fucking headache never lets up. This is the only thing that helps," Sidewinder complained, but he crossed to the other side of the seating area.

"Give me a hit, will ya?" Whip Girl joined him, holding out her hand. Sidewinder passed the vaporizer to her, and she took a deep hit. "You takin' the tabs?"

"Fuck the tabs. They don't do shit for me."

They crossed over to my end of the atrium. Sidewinder held up his hand. "What's that?"

"What's what?" the woman asked.

"My Insight's picking up a signal."

Whip Girl jerked her head toward Wright and DeAjamae. "Probably one of their cuffs. Where'd you toss 'em?"

"Back of the storage room."

The woman's face pinched. "Now I got it, too."

A coil of metal rope distended from her right wrist as she scanned the perimeter of the court. It would only be a moment before she spotted me perched above her.

"Shit," I said under my breath. "So much for the element of surprise."

I drew my blaster and aimed it at the woman. From what I'd seen on the drone feed, she was the greater threat. Then I directed my Intell's hacking program to chomp away at their Insights' firewalls. Like their colleague in the woods, these two had chips with enhanced security measures.

The high-pitched whine of the blaster drew their attention to me. I fired. The energy bolt slammed into the woman's shoulder. Not a lethal hit, but bright-blue sparks shot out from the impacted area, and her arm went limp. Her bionic limb must go all the way up to the shoulder joint, which explained how such long whips could be stored within them.

She cursed and swatted at the sparks that flew too close to her face.

I holstered my blaster, grabbed the railing with my free hand, and vaulted over the top. My Intell calculated my speed, angle, and trajectory, allowing me to twist at the last second to land on top of Sidewinder.

He dove to get out of the way but wasn't quick enough. Our bodies crashed to the floor in a tangle of limbs. His metal fingers latched onto my collarbone and squeezed.

"Reliance!" In the distance, I heard Wright call my name.

Pain flooded my neck and chest. Multicolored spots of light swam through my vision. My knee found his diaphragm, and I drove it in repeatedly until the assassin gasped for breath. Distracted, his grip loosened enough for me to slip out and roll off him.

I grabbed the electric baton at my thigh, shoved the blunt end into his side, and delivered twenty-five thousand volts of electricity to his midsection. His body convulsed.

I scrambled up and bolted for the room where I had seen Wright and DeAjamae. Three steps in, something bit into my ankle and yanked me off my feet. I lost hold of my baton. It clanged to the floor, rolling out of reach.

Hard ground rushed to meet me, and I barely got my arms up to break my fall before landing hard. My shoulders jarred from the force, lighting my previous shoulder injuries on fire. Hot, sharp pain sparked at my ankle followed by strong tug that had me sliding backward.

Behind me, Whip Girl grunted as she wound back the metal rope lashed to my ankle. It creaked and groaned as it retracted back into her bionic arm.

My fingers clawed at the floor, not finding any purchase against the smooth tile. I flipped over onto my back, drew my blaster, and shot her three times, center mass.

She fell backward with a heavy thud. Those bionic arms had to weigh twenty-five or thirty kilograms. I couldn't tell if I'd killed her or stunned her, but the tension on my ankle relaxed and I kicked my leg free of the whip.

I sprinted for Wright and DeAjamae, snagging my baton from the floor as I passed it.

"Can't you idiots keep it down out here?" Doctor Adler asked, stepping out from a kitchen area. She wore a blue medical coat and was pulling off a pair of nitrile gloves. Her brown hair was pulled back into a low bun and a surgical hat covered the rest. "It's bad enough I have to work in these subpar conditions—You!" Her voice broke as she looked up and took in the scene. "What are you doing here? Ophidian!" she yelled.

Whip Girl groaned and rolled over onto her hands and knees, but I made it to the storage room where my teammates were being held before she got back on her feet. Rows of crates stacked head high and five deep filled the back half of the room. They were the grav-assisted type often used for interplanetary shipping.

DeAjamae's hands and feet were secured to the metal frame of a chair from the dining area. She'd tried to wiggle out of the tape, but it had only rolled and stuck to itself, making it impossible to tear.

They'd used Wright's augmented restraints on him, twisting his arms through the chair's frame and locking them in place behind his back. If he struggled at all, tiny syringes inside the restraints would inject him with a sedative.

"What are you doing here?" DeAjamae asked. "You should have left and requested reinforcements from the Ritru-6 office."

"They would have killed you by the time I got back—or worse." I found a utility knife on a table set up for packing boxes and used it to cut through the tape on DeAjamae's hands. "Where are your cuffs?"

The augmented restraints were keyed to DECA agents' cuffs, allowing agents to unlock them. Wright jutted his chin toward the far end of the room. "In that box near the climate control vent."

We only had seconds before one of the gang members would be here. I freed DeAjamae's left arm, handed her the knife, and dashed in the direction Wright indicated. As soon as I got within range of the cuffs, they pinged on my Intell. I hacked into Wright's cuff and triggered the command to unlock his augmented restraints.

DeAjamae cut through the last of the tape around her ankles and knelt to unclasp the restraints from Wright's wrists.

I found three sets of cuffs in the box and tossed DeAjamae's and Wright's to them. "Where's Ravi?"

Wright stood, shaking out his hands. "They took him into another room to question him about how much we've reported back to the Department."

"Let's find him and get out of here."

I tossed Wright his spare blaster from my bag and handed DeAjamae the electric baton since my DECA blaster was DNA coded to me and wouldn't work for her. She spun the baton in her hand, testing the weight of it.

Wright powered on his blaster. "We can't leave. I overheard them say those crates are filled with bionic weapons."

"We'll be lucky to get out alive," I said. No way we were hauling that many crates with us.

"Just one of them has pushed the Ritru system to the brink of war. If these bionic weapons leave Valla, millions could die."

DeAjamae peeked around the doorframe. "The room next to us has explosives. I saw them when they brought us in. They looked like parts for the bionic weapons—energy packs and stuff. I might be able to rig up something to destroy the weapons."

"Find Ravi, then see what you can do," Wright said. "We'll buy you time."

We ran from the room. DeAjamae split off at the door and made for the kitchen-turned-parts room of the restaurant. She hunched low along the counter when Ophidian sent a volley of blaster fire her way. Wright and I fired back, providing cover until she got to the parts room.

Ophidian, Whip Girl, Sidewinder, and another man had fanned out along the outer perimeter of the food court. Sidewinder moved stiffly, favoring his side. I didn't see Adler.

Whip Girl's left arm hung limp at her side, but she cracked the metal coil of rope coming from her right arm while staring daggers at me. It was possible she held a grudge. Awesome.

Wright and I hunkered down behind the restaurant counter. The flimsy construction material wouldn't provide much protection, but something was better than nothing.

Signals pinged against my Intell as the group of four advanced on our position. It still hadn't broken through the firewalls. A dull pain in my head pulsed in time with my heartbeat. I cracked my neck in a futile attempt to relieve the pressure.

"They're all fitted with Lourde's Insight neural implants," I warned Wright. Not Intells like mine, and that might give us a slight advantage.

The new guy stepped forward. I recognized him as the big guy who had been with Ophidian at The Wandering Star. He was built like a military spacecraft carrier and took up the same amount of space.

He grabbed two handfuls of his shirt, ripped it open down the middle, and let the pieces fall to the floor. Giant, flat slabs of pectoral muscles bobbed up and down as he flexed. A tattoo of a hissing five-fanged snake decorated much of his exposed skin.

"Is he trying to intimidate us?" Wright asked.

The man made two fists and curled his arms in front of him, straining his muscles until veins popped out along his forearms, biceps, and neck.

"Is it working?" I asked.

Wright adjusted his grip on his blaster. "A little."

A sickening ripping sound came over the man's bellows. The skin over his spine rent in half. Two appendages rose from the back of either shoulder like twin mechanical scorpion tails. They stabbed the air with lightning-quick strikes.

"Oh … oh, ick! I don't think I can ever unsee that."

Wright swung his blaster from Ophidian to the new guy—who I dubbed Scorpio and who was by far the scarier threat at the moment. "Where did they even fit? I'm not sure what to aim for. Is his entire torso bionic?"

"Go for the head," I offered, shrugging one shoulder. "Always works in the holovids."

"Humph."

I activated the Artemis program. The automated targeting display blinked on, overlaying my natural vision with crosshairs centered on each of the four gang members, along with lines and numbers denoting distance, relations, and optimal order of attack.

Heat flushed my neck and face, and the throbbing at the base of my skull extended up through my jaw and ears. Blood thrummed so loudly in my head that I almost missed what Wright was saying.

"We need to draw them away from this door so Leahy can get back with the explosives. Once things get going, we'll circle counterclockwise toward the staircase."

"Aye, sir."

My hands trembled, making the muzzle of my blaster shake like a dried leaf at the end of a stick. I wished it was only the result of an adrenaline dump, but I knew the chase from earlier in the night and linking with Walnut to navigate the mall had taxed my body's ability to cope with the Intell to the limit—even with the Blue Lace.

I focused on Scorpio and engaged Artemis.

Micro impulses traveled from the chip in my brain to my hand, stilling the tremors and adjusting my aim. It was unnerving turning over control to the Intell, but it might make the difference between us walking out of here alive or not.

Scorpio bellowed and charged. I fired three shots, center mass. Those long appendages snapped forward, deflecting each energy bolt.

"Not good!" I yelled.

Wright focused on Sidewinder, who followed close behind in the big guy's wake. They exchanged blaster fire, but the assassin used Scorpio as a personal shield.

At this rate, they would reach our side of the food court in seconds. We needed to move so they would follow us away from this section and give DeAjamae a chance to do whatever it was she planned on doing.

"Cover me," I yelled to Wright and dashed to the stack of furniture and cooking equipment piled near the stairs.

Scorpio veered to follow me, leaving the assassin open to Wright's assault. I lost track of them when I dove behind an upside-down industrial reclamator. Scorpio waded into the pile of furniture, flinging tables and chairs out of his way like they weighed nothing at all.

I shot at him several times. Even with the Artemis program adjusting my aim, those void-damned appendages of his moved too fast. They intercepted each bolt.

Did he have a program to counter my shots? And what were his appendages made of?

My next two shots were at his feet. If I couldn't hit him directly, maybe I could immobilize him.

One blast found its mark, but it only seemed to enrage him further. A chair sailed over my head, missing me by a hairsbreadth.

DeAjamae emerged from the parts room. She had Ravi with her and supported some of his weight on her shoulder as they ran for the room Wright and she had been held captive in.

Ophidian—who had been hanging back from the fight—must have sensed their movement, too, because he turned their way. I took a few potshots at him, even though Scorpio blocked most of my view.

My arm jerked up of its own volition. The Artemis program targeted automatically, which meant my stray shots that hit the second-floor overhang weren't so stray after all. A critical bracket connecting the support beam to the wall melted under the intense heat of the blaster bolt.

It groaned. With a tremendous roar, an entire section of the second-floor walkway crashed on top of Ophidian. Dust and plaster broke free, clouding the air in fine particulates.

I coughed and waved my hand in front of my face. The move had saved DeAjamae and Ravi, but it cost me time I didn't have.

Scorpio heaved the last reclamator out of his way, grabbed me around my ribcage, and hoisted me up like a disobedient puppy. I prepared to be hurled across the room like one of the chairs.

Over Scorpio's shoulder, I saw Sidewinder's blaster misfire. Orange sparks lit his face with a hellish glow before he was forced to detach the bionic arm at his elbow and drop it to the ground. Smoke poured out as Adler's replacement arm overheated and the acrid smell of burnt electronics filled the air. Getting shocked with my baton earlier probably hadn't done it any favors.

Wright used the assassin's momentary distraction to come to my aid. He sprinted across the open courtyard and rammed into Scorpio from behind.

Scorpio stumbled into a table, tripped on one of the protruding legs, and we all fell into the furniture. He lost his grip on me somewhere between Wright's fist to his face and my boot to his groin.

I got tossed free and hit the ground a few meters from the guys. My injured shoulder took the brunt of it. Pain zipped through the joint and across my back. I tucked my arms and rolled to disperse the energy from the throw.

The world continued spinning even after I came to a stop and pushed myself up to my hands and knees. Nausea rose up from my stomach, and I swallowed back the feeling with some effort. Somehow, I got my feet under me and stood.

A series of earsplitting cracks commanded my attention. Whip Girl approached. She snapped her working whip like this was a party and she was the musical guest.

"You like that?" she asked. "I can make it sing, too."

She lashed out. Her whip coiled around my torso, trapping my arms against my body. It squeezed, the unforgiving metal bands cutting into my soft flesh and making it a struggle to draw in air.

My blaster clattered to the floor. It was all I could do to stay upright as she reeled the whip back in. I braced my feet to keep her from pulling me closer.

"Nuh-uh-uh." She waggled a finger at me. "The doctor lady says you got one of these chips in your head that's real valuable, and she wants it back."

Behind her, Wright struggled with Scorpio. The behemoth of a man had him pinned to the floor. With the added weight of the bionic appendages, Scorpio must have outweighed Wright by almost twice as much.

Scorpio stabbed downward, missing Wright's head by centimeters. The sharp spikes dug deep holes into the tile floor.

Wright dodged another blow by whipping his torso in the other direction, but he wouldn't be able to dodge them much longer. It was just a matter of time before he was a little too slow or Scorpio a little too lucky.

"I suppose we should thank you," Whip Girl said, tugging on the whip. "The doctor lady said you were the reason the big boss moved up the schedule. They were supposed to work out of that swanky lab for another year before they started production on the brain chips and the bionic weapons, but you messed it all up. You're why we got this job and these cool upgrades."

I strained against the rope around me, trying first to spin out of them, and when that didn't work, attempting to muscle my way free.

Sidewinder sorted himself out from his malfunctioning weapon and stomped toward us with revenge in his eyes.

"She's mine," he snapped at Whip Girl.

"You lost two bionic arms in one week. That has to be some kind of record," I said between clenched teeth. I went back to digging my feet in. "Stick around, and I'll make it three."

His lips curled into a sneer. "Doctor Adler didn't say she needed you alive."

My Intell pinged with a notification that it had broken through to his Insight. "Fuck, yes."

Sidewinder stepped closer and raised his blaster to my head. "What did you say to me?"

My hands were still pinned to my sides by the whips, but my fingers were free enough to do the minute aerial scribes needed to operate my Intell. It only took seconds for the Intell to break through the rest of his security measures. A new viewscreen opened in my mind's eye, giving me access to all of Sidewinder's Insight controls.

I navigated to the program that ran his bionic limbs—disregarded the now useless options for the right arm—and entered a new set of commands for the left.

His blaster swung from pointing at my head to pointing at Whip Girl.

"What in the void are you—" she hissed.

I squeezed my index finger, and the assassin pulled the trigger. His arm was already moving before her body hit the floor. I leveraged my Artemis program to line up the next shot.

Scorpion still had Wright pinned to the ground. He didn't see the shots coming and had no time to block them. His head exploded in a gory mess.

The whip loosened and fell around me. The assassin looked at what he'd done, a horrified expression on his face.

I triggered the auto-disconnect command on his bionic arm. Gears spun, and with a mechanical click, the arm ejected from its socket and clattered to the ground.

"That's three. Don't say I didn't warn you."

My victory was short-lived, however, as an intense stabbing sensation tore through my brain.

No, no, no! Not now! The Blue Lace should last longer than that.

My muscles suddenly weakened. My vision blurred, the rainbow lights of an aura dancing at the edges. I backed out of the assassin's Insight and shut down all the programs I had running, but my whole body trembled and shook as a spasm racked through it.

Light was too bright. Sounds were too loud. I clutched my head and found my skin burning to the touch. I stumbled away from the assassin, not seeing where I was going.

DeAjamae ran from the storage room with Ravi in tow. "Get down!" she screamed.

When I didn't comply, Wright tackled me to the ground and shielded me with his body as a deafening explosion rocked the food court.

Chunks of concrete, drywall, and mycelium block rained down on us like hail. We coughed, trying to clear our lungs of smoke and dust.

When we could breathe again, Wright pushed himself up. "Are you okay? Reliance, you're bleeding."

My head rolled to the side. Wright's hand cupped my jaw and directed it forward. He used the hem of his shirt to wipe blood from my upper lip.

"Stay with me." He patted me down, searching for wounds. "Were you hit?"

"No, it's from..." My voice trailed off.

"The implant?"

I thought about denying it, but I was through lying to the team. I nodded. The world tilted at the movement. Bad idea.

"Are you still using it?"

I grunted something I hope sounded like no. Things got muddled after that. I may have lost time, because the next thing I knew, I was no longer in the center of the food court. Someone had carried me over to the stairs where I'd be more sheltered.

Wright must have seen me stir, because in the next instant, he was kneeling beside me. "Things are under control. Rest here. Leahy and I will take whoever is alive into custody."

"DeAjamae!" I forced myself into a sitting position and looked for my friends.

Wright held up his hand. "Singh will need a doctor, but they're both up and walking. Sit back. I'm going to give them a hand." Wright began to rise, then crouched back down. "Thank you for coming for us."

"You came for me at the lab."

He squeezed my shoulder and then left to take the assassin into custody.

I scooted myself over to a pillar and used it as a backrest while my vision and hearing returned to normal.

A flash of blue near one of the back rooms caught my eye. I squinted, still not trusting my vision one hundred percent.

Adler stepped into the courtyard and screamed.

It was the unhinged sound of someone watching their world crumble. Splotches of dirt and blood marred her pristine doctor's coat, and her hair had torn free of her neat little bun. She turned and fled up the stairs.

My legs felt like gelatin as I struggled to my feet. I scooped up my blaster and charged after her.

Chapter 32

I STAGGERED UP THE stairs, using the handrail to pull myself up when dizziness threatened to overtake me. It took longer than it should have to reach the top, but the combination of movement and adrenaline helped clear my head. Adler couldn't get away. Not after all of this.

She'd made it about three storefronts away from me and was heading for the next set of stairs that would take her to the ground level.

"Stop!" I yelled. "It's over, Adler. You're done."

The doctor turned toward me. Before I could move to arrest her, a crashing sound drew our attention to the food court.

Ophidian launched himself straight from the first to the second level. He cleared the distance, sailing over the railing to land in between Adler and me.

The leader of the Five Fangs must have dug himself out of the rubble, because gray dust covered his skin and tattered clothes. His bionic legs had doubled in size, shredding his pants and splitting the synthetic skin until only scraps clung to the mechanical structure underneath.

He no longer wore shoes. Thick metal bars replaced his feet, spread out to compensate for his increased size. They dug into the floor, puncturing through the regolith tile with every step.

"You killed Mamba and Rattler."

I eased back, bringing myself closer to the stairwell. "Who now? Doesn't ring a bell."

"They shot down your ship. Rattler said they lost you in the atmosphere, but Mamba thought there might be something worth salvaging."

"Mamba and Rattler were your two lackeys that attacked us out in the woods. Quite the enterprise you have going here. Aurelian Tazza not paying you enough? You have to resort to piracy to pay the bills?"

"Tazza's been under a lot of scrutiny thanks to you. We have to be creative in where we source our material so it can't be traced back to him. Once the Ritruvian system goes to war, nobody will give a shit where the weapons come from. Only how fast they can get them."

Ophidian took another step toward me. His body mods undulated beneath his tattooed skin, reminiscent of a mouse being swallowed by a snake.

"Mamba had finished training on her arm," he continued. "Rattler would have gotten his next week. Mamba'd been with me for over twenty years. Since we were kids. We started the Seven Serpents together."

Ophidian ran at me in that exaggerated side-to-side motion. The damaged walkway shook each time he landed. One, two, three loping strides, and he was almost on me. I looked for a way out, but the floor had collapsed behind me, and the hallway wasn't wide enough to get around him.

I was about to dive back down the stairs when a bright-blue energy bolt slammed into Ophidian from the lower level, throwing him off-balance and spinning him in a circle. His mechanical feet dug huge gashes into the floor.

I ran at him, leaped, and drove my foot into his chest with a side kick. It felt like kicking a brick wall, but combined with the momentum of his spin, it sent him staggering into a pillar beside the staircase. I regained my footing, spun, and hammered my heel into his torso with a back kick.

A second energy bolt hit Ophidian, this time right above his ear. His head rocked to the side, slamming into the cement support behind him.

Both bionic legs shook and rattled, then emitted a grinding noise before collapsing. Ophidian slid down the pillar, a bright-red streak of blood following where his head made contact. He made burbling sounds, and pink-tinged spit dribbled down his chin.

I knelt beside him. "Lady Ilymechina sends her regards."

His brown eyes widened for a second, then he sputtered and gasped out his last breath. I checked his pulse. Nothing.

Exhaustion drained me, and I grabbed onto the railing to steady myself. Below in the courtyard, Wright stood with his blaster still raised to the second level. He lowered it when he saw me.

Ravi leaned propped against a pillar by the staircase. He held a blaster with his off hand on Sidewinder while DeAjamae finished locking a pair of augmented restraints on the assassin's ankles. She'd gathered both of the detached bionic arms and set them aside to take back to the ship.

I gave Wright the all-good signal.

With Ophidian down, my aches and pains came rushing to the forefront of my attention. Everything hurt from the roots of my hair to the blisters on my feet. Collapsing into a puddle of goo sounded really appealing.

I turned to rejoin the team on the first level. Adler stood behind me. Her hands balled into tight fists at her side, and her entire body vibrated. Hatred burned in her good eye. Something else burned in the bionic one. It glowed bright red and swiveled in its socket as she tracked me.

"Why must you ruin *everything*?"

"Me? Doctor Lourde is going to be so disappointed when I tell him how you fucked up his designs," I said. "Does he even know Aurelian Tazza put you in charge of the bionic weapons project?"

"There have been a few setbacks, but Kandall's legacy is in excellent hands."

"Excellent hands?" I scoffed as I moved closer. "Pirate ships and scrounging for scrap metal, unsanitary conditions, artificial skin that barely holds together—it's a far cry from the sophisticated operation he envisioned. He may be morally destitute, but at least his designs were elegant. Yours looks like some kid's science fair project that got put off until the last minute."

"Do you see these conditions I'm forced to work in?" She waved her hand at the food court. "That's your fault!"

"My fault? You kidnapped me and put this thing inside my head! I never asked to be turned into a lab rat."

I crept closer to the wall. If I could circle behind her, she'd have no way to escape. Her only options would be to surrender or go back down the stairs where the team waited.

She sneered, her red eye eerily fixated on me. "Kandall's work is nothing short of brilliant. What you and your people have done to him is reprehensible. You should be honored to have an Intell."

"This thing is killing me, so excuse me if I'm less than grateful."

"We were working on that. Our latest formulation of the anti-rejection medication was near perfect."

"Is that what you told Ophidian's crew to convince them to accept the implants? Did they know the tabs you were giving them were just Blue Lace? That Lourde never trusted you with his formula?"

Pink splotches crept up the side of Adler's neck. Her weight shifted from side to side, and she repeatedly clenched and unclenched her fists.

Oh, yeah. I hit a nerve with that last one. I had to keep her talking a little longer. A few more steps and I would pass the halfway point, putting myself between her and any easy exit.

"Kandall trusts me. It wasn't my job to make the tabs. I implanted the chips and limbs and handled the subject testing."

"I see. You were the assistant."

"I was more than his assistant! Kandall and I are *partners*."

The way she said partners left a gross taste in my mouth.

"Do you really think Lourde sees you that way? As anything more than hired help? You're smart, Yelena. Surrender now, and you might cut a deal if you testify against Aurelian Tazza."

"Nobody crosses Aurelian Tazza. Even now, presidents curry favor with him, and mega corporations whisper promises in his ear.

Soon, his products will start wars, arm the participants, and supply enough information and disinformation to ensure that the market never goes dry. He'll be the most powerful man in the galaxy. I'll carry on Kandall's work, and you will be dead."

Adler popped her bionic eye free from its socket, twisted the two halves until they clicked, and threw it at me. It beeped, slowly at first, and then increased with an alarming frequency.

I dove behind an empty planter box—the only solid object near me.

BOOM!

The bionic eye exploded. It tore a hole through the storefront I had been standing by. Plastiglass and chunks of debris flew past me as I huddled by the planter.

My ears were still ringing from the blast when Adler charged me. I raised my blaster, and the high-pitched whine wheezed and died. Out of power.

Shit. I holstered the useless weapon.

The deranged doctor barreled straight into me. I grabbed her coat at the lapel and sleeve and deflected her momentum into a spin. She stumbled but got her hands around my throat before I could turn the hold into a throw.

She squeezed, cutting off my air.

Panic gripped me. I clawed at her fingers, but her hands were locked tight. Darkness flirted with the edges of my vision. I kicked her in the shin, and when that didn't work, I went after her good eye.

She laughed, and it was the sound of a crazed woman. "I should have put you down the night you broke into my lab. We were doing great things. Making history. I loved him, and you took him away from me."

Her fingers dug deeper into my throat. My vision tunneled and the darkness of unconsciousness threatened to pull me under.

"Wheek!"

A little blob of brown fury raced out from one of the stores. Walnut sank his teeth deep into Adler's ankle. She howled in pain, shaking her leg to dislodge him.

He released his bite and scurried away.

I punched her with an uppercut to her diaphragm. It knocked the wind out of her, and she dropped her hands, doubling over. We separated, both gasping for air.

I took a pair of restraints from my bag and held them up. "It's over. You're under arrest for escaping custody, bionic weapons development, resisting arrest, accomplice to murder, attempted murder, and—I don't know, a whole bunch of stuff. Hold out your hands."

Adler shook her head while backing away. Her hair had come undone during our struggle and stuck out around her face in a tangled mess.

"No. No, I won't go back to that psychiatric facility." Her back bumped into the rusty railing overlooking the food court.

I raised my empty hand, palm out, in a placating gesture. "There's nowhere to go. Make it easy on yourself and give me your hands."

She twisted, looking behind her shoulder at the drop below.

"Tell him I loved him."

Adler leaned backward. The railing creaked but held. Spiderweb fractures splintered throughout the plastiglass pane beneath it. Then it shattered, taking the railing and Adler with it.

"No!" I raced to the ledge, but she was already gone.

Chapter 33

I BELLY FLOPPED ONTO the hard floor and slid the last few decimeters to the edge of the overhang. My hand snagged a fistful of Adler's doctor's coat, clenching the thick material. The other hand grabbed hold of the rusty post to the railing. Pain erupted in my shoulder as the force of stopping Adler's fall about wrenched it out of its socket. Whatever shreds of GraftPatch were left on my shoulders gave way under the strain. Shards of plastiglass rained down around Adler, only to make a tinkling sound as they shattered against the tile several meters below.

"Reliance!" one of my teammates yelled.

Momentum spun me sideways. My cross-body bag flung itself around my back, threatening to tangle me in the strap. I kicked out, hooking my foot on the opposite post. Adler swung like a pendulum. Each arc dragged me closer and closer to going over the edge with her.

"Must you ruin everything?" Adler screamed. "Let me die!"

"You're not ... getting off ... that easily," I grunted between clenched teeth.

She clawed at my hand, rage driving her past the point of reason.

My fingers cramped, and I didn't know how much longer I could hold her. Sweat ran from my forehead into my eyes. I tried to pull her up, but I didn't have any strength left in my arm. My grip was slipping.

Adler shook her body, and the coat fabric started to tear. I lost another few centimeters.

The post at my feet creaked and groaned. I felt the bolts securing it to the floor begin to loosen. Slowly, my foot slipped upward as the pole tipped toward the open courtyard below.

I grunted and attempted to pull Adler up, again. She didn't rise a centimeter. I had nothing left in me. Between the fight, the Blue Lace, and pushing my Intell to the max, I had nothing left to give. My energy was spent. No sinnafuel left in the tank.

Adler's coat tore a little more. Her weight dragged me closer forward. Half my torso dangled over the edge. Any more and we'd both plunge to our deaths.

I kicked my back leg, searching for something else to anchor me. If that post gave way—

Arms wrapped around my torso, preventing me from sliding any farther.

"Gotcha!"

I craned my head around and got a face full of DeAjamae's hot-pink-and-brown hair. It smelled like bubblegum, which seemed so out of place that I almost laughed.

Then Wright leaned over my back, and his hand joined mine, grabbing onto Adler's wrist. Together, we hauled the doctor up over the ledge.

I sprawled on the floor, sucking in oxygen like a vacuum seal had just burst open on my lungs. Something lumpy dug into my lower back, and with great effort, I fished my bag around from where I'd flopped on top of it. I sighed. That was better.

My head lolled to the side, and I watched Ravi give Wright a pair of restraints for Adler. His arm was in a makeshift sling fashioned from DeAjamae's jacket and his face looked a little ashen, but he was still on his feet. It didn't look like Ophidian had gotten too far in questioning him.

After reading Adler her rights, Wright marched her down the stairs to join the assassin.

Ophidian, Sidewinder, Whip Girl, Scorpio, and Mamba—the woman from the jungle. We'd done it. We'd tracked down all five prototype bionic weapons and neutralized them, arrested the Ritruvian representative's assassin, and recaptured Doctor Yelena Adler. The two would be questioned and, hopefully, provide us with additional evidence we could use against Aurelian Tazza. He may have squirmed out of the kidnapping, assault, and murder charges for what he did to my friends and me, but illegal weapons development and trafficking carried life sentences, too.

I rolled my head back to stare at the ceiling and laughed.

DeAjamae plopped down beside me. "Is this like a cathartic thing or a hysterical thing?"

"Cathartic, I think."

"Cool, cool."

She lay with me until my breathing returned to normal. Then we heaved ourselves up and surveyed the surrounding damage. I noticed she favored one leg.

"What did you do down there?" I made the sign for an explosion with my hands. "*Kaboom!*"

"Daisy-chained the fuel cells of a few blasters together, overloaded them, and threw them on the pile of bionic weapons."

We watched the dying flames for a minute, listening to random pops and bursts as a few holdout weapons gave up the ghost. Luckily, the Five Fangs had cleared out most of the flammable material from the food court to make room for their fancy equipment.

My Intell picked up a familiar signal, and I bent down to pick up Walnut when he waddled out of his hiding place. I planted a big kiss on the top of his little furry head.

"My hero! You're going to get *all* the carrots when we get back to the *Soteria*."

He snuggled his nose into the crook of my neck and sniffed around until I laughed.

"Okay, okay. Back in my bag for now." I placed him inside with a pat and dumped out the remaining treats for him to munch on if he wanted. He'd earned every one.

We met the guys downstairs where Wright was securing Adler and the assassin. The gash above his eye had stopped bleeding. He looked a little worse for wear, but then again, so did the rest of us.

"Let's put out the last of the flames, gather whatever evidence we can, and transport these two to the cruiser. You'll have to patch yourselves up as best you can on the ships. We've already pressed our luck being on Valla this long."

Ravi shepherded the prisoners toward a bench while DeAjamae doused the fire with water from one of the kitchens.

"Do you want me to retrieve the Insights from those three?" I asked, indicating the bodies of Whip Girl and Scorpio on the floor and then Ophidian up top.

"No, you can help Leahy. I'll see to that."

"What happens next?" I asked Wright.

He ran his hand through his hair. "We'll take Sidewinder to Ritru-6 to face trial for the assassination of Representative Delligatti. I have a feeling the DECA office there will be more than willing to cooperate with our investigation. They can send a team here to process any additional evidence and remove the bodies. Adler will come with us to Andaress-4. We'll request a permanent transfer for her from the Tylo facility. Shouldn't be too hard to get, considering they let her escape custody once already. It might be a long shot, but maybe with time and space away from Brione-2, we can convince her to turn on Aurelian Tazza."

"I might know something to help with that," I said.

"Yeah?" Wright arched an eyebrow.

"Love."

Wright eyed me skeptically.

"Adler is in love with Lourde. People do crazy things for love."

He gave me a funny look that I wasn't sure how to interpret. "I can't disagree with that."

Chapter 34

I was the last one to arrive. Wright remotely unlocked the door reader to his place, and I climbed the wrought-iron staircase to his rooftop patio.

"Where do you want the wings?" I asked, holding up a box of chicken wings ranging from mild to Ceti-lava-fields hot.

"Right in front of me," DeAjamae said, shoving a tray of raw veggies and a bowl of potato salad aside to clear a spot. She made grabby-hands motions.

I deposited them on the table and fished out a handful of sauce containers from my messenger bag. She transferred five wings to her plate and snagged the single container of Existential Crisis.

"Unless someone else wants it?" she asked, holding it up.

Ravi made a face of disgust. "All yours. My stomach hurts just looking at it."

DeAjamae pulled a funny face. "It's not *that* hot."

"It comes with a legal disclaimer!"

A doctor in Lapidea had tended to Ravi's shoulder, but his arm was still in a sling to prevent him from moving it too much. He'd gotten one week off for medical leave and after that, he'd be on desk duty for a couple of weeks until it healed. Nobody had told him he couldn't join our traditional post-op celebration, though.

"Whisky?" Wright asked.

"I'd be much obliged," I said, pulling up a chair.

He handed me a glass of ice water and then poured me two fingers of my favorite Lonnie Powell whisky in a separate glass. The silky, amber liquor sparkled under the overhead twinkle lights. The lights were an old-fashioned kind that operated on a battery pack. No electrical signals. In fact, Wright had stripped out most of the electronics from the patio. A few candles lit the table, and he'd replaced the zapper with a grill that used little bricks of charcoal to cook the food. Besides the team's cuffs, there was little here to set off my Intell.

I added a few drops of water to my whisky, swirled it in, and sipped. Despite being in the city, it was quite peaceful here.

"Did you know Felix had converted half of my cleaning bots into search-and-rescue bots? He hid them in the engine room. I found a box of them when I checked on the new high-pressure pump yesterday after we got back to Salin."

DeAjamae licked sauce from her fingers. "What did Felix use as a design? Or does his programming allow him to create on his own? That's pretty advanced."

"I don't know, but he ran me out of raw materials. I'll have to restock before I take the *Soteria* anywhere or we might end up stranded and unable to print replacement parts."

Wright held up his glass. "Well, I, for one, would have welcomed the backup. I've seen what Felix can do with those cleaning bots, and they are a force to be reckoned with."

"To backup," Ravi said.

"To backup!" We all raised our glasses in salute.

DeAjamae leaned forward, elbows on the table. "Okay, so I'm dying to know—Boots?"

Heat crept up my neck, and I was sure my cheeks were stained pink. "Oh, that."

"Yeah, that. Spill!"

Ravi turned that megawatt smile on me. "Yeah, Boots. How did you come by that particular nickname?"

"Stop it, you two. It's not that bad. It's not even that interesting."

"Then you won't mind telling us," DeAjamae said. I could see she wasn't going to let it go.

Wright traced a finger over the rim of his glass. His expression was painfully neutral. He hadn't asked me about the nickname since that first night in Newtown, but I knew it bothered him every time Pierce used it.

"Fine. I was on a team investigating a string of spaceship thefts—mostly luxury and high-performance fox hunters. It was a pretty big ring of thieves with ties to a bunch of planets. I drew the short straw and had to go to Valla."

"Is that when you met Pierce?" DeAjamae asked.

"No, but he helped me find the guy I was looking for. Only it turned out, we sort of stumbled on the ring's central chop shop. Instead of finding one fox hunter, we found twenty-three. There were five guys running the place. I knew if I went in to arrest them, at least a few would use the ships to escape. So I clamped immobilization devices around the landing gear of all twenty-three ships and hooked them together so they couldn't take off."

Ravi's eyes sparkled with laughter. "You *booted* twenty-three ships?"

I grinned. "Biggest single score my department ever made. It earned me my promotion to agent and a nickname—at least from Pierce." My smile faded. The memory was bittersweet. That promotion had gotten me out of patrol purgatory and partnered me with Hal Cavender in homicide.

After we finished eating, Ravi picked up his guitar and strummed the first few chords to the new song DeAjamae had been playing at the bar. He grimaced, tuned the strings, and readjusted his grip.

"You aren't going to play with your shoulder like that," DeAjamae said.

"We never got to hear the ending," he retorted.

She sat next to him on the ledge and hummed the melody for a few bars. "Okay, but only if you promise to stop if it hurts."

He flashed her one of his charming smiles and launched into the song. It was an acoustic version—slower and more emotional than the rocker rendition DeAjamae's band had played at the bar. Ravi messed up a chord. They laughed while they worked out how the section went.

Once they got it sorted out, DeAjamae sang it from the beginning. Her voice was low and raspy and sent a shiver of goosebumps down both my arms.

Wright refilled my glass of whisky. "What did the doctor say this afternoon? If you don't mind me asking."

I didn't mind. I'd decided back on Valla that keeping my Intell issues from the team didn't help any of us. No more secrets.

"She's restricting me to light field work for now. I'm supposed to go in for weekly checkups, aka monitoring for Intell side effects. It's weird, though."

"What is?"

"My doctor didn't bring up the Blue Lace. She could have recommended suspension."

Wright glanced over to Ravi and DeAjamae, who were starting on the second verse. He finished his drink and set the glass on the table. "We talked it over. A lot happened on Valla. Not everything made it into the official report."

He reached into his pocket and pulled out a small box. After hesitating a moment, he slid it across the table to me.

I raised my eyebrows. "What's this?"

"A gift from my mother. Her position as ambassador comes with certain useful connections."

I opened the lid. Inside were ten packets of Blue Lace. That would be one hundred tabs. "I don't understand."

"They're pharmaceutical grade. Tested and guaranteed not to be cut with anything dangerous. Officially, the Department has a zero-tolerance policy on officers taking narcotics." He leaned forward until I smelled the citrus scent of his soap. "Unofficially, I never want to watch you collapse from using that chip ever again. Not if these can prevent that."

My fingers closed around the box. "Please tell your mother thank you."

His hand covered mine. "I'm sorry you felt you couldn't tell me about your symptoms before. I know you said you weren't interested in a relationship—and I respect that—but I hope we're good enough friends that you'll come to me if you need help. For more of these tabs or anything else."

My traitorous stomach did that flip-flop thing. Because the thing was, I was interested in Wright. A lot. But I had to get my life sorted out before I was in a position to be in any relationship.

"Grayson, I—"

Wright's cuff beeped, signaling an incoming comm. He gave me an apologetic smile. "Hold that thought? I'm expecting to hear from the lieutenant."

"Of course," I said, reluctantly letting my fingers slip free from his hand. I tucked the tabs into my bag while he stepped to the other side of the patio for privacy.

The song ended. I clapped as DeAjamae and Ravi took exaggerated bows and moseyed back to the table.

DeAjamae passed around a plate of brownies she had made for dessert. They were sweet and fudgy, with chopped nuts sprinkled onto the frosting. I was contemplating a second one when Wright closed his comm and joined us. He had a grim expression on his face.

Ravi set his brownie down. "Bad news, boss?"

"That was my mother," he said. "In exchange for a more lenient sentence, Sidewinder agreed to provide information on their operation on Valla. They are still hammering out the details of the agreement, but in a show of good faith, he told them that prior to the assassination of Representative Delligatti, he transported a full shipment of Adler's bionic weapons. He won't say anything else until the agreement is signed. She requested we return to Ritru-6 and take the lead in retrieving them. Her bosses are satisfied for now with showing the public that Representative Delligatti's assassin has been apprehended. However, they haven't taken war off the table if the buyers turn out to be from Ritru-3 or connected to Sinna Energy."

The coming months would be difficult. With Lourde and Adler both locked behind bars, Aurelian Tazza's plan to manufacture bionic weapons would be significantly compromised. However, he'd proved himself a man willing to pivot. If Adler was correct, and Tazza's primary goal with the bionic weapons was to start a war so that his company could sell mass-market weapons and tech to both sides, then the damage may have already been done.

"When do we leave?" I asked.

"Not for a few days. The agreement will take at least that long to complete. Take the time to rest and recover. This operation was a big win for us and for the galaxy. You deserve to celebrate." Wright raised his glass. "Cheers!"

I lifted my glass and watched the happy but determined faces of my friends. Whatever the new challenges, we'd face them together. As a team. "Cheers!"

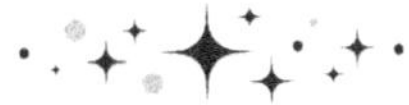

The next morning, I parked my hoverbike in the maximum security penitentiary's parking lot and stowed my helmet. Gravel crunched beneath my boots as I walked to the entrance.

"Are you sure you want to go through with this?" Felix asked over my comm. "It's not too late to change your mind."

"I'm sure."

I'd lain awake all night trying to come up with another option. The Blue Lace was, at best, a GraftPatch on an open wound. Sooner or later, the underlying issues with my Intell would bleed through, and when they did, there would be no patching me back together. I knew that as surely as I knew the stars revolved around a black hole.

Even now, I felt the pull of the drug and the temporary release it offered. My last tab had been less than twelve hours ago. How long until I was just going from one hit to the next? I'd be no more good to the team on it than off it. I quickened my pace.

It was early. The sun just peeked above the horizon and cast the buildings of Salin in a warm glow. Air traffic had been light, but it would be busy soon. Thousands of people going about their lives, not realizing how close the galaxy stood on the brink of war. Hopefully, they never would.

I owed it to them, my team, and myself to use every tool available to make that a reality. That meant doing something I swore I would never let happen again.

"Can I help you?" asked the guard.

"Yes. I'm here to see inmate Kandall Lourde. We have something important to discuss."

THANK YOU FOR READING!

I would love to know what you thought of Reliance and the gang.

If you enjoyed the story, please consider leaving a review wherever you purchased the book or on your favorite review site, like Goodreads or Amazon. Indie authors depend on reviews like yours to help find new readers so we can keep writing the stories you love.

Don't Stop Now!

Dive deeper into the stars at
heathertexle.com

★ Curious about Reliance and Jarrett's adventure to take down Lady Ilymechina?
Get *On Instinct*, the *FREE Reliance Sinclair* prequel!

★ Find bonus content like book club questions, inspiration boards, and more!

★ Be the first to know about new releases, deals, and upcoming events!

Acknowledgements

This book wouldn't exist without the help of many people, both friends and colleagues.

Thank you to my best friends and beta readers extraordinaire Shawn, Tawnie, and Rosa for reading everything I've ever written—including the really, really, *really* bad stuff. You put up with my "What if...?" texts, conversations about imaginary people, and error-riddled early drafts while being both my reality check and greatest cheerleaders. You keep me pointed to the stars.

My editor, Kat Betts of Element Editing, is to be thanked for every time you think, "I want more Felix," and then he magically appears in the next chapter. Her suggestions never fail to elevate my story. Any mistakes are entirely my own and included to prove this story was written by a human, not AI.

MiblArt came up with yet another amazing cover design. They truly bring my vision of Reliance to life.

Since the publication of my first book, the indie author community has welcomed me with open arms and endless advice whenever I have asked for it. They have all my gratitude. Thank you to my friend and mentor, Elicia Hyder for continuing to light my path; Jessie Kwak for grabbing my hand and pulling me along; Kate Sheeran Swed for introducing me to new travel companions; and the Sci-Fi Unity group being my interactive travel guides and putting up with my endless questions. The journey is better with friends.

And finally, thank you to my husband, Justin, for his unwavering support of my authorial dreams. I'll never know how I was so lucky to get you as my copilot through life.

Also by Heather Texle

Full-Length Novels

On Impulse (Reliance Sinclair, #1)
On Impact (Reliance Sinclair, #2)

Short Stories

On Instinct (Reliance Sinclair, #0.5)
"On Ignition" (Reliance Sinclair, #0.9) – In *Crooked v.3*

About the Author

Heather Texle is the author of the *Reliance Sinclair* science-fiction series who finds inspiration in the quirky, weird, and I-can't-believe-that's-true things. With a lifelong passion for learning, Heather is fascinated with the creativity and ingenuity of the human spirit. She also adores a good conspiracy theory.

After graduating college, Heather moved to Minnesota where she attained her law degree and continues to live with her husband and two cats, Mew and Spots. Despite once being stranded in the Gulf of Mexico on a burning cruise ship, she loves to travel and can often be heard muttering "I miss Scotland" on cool, rainy days.

For more information about Heather and her work, follow her online on FaceBook, Goodreads, and BookBub. You can also sign up for her newsletter and receive a free *Reliance Sinclair* short story at heathertexle.com.